It Had to Be You

A romantic comedy by
Lynda Renham

About the Author

Lynda lives in Oxford, UK. She has appeared on BBC radio discussion programmes and is a prolific blogger, Twitter and Facebook contributor. She is author of the best-selling romantic comedy novels including *Croissants and Jam*, *Coconuts and Wonderbras, Pink Wellies and Flat Caps* and *The Dog's Bollocks*.

Lynda Renham

The right of Lynda Renham to be identified as the author of the work has been asserted by her in accordance with the Copyright, Designs and Patents Act 1988.

ISBN 978-0-9571372-8-8

first edition

Cover Illustration by Gracie Klumpp
www.gracieklumpp.com

Thanks to:
The real Muffy for allowing me to use her name.

Printed for Raucous Publishing in Great Britain by
SRP (Exeter)

Copyright © Raucous Publishing 2013
www.raucouspublishing.co.uk

Chapter One

Don't you just hate Christmas bonuses? Well maybe you don't and generally I don't either, so when my boss drops a subtle hint about giving me one I didn't for one minute imagine he was talking about a quickie up against his desk. Well you wouldn't would you? A bonus normally smacks of a little brown envelope with a nice wad of crisp new notes inside doesn't it? Well it does from my experience but maybe it smacks of a quickie up against a desk for you. I avert my eyes from the developing bulge in his trousers and scan the desk for the said brown envelope.

'It's Christmas,' he says, like I've somehow overlooked the fact, and takes my hand, rubbing it erotically over the bulge. God, I feel sick. I fear the overload of Christmas sausage rolls, turkey sandwiches and mince pies that I had guiltily consumed thirty minutes earlier at the office Christmas lunch will burst forth and decorate the lovely oak desk I am pressed up against.

'I'm not sure what that's got to do with it,' I say hesitantly. Well you have to agree I do have a point. The boss is supposed to give me the present isn't he, not the other way around? Although, on reflection perhaps he considers a quick shag over his desk on Christmas Eve is a good present; I'd much prefer a Body Shop voucher to be honest, or a family bag of M&Ms.

'Goodwill to all men and all that crap,' he whispers, launching his open mouth towards my neck like a vampire, engulfing me in champagne fumes. I think a vampire would be preferable, at least it would be over quicker. I don't believe this is happening. I mean, this sort of thing doesn't happen to women like me. Don't get me wrong, when I say women like me; I'm not saying I'm twenty stone with unsightly moles on my face. Not that there is anything wrong with being twenty stone of course, or having moles on your face come to that. If you're happy that's what counts right?

But you know what I mean. I'm just your standard size fourteen, ordinary looking woman. I wouldn't call myself a blonde bombshell by any means. That's the thing with Christmas, isn't it? Things happen in offices that would never happen at any other time of the year. When else would you consume alcohol at lunchtime and it be deemed acceptable to continue working half-pissed for the rest of the day? Not to mention that secret Santa thing. I always get unstuck with that bugger, and this year has been no exception. I usually pay over the odds too. Well, what can you buy for a fiver these days? And what happens? The one who was supposed to buy my present didn't bring it in and is now off sick, with a hangover no doubt, which means I go home empty-handed. Obviously I shrug it off as no big deal and I don't really mind, but I know I won't get anything now and it does seem a bit unfair. I'm Binki Grayson by the way, and that's Binki with an i by the way. I don't mean I only have one eye obviously. I most certainly have two and I'm not off the telly. I live in Notting Hill which I assure you, is very different to Chelsea. Just as nice you understand but different. I may as well tell you this now while I'm pinned up against an office desk by my sleazy boss as I may not get a chance later. You're probably wondering how I came to be in this pickle, and I'm wondering that too. My boss, who I have to say is very much a wolf in sheep's clothing, has taken me totally by surprise. I never imagined he had it in him. I've worked at Temco Advertising for five years now. Three of those I was a junior sales assistant but the past two years I have been working as the senior sales assistant directly under Ben Newman; not literally under him you understand, that would be a bit gross. In all that time he has never had me pinned up against a desk. I've worked really hard to get here too. I don't mean pinned up against Ben Newman's desk with an unsightly bulge pressed against my thigh, just in case you thought I did. I mean, I've worked hard to climb my way up in the company and this is the last thing I need. I am, after all, a soon-to-be-engaged woman. At least that is what Oliver has been hinting. I know he has visited Hatton Garden on the quiet because my friend, Muffy, saw him there in her lunch break last week. I'm expecting him to propose over the Christmas holiday, and I can't begin to tell you how excited I am. Oliver is my boyfriend by the way, but I expect you guessed that.

'I've wanted you for months,' Ben Newman mumbles, salivating so much that I feel sure that's a dribble running down my neck. I shudder and attempt to duck under his arm but he pushes me back and I feel the desk cutting into my buttock. His hand slides up the inside of my thigh and I start to panic. Good heavens, this has never happened to me before in my life.

'You know you want it,' he says huskily. He releases one hand to yank down the zipper on his trousers.

'Your gorgeous silky blonde hair and cute little dimpled cheeks really turn me on, and that tight little arse of yours. Ooh sugar, you drive me crazy.'

'Oh,' I hear myself squeal. I don't think I have ever driven a man crazy in my whole life, and that includes my boyfriend Oliver.

'I've seen you giving me the come on,' he slurs.

He has? I wonder when that was. I hope he isn't mistaking me for someone else. I don't know if I should be relieved or insulted if that is the case. It is rather flattering to be lusted after, it's just a shame I couldn't do any better than Ben Newman.

'You want it don't you?' he dribbles as his hand swoops down the front of my dress and grabs a breast.

I've never wanted it less in my whole life.

'Surprisingly enough I don't,' I say firmly as my elbow squashes a sausage roll that sits drying up on his desk.

What is it with these creeps? And what does he imagine I find so irresistible about him? He surely can't think it's his disgusting alcohol and tobacco breath, or his greasy floppy brown hair? Or maybe he thinks it is his enormous erection that I want so desperately. I can't think of anything worse than being rammed by that awful ... Oh my God, he's got it out. It's all purple and veiny. Now I am going to be sick. I slide sideways and get a prick from a cocktail sausage stick. It seems pricks are everywhere but this one is way out of control. I so wish I was back, thirty minutes earlier, at the lunch eating a cocktail sausage rather than being pricked by one.

'You can't tease me all these weeks and then start playing Miss Prim,' he hisses as he tugs at my knickers. 'You know you want my thrill drill in your pussy. I know you're gagging for it.'

Oh purleese, thrill drill? I've heard it all now. I really can't imagine being thrilled in the least by this veiny looking drill. I bring my knee up and thrust it roughly into his well-exposed groin. He falls back groaning and I quickly pull my panties up. Oh dear, I somehow feel this is not helping my job prospects.

'For fuck's sake, what was that for?' he cries, clutching the pink and now very soft appendage.

I can't believe he has the cheek to even ask.

'You can stick your thrill drill somewhere else Mr Newman, Christmas or no Christmas,' I say haughtily, straightening my dress.

He gives me a filthy look and zips up his trousers.

'Playing Miss Innocent are we? I tell you what, why don't you think this through, we'll discuss it again at the New Year's Eve party,' he says breathlessly, tucking in his shirt before taking a brown envelope from a drawer.

I don't think we will. He leans towards me and I back away. God, he's so ugly I swear he would win the world finals of the Ugliest Man competition. I mean, that wart on his nose, what's that about? He scoffs and flicks his hair back with his hand.

'Here's a little bonus, but I expect you to work harder next year. Do you get my drift? Put in a few extra hours, that kind of thing.'

I seriously don't believe this. Christmas Eve and I'm about to throw my job in. What else can I do? I can't have this moron drooling over me for the whole of next year, it doesn't bear thinking about. I snatch the envelope just to be on the safe side.

'Mr Newman, I really can't do any extra hours. Forty hours a week is more than enough, and my boyfriend would be really unhappy.

His hard eyes meet mine and I realise, right there right then, that I really have no choice but to resign.

'I think you will do extra hours Miss Grayson. I really wouldn't want to tell the powers that be how you threw yourself at me, a happily married man with two children, on Christmas Eve because you couldn't hold your drink.'

What a pig.

'They would never believe you,' I say lamely, knowing full well they would. He's a bloody director after all. He gives me a smug smile and I cave in.

'Under the circumstances, I think perhaps you should find yourself another sales assistant for the New Year,' I hear myself say and cringe inwardly. What am I doing? Oliver and I have only been in the new *luxury apartment in the most sought-after residential area of Notting Hill* for two months. I'm twenty-nine years old with ten months on a tenancy agreement. I've a gorgeous boyfriend who is climbing the surveyor's ladder and is most certainly going to ask me to marry him over Christmas because men do that at Christmas don't they? I mean, they do, don't they? All I need is to be out of a job now with a wedding coming up. I hold my breath, you never know, Christmas may just bring out the good side in my boss.

'Well, if that's how you feel Binki,' he says, leaning forward and reaching for the envelope.

I quickly push it into my bag and head for the door.

'Thank you very much,' I say shakily. 'Shall we say it is for services rendered? Or shall we take our chances in court, sexual harassment and all that. What would the wife say?'

'Why you ...'

The thing is I can't stay, can I? He'll make my life unbearable and the last thing I want is the stigma of sexual harassment. Everyone at work looking at me and thinking, maybe she asked for it. Like anyone would choose to throw themselves at wart-nose Newman but all the same, you get my drift don't you?

I dive out of the office faster than you can say Father Christmas and wonder if I offer Oliver sex when I get home he'll take the bad news better. Maybe he'll even storm up to the office and punch Ben Newman's lights out; then again, knowing Oliver and his bad back, maybe not.

Chapter Two

I saunter miserably towards my car, juggling a tin of Foxes chocolate biscuits under one arm and a box of Roses under the other.

'A little something from the company,' Brian, our office manager had said proudly. 'Everyone gets something at Christmas.'

It would be my luck that my little something turned out to be Ben Newman's erect penis wouldn't it?

'Yeah, like another stone overweight you mean?' Sophie had quipped.

'An extra fifty quid this month would have been better,' Sally the receptionist had moaned. 'I've just started dieting.'

Honestly, who starts a diet before Christmas? That's plain self-torture isn't it?

'Well,' a confused Brian had said, 'a couple of days off your diets won't do any harm will it?'

Men honestly, what do they know about diets? I'd accepted my biscuits gratefully, after all, in the next few weeks that may be all we have to eat with me not working and us coping on just Oliver's salary. I'd discreetly swiped the photo of Oliver and me from my desk, along with the M&Ms I'd kept in the drawer, and said brightly,

'See you all after the holiday.'

Well, I don't want everyone knowing do I? Not just yet anyway. I can just picture their sympathetic smiles while knowing they are thinking,

'Poor cow, and at Christmas too.'

I sigh at the sight of a traffic warden hovering by my Kandy and hurry towards him. *Kandy* is my lovely little Ford *KA* by the way.

'Excuse me,' I call. 'I work here, so I am allowed to park there. I have a pass.'

Honestly, it comes to something when you get booked for parking in the office car park. What is it about the sight of a traffic warden that brings out the murderous in even the most placid of people? I don't know the guy but already I want to throttle him.

'Sorry love, *you're nicked*,' he says in a bad Sweeney imitation. 'The pass is not clearly evident and you're in a disabled parking space,' he adds bluntly before slapping the ticket onto the windscreen. I feel like he has just mugged me of my little brown envelope.

'Oh come on,' I say in my *let's be mates about this* voice. 'It's the festive season. Goodwill to all men and all that,' I trill, accidentally dropping the box of Roses at his feet.

Blimey, I sound like Ben Newman. Not that I'm asking the warden to get out his thrill drill just in case you thought I was. God, the end of my day is becoming more sordid by the minute. But seriously, who gives parking tickets on Christmas Eve? He steps back feigning a surprised look.

'Are you trying to bribe me miss?'

What? I didn't mention thrill drills did I? I only thought it. He tips his head towards the Roses.

'Because it won't work I'm afraid.'

'I dropped them,' I say innocently, 'but if ...'

He holds his hand up.

'I'd stop there if I were you miss. The ticket is on the windscreen now,' he says, and I swear he clicks his heels. Bloody little Hitler, don't you just hate them?

So now, because it is on the windscreen, it can't be removed. Has he stuck it on with superglue or something? I look at my pass which is, to be fair, upside down but ...

'The pass is in date though,' I argue. 'Couldn't you have just twisted your neck a bit then you would have seen it was in date?'

'Not with my ankylosing spondylitis,' he says dryly. 'I'll end up in a neck brace.'

He may still end up in a neck brace if he carries on like this. I was only asking for a small twist, not a full 360 degree turn like Regan Mcneil in *The Exorcist*.

'What if I put it the right way up?' I suggest hopefully, giving him my nicest smile.

'That won't take you out of the disabled space will it?' he says gleefully.

What a pig. I hope he isn't expecting a chocolate after this. He takes a tube of fruit pastilles from his pocket and sucks on one slowly. I find myself wishing he would choke on it. No, that's awful Binki, stop it.

'I only like the black ones,' he says, offering a red pastille to me.

It's all right for him but if I'd said that I'd be hauled in for making a racist comment.

'I'm actually not in a disabled space,' I say patiently.

He points nonchalantly and I follow his grubby finger to a rusty sign.

'But no one takes any notice of that,' I argue. 'Look, I've just lost my job,' I say appealing to his human side.

'Huh,' he scoffs, 'If I had a pound for every time I heard that. I suppose your mum is sick too.'

'Actually she is,' I say tearfully. 'How did you know?'

Well, OCD is a sickness isn't it? So it does count.

'It's on the windscreen now, so that's it.'

He makes it sound like sodding bird shit. I sigh and unlock the door.

'I hope you can sleep at night,' I quip before climbing into my car.

'I take Boots extra strong sleeping pills, works a treat.'

Bastard. I start the engine, give him the finger and drive out of the car park. God, I hope the saying that things come in threes that my mum rants on about isn't true. I don't think I have the energy for a third calamity on Christmas Eve.

Chapter Three

I'm winking at everyone, including the bloody greengrocer. What's worse, I'm standing under a huge sprig of mistletoe. I look like I'm giving the biggest come on ever. I've just dragged a heavy Christmas tree into the shop, practically poking my eye out with the stupid needles in the process. My hands are blue with cold and I can barely feel my toes. Christmas trees, who invented them? They're lethal, they really are. Whose bright idea was it to put a tree inside your home? Now, I'm stuck with this needle in my eye, and I can't get it out for love or money. Brian, the greengrocer, gives me an odd look as I continue to wink in a *say no more, say no more* manner.

'Something up?' he asks as I knock over a tray of satsumas.

'No, everything's fine,' I say, fumbling to retrieve the little suckers while hanging onto the tree and winking at the fifteen-year-old behind me. Christ, I'll be arrested for consorting with minors next.

'You sure?' pushes Brian.

'Absolutely,' I smile through a watery eye.

Oh yes, everything is dandy. I've only just lost my job and what now feels like my eye, not to mention half of my bonus on the exorbitant fine for parking in the right place. I reach the front of the queue.

'I did put a tree by for you,' he smiles. 'I thought you weren't collecting until after six.'

'Early finish,' I lie.

'That's nice of your boss,' he grins.

'Oh yes, he's all heart,' I say through gritted teeth.

I pay for the tree and schlep it, with great difficulty, to the car, cursing bloody Christmas the whole time. My eye is so red I look like Arnold Schwarzenegger in *The Terminator*, without the muscles of course. It is seriously horrific. I almost expect my eyeball to burst out along with an unexpected alien. I lift the bags of fruit into the boot and blow onto my hands. Snow begins to sprinkle and I pull my scarf tighter around me.

'Merry Christmas,' says a passing lady with a white poodle who cocks its leg up against my tyre. I try to tell myself it is good luck, you know, like when the bird shits on your head and everyone says,

'That means you're going to have good luck.'

I don't imagine the good luck started with the bird actually shitting on your head did it? Because that is the shittiest kind of luck ever isn't it? I want to ask her what is so merry about it, but of course I don't bother. I smile, wish her one too and drive the short journey home with the Christmas tree poking out of the passenger side window. It's only four o'clock and Oliver's car is there already. Maybe he got let off early too. Christ, I hope he didn't lose his job as well. I heave the Christmas tree from the car and drag it to the front of our block. The doorman rushes out and relieves me of its burden.

'Merry Christmas Miss Grayson,' he smiles.

Why is it at Christmas no one greets you with *Good afternoon* or *Good evening*? Only bloody *Merry Christmas*? God, I'm becoming a real bah humbug.

'Hi Taylor. How are you?'

'Very well,' he says gawping at my eye. God, the eyeball hasn't gone and popped out has it? Heaven knows I can't see bugger all.

'What happened to your eye Miss Grayson?'

'Christmas tree attack. There's a lot of it about this time of year.'

'You should get that seen to,' he says walking to my car. 'I'll bring your bags up shall I?'

I nod. I so love my flat and all that goes with it. I hit the lift button and fall against the wall, grateful for the blast of hot air that blows from the vents. Oh well, at least the needle in the eye thing means I no longer have to fear the dreaded third catastrophe. I get to the flat and fling open the door. The hot air from the heating system hits me. The windows are steamed up and I make a mental note to open one as soon as I have showered.

'I'm home. Let out for good behaviour,' I call, throwing my bag and scarf onto our new John Lewis couch and kicking a parrot underneath it. Not a real one, obviously. I'm not that cruel.

No reply. I hear a scuffling sound from the bedroom and the faint sound of music. He must be in the shower. There is a light tap on the front door. I open it to let Taylor in with the bags and tree.

'Merry Christmas,' I smile, giving him a twenty-pound note from the brown envelope. I must remember to get that back from Oliver later.

'Thank you, Miss Grayson and a good one to you and Mr Weber too,' he grins.

I close the door and stroll to the bedroom.

'You're bloody quiet, what the hell are you up to? Wrapping my very expensive present I hope,' I say flinging open the door.

What was that I said about a third thing? No one ever mentioned a fourth. I stand frozen in the doorway. In front of me, in my, no our bed, is Oliver and some woman I don't recognise. Mind you I'm only looking at her huge brown nipples which are bouncing up and down. I don't normally recognise people by their nipples. Oh God, what am I thinking? What the hell is happening? Why do I suddenly feel guilty, like I've walked in on my parents having sex? I feel the words 'I'm sorry,' forming on my lips and nearly turn back but instead ...

'What the fuck,' I utter in a disbelieving voice.

Oliver throws the woman off him so roughly that she almost tumbles off the bed, our bed. I can't bear this. I've never felt so humiliated. Maybe I'm seeing things; it's this bloody alienated eye, that's what it is. But no, I'm not seeing things. That really is Oliver's penis, rapidly diminishing admittedly, but his nevertheless. I don't believe this. Please God, Jesus and Santa say this isn't happening, please don't tell me Oliver is giving the bitch her Christmas bonus? Oliver attempts to stand but gets caught in the sheets, our sheets. Oh my God. He falls from the bed and I'm left staring at her. Her long black hair hangs sensually around her face. She looks vaguely familiar but I can't remember from where. I can never achieve that kind of look, in or out of bed. She's extremely pretty and looks stunning. I suddenly feel ancient. I've always wanted hair like that but I've been blessed

11

with fine wispy honey-blonde hair instead. This certainly proves the saying *blondes have all the fun* is totally crap. Her make-up is flawless and her lashes are long and thick. I need three coats of mascara to get that look. If there was a knife close by I swear I would kill her and all because she looks so good.

'Binki,' Oliver says, crawling pitifully towards me, and dragging our Laura Ashley throw behind him like a wedding train.

'How could you?' I say kicking at him.

I turn to the door. My legs feel like jelly. Damn it.

'Binki, it didn't mean anything. It's just because it's Christmas,' he says, a pained expression on his face. What the fuck has Christmas got to do with it? Bloody Christmas, I fucking hate it. He stands in the doorway with the sheet wrapped around him like a Roman emperor and looks pleadingly at me. I feel my heart melt.

'You look bloody stupid,' I say, feeling tears running down my cheeks. 'And you are bloody stupid. How could you do this to us?'

'I had too much to drink at work. I didn't know what I was doing. Come on Binki, please.'

He lurches towards me. I quickly sidestep and he stumbles.

'You knew enough to bring her to our flat when you thought I was at work,' I yell.

'It isn't what you think and ...' says Brown Nipples.

'And you can shut it,' I snap, grabbing the tissues from the bed and wiping my snotty nose. The soft smell of her fragrance wafts across and I feel suddenly sick.

'Come on Binki, don't throw everything away just because of a little Christmas indiscretion,' Oliver says while grabbing my arm.

'I didn't throw it away. You did.'

Why is everyone allowed a little Christmas indiscretion is what I want to know? First Ben Newman and now Oliver. I mean, what the hell? If this is Christmas then you can stick it. That is of course if you haven't already.

Chapter Four

Too upset to drive my little Kandy I decide to take a taxi. I wave at the first black cab I see and it stops. I nearly pass out on the spot. Christ Almighty, when does that ever happen? I can only imagine I have one tit hanging out, or my skirt has got stuck in my knickers and half my arse is on show. I never get a cab that quick at the best of times and on Christmas Eve it is unheard of. Maybe I look distraught, that must be it. Then again, when has a London cabbie given a shit about a distraught woman? Let's face it they are always the first to drive past aren't they?

'Are you free?' I ask, not quite believing my luck.

'No not even at Christmas. You still have to pay,' he quips.

'I meant, are you for hire?'

'Not really, but if you don't mind sharing with Bradley Cooper,' he says sarcastically.

Honestly, don't you just hate cab drivers with a sense of humour? I mean, it's not natural is it?

'Where to then darling?'

Tower Bridge seems a good idea. I could throw myself off. After all, no one would give a shit. I'd just be one more Christmas statistic. There is probably a queue there already and I'll most likely find a ticket system set up to make us wait until our number lights up before we can jump. Yes, that's about my luck at the moment.

'You do want to go somewhere don't you love?' he asks irritably.

'No, I just fancied a sit down,' I snap.

I sigh and look back at my apartment block, and oh God, is that Oliver running out in his pants and T shirt?

'Westbourne Grove and make it snappy,' I say, feeling my heart race.

'What do you think this is, a movie take?' says the cabbie.

Bloody hell, I'm paying aren't I? And most likely at some exorbitant Christmas Eve rate.

'Yes, so could we have some sodding action here,' I say averting my eyes from the embarrassing sight of Oliver. I can't believe I was hoping this man would propose to me over Christmas. Oliver I mean, obviously not the taxi driver. After all, I barely know him. I suppose that won't happen now will it? The cab shoots off leaving a waving Oliver hanging onto his loose underpants. It's not a pleasant sight. I fumble in my bag for some tissues and pull them out along with the stupid parking ticket.

'Got done?' asks the driver.

Oh God, yes I've been done all right.

'The bastards love to get you at Christmas,' he says with a snarl.

'Well they all got me,' I say hiccupping. 'All the bastards got me.'

He shifts uncomfortably in his seat.

'Yeah, well don't let it ruin your Christmas,' he smiles, tinkering with a Saint Christopher lucky charm. 'Worse things happen. You could have lost your job.'

'I did lose my job,' I mumble, before popping a handful of M&Ms into my mouth.

He sniffs and goes quiet. Why me? I look out into the snow-dusted streets of London where happy couples are walking hand in hand. I don't understand it. I did everything right. Well, I thought I did everything right. I can just hear my mother's words. *What doesn't kill you makes you stronger.* Bloody stupid saying that is. Damn, we were driving down to my parents tomorrow. That means I've now got to face the M4 in a filthy mood which will inevitably result in road rage and missing the bloody exit. I hate driving at Christmas. Oliver never seems to mind. Honestly of all of the times to shag someone else he has to do it the day before visiting my parents. I find myself wondering if he was telling the truth. What if this wasn't the first time? What if he's been shagging her for weeks? No, mustn't think about it. It probably was just a Christmas thing. God, I'm excusing it now. Like that makes it perfectly okay if it was just a Christmas thing. But in our bed of all places, I mean, he could have used the couch, or the floor. Oh do shut up Binki, you know he could never do it on the couch with his back. Christ, the whole thing has turned my head. Why the hell am I thinking of his sodding back. Hopefully he'll be crippled by the morning. That will teach him.

'Where in Westbourne Grove do you want me to stop love?'

I see Muffy's street approaching.

'Here will be fine,' I say.

I climb out reluctantly. The last thing I want to do is tell my closest friend that the love of my life has just cheated on me with some huge brown-nippled woman on Christmas Eve. Maybe I won't. Perhaps I'll just say I was passing and thought I'd drop in for coffee. I pay the exorbitant fare out of my brown envelope. Blimey, that little bonus didn't last long did it? He stares at the notes like they're Scottish currency or something. I'm not giving him a bloody tip if that's what he's waiting for.

'Thanks very much,' I say, slamming the door. 'The quickie with Bradley Cooper made all the difference.'

'And a Merry Christmas to you too,' he says before shooting off.

Don't you just hate people who wish you a Merry Christmas with attitude? It's obvious they are really wishing you the worst one possible. He got in a bit late didn't he? Let's face it; my Christmas couldn't get less merry if it tried. I trundle down the steps to Muffy's basement flat and put on a brave face. She opens the door, takes one look at me and the tell-tale M&Ms in my hand and says,

'Don't tell me. You found the bugger in bed with some tart from work.'

* * *

'What a bastard thing to do at Christmas,' says Muffy, crashing about in the kitchen.

What a bastard thing to do, period. I'm stretched out on her couch with a cold compress on my head and two aspirin fizzing away in a glass of water. I've got a box of tissues in one hand and my mobile in the other, although I'm ignoring every call from Oliver, and there have been seven so far. I can't even bring myself to listen to his voicemail messages.

'What is it with bloody men and Christmas?' She yells. 'They always seem to end up naked with a bimbo balanced on their balls. Christ, if we did that, can you imagine?'

I sigh.

'No I can't imagine balancing a bimbo on my balls,' I say stupidly.

'What was she like anyway,' she asks curiously, popping her head around the kitchen door.

'Oh, you know, young, with massive nipples, gorgeous hair and a voluptuous body. Everything I don't have,' I say miserably. 'The perfect balls-balancing woman I suppose.'

'Christ,' she mumbles, putting a plate of mince pies on the table beside me. 'Don't you start feeling bad about yourself? Did you read the Robin Norwood book I gave you?'

Oh God, not the one about women who love too much. It was so bloody depressing. Muffy is my closest girlfriend and staunch feminist, who thinks all men are dysfunctional little shits and who will finally let you down one way or the other. I'm slowly coming round to her way of thinking.

'I tried,' I mumble.

'I give up with you,' she groans.

It seems everyone gives up on me. I so wish I was like Muffy. She is so comfortable with herself although not so comfortable with men mind you. I think she hates them. Muffy has a brilliant job in public relations and always looks terrific whether she has just stepped out of bed or at the end of a stressful day. Men fall at her feet, seriously, and she just walks all over them. If I didn't love her so much I would have to kill her. I swallow the last M&M and say,

'I can't eat a thing.'

'Don't let the bugger put you off your food. He's the one who's always nagged you about losing weight isn't he? Well sod him.'

She's quite right of course, and I do feel a bit peckish. I can't help wondering if it was my fault. Maybe I did give Ben Newman the come on without realising it. I can't imagine what I did mind you, unless he finds being totally ignored most of the week a sexual turn on. Perhaps I didn't meet Oliver's sexual needs enough. Not that he ever was that demanding you understand.

We made love three times a week, that's average isn't it? Well it was always enough for me, I never complained.

'If you ask me, he doesn't want to commit. It's easier for him if you leave, that makes more sense. He probably feels you're too good for him. You've *over loved* you see,' says Muffy with an authoritative tone of someone who knows what she's talking about.

I don't see in the least. In fact, I'm having great difficultly seeing altogether with my blood engorged eye that stings like mad. I'm sure it is deteriorating by the second. It must be the stress. Surely if Oliver didn't want to commit he wouldn't be looking at rings in Hatton Garden would he? Suddenly a terrible thought enters my head. What if he wasn't looking at rings at all? Oh, my God, he was most likely looking for some very expensive jewellery for Miss Brown Nipples. Oh how could he?

'You're *stereotypical*, that's your problem,' continues Muffy.

Great, at least there is a name for someone like me.

'Can you take a pill for that?' I ask cynically.

'You're blaming yourself already aren't you?' fumes Muffy, launching into her favourite topic, the complex dipstick male mind. 'He'll do anything to wriggle out of ...'

She stops and stares at my eye.

'Jesus Christ, how did that happen?'

'A Christmas tree,' I say flatly.

She jumps up and slaps her thigh.

'God,' she thunders. 'He went at you with a bloody Christmas tree. What a sodding brute. You should report it Binki, like *now*,' she thrusts a mobile at me. I point out I'm already holding one.

'I got a needle in my eye from the tree I brought home. Oliver could barely untangle himself from the sheets let alone go at me with a tree. He's got a bad back remember?'

She scoffs.

'That didn't stop him humping some bimbo did it?'

'I'm surprised she didn't send it into spasm. You should have seen the size of her tits.'

Don't think about her tits Binki. Think about something else, anything else, but not tits.

'Pity he didn't go into anaphylactic shock, swallow his tongue and die,' says Muffy evilly.

I gawp at her, blimey that's a bit harsh. Death by tongue swallowing, even I wouldn't wish that on Oliver, and I'm feeling worse by the minute. It's Christmas Eve and it has been a day of award-winning horror, definitely worthy of a film. Maybe Carey Mulligan could play me.

'You need to change your pattern of thinking. You still believe being *in love* means being in pain. You were expecting him to propose weren't you? Instead you find him balls deep with some floozy from work,' she says nonchalantly, biting into a mince pie.

'You were the one who told me he was in Hatton Garden,' I say defensively.

'It all stems from problems in your childhood,' Muffy spouts, cracking open a walnut.

I knew my mother was to blame for something.

'Did you see yourself as a co-dependent?' asks Muffy, looking at me intently.

'Only on M&Ms,' I answer honestly.

I feel like I'm having a therapist's session. I wonder if this has something to do with the fishnet tights and suspenders. Oliver has a fetish for them, that and pirate outfits, but I always felt stupid with them on. I struggle to remember if Brown Nipples was wearing anything pirate related. No, I feel quite sure she was wearing absolutely nothing and feel the mince pie lurch up my diaphragm. I must put the whole thing out of my mind. Oh God, all the presents we were taking to my parents are back at the flat, as of course are my clothes.

'You'll have to go back and get my clothes,' I blurt out, 'and the Christmas presents.'

Her mouth drops open.

'I can't go there, what if ... Well you know, what if she is still there?'

God, I don't believe this.

'Tell her to bugger off if she is.'

I shudder at the memory of Oliver's pained expression.

'Who does this sort of thing at Christmas,' I say with a little sob. 'It's so cruel.'

'Half the male population if you ask me. Little shits,' she snarls. 'If I go round there I'm likely to give him a knuckle sandwich.'

'Can you get my chocolate teapot,' I say, the thought of it comforting me. 'You can't pop round now can you?'

She tsks at me.

'I'm stressed,' I urge.

'Yes, and you'll eat the whole pot. Honestly you and your M&Ms. Has it ever occurred to you that most women don't hide sweets in teapots just so their boyfriend won't nag them?'

I sigh.

'His parents were coming on Boxing Day,' I say stupidly. 'I bought ham on the bone and tons of salad. The fridge is bulging. I nearly bought a whole turkey. I never buy that much food.'

I grab another mince pie.

'You don't have cream do you?' I say miserably.

'Don't comfort eat or you'll end up huge.'

I so need my chocolate teapot.

'I don't care. I never want to look at another man. Food is my best friend and lover now,' I say with a boldness I really don't feel.

'I'm never making myself nice for a man again. I shall end up like that woman in the film *Monster* and become a lesbian.'

Muffy steps back slightly.

'Christ Binki, don't do anything extreme.'

That reminds me.

'Ah, too late. I threw my job in too, so it couldn't get any worse could it?'

Muffy stares at me.

'Why on earth did you throw your job in? Are you out of your mind? Have you been drinking?'

That's great isn't it? My best friend thinks I can only do something drastic when intoxicated.

'No, I just kind of had an epiphany. There I was waiting in the queue for my morning cappuccino and I thought I'm going to chuck my job in today. Of course I hadn't been drinking,' I snap. 'Ben Newman tried to thrill drill me over the office desk and that just kind of clinched it,' I add scornfully.

I stuff a mince pie into my mouth. Muffy stands over me with a carton of single cream. I'm wondering if she needs me to tip my mouth up so she can pour some in. She places the carton onto the coffee table with shaking hands. That's the only good thing about your boyfriend balancing a bimbo on his balls isn't it? It's the one excuse to eat exactly what and as much as you like, and no one likes to tell you off. After all, if you can't stuff your face at a time like this then when can you?

'Ben Newman tried to give you one?' she says wide-eyed.

I nod.

'And we're not talking bonus. You'd never believe it possible would you? At the same time my boyfriend was ...' It's no good I can't say it. I hate men, I really do. I'm giving them up. No more men for me.

'While he was, you know with her, my boss was also trying to have me over his desk. On Christmas Eve, can you believe it? He was all fired up to give me his thrill drill. So I bluntly told him where to stuff his thrill drill. He then kind of blackmailed me so I had no choice but to leave. I was stupidly hoping Oliver would give him a black eye.'

Her mouth gapes open and tiny pieces of mince pie drop out. I look at her in disgust as she grabs a tissue.

'Ben Newman?' she says aghast. 'Ben Newman with the wart on his nose tried to have you over the desk? Ben Newman?' she repeats like a parrot. I think we've now established my boss's name is Ben Newman.

'Don't look that bloody shocked. I still have some pulling power. I'm not twenty stone yet you know,' I say trying to hide my hurt feelings.

'I suppose you should be grateful he didn't ask for a blow job,' sniffs Muffy. 'Then again, I suppose you wouldn't have had to look at the wart.'

I stare at her.

'Okay, just a thought,' she mumbles.

'Christ Muffy, I'm eating,' I groan.

Her phone erupts and we both jump. I stare at it in horror.

'Don't answer it,' I scream. 'It's Oliver.'

Muffy gives the phone a despairing look.

'No it isn't. No one calls the landline except my mother.'

I watch her stroll towards it. If this was a Hollywood film then I am sure this would be one of those *No-o-o-o-o* moments with her moving in slow motion.

'But what if it is him?' I say, my heart hammering in my chest.

She shakes her head and picks up the phone. 'It won't be.'

'Oh Oliver, hello,' she says meekly, and mouths *cock it* to me.

Great, why does no one ever listen to me? I hear the murmur of Oliver's voice and feel myself turn to jelly.

'She is very upset Oliver,' she says angrily.

Oh no. Now he knows where I am. She holds the phone towards me.

'It's Oliver,' she says.

I'd never have guessed. I hiccup my way to the phone and take it with shaking hands.

'Binki, I'm really sorry baby. Please come home so we can talk.'

Huh, talk about what?

'How could you Oliver? How could you do this to us?'

'I'm sorry baby. I didn't know you were coming home early. I …'

What the fuck?

'So it's my fault now is it? It's my fault for coming home early?' I say fighting back a sob.

'No, I didn't mean …'

'What did you mean then?'

'I don't know … I'm not sure,' he says stupidly.

'Oh Oliver, you're such a prick,' I say and hang up.

'It wasn't your mother,' I snap at Muffy.

She jumps up and rushes to the kitchen, returning with half a loaf of bread, olives and a cheese board.

'Down with men,' she declares. 'I'm sick of going without bread and cheese and all the best things in life. Let's get bloated and then I'll fetch your stuff. Bastards. We don't need them. We have equal rights now.'

Crikey, I'm lost for words. What do you say to the woman who thinks bread and cheese are the best things in life?

'To giving up men,' she declares holding up a piece of Hovis. I follow suit.

'Amen to that.'

'To Emily Pankhurst,' I say stuffing my mouth full of olives.

Chapter Five

Dad opens the door wearing a red and green apron with the words *It's All About The Cock Not The Cook* splashed across it. No doubt a Christmas present from my mother who I hear shouting in the kitchen.

'Merry Christmas, Merry Christmas,' he shouts. 'Bella, she's here. Your mother's on her mobile,' he adds, ushering in Muffy. 'Probably phoning the mortuary, you do know we were expecting you over an hour ago?'

I can't take my eyes off the apron. God, I hope they haven't got friends coming. I hate it when my parent's friends look at me with pity.

'Yes sorry, we took the wrong exit,' Muffy says, averting her eyes from the apron.

'Junction ten was it? It's a bugger that one.'

'Cool apron,' I say, quickly closing the door before their 80-year-old neighbour spots it through her binoculars.

'Oh yes, your mother didn't want the new shirt she bought me ruined.'

'Right,' I say, handing him the carrier bag full of presents. 'I think a ruined shirt may be preferable.'

He looks behind me.

'Where's Oliver?'

I can't very well say balancing a floozy on his balls can I? Although I imagine his balls are pretty tired by now.

'Erm, he's not coming. There's something I need to tell you and Mum.'

'Oh dear,' he says adjusting his glasses.

I stroll into the lounge where the tree lights are flashing like crazy. It's enough to give you an epileptic fit.

'It's the middle red one that keeps doing it. I'll have another look in a minute,' says Dad, sighing.

'Oh, don't worry,' smiles Muffy. 'We'll just all convulse after dinner, much more fun than charades.'

I stroll into the kitchen, which is hotter than India and steamier than a Turkish bath. Mother is leaning out of a window with a finger jammed in one ear and a mobile phone glued to the other while a saucepan of Brussels sprouts bubbles over. My God, what is she wearing? It looks like The Amazing Technicolor Dream Coat. I'd have brought my sunglasses if I'd known. The table is covered in stuffing balls and tiny sausages rolled up in bacon. I feel my stomach rumble and dive into the biscuit bin for a Rich Tea.

'Hello Sylvie, are you still there? Just bring wine. No, white would be good. Hello, are you there? Oh, I thought I'd lost you. Yes, that will be great. Shit, buggery phone, you're cutting out again. Are you still ... Bugger it. Shall ... bugger.'

She turns, sees me and drops the phone.

'Darling,' she cries, opening her arms and like a child I fall straight into them. 'I thought you and Oliver had run off to elope.'

If only. What a different Christmas I'd be having. I smell her Estee Lauder perfume and feel immediately comforted.

'I tried your mobile but you know what this one is like,' she says releasing me and pointing to the Nokia. 'Bloody thing, I said to your father we should take it back. I've got to be in the bloody shed before anyone can hear me. I sometimes think that was his plan you know.'

She looks at me closely.

'What's the matter, something's happened I can feel it?'

I turn the sprouts down.

'Everything's fine,' I say. 'Well kind of.'

She flings open the back door to let the steam out.

'I knew it,' she says falling onto a kitchen stool. 'Is it your breasts?'

What have my breasts got to do with anything?

'No, I ...'

'You do check them don't you? What is it then?'

I dip in the biscuit barrel again.

23

'It's Oliver ...'

'Oh God, it's his prostrate isn't it? I had a feeling.'

I wish he was bloody prostrate.

'Mum, it has nothing to do with body parts, at least nothing to do with parts gone wrong or not working.'

I sound like Jeremy Clarkson talking about cars.

'And it's *prostate*, not prostrate.'

'Well, it's all the same.'

Her face lights up.

'He's proposed hasn't he? Oh and at Christmas, that's marvellous news.'

I really don't know how my mother manages to go from my breasts and Oliver's prostate problems to us getting married, all in the space of twenty seconds and still manages to get it all wrong.

'Not quite,' I say softly.

Her face darkens.

'Oh dear, I'm not sure I want to hear this. Is he in the lounge with your father? I hope he can fix those lights. It's like a nightclub in there. I can't imagine what the neighbours think we're up to in the evenings.'

'Binki darling, have a drink,' says my dad.

I see Muffy is already holding a glass with yellow liquid in it.

'What's that?' I ask.

'I'm not sure,' she says looking at it curiously. 'Something with egg in it.'

'It's eleven in the morning,' I protest.

'I could make tea,' says Mum, sniffing the top of a milk bottle. I so wish she wouldn't do that.

'It's Christmas,' Dad laughs. 'We don't want tea at Christmas.'

Oh of course, stupid me. It's Christmas, so that explains why my dad is wearing an apron with the word COCK splashed all over it. I mean, for goodness' sake, what is it about Christmas that makes people think everything is acceptable? Oh, you can bang your boss up against the desk, after all it is Christmas. I can almost hear my mother telling me not to be so silly about Oliver giving his colleague one. It is Christmas after all and if you can't get your leg over at Christmas when can you. Only at the festive season is it acceptable to knock back the cocktails at nine in the morning and not be called a lush.

'Do you want eggnog?' asks Dad, pulling me into the lounge where Mariah Carey is singing. I feel like smashing the hi-fi and telling Mariah that I couldn't give a toss what she wants for Christmas.

'Ah yes, that's what it's called,' pipes up Muffy, taking another sip.

That's another thing. When does anyone ever drink something as obnoxious as eggnog except at Christmas? I mean who seriously goes to the pub after work and says *Mine's an eggnog?* Well you don't do you? I fall onto the couch and bury myself in the overabundance of cushions and throw back half a glass of eggnog. Well it is Christmas after all. All I want to do is climb into my fleecy pyjamas and pig out in front of the telly. I grab Dad's bumper issue of the Radio Times and study the Christmas Day schedule. Oh lovely, they have an omnibus edition of Coronation Street. There is bound to be something in that to match my misery. I'll overindulge on the Turkish Delight and eggnog, and feel very sorry for myself.

'She found Oliver at it in their bed with some tart from work,' announces Muffy, helping herself to a handful of peanuts.

There is a deafening silence broken only by Muffy's crunching.

'And on Christmas Eve,' she adds for extra impact. I want to hide behind the cushions. 'How shitty was that?'

My mother falls onto the couch beside me.

'I see what you mean about his prostrate being okay,' she mumbles.

'Prostate,' I correct.

'Well whatever, it doesn't really matter. His thingy is in working order then. What a little arse.'

'Bella,' admonishes Dad.

'Well at Christmas, it really isn't on is it Bernard? Stella's husband Rupert was at it too,' she says, lowering her voice. 'She said Rupert pretty much always had a dolly bird sitting on his balls at Christmas. So you're not alone.'

'Amazingly that isn't much of a comfort,' I say.

'No, of course not darling,' she says hugging me.

'For God's sake Bella,' says Dad, topping up my glass. 'Do we have to hear all the gruesome details?'

'I haven't told you them yet, I'm only relaying the story. They were her words. It seems men do this sort of thing at Christmas. No bloody control, that's their problem.'

'Little shits,' agrees Muffy.

'Well, I've never had a bimbo on my balls at Christmas, or at any other time come to that, either at work or home,' says Dad with a sigh. 'And I don't see what makes it acceptable at Christmas.'

'Nor do I,' says Muffy pouring more eggnog into her glass. 'This is nice isn't it Binki?'

What's nice? Discussing my horrendous Christmas, or the eggnog?

'I should hope you haven't Bernard. And do fix those lights before they give me a headache.'

I'm trying hard not to cry. I was so looking forward to Christmas with Oliver. I had bought him some CDs, a new shirt and the *Pirates of the Caribbean* DVD box set as he is so into his pirate stuff. I'd also splashed out on one of those red letter day experience gifts. I saw it and thought Oliver would love to race a car around Brands Hatch. Now all I can think about is him crashing the car at Brands Hatch. I know, it's cruel of me, but do you blame me? I'll never get my money back. There was me stupidly thinking he was going to propose over the holiday season. I'd even bought a sexy lacy top and undies from Ann Summers. One of those split open tops where you simply untie the bow and your tits pop out. I remember thinking that will turn Oliver on. I'm such a fool. Obviously huge brown nipples turn him on and I'm not blessed with huge tits. I've always been a bit flat-chested, I so hate my breasts. I'm never getting involved with a man again, not ever.

'She's also lost her job. Well, she chucked it in actually,' says Muffy.

I'm sure she's just trying to help break the bad news but Christ, has she never heard of sensitivity?

'Her boss tried to shag her over the desk. Perverted little shit. I hate bosses that think they can do that,' she finishes, opening a box of Thorntons.

God Almighty, talk about staggering the bad news. Dad flops into a chair and his apron crinkles into *It's All About The Cock*. It sure is. Don't you just love Christmas?

'I've heard nothing like it,' he mutters.

There is silence as we all sip our eggnog.

'I bought your favourite perfume,' says Mum. 'That Lizzy Malarkey one'

'Issey Miyake,' I correct.

'Yes, well the same thing,' mumbles Mum.

More silence and Dad tops up our glasses.

'Your Great Aunty Vera died,' says Dad, adding to the gloom.

We all nod solemnly like that's about right. Christmas is not all it is cracked up to be. Roll on bloody Boxing Day.

Chapter Six

Two weeks have passed. Christmas has been and gone and I've moved in with Muffy, and I'm going slowly insane. Christmas means that everywhere has been closed like forever. I haven't had one reply from the job agencies, not that I am in any fit state for an interview. I spend my days in my pyjamas and sit on Muffy's couch with my computer on my lap and the chocolate teapot beside me. It's not a teapot made of chocolate, just in case you thought it was. It wouldn't have lasted this long if it had been I can assure you. I bought it when Oliver and I holidayed in St Ives last year. It's a lovely white teapot with red polka dots. Of course, the thing with teapots is that you never use them do you? It's far easier to throw a teabag into a mug isn't it? So when Oliver started nagging me about my addiction, I decided the teapot was the best place to hide my stash. Chocolate that is, not cocaine just in case you were wondering. Although I'm beginning to think at the rate I'm going through M&Ms that cocaine may be cheaper and carry far less calories. I've hardly been out of the flat. Well, I went out once to get some supplies and even then with my coat over my pyjamas. It was freezing, but any hope I had of dying from pneumonia never materialised. I just ended up with a filthy cold. I haven't stopped eating, mostly popcorn, marmite sandwiches and cheese crackers. My keyboard is covered in crumbs and the 'F' key keeps sticking. Just as well. I keep looking at Oliver's Facebook page but his profile gives nothing away except for a daily update on the state of his bad back. Well, if he will get his leg over Brown Nipples what does he expect? Muffy says he puts on a pained look when she pops round and says things like *Tell her I'm okay. She needn't worry.* Ha, as if I do. I wonder if he has seen her again, not that I'm interested of course. I'm totally over him, I mean I really am. As for Muffy, well she soon let the side down. As soon as Christmas was over she was back on the Ryvita and tuna salad. She's so boring. Still, at least she has a flat and a job. I've got neither. She's also got plenty of food. I promised to join her at the gym today, and I was intending to but you know what it's like. So I've stuck a Rosemary Conley DVD on instead and I will make an effort to Salsa with her. Just as soon as I've finished this fried egg sandwich, I really will. Oliver has given up phoning me. I had hoped he would offer me the flat but oh no, the bugger is still there, living in luxury while I just fade away. Muffy gets my post on the way home from work each day and a pile of unopened letters sits on the coffee table. I stare at it thinking I really should check them. I lean forward and drag the pile towards me and begin the painful process of going through the post. The first one is a glitzy Christmas card with a little note inside. Don't you hate those round robin things? I think the post office should supply sick bags when they deliver them. I unfold the note as I pop another cheese cracker in my mouth. From Ruth and Greg, do I even know a Ruth and Greg? Well, obviously we don't see each other often do we else they wouldn't have seen fit to send me an A4 sheet with their life story printed on it. Oh well, might as well read it now, after all I've got sod all else to do with my time.

'Oh what a year it's been! [*You can say that again, mine was great up until Christmas Eve.*] So let me tell you all about our wonderful life this year. January was a bit of a struggle; Greg broke his thumb and couldn't work for a couple of weeks. [*Oh God no, how absolutely tragic.*] It was a tough fortnight and we had to help him out with our savings, poor thing. [*Crikey, you should have had my fortnight. I wonder if they have any savings left for me.*] February saw me start my much anticipated Pilates class; I'm now a fully qualified Pilates teacher. I feel so blessed. [*Pass the sick bag*] Tom turned four and we are preparing him for school in September. He has already started playing the piano and has a real talent for music. [*Yeah right*] In March we whisked the family off on a mini-break to Austria for one-to-one skiing lessons, we felt we deserved it. Our swimming pool dream came true, just in time for summer. We had a lovely party to celebrate which was attended by the local councillor no less. [*Deep envy, NOT*] We hired private caterers, it made such a difference. A bit more expensive but Greg's bonus more or less paid for everything, and we give thanks for that. [*Ha, my bloody bonus did well too. Paid all of a parking ticket, an overpriced taxi, and a Christmas tree that almost took my eye out. Beat that if you can ... But I do give thanks, I think.*] In September Gabrielle was offered a place at an all-girls school and now she is the most popular girl of her year. [*Bloody lesbian, no doubt*] She is doing amazingly well. [*I bet*] Her teacher predicts all As for her GCSEs, we are so proud. An Oxford graduate if ever there was one. [*More sick bags please*].

Are these people for real? Who the hell are they anyway? How can you get letters like this from people you don't even remember? Maybe I should write my own belated round robin. Yes that's what I'll do.

'Hi Everyone,

I don't suppose you give a toss but I've had a shit year. Things were going well up to Christmas Eve and then my boss decided to give me my Christmas bonus – oh, did I say Christmas bonus? I meant to say Christmas boner. So, this next year will be 'challenging' and 'full of new opportunities' as I struggle to survive jobless and homeless. Did I say homeless? Yes, that's because I left my prick of a boyfriend at just about the same time as your little angels were passing their grade three piano exams and getting the school prize for being the best child ever, and not to mention coming out as lesbians at their all-girls school. So, spare a thought for me as your teenage daughter embarks on her gap year mission to feed the starving of Africa, as I will be on a mission to feed myself, and will be en-route to the job centre. And no, I didn't have a holiday of a lifetime in the Bahamas last year as you all did, nor will I be having one this year. I may have a day trip to Skegness and I give thanks for that, and now you can all sod off. You boasting up your own arse pricks.'

I sigh heavily and throw all the Christmas cards in the bin without reading them. There's a limit to how much you can read of other people's good fortune without tying a noose around your neck isn't there? Honestly, I was never this bad tempered until Oliver slept with what's-her-face. I turn off Rosemary Conley, I mean seriously, who wants to look like her anyway? And switch on Jeremy Kyle instead, far more entertaining. It's always nice to see someone else suffering like you isn't it? I glance nervously at the bills and breathe a sigh of relief when I see they are not so bad after all. I study another letter curiously. It looks frighteningly official. Oh no, what if my parking ticket payment didn't go through? The postmark is the 28th December. It's the 9th January now. I wonder if a relationship break-up counts as mitigating circumstances. Shit, this is all I need. My mouth goes dry as I rip open the letter. If I have to pay out any more money I seriously will have to consider selling my body. I scan the words quickly.

Dear Miss Grayson,

Please contact Mr Hayden, of Hayden and Carruthers to discuss your inheritance from Mrs Vera Cramton. The reading of the will is to be heard on the 2nd January at 10.15. We look forward to seeing you.

Yours Faithfully
Martin Hayden.

Oh my God. Great Aunt Vera left me something in her will. That's just amazing. I mute Jeremy Kyle and grab my mobile with my heart pounding. But I've missed the will reading. Hell, why didn't I read my stupid post? I punch in the solicitor's number and wait. It seems like forever before anyone answers. Please let it be money. I don't care if it's not a lot, just a little will help right now. Maybe my luck is finally changing.

'Hayden and Carruthers, solicitors of repute, Samantha speaking, good afternoon, how can I help you today?' says a woman in a squeaky voice.

Blimey, that was a long speech. I've almost forgotten what I was going to say.

'Hello, can I speak to Mr Hayden please?'

'What is it concerning?' she asks sweetly.

'I've received a letter from you ...'

'Reference number please?'

'I'm sorry, what,' I say, quickly scanning the letter for a number and feeling the first stirrings of panic.

'I can't see one but ...'

'Just putting you on hold, are you okay to hold?'

Well no I'm not. I'm very anxious actually, but before I can reply there is a click and I'm listening to music. Correction, I'm listening to something, but I wouldn't have the gall to call it music. It's that *drive you to despair* stuff that should be banned. It's seriously criminal. I'm sure they play it in the hope you'll hang up before they get back to you. You can almost hear them saying, 'Another one bites the dust'. They can't even play it at the right speed. I crush a cheese biscuit between my fingers and feel my teeth grind. Seriously, if it wasn't for the fact that I may be inheriting a fortune I would hang up. The music sounds like it is coming from an old gramophone with a slow turntable. It's excruciating, it really is. It's the music you hear at a crematorium service, you know, at that moment when someone's coffin goes through the curtains. That painful moment when you want the whole thing to be over and, just in case you don't seem upset enough, they play this music to induce the tears. My heart races and I feel sick. I feel my finger hover over the off button on the phone. If I wasn't depressed when I made this call I will be soon. There is a click.

'All our operators are busy at the moment. Your call is important to us, please hold,' chirps a slightly robotic voice.

Yeah right. And back to the droning music.

'Hayden and Carruthers, solicitors of repute, Samantha speaking, good afternoon, how can I help you today?'

Déjà vu or what?

'Hi Samantha, you had me on hold. It felt a bit like a pre-execution dinner to be honest.'

'Oh yes, do you have your reference number?'

She's totally ignored me.

'No, there isn't one actually. I have …'

'There is always a reference number, right at the top of the letter.' she says abruptly.

I feel the hairs on the back of my neck bristle.

'I assure you Samantha, there is no reference number,' I say firmly.

Silence and then,

'You're sure the letter is from us?'

Does she think I'm some kind of dimwit?

'The letter has your name on it,' I say.

'My name?' she asks puzzled.

'Not you personally, but the solicitor's name ...'

I'm beginning to wish I had never started this.

'And your name is?'

I'm so tempted to say Lady Gaga.

'Binki Grayson.'

'Binki did you say?' she repeats.

Blimey she recognises me. It must be millions that Aunty Vera has left me. Wait till I tell Muffy.

'Yes, that's ...'

'That's an odd name.'

What a cheek.

'I say, you're not ...'

'No I'm not. It's Binki with an ...'

'Oh, are you okay to hold?'

'No,' I shout.

Click and I'm back in the crematorium. I'll be stabbing myself soon. I groan and the phone clicks again just as the television automatically turns Jeremy Kyle back on.

'So you've slept with fifteen of your fiancé's friends?' shouts Jeremy to a spotted face woman.

I don't believe this.

'Hello, Miss Grayson?'

I wonder if I should explain that it isn't me that has slept with fifteen of my fiancé's friends.

'Yes,' I answer quietly, thinking it best not to get on the wrong side of her.

'Putting you through to Mr Hayden now.'

Thank goodness. Another click and there is a male voice.

'Miss Grayson? I'm pleased to hear from you. We were thinking you had perhaps gone away for Christmas.'

'Something like that,' I laugh.

'Right, let me have a look at what we have for you,' he says thoughtfully.

I cross everything and say a quick prayer.

'Ah yes, I remember. Mrs Vera Cramton.'

I hear a rustle of papers.

'Here we are. Yes, your great aunt has left you Driftwood.'

I don't want to seem ungrateful but what did Aunty Vera expect me to do with an old plank of wood?

'Driftwood,' I say feeling my heart sink.

'We have the key if you would care to collect it. If you could bring your passport, we can hand it over.'

'Key?' I echo.

He laughs.

'To the property. *Driftwood* is a house just on the outskirts of Hampstead Heath. Lovely name don't you think?'

'Great Aunty Vera has left me a house, are you sure?' I ask.

'There's no mistake. If you could bring your driving licence if you don't have a passport.'

What a cheek, of course I have a passport. I'm a woman of the world after all. A property in Hampstead Heath? Oh my God. I never even knew Great Aunty Vera had a house. She never mentioned it. Thank you, thank you so much Aunty Vera. It is bound to be worth at least a hundred thousand, if not more. I can barely control my excitement and have to fight back a scream.

'Yes yes of course. Is it a large house?'

'I don't have those details I'm afraid.'

Oh well, it's a property. He didn't say caravan did he?

I arrange to pick up the key tomorrow. I click off the phone and cheer. I feel vindicated. I call my hairdresser Wesley, and book myself an appointment for the morning. Oh yes, I am a woman of property now. Stick that up your arse Oliver Weber.

Chapter Seven

My exuberance is quickly dampened by Muffy and totally quenched by my mother.

'It's probably a complete dump,' says Muffy, chopping a green pepper.

I'm sure they were happier when I was falling apart. I was just starting to get a new perspective on everything too. This could be a turning point for me but oh no, not according to Muffy and Mother.

'Yes, she is probably right darling,' agrees Mother as she cleans up behind Muffy.

I wouldn't mind but it isn't even her kitchen. Honestly, talk about dissing the first bit of good luck that comes my way.

'It may not be,' I say while feeling a little twinge of doubt.

Supposing they are right and it is just a dump? No one seems to know about this house that Great Aunty Vera apparently owned. It will probably turn out to be a tiny tumbled down studio apartment in the back streets, well that's not so bad is it? It's more than I have at the moment, and I can always sell it.

'She never said a word about a house. Mind you, she was very secretive. Even your gran doesn't know about it and she was her sister. I can't for the life of me fathom why she left it to you though,' mumbles Mum while emptying the dishwasher. God, I so wish she would sit still for five minutes.

'Gran can barely remember *me*,' I scoff. 'So we can't really take anything she says as gospel.'

'Well, that's true,' quips Dad from behind the paper. 'And you did visit her from time to time when you were younger. She probably had no one else to leave it to. Old people do that kind of thing don't they? At least she didn't leave it to her cats.'

'You see,' I say triumphantly. 'I'm the youngest relative she had and she wanted someone to make the most of it.'

'Well I don't know why she rented a flat in Knightsbridge if she owned a house.'

'Perhaps it was an investment and she rented it out,' I venture.

'We're only trying to prepare you, just in case,' says Muffy. 'You don't want to get a shock. Not another one.'

Thanks for reminding me.

'But you should still get your hair done,' says Mum tactfully, taking the salad into the living room. 'Just in case you meet a nice man.'

'Men are off limits,' snaps Muffy. 'Don't even go there. Isn't that right Binki?'

I nod and think of Oliver. I wonder if he will ask for my half of the rent now that I have moved out.

'Just be prepared is all we're saying, just in case it is a pile of rubbish,' says Dad.

For goodness' sake, not my dad too.

'Can't one of you be positive about this? It might be a really nice house that I can sell for a good price.'

'Can't think why we didn't know about it then,' says Mum, gently dusting breadcrumbs from the table.

I give up.

'Anyway, at least you're getting your hair done,' says Mum. 'That's good.'

I really do give up.

* * *

'Where have you been *chérie*?' cries Wesley. 'I thought you had died or something worse.'

Is there anything worse than dying I wonder? The wonderful fresh smell of shampoo and hairspray reaches my grateful nostrils. You have to admit there is nothing like a bit of pampering is there? I shall emerge looking like *Pretty Woman*. If only I had her spending power, now that would be cheering. Wesley gingerly touches my shoulder-length blonde hair and pulls a face.

'You look like you've been reincarnated as a horror film heroine,' he says bluntly.

'That's a bit unfair,' I grumble.

'Tsk, what have you been using, Lincoln Beer shampoo, or simply beer? I don't know if I can do anything with this. Anyway this is my battle, come along, come along. If Wesley Dumont cannot make you beautiful then no one can.'

With a swish, in the manner of Derren Brown, he produces a robe and I glide into it. Oh, a bit of luxury. It feels so good. I'm gently led to a chair and within seconds I am surrounded by helpful trainees offering me *Hello!* magazines, coffee and biscuits. I'm stuck in front of a mirror and forced to confront myself. I look at my reflection in horror. I've developed lines and my eyes are all puffy and swollen. It's all this crying and emotional stress, either that or it's the bad lighting in here. I wonder how Oliver looks. He's probably too busy to give me a second thought. No, that's not true, he has been texting me every day. I really should answer him. I wonder if he's got lines. He certainly won't have puffy eyes. I can't imagine Oliver crying all day somehow. He says I'm overreacting. My God, what a nerve, I mean it's not like I found him masturbating on the loo is it? That would have been shocking enough, but I found him humping some bimbo with a look of ecstatic pleasure on his face. I shudder at the memory. Maybe I should put it behind me, but then every time he has a work do, or goes out with his mates I'm going to think he is with Brown Nipples again aren't I? Anyway, I don't know if I could have sex with him again knowing it has been, well, you know where? And who knows what she's got, apart from huge nipples, and voluptuous hair. I wouldn't mind some of her looks but I don't particularly want her brand of chlamydia, thank you very much.

'Mince pie?' asks Lucy. 'We've got tons over from Christmas?'

I grab two and stuff one into my mouth. What if he's been with her before? I may already have her brand of chlamydia. Why was he humping her anyway? It's not like I said no that often, apart from the suspenders and the saucy sailor outfit. Well, I looked ridiculous. I felt like something out of a cheap porno film and Oliver dressed as a pirate rather dried up any sexual juices I may have produced and I felt like we were in an X-rated version of *Pirates of the Caribbean*.

My hair looks lank and miserable, rather like me. I pop a Ferrero Rocher in my mouth.

'We have loads over,' Lucy repeats.

You won't by the time I'm finished I think. Why is it hairdressers have such stark lighting. You'd think they'd soften it to make you feel a little bit better about yourself. Wesley picks at my hair with a gruesome look on his face. Jesus, he'll be telling me I've got nits next.

'Oh dear, we have let ourselves go haven't we? Brittle, brittle.'

I bow my head in shame.

'Lucy, wash this will you,' he orders, making me sound like a poodle at a dog parlour. He pushes me towards the freckle-faced teenager with a tartan bow in her hair.

I drop my head back into the little curved basin and feel my neck crick.

'How are you today?' Lucy asks sweetly, lifting my head to put a towel under me.

'Mmm fine,' I reply.

'Comfortable?'

'Oh yes,' I say, feeling my neck go into spasm.

She blasts me with scalding hot water and I fight the urge to cry out. Holy shit, what happened to the pampering? This is torture.

'Is the water too hot for you,' she asks kindly.

Has she got asbestos hands? Can't she tell it is scalding me?

'No, that's perfect,' I lie in a high-pitched voice. It's probably giving me tiny blisters but God forbid I should admit to anything.

'Did you have a nice Christmas? She asks.

Is she taking the piss or what?

'Bloody awful actually,' I say honestly, 'but you really don't want to hear about it.'

'Oh dear,' she responds with a falseness that makes me cringe and then proceeds to squirt shampoo into my eye. It would have to be the bad eye wouldn't it? She could at least have aimed for the other one.

'Oh well, at least you got a break from work.'

She continues massaging my head for all she's worth. Yes indeed, I got a lovely long break thanks to my wanker boss.

'Yes,' I say with a sigh.

'Going anywhere nice this year for your holiday?' she persists.

'Actually no, I'm not having a holiday this year ...'

'Oh that's nice,' she says. 'At least you'll save some money.'

Not if I'm not earning it I won't. I move my head to allow some water to dribble out of my ear.

'Is the water okay for you?' she repeats, rinsing off the shampoo.

I'm adjusting.

'Yes lovely, thank you.'

Why can we never speak up at hairdressers? We are paying after all.

'Saving up for something nice instead are you? I'm saving for my wedding, so we're not going away either.'

I feel a lump in my throat.

'That's nice,' I say in the same monotone as her. I feel water run between my breasts.

'What are you saving for? Oh don't say your wedding as well,' she laughs.

Okay I won't then. She wraps a towel around my head and I feel an earring pinch my earlobe and I wonder why this is called luxury. Still, at least I'll look good to see the solicitor this afternoon. I'm led back to my chair and I dab carefully at my watery eye. I glance towards the door and fight back a gasp as Brown Nipples walks in. Oh no, I'm sitting with a turban on my head, without a scrap of make-up on, and to top it all I've got lines. Any dignity I had left disintegrates into little pieces. I quickly hold the *Hello!* magazine up to my face and struggle to read it out of my one good eye. I'll need an eye patch soon.

'Amanda darling,' cries Wesley. 'Look at you, you're looking amazing. You don't have an appointment *chérie*? You certainly don't need one.'

So that's her name. I think I preferred it when she was anonymous. How dare she come to my hairdressers? That's just plain off isn't it? The bitch, I hope she bursts into tears and says how it's all falling out and bald patches are sprouting everywhere.

'I've come to buy some shampoo,' she says in a sultry voice.

I hope it gives her a severe case of alopecia.

'Binki, can I get you another coffee?' asks Lucy.

A double whisky would be good but they don't offer you that in the hairdressers do they?

I shake my head. Please go away. Besides, I still have one cold cup of coffee to get through. I pretend to be engrossed in an article on Victoria Beckham, guaranteeing myself a reputation as a true bimbo for life.

'Well you so deserve it, *chérie*,' Wesley says loudly.

And for a moment I'm not sure if he means my coffee, or her shampoo?

'You're too sweet,' she says huskily.

'How are things at Mansill Enterprises? Those men under you working hard are they?' Wes laughs.

Oh, they're under her all right at least one of them has been, the rotten bastard. She laughs huskily. I so want to scratch her eyes out.

'Kelly, a bottle of Miss Rowland's shampoo please.'

Oh my God, Rowland. Amanda Rowland. She's Oliver's boss. No wonder she looked familiar. I met her at last year's Christmas party. Oh God, was she shagging him then too? What the hell is he thinking of shagging the bloody boss? Now I know he is crazy.

'You're a darling, Wes.'

Oh it's *Wes* is it? I somehow feel her coffee never goes cold and the water is probably always warm. I hate the bitch more than ever. She didn't deserve my boyfriend, that's for sure. I should tell her so. I turn the page to an article and focus on George Clooney and plead for her to hurry up and leave. I hear the sloppy sound of kisses and then thankfully she has gone. I lower the *Hello!* magazine and beckon to Lucy for a fresh coffee. I'm not sure why I bothered though because as soon as it arrives Wesley pushes my head forward and starts snipping at the back. Not until blow drying do I make another attempt to reach for the coffee but I am yanked back from the cup with such force that I decide to give up and eat a chocolate finger instead.

'Did you have a lovely Christmas darling, lots of sex and mince pies?' he laughs.

Oh not again.

'Crap Christmas, no sex, too many mince pies and a broken relationship. '

'Oh God, I'm sorry love. Bloody Christmas, I always said it should be banned. Never mind, you've got good old reliable Wesley to make you shine again. You'll have a new man in no time.'

Yes well, it's not quite like buying a handbag is it? I wipe my tears and stuff another mince pie into my mouth, after all Lucy did say they had tons over didn't she?

Twenty-five minutes later and I am a new woman. My long blonde hair is shiny again and looking thicker with lovely layers, courtesy of Wesley.

'I've taken ten years off you my dear,' he smiles.

I wouldn't quite say that, unless he gave me a face lift when I wasn't looking. He's right though, I do look much better.

'Bugger him,' Wesley says, kissing me on the cheek. 'The sod isn't worth crying over. Bad hair styles yes; men never.'

'Thanks *Wes*,' I say.

Stick that in your 38D Brown Nipples. I leave the salon feeling ten times more confident than when I arrived. I also leave ten times poorer than when I arrived but hey, beauty doesn't come cheap right? And I'm a woman of means now, a landowner. I can't believe I tipped Lucy two quid though. I should have put it towards the skin graft I'll need on my scalp.

Chapter Eight

I'm thirty minutes early. I don't know whether to go in and hope Mr Hayden will see me, or drive around for another fifteen minutes. Parking in London is such an ordeal. If I park now it gives me one hour on the clock, and you can be sure that one minute before my time is up there will be a warden standing at the side of my little Kandy, dribbling with pleasure at the thought of slapping a ticket on the windscreen. The trouble is I can't be sure of being seen early, which means I will certainly go over the hour. I could drive around and hope there will be another space but if there isn't I'll most certainly be late. I chew my nails and decide to take my chances and grab a Starbucks to kill some time. Hopefully what I make on the house will more than pay for a parking ticket. I stroll into Starbucks and order a latte to take out. My stomach is fluttering with butterflies. I'm so excited and nervous all at the same time. I'm trying not to raise my hopes and tell myself that the property is probably only a tiny run down cottage and is only worth a few bob, but right now even a few bob would balance my bank account very nicely. Maybe I can do it up, not my bank account obviously but the house. After all, I've got plenty of time on my hands. That's all I've got plenty of, mind you, as my credit card bill practically wiped me out. Christmas, why do we have it? I wonder if there is furniture in the cottage. I pull my phone from my bag and text Muffy and take a sip of latte as I turn the corner towards Hayden and Carruthers Solicitors of Repute, and bang. My latte and phone are knocked out of my hand, and my handbag slips from my shoulder as I collide with a hard firm body. I feel myself lurch backwards as I try to recover the handbag. The latte splashes over my hand, down my coat and onto my boots. Oh great. They're only real suede and cost over a hundred quid. The contents of my handbag are strewn all over the street and I watch miserably as a black cab squashes my make-up bag.

'Christ,' I exclaim as the scalding liquid runs over my hand.

'Nathan, I'll call you back,' says the firm hard body in a deep well-cultivated voice.

'I'm sorry, are you okay?' he asks, pushing his phone into his jacket pocket. His soft fragrance wafts over me.

Do I look okay? I'm covered in latte and half my life is strewn all over London. Bloody typical city ponces, prancing around and conducting their businesses on their mobile phones. God forbid us mere mortals should get in their way. They think they own half of London.

'Perhaps if you hadn't have been chatting to *Nathan* in the first place this wouldn't have happened,' I snap, rubbing at my coat with a tissue. 'Don't you have an office to go to?'

'I think you walked into me. You're making a terrible mess of your coat.'

I look down at the coat to see it is covered in bits of tissue. Bugger it. I look at my boots and sigh.

'You've ruined my boots,' I say, kneeling on the ground to retrieve the contents of my handbag. He scoops up my phone and a bottle of aspirin.

'I think you've lost a few of these.'

'Well that's the suicide cancelled then isn't it,' I say sarcastically. 'I was looking forward to that too.'

'I'm sure things aren't that bad.'

I lift my head to look at him. Mr firm hard body has a gorgeous face to go with it. His dark curly hair has been combed back expertly revealing a high forehead. His grey eyes are twinkling and his lips have a half-smile on them. I stare at his appealing cupid's bow. His perfectly tailored suit has escaped my latte. Yes, that's about right. He's as cool as a cucumber in his dark blue shirt.

'I'm very sorry about the boots. Let me pay for the dry cleaning of the coat at least,' he says casually, pulling out a leather wallet from his pocket.

Oh that's right, pay off the peasant.

'Are you offering to pay for the skin graft on my fingers too?' I ask.

'You don't even take part blame do you?' he says smiling, handing me a fifty-pound note.

'You walked into me,' I insist, feeling rather glad I had my hair done.

'You were on your phone too. This should cover it.'

I stare at the fifty-pound note. God, I feel sure my eyeballs are whizzing round like a one-arm bandit arcade machine. Fifty quid, I mean, every little bit helps doesn't it? But I can't take money from a stranger can I, especially in the middle of London? Good God, it looks almost sordid.

He looks at me curiously.

'You don't think it's enough?' he says questioningly.

'No, I mean yes,' God what do I mean? 'It's just I don't often get offered money by men in the street.'

What do I mean often? I *never* get offered money by men in the street. What am I talking about? I never get offered money by men, period. What will he think of me?

He raises his eyebrows.

'I assure you it's only for dry cleaning,' he says impassively.

Oh God, I didn't mean. Is that what he thought? He is no doubt thinking the worst of me now.

'Well obviously,' I say blushing.

'Would you be more comfortable sending me the dry cleaning bill,' he says in matter-of-fact voice and offering his card. I wonder what he'll be offering next. Binki, what is wrong with you? Men are off the menu remember. And this one would be a very expensive item and has probably been purchased cooked and consumed already. Ooh what a delicious thought. He smiles and his eyes crease into a sultry gaze. I take the card and glance nonchalantly at the name printed in gold lettering, 'William Ellis, Investment Consultant.' Well, I won't need his services in the near future will I? The only thing i'll be investing in is the Notting Hill job advertiser if this bloody inheritance turns out to be a park home.

'Thanks but no thanks. I'm sure it will come out,' I say, reluctantly handing back the card. I push my hands into my coat pockets so as to stop myself from snatching the fifty-pound note off him.

'If you're sure?'

I'm not in the least sure. He crouches down to pick up my scarf.

'Sorry again,' he says and before I know it he has turned the corner and the soft fragrance of him has gone. What an idiot. I should have at least taken the business card. No, I am resolved not to have a man in my life. I sigh and check my phone. Shit, I'm late. Typical that it should be a man who messes up my plans yet again.

* * *

I burst into the solicitor's office and almost pass out from the heat. A girl with bleached hair and bright pink lips smiles at me. Her top is cut so low that I can see the swell of her breasts; it seems that I am destined to be reminded of Miss Brown Nipples everywhere I go. I pull off my coat and fan my face. It's hotter than the Caribbean in here.

'Cold out there isn't it?' she says.

'Lovely and warm in here though,' I say as I feel a bead of perspiration run from my forehead.

'How can we help you?'

'I'm Binki Grayson,' I say, feeling the temptation to remove my jumper but not wanting to compete with her huge breasts. Why is it that everyone has bigger tits than me?

'I have an appointment with Mr Hayden. My aunt has left me a property,' I say excitedly. 'I'm here to collect the keys.'

She chews her lip as she checks her computer screen.

'You know,' she drawls, 'that appointment was for two.'

I follow her eyes to the clock and to the minute hand that shows I am ten minutes late.

'I had a little accident on the way here,' I say apologetically.

'With some coffee?' she says, wrinkling her nose.

God, does she have to rub it in?

'Still, I'm only ten minutes late,' I say cheerfully.

She studies her purple painted nails.

'Mr Hayden has a tight schedule,' she says, making him sound like the bloody prime minister.

'Yes well, I'm not here to discuss world peace so I shouldn't be with him too long,' I say sweetly.

'I'll see if he is free,' she says nonchalantly.

'Oh why, did you have him tied up?' I say with a chuckle.

She gives me a stony stare. Obviously no sense of humour with the solicitors of repute then.

'Right,' I say. 'Thank you.'

'First door on the right,' she says while checking her nails.

I open the door and step into a smoke-filled room. The smell of pipe smoke sends me reeling.

'Miss Binki Grayson, a pleasure,' says a grey-haired man wreathed in smoke. 'An unusual name,' he adds questioningly.

'Yes, I suppose it is,' I say, not wishing to explain that my mother, when she was expecting me, found the name in a novel. I should be grateful I suppose. I could have been Scarlet, or Vanity or God forbid, Constance. Still, it would have been nice to have been named after a classic rather than a Mills and Boon romance called *Hot Surrender*.

I shake his hand.

'First of all, let me wish you a Happy New Year,' he smiles. 'I trust you had a good Christmas.'

I sigh.

'An unusual one,' I say, staring at his grey bushy eyebrows that have a yellowish tinge from the tobacco smoke. And there was me thinking it was illegal to smoke in a public place but I refrain from saying anything.

'Lovely, now let's have a look at what your aunt left you. A property in Hampstead Heath, a lovely part of London. Very much sought-after area and *Driftwood* is a nice little house I'm told.'

I'm beginning to feel like I'm in an estate agent's office.

'Although, I can't tell you much about it I'm afraid. We don't even have a photograph.'

He sucks on his pipe making it emanate a little squeak. I half expect him to swallow the damn thing as he is sucking it so hard.

'Is there anyone living in it?' I ask.

'Maybe the odd bit of driftwood,' he snorts.

I roll my eyes.

'No, not unless it has a poltergeist,' he laughs heartily, his laugh turning into a fit of coughing by virtue of the pipe smoke. I stare at him stony faced.

'I always carry a crucifix,' I say in a deadpan voice.

'Erm yes,' he mutters. 'The thing is, we don't even know if it is habitable. Best you take a look. Obviously we would be happy to handle the sale if you decide to move in that direction.'

I splutter on his pipe smoke and pull off my jumper. I'm thinking I should make a hasty exit before I end up stripping off completely.

'Did you know my Aunty Vera?' I ask.

He shakes his head.

'I'm afraid not. Now, if you could just prove you are who you say you are.'

Oh trust me no one would pretend to be me. I pull my passport from my handbag. He studies it intently before handing me a brass key. I feel like a character in a horror movie, you know the kind of thing, where everything starts off nice and calm in a solicitor's office where they pass over the innocent-looking key which everyone knows will end in high-pitched screams and figures moving through the darkness. I shudder and pop it into my bag.

'Now here are the directions to Driftwood and I hope it is everything you dream it to be.'

Now, that's a typical line from a horror film if ever I've heard one. He points to a map with the tip of his pipe.

'Thank you,' I say, choking on the smoke.

I tuck the instructions neatly into the zip compartment of my handbag and fight back the impulse to jump up from my seat and shout YAY. I'm the owner of my own house. Okay, so it may not be in the best condition, but the important thing is it belongs to me.

Chapter Nine

'I heard you broke up with Oliver,' says Ben Newman, in what I presume is his sexy voice. 'I'm not surprised, he was a bit of a wimp.'

I can't believe the guy has the gall to phone me and insult my ex-boyfriend too.

'I imagine you're pretty desperate aren't you?' he drawls.

I'm desperate to get off the phone that's for sure. This guy really is a professional pervert isn't he?

'For a job I mean darling. There's a good one waiting for you here. I'm sure I could talk to the powers that be and get you a little pay rise, as well as a few other rises.'

It's all I can do not to throw up into my handbag.

'Thanks Mr Newman, that's very kind of you but I think it is time for me to move on,' I say haughtily.

'Don't be a fool Binki. This is a good opportunity I'm offering you. There are hundreds of women that would jump at this offer.'

Until they realise that you are going to be jumping on them.

'Well, I'm happy to give someone else a chance,' I say.

He sighs irritably.

'I imagine there will be a little promotion in it for you too. All you have to do is a little overtime; help me get on top of things, so to speak.'

Oh God, he really is obnoxious isn't he? And I can't believe he is phoning me today of all days. I am going to see my house, my very own house, and I'm not going to let wanker Newman spoil it for me.

'Mr Newman, I couldn't possibly work for you again. You see, I find looking at you very difficult. I don't know where you got your looks, but I hope you kept the receipt because you so deserve a refund.'

There is a long silence and I am about to hang up when he says in a sinister tone,

'I hope you're not expecting to find a job elsewhere Binki.'

Oh my God, is he threatening me?

'Well I'm thinking as long as I avoid *Warts R Us* employment agency I'll find something,' I say, forcing bravery into my voice that I don't feel. I know he is big in advertising but he can't be that powerful can he? I push the thought from my head, it's ludicrous.

He sighs.

'It's your decision Binki. Let me know if you change your mind. I'll be using temps for a few months. I can't be fairer than that now, can I?'

The phone goes dead. I push it into my bag and glance at my map. My initial confidence has evaporated and I don't expect Great Aunty Vera's house to be anything more than a ramshackle old shack. I'd packed a suitcase because I'd figured if the house was habitable then I might stay the night. As much as I love Muffy, living with her is a nightmare. She plays Mahler in the mornings at full volume for Christ's sake, and God forbid you criticise Mahler. Anyone would think she'd known him personally. All I'd said was,

'Don't you find Mahler a bit dramatic first thing in the morning?'

Only to be quoted by Mahler himself, through Muffy's lips of course, just in case you thought we resurrected him.

'To judge a composer's work, one must consider it as a whole,' she'd snapped.

I agree totally but personally I prefer to wake up to Robbie Williams and consider him as a whole rather than Mahler. It just proves that saying *you never know someone until you live with them*. But then again, I lived with Oliver and was sure I knew him. I so hope I can live in this house. I really can't continue living with Muffy. Even if this house is all run down I can make the best of it. I must be positive and look on the bright side. My phone bleeps with a message. Oh God, I hope it's not Ben Newman again. I fish for my mobile in my bag and squint at the screen. It's from Oliver.

'I think you've gone mad. Since Christmas you've been acting really strange. Maybe even before that Chrissie said. No wonder I went a little crazy at Christmas. Chrissie says it was to be expected.'

Who the hell is Chrissie? If I don't know her how can she know whether I've gone mad or not? Jesus, is he telling the whole world and his dog about us?

'Oh well,' I text back. 'If Chrissie says it was to be expected than I suppose it was okay for you to hump some tart then.'

I click send and instantly regret it. I hear my mother's voice echo in my head *don't be so impetuous Binki, stop and count to ten,* and she is quite right of course. I frantically punch the keys in a vain attempt to stop it sending. Shit and double shit. I must not feel guilty. I wasn't the one bonking my boss was I? I push the image of Ben Newman from my mind, start Kandy and continue on with my journey turning left as instructed by the satnav. The road curves and I pass a little white house with smoke billowing from the chimney. That's a thought. It will be freezing in the house. I wonder if there is a fireplace. Maybe I should get some logs, but then again, it may have electric heaters, but the electricity is probably disconnected, best to wait and see. I drive for another thirty minutes down a quiet secluded lane before the satnav announces that I have reached my destination. I stop the car and stare breathlessly at the driveway. Oh my God, the house is beautiful, a chocolate box cottage with clean white walls. My excitement is soon quenched when I see a group of workmen drinking tea by some outbuildings, and a blue Lamborghini parked at the side of the cottage. I should have known. I am about to reverse when one of the builders approaches.

'You alright love, you look a bit lost?'

Don't you hate it when men think that because you're a woman you must be lost? I mean what a bloody cheek. Except the truth is, I have no idea where I am going. If this isn't *Driftwood* then where is it?

'I'm fine thank you,' I say, feeling as far from fine as fine can be.

'Where you aiming for?' asks another.

Driftwood I want to say but they'll probably think I'm mad. I am also terrified to ask where Driftwood is in case I make a fool of myself and it is actually the shed at the bottom of the garden, but Mr Hayden did say it was a *house* didn't he? I decide that looking a fool is preferable to driving around all afternoon.

'I'm actually looking for a house called *Driftwood* I say, fumbling with the solicitor's letter.

'Let's have a butchers,' he says, snatching the letter from my hand.

I look on as all five builders have a so-called butchers. After examining my letter I am half expecting them to rummage through my underwear bag but they simply grin at me.

'This is *Driftwood'*, says the one I think is the main man. He is wearing loose jeans and a baggy top but I can still see his belly. They all look towards the white house.

'Yup, this is it,' he says in that tone that hints at wanting to know more.

'Thanks so much,' I say.

I park next to the Lamborghini. Bloody hell, what are they paying builders these days if they can arrive at work in sodding Lamborghini's. Perhaps I should train to be a builder. I mean how hard can it be? I debate asking who owns the outbuilding they are working on, but think better of it. I jangle the key in my hand and climb from the car. This is amazing. I never dared even dream it would be like this. Oliver will be so sick with envy. I walk towards the door with the workmen staring at me over their steaming teacups. I turn the key in the lock but the door is already open. A little wave of panic washes over me. I walk straight into a cosy living room. Katie Melua is playing and I feel like an intruder. My God, someone lives here. Strewn across what looks like a new couch is a briefcase and numerous papers. Mr Hayden was quite insistent that no one lived here, unless the house had a poltergeist. It seems this one likes Katie Melua. I must have the wrong house. As I try to get my head around the situation I hear movement from upstairs. A man looks down from the landing wearing a bath towel, and chats animatedly into a mobile phone. He sees me and waves.

'Hold on a sec,' he says into the mouthpiece.

He looks vaguely familiar. Don't I know him from somewhere? And what is he doing in my house? What's more, what is he doing in my house half naked?

'Oh good you're here. Can you start in the bedroom, the cleaning materials are under the sink and the kitchen floor needs a good scrub,' he says casually before slamming the bathroom door behind him.

Chapter Ten

Cleaning materials? Do I look like a scrubber? I feel myself seethe with anger. What a sodding cheek, and how dare he shut the door on me. Who does he think he is, and what the hell is he doing in *my* bathroom and what's more, wearing what is obviously one of *my* towels? Well I will soon sort him out, sodding builders. He can get back to work right away. I have had enough men shit on me in the past few weeks. I'm buggered if I'll let another one do it. I throw my handbag onto the chair and march upstairs to the bathroom. It's like an oven in here. I hope I'm not going to be paying the heating bill. I pull my jumper over my head and fling open the bathroom door only to find him completely naked.

'Oh,' I squeal, my eyes inevitably dropping to you know where, well that's what happens right? It's plain inevitable isn't it? God, he's got firm thighs. I blush and open my mouth to speak but he holds a hand up to stop me. What a rude bugger. A well hung rude bugger admittedly.

'Just a sec,' he says dismissively, grabbing a towel. 'I'll need to get back to you Nathan. In the meantime go with that price if you feel comfortable.'

He lowers his eyes.

'Right, erm, what's going on?' he says hesitantly.

What the hell's going on indeed? And why is he staring at me like that. I follow his gaze. Oh Jesus, I'd only gone and pulled off my shirt with the jumper. I stare horrified at my pink and white spotted bra and cringe. Shit shit, of all the times for that to happen.

'Sod it,' I mumble, fumbling with the shirt and pulling it over my head, grateful to have my red face covered if only for a short time. 'It is hot in here.'

His phone trills again.

'I'll get back to you Nathan,' he says abruptly and then turns to me. 'You are here to clean right? You do know that?'

Oh hell, he thinks I've followed him into the bathroom because I'm after his cute body. How arrogant is that, and why does that name *Nathan* ring a bell? Then I remember where I've seen him. He's the guy who sent me reeling outside the solicitors. What the devil is he doing in my house?

'I remember you,' I say. 'What are you doing in my house?' My feet slip on the wet floor and I grab the sink for support while thinking what a nice bathroom I have. Just a shame Mr Lamborghini is standing in it.

'You're not the cleaner?' he studies me.

I inhale the fresh smell of him and pull myself up straight.

'Do I look like a bloody cleaner?'

'I've no idea, do they have a special look about them?' he says in an upper class drawl.

I feel my hands turn to fists.

'I own this house and I'd like to know what you're doing in it?'

He smiles indulgently and glances at his phone as it rings again. He clicks it off.

'I don't know what house you own but I assure you it isn't this one ...'

What an arrogant little git. How dare he patronise me.

'You're so bloody arrogant. First you toss fifty quid at me like I am some peasant to be paid off and now you treat me like a cleaner. You're a real arsehole.'

'You swear a lot don't you?' he states.

I blush. He turns to study me and I see recognition spark in his eyes.

'I'm phoning my solicitor,' I say storming past him. 'My Great Aunt Vera left me this house. I demand you leave immediately.'

'Hang on a sec,' he says so casually that I am left speechless. He disappears into another room, which I presume is the bedroom, my bedroom. Honestly, only I could have a poncy squatter. He returns a few minutes later wearing jeans and a blue short sleeved shirt. His hair is swept back and his cheeks are still slightly flushed from his shower. He's incredibly good looking and he knows it. His phone trills and he holds a finger up at me before taking the call.

'Hi, Anna, yes of course we are. Can I call you back? I've got a bit of a situation here.'

Oh, so I'm a situation now. He clicks the phone off and turns to me.

'Aunt Vera did you say. Would that be Vera Cramton by any chance?'

I gasp. He knows her. How can that be possible? Before I have time to reply he says in a cold voice,

'I don't know who you are or what you're up to or what you stole from me in that little incident in town, but you can leave now. I'm not easily fooled. Now if I were you I'd go quietly or I'll have no choice but to call the police.'

He walks downstairs, holds my handbag out towards me, opens the front door and gestures for me to leave. I feel my mouth open in shock. What a nerve. My God, the guy is unbelievable. First he treats me like a prostitute and then a scrubber and now a bloody thief. The builders watch intently. Great, this is so not what I was expecting. I snatch my bag and pull out the letter from the solicitor.

'How dare you accuse me of theft? That's outright slander. Here is the letter that says I own Driftwood.'

He studies the letter casually, closes the door and then punches the solicitor's phone number into his phone. The builders resume their hammering.

'Let's get this cleared up once and for all shall we, and then you can leave,' he says, his voice cold and his sultry blue eyes hard. His cupid's bow lips are drawn tight. I feel like slapping him. How dare he call me a fraud?

'Ah, yes. Hi, Mr Hayden please. It's regarding Mrs Vera Cramton's will and her supposed legacy to Miss ...' he raises his eyebrows at me. 'Binki Grayson.'

Supposed legacy? I feel myself fume even more and if I fume much more I am sure I will self-combust.

There is a short pause.

'Yes that's right, Binki,' he adds. 'My name is William Ellis.'

He studies me intently and I fidget as though guilty. What am I doing, it's my bloody house isn't it? Maybe I should get the burly builders to throw him out. That would wipe that arrogant smug smile off his face. I watch as he listens to someone at the other end of the phone.

'When was that?' he asks, his brow creasing.

Oh yes, got you now you poncy squatter.

'I see and there is no mistake? Right, thank you very much.'

He hangs up, hands me the letter and shakes his head.

'It seems Vera did leave the house to you,' he says grimly. 'She was ...'

Before he can finish I have opened the front door. The builders stop work and turn as if I am about to make the announcement of the century.

'Now *you* can leave,' I say angrily. 'I don't know what you're up to but if I were you I'd go quietly or *I'll* have no choice but to call the police.'

I make no attempt to hide my smirk.

'And take your phone and bloody Nathan with you.'

The builders glance at each other. Mr Lamborghini smiles and his eyes sparkle. It's all I can do not to slap his face, in fact, perhaps I should. I'm not likely to get arrested for slapping a squatter am I? Even if he is a posh upper crust squatter that drives a Lamborghini. Honestly, they say those with money are the worst don't they?

'It seems we have a situation,' he says, waving to the builders.

We have a situation all right and I'm about to remedy it.

'Okay to make a cuppa Mrs Ellis?' responds the builder.

I reel round. Mrs Ellis? Is he having a laugh? Do I look like the kind of woman who would marry an arrogant ponce?

'I'm not his wife,' I say haughtily.

'And thank goodness,' retorts Mr Lamborghini. 'Go ahead Andy,' he tells the builder.

Excuse me, this is my house.

'Hang on a minute Andy,' I say forcefully.

Andy stops halfway to the house, mugs in hand. The other builders are giving me daggers. Who are these bloody builders anyway? And didn't they have a tea break just a few minutes ago? I look down at his muddy boots.

'You can't come in here with those muddy boots,' I say primly.

'It's not a problem,' says Mr Ellis Lamborghini. Not a problem? No, it wouldn't be for him would it? It's not his house. Andy looks first at Mr Lamborghini and then at me. He finally turns and shrugs his shoulders at the other builders. Right, I need to stand my ground here. Be firm and strong. I pull my shoulders back. At that moment a Mini pulls into the driveway. We all turn and stare as a petite young blonde climbs from it.

'Hi,' she says cheerfully, obviously oblivious to the atmosphere. 'I'm from the cleaning agency. Sorry I'm late. Where would you like me to start Mrs Ellis?'

Mr Lamborghini's face lights up.

'Great, can you start in the ...' he begins.

'I'm not Mrs Ellis,' I snap, 'and can you all just hang on a minute.'

This is getting out of hand.

'Right,' I say, taking a deep breath. All eyes are now focused on me. I turn to Andy.

'Andy, why are you working here? This is my house and I didn't hire you.'

Andy looks apprehensively at William Ellis and then to the other builders before yanking up his trousers and saying,

'Your husband hired us to turn them there outbuildings into offices.'

I sigh heavily.

'He isn't my husband,' I snap.

'Shall I get started?' says the blonde eagerly.

'No ...'

'If you could, the cleaning things are under the sink,' interrupts Ellis.

'Just a minute ...' I hold my hand out like a traffic policeman.

'The thing is,' says Ellis. 'It seems your great aunt left the house to me also. Two wills, two solicitors, same day, very confusing.'

It seems like everyone is frozen, motionless as if the pause button has been pressed, and then, in unison, the blonde enters the house and the builders resume their building.

'I'll put the kettle on then Mrs Ellis,' says Andy as he follows the blonde into the house.

Chapter Eleven

'You've got to be kidding; she must have lost the plot. But if she wasn't of sound mind, as they say, when she made the will then you can argue the case, after all, he isn't family like you is he?'

I rummage through the suitcase for my facial wipes, pressing the phone against my ear. I really am finding this hard to believe. How could Aunt Vera have left the same house to two people? She had to be crazy right? Trust me to have a crazy aunt. And why is it I have never heard of this William Ellis?

'Huh,' I scoff. 'Apparently he's phoned just about everyone. He's as keen to get me out as I am him.'

'You can't stay there,' squeals Muffy. 'What if he's a nutter or something? You hardly know the guy.'

'Which is exactly why I can't leave. He will no doubt change the locks, and you know what they say about possession being nine-tenths of the law, I daren't leave. The whole thing is a bloody nightmare. I have to risk him chopping me up and burying me under the floorboards. Anyway I thought I knew Oliver but look what he did to me, not to mention bloody Ben Newman.'

'Little shits,' she affirms.

'Exactly, it would be a bloody man who takes my inheritance. Honestly, I never get left anything and when I do a man comes along to steal it from me.'

Muffy sighs.

'Is he good looking?' she asks.

'Muffy! Don't let the side down,' I grumble, pulling my socks off. If it gets any hotter in here I'll pass out.

'Just curious,' she says nonchalantly.

'Well yes, but I'm not interested in men, and most certainly not in this one,' I say, hanging my things in the pinewood wardrobe.

She gasps.

'God Binki, what if he's a sexual predator?'

I feel a tiny tingle run through me. I've been too long without a man if the thought of a sexual predator turns me on. Well, that's not strictly true is it? If a sexual predator turned me on I'd be flinging myself on Ben Newman right? Who is most certainly a sexual predator and I can categorically state that the thought of Ben Newman and his wart does not turn me on in the least. Call me weird, but there it is.

'Well, he is quite good looking and he has a nice body, I saw it in the bathroom remember?'

'Binki!' she exclaims.

'I know, only joking, but I can't leave, not tonight anyway. Honestly, if Aunt Vera wasn't already dead I'd kill her myself. How could she do this and on the same day too, can you believe it?'

'Surely whoever she left it to last is the owner, it's her *last* will and testament that counts isn't it?'

Oh yeah Muffy, like we hadn't thought of that. Seems Aunt Vera made both wills on the same day three years ago. His was at 2 p.m. but my solicitor doesn't have any record of when my will was made, no appointment book or anything. He probably put the appointment book in his pipe and smoked it for all I can tell. Honestly, what a bloody cock-up.

'I don't believe it,' mumbles Muffy. 'How did he know her anyway? You don't think he was her bit of posh do you?'

God, what an awful thought. Then again, William Ellis as a bit of posh doesn't seem so bad. Obviously only if you're desperate I mean. I wouldn't give him a second glance, obviously.

'Apparently he helped her with investments and stuff,' I say, placing my teapot on the dressing table.

'I bet he did,' she scoffs.

'No, that's what he does and a lot he did for her free of charge.'

'I bet he did,' she scoffs again. 'Little shit.'

I exhale.

'Not all men are little shits, Muffy.'

I suppose she's right though. So far all the men I've met have been little shits, apart from my dad of course, but for all I know he could be a little shit too. I look out of my bedroom window to a view of a field with horses grazing. Oh, it would all have been so lovely if only William bloody Ellis wasn't here.

'Want to bet?'

'He's been here two weeks already. The place is furnished and everything. I think Aunt Vera was renting it out. He's renovating the outbuildings and turning them into offices, and he's got a Lamborghini, and oh Muffy, what am I going to do?' I say, beginning to cry.

'It will be okay Binki,' she says.

'Don't tell Oliver will you? I don't want him to know it all went wrong. He would love that,' I hiccup, wiping my eyes on the facial wipe.

'Of course not, but he is sorry Binki. You could come back and start again.'

Bloody hell, is that Muffy speaking. Feminist, down with men and up with the Hovis Muffy?

'Are you serious?'

'I hate you being upset.'

There is a rapping at the door and Ellis pops his head round. I tell Muffy I will call her back.

'I could have been naked,' I snap.

He cocks his head and says,

'Then we'd be even. I'm popping out to get some Chinese. Do you want some? We could talk things through over a chow mein and a glass of wine. What do you think?'

I think you can't get me to change my mind with a chow mein is what I think. God, some men are unbelievable. Mind you, I am starving and if he's paying, God knows he can afford it with that bloody Lamborghini sitting outside.

'Well …'

He grins.

'Great. Chow mein, sweet and sour and maybe a satay, you okay with that?'

That sounds fabulous.

'I guess it will suffice,' I say huffily, hesitantly reaching for my purse.

'It's on me,' he says.

'I couldn't possibly,' I protest.

'Oh yes you could, or else you'd have been in your purse a lot quicker. Don't think of locking me out. I'm quite capable of climbing through a window and if I have to smash one you can bet it will be yours. See you in a bit.'

What an arrogant bugger. I call Muffy back.

'Oh well, at least it was chow mein and satay, better that than kwik wank or vee dee,' she laughs.

'It's not funny,' I snap. 'He's obviously trying to get round me with food and wine. Well it won't work. I'll phone you later. I'm going to nose around *my* house while he is gone.'

I hang up and watch him reverse out of the driveway. I look around my bedroom which is very cosy with lovely pine wardrobes and dressers. Just a shame it doesn't have an en suite. It seems I've got to share the bathroom with Mr Arrogance which is just what I don't need. I wander along the white painted landing and open the bathroom door. His scent hits me and my stomach flutters, and I find myself wondering if he has a girlfriend and where he lived before. I bet Muffy is right and he did take advantage of poor Aunt Vera. Maybe if I can prove that then I'll get him out of the house.

The bathroom is clean but his things are everywhere. A razor sits on the sink with shaving gel beside it, the top off of course. What is it with men and shaving gel? I sigh and replace the top. I gingerly open the bathroom cabinet and look inside. Maybe I can find something to incriminate him. Dental floss, yes well flossing hasn't yet become a crime has it? Painkillers, they're still legal aren't they? Multi-vitamins, at least he looks after himself. Deodorant, nail clippers and aftershave balm. No illegal drugs then, that's a relief I suppose. He's pretty clean living. Not even a bottle of aftershave. I sniff his shower gel, and realise that is the fragrance that lingers about him.

I move a comb to one side and see a small packet of something. Ah, what's this? I pull the pack towards me and drop it in shock. My God, *condoms* and not one pack but two. Muffy was right, he is a sexual predator. I quickly replace them with shaking hands. What's the matter with me? The man is entitled to condoms isn't he? He must only be about thirty, so he's obviously having sex with someone. I curiously find myself wondering who she is and what she looks like.

I close the bathroom cabinet and head to the bedrooms. The smaller one at the end has a rowing machine and treadmill in it. God, he's not one of those health freaks is he? Don't you just hate those types? I tried running once. Oliver was into this health kick or it may have been a 'kill Binki week kick', it certainly felt more like that anyway. I'd downloaded some drum and bass onto my iPod in preparation. Oliver said it was a real motivator but it only managed to motivate me for six minutes before my lungs gave way. I'd felt like a real jogger. I was full of determination and it felt like I was running for a long time but it had only been six minutes and bloody drum and bass was still pounding away. At this point my thighs were trembling and there was a burning in my throat. Oliver was way ahead of me and I tried to signal that I was dying and needed oxygen. He'd beckoned me to hurry and catch up and rather than admit I actually couldn't take another step I had shamelessly pretended to have twisted my ankle and popped into the local pub. Well, sometimes you have to lie in relationships. I wonder if Oliver has been lying all this time about Miss Brown Nipples. No, I must not think about that.

I reach the other bedroom and hesitate. What am I doing? But it's my house isn't it? Of course I can explore. I open the door cautiously. His soft fresh fragrance pervades the room. The bed is made, that's a surprise, but then again Cara, the cleaner, has just been. There are shirts hanging outside the wardrobe, God forbid he should go that extra mile and hang them inside. A laptop sits on the bedside cabinet and another on a table by the window. A PDA lies on the bed. My goodness, the man is technology addicted. A row of green envelope files sits on the windowsill and several boxes clutter the floor. Well, he'll have more boxes soon if I have my way. This bedroom is huge. Trust him to take the biggest room, and actually he has two rooms if you count the exercise room, that's not fair is it? He's an arrogant pushy bugger, who has far more money than me. That's it! I fall onto the bed as the epiphany hits me. If he wants the house so much then he can buy me out. Of course, why didn't I think of that before? I glance at the folders and study the labels. I stare at the one labelled *Bank Statements*. I could just peek couldn't I? After all, it is best to know your enemies isn't it? Don't they say keep your friends close but your enemies even closer? Yes, I'm doing the sensible thing. I need to know all I can about this guy. I quickly check the drive and see that there is no sign of his Lamborghini. I carefully pull out the folder and scan the sheets for a balance. I gasp. I don't believe it. The guy is loaded. I close the folder carefully and slot it back into place feeling myself pant with excitement. Yes, oh yes. He can't possibly refuse to buy me out. I can't think why he didn't suggest it in the first place. Oh relief. I find myself actually looking forward to the chow mein. I wish I'd asked for a portion of chips and a curry sauce to go with it.

Chapter Twelve

Muffy said to play it cool.

'Wait until he's had a few glasses of wine before you ask him. I spoke to Geoff and he knows about these things, he says don't leave. The minute you do the guy will change the locks and you'll have him as a squatter. Geoff said it will cost you thousands to get him out.'

By the time William Ellis walks through the front door I've laid the table and changed into a dress which I've topped with a cream cardigan. I'd tidied my hair and applied some lipstick and blusher. My aim is to get on his good side but it suddenly occurs to me that he may think I am coming onto him. He looks at me curiously and plonks the food on the table. I blush and feel myself grow hot as I remember the condoms in the bathroom cabinet.

'You shouldn't have gone to such trouble,' he says brusquely.

I grow even hotter. I wish the heating was not so high.

'It's only a dress and a bit of make-up,' I say blushing.

He frowns.

'I meant the table,' he says, removing his jacket and casually turning a switch by the door to dim the lighting. God, I really dislike this man and his hurtful comments. He walks past me into the kitchen and helps himself to the wine rack. He's very much at home in my house isn't he?

'Red or white?' he calls.

Right now I'd drink anything as long as it has alcohol in it.

'I'm easy,' I say and bite my lip. Jesus, I can't believe I said that. I am playing it far from cool. I think I see a smile pass his lips but it's gone before I can be sure. He returns to the table with a bottle of red which he uncorks expertly.

'I got some chips and curry sauce,' he says while pouring a little wine into a glass.

He must have read my mind.

'But if you're watching your figure,' he adds, glancing at me. I feel myself blush and fight the desire to stab myself with a chopstick. Honestly, how can three men in the space of as many days manage to make me feel so bad about myself? Is he trying to insinuate I'm fat? I blush and curse myself. Anyone would think I was having dinner with Daniel Craig the way I'm carrying on. It isn't like I'm not used to good-looking men. Oliver is very handsome; I wonder what he's doing now. We always used to get a takeaway on a Saturday night. I loved our evenings in with a Chinese and a good DVD. I hope he isn't with Amanda Rowland. Maybe Muffy is right, perhaps I should go home. What the hell am I doing in a strange house, and what's more, eating a Chinese with a strange man. I can't possibly sleep here tonight. I barely know the guy. He sits opposite me at the table and removes the lids from the cartons. I expect him to offer me something but he just helps himself and fills his plate. Oliver would never be so rude

'So, I'm thinking you could buy me out,' I announce. 'After all, you're good at spending money.'

Whoops, that was a bit uncalled for. I don't know what came over me. He dips a chip in the curry sauce and lifts it to his mouth in such a way that I have to fight a swoon. His lips are a soft pink, tinged slightly from the wine. Seriously, he is that good looking he could be a film star. No wonder he has condoms. He probably gets through a crate of them each week. I imagine he has a different woman every night. He is probably quite accustomed to slipping them fifty quid, not to mention slipping them a little something else. My dear aunt's house has become nothing more than a knocking shop. He looks the type who works hard and plays hard. I'm surprised he has got time to do fuck all else, let alone eat Chinese, but I suppose he needs to keep his strength up. I wait patiently and feel myself grow hotter as he deliberates. He lifts his glass and clinks it against mine. I see I still have half a glass left and it suddenly occurs to me he may have spiked the glass before pouring the wine. I don't normally feel this light-headed after just half a glass.

'*To Driftwood*,' he says, 'which I can't possibly buy from you because there is nothing to say you own it.'

I scoff.

'My Aunty Vera says I own it actually. She left it to me, remember?'

He might be good looking but he's a bit brainless. He grins in that annoying way of his. His eyes twinkle and his nostrils flare.

'She also left it to me, remember?' he says, mimicking me. 'Only one of us can own the house so I'm not able to buy you out of your share. In fact, neither of us actually has a share, that is until we know which of our two wills is the *last* will and testament of Vera Cramton.'

This is ridiculous.

'She was my great aunt so she obviously left it to me.'

He tops up my glass before I can stop him.

'Both wills were made on the same day, albeit at different solicitors, and they were both titled the *last will and testament of Vera Cramton*. So, until the solicitors can find evidence to show the time each will was made, both wills are worthless and the cottage remains intestate I'm afraid,' he says, smiling over his glass.

I look at him suspiciously. I visualise myself being dragged into his bedroom and chained to the bed in the manner of Anastasia Steele. I have to say it is a rather delicious thought. He is a rather appealing Christian Grey lookalike. I imagine being flogged by William Ellis is much more fun than when Oliver tried to do it. Oh, the thought of Ellis saying 'Come for me baby, come now,' is too much. I shudder and blush furiously. Good heavens, what is in this wine? It's turning me into some kind of dirty bitch. Oh God, what am I thinking? I may not get out of here alive. I look into my glass and feel his eyes on me.

'Don't panic. I've run out of Rohypnol and you've exhausted me already. I don't have the energy to molest you. Do you want the last spring roll?'

He has read my mind. How embarrassing as mine is a definite 18 certificate at the moment. I shake my head. He gleefully picks up the spring roll with his chopsticks.

'Don't you have somewhere else you can live?' I hear myself say.

He tips some chips onto my plate and helps himself to the rest.

'I want to live here,' he says stubbornly. 'Are you homeless or something?' he adds, looking at me curiously.

Don't answer Binki, don't give anything away. I despairingly knock back the rest of the wine.

'I have a luxury flat in the most sought-after residential area of Notting Hill actually,' I say proudly.

'Oh really,' he says looking impressed and leaning back into his chair.

I nod with that *oh yes* proud look on my face.

'How long have you owned that?' he asks, toying with a tooth pick.

I stare at him. Own? Bloody hell, who owns their own property these days? I fidget in my seat.

'We rent it,' I say. 'They're very sought after.'

'We?' he questions, raising his eyebrows.

I look away. He nods and says *right*, in that dismissive way, the way that arrogant little pricks like him do. You know the kind of *right* I mean, don't you?

'So why aren't you living there?' he asks pointedly.

'Because I'm here, sorting out Aunty Vera's house,' I say, not sounding in the least convincing.

He collects the dishes and walks to the kitchen.

'Well you needn't worry about this house. I'll take care of it until we know who it belongs to. I can send you regular updates if you like.'

I don't believe this guy. What was Aunt Vera thinking of leaving it to Mr Casanova? How the hell did she know him anyway? It's obvious to anyone with a GCSE that Aunty Vera left the house to me. He must have worked on her when she wasn't all the ticket. I gasp when I think of the Lamborghini outside. I bet that was bought with Aunty Vera's money too. Muffy was right, he was Aunt Vera's bit of stuff. A young stud that made her feel good in her old age. All this rubbish about helping her make investments is just bollocks. No one leaves money to people who help them handle their money do they? It's like me leaving the bank manager everything I own because he helped me set up a savings account. My heart sinks at the thought of the savings account a.k.a. my wedding fund. I'll have to break into it. That seems like bad luck doesn't it, I mean, who breaks into the wedding fund for anything other than a wedding?

'I'm not leaving the house because I know it's mine. It's pretty obvious that Aunty Vera was confused when she left the house to you. You're not even family and personally I think you should be ashamed of yourself,' I say boldly, pouring the last of the wine into my glass.

He spins round holding a box of mince pies.

'I've got two left over. As you're not watching your figure ...' he says, deliberately leaving the words to hang, and looking me over critically. Bloody cheek. I suppose all the women he humps are like stick insects. I accept the mince pie feeling I need a sugar lift. He takes a bite from his while stacking the dishwasher.

'So, are you staying?' he asks, deliberately squeezing past me to the kitchen sink. His hips brush mine and I fight back a gasp as the heat of his body washes over me.

'Are you leaving?' I reply.

He shakes his head.

'And have you changed the locks? Don't get me wrong, I'm sure you're a nice person but I don't know you that well. For all I know you may have a deceitful scheming evil side and I'll be locked out the minute my back is turned.

I open my mouth to feign shock.

'Now if you intend staying, you'll need to pay your share towards the heating ...'

'Well that can go down for a start, it's much too high.'

'And I'm afraid there is only one bathroom so I suppose we should organise times so we don't barge in and ...'

'I'll set up a rota,' I say primly.

'Whatever. I imagine you'll need more time in there than me.'

What the buggery does that mean? First he calls me fat, now what is he insinuating?

'As for the heating, turn it down if you wish, the thermostat is on the landing I'll tell you now though, as soon as you do the place turns into an ice cube. I was going to get it repaired next week but I'll leave that to you shall I?'

Oh, he is such a bastard. Poor Aunt Vera, she must have been a sitting duck for someone like him. I'll ask Muffy to see if she can check him out. She knows all kinds of people, one of them must do that kind of thing.

'As for the builders ...' I begin.

'They can carry on,' he interrupts, closing the dishwasher. 'It is in both our interests to get the most out of the outbuildings. I'll pay. I'll also work out there. So that's sorted. I go running every lunch time. Don't get any ideas though; otherwise I'll have to get Andy to keep an eye on you. There are a few shops about a mile away. The nearest supermarket is a bit further out. There isn't much in the local town but it does boast a post office and a sex shop.'

'Huh, I imagine you're keeping them in business.'

I bite my lip when he raises his eyebrows.

'They need staff if you're interested,' he smiles. 'I think they prefer women without sex appeal; you'll be perfect. Stops the leeches and makes sure they focus on the goods.'

I feel my lips tighten. I could knee him in the balls. I really could. How dare he call me unattractive? Ben Newman didn't think so did he? He would have had his thrill drill in me in an instant if I had been obliging. Then again, Ben Newman with the wart on his nose; not exactly your dream man is he? And then I did find Oliver with some tart on Christmas Eve. Oh God, what if Mr Lamborghini is right and I am totally without sex appeal and that the only men who want me are sleazeballs like Ben Newman. Ben Newman, God, what's happened to me? His phone bleeps. He studies the text.

'I've got work to do. I'll see you in the morning. Oh by the way, I hope you don't mind spiders, the place seems to be crawling with them. Check your bed. Goodnight.'

I feel my body turn cold. He's not serious is he?

'Really,' I say with a quiver in my voice.

'You're not scared of them are you?'

The bugger. He's just trying to scare me into leaving.

'Of course not.'

He smiles.

'I'll check your room if you like, you know, like do a spider search.'

I force a laugh.

'I'm not afraid of a little spider,' I say turning to the stairs while feeling my thighs turn to jelly. I hate the little buggers.

'Good. See you in the morning then,' he says, strolling past and leaping up the stairs. 'Don't forget the lights.'

I hear his door close and shut my eyes. Oh my God, what am I going to do if there is a spider in my room?

Chapter Thirteen

I'd pulled the bedcover back and almost died when a little black thing dropped onto the white sheet. I had to fight back a scream and I quickly threw the sheets back over the little bugger in the hope that would kill it. I had considered fetching the bastard, but the thought of his smug smile stopped me, so I grabbed my shoe, pulled the sheets back and whacked the thing with all my might. It took me a while to realise I was murdering my earring. I fell onto the bed cursing William Ellis, Oliver and Ben Newman, my curses turning into tears, and tears turning into sleep.

* * *

I open my eyes and look around. Panic engulfs me. This isn't my bedroom. I lift my head and groan as a pain shoots through my neck. These aren't my pillows either. I listen to the strange noise emanating from the other end of the landing and then I remember. I'm in the house Aunty Vera had left me and with Mr Arrogant. What is that noise? Whoosh, whoosh, whoosh. I fumble for my Blackberry, check the time, groan and pull the duvet over my head. It's only 6 a.m. Whoosh-whoosh whoosh. For pity's sake. I pull the curtains open and squint outside to try to find the source of the noise. No builders. Maybe it's the faulty heating system. Whoosh, whoosh. I feel my shoulders tense. My head is thumping from the wine and my tongue is stuck to the roof of my mouth. I untangle myself from the duvet and fall out of bed. My clothes lie in a heap on the floor and I fumble in the suitcase for my wrap. Oliver had bought me a lovely Japanese silk kimono for my birthday last year and then with a jolt I remember that tomorrow will *be* my birthday. I'll be thirty. Oliver had planned to take me to Romeo's to celebrate. I feel the tears spring to my eyes. Am I being stubborn not forgiving him for a little Christmas indiscretion? After all, it was Christmas. God, what am I thinking? I'm doing the *It's okay at Christmas* crap. I bloody hate men. Whoosh, whoosh. I grab two aspirin from my handbag and throw them into my mouth. Whoosh, whoosh.

'Oh for God's sake,' I groan, flinging open my door to find the source of the sound.

It's coming from the end bedroom. Bloody heating system, I suppose I'd better let *knob head* get it fixed. I smile at my new name for him and fling open the door. I stare transfixed at knob head who is rowing rhythmically with sweat staining his running top. Don't you just hate keep-fit addicts? They have this marvellous way of making you feel stiff and inadequate. He turns to look at me and continues rowing, his firm thighs rippling with the effort. I force my eyes away from his lean athletic body and grasp the door handle as a wave of nausea washes over me.

'Some of us are trying to enjoy a hangover you know,' I groan.

'Oh dear,' he smiles. 'There's coffee downstairs.'

'Can't you go somewhere to do this kind of thing?' I mumble, turning to leave. 'Like a gym.'

'I'll be finished soon and we can go over that rota of yours, I presume it's done?'

Wanker. I give him the finger under my wrap and slam the door. I hear his low laughter.

'I like the scarecrow look by the way,' he shouts. 'Kept the spiders away did it?'

What? Oh no. I rush back to my room and check my reflection in the mirror. Oh sod and piss it. I'd only gone in there with mascara-streaked eyes, and as for my hair ... I sigh and run to the bathroom. I don't care if the bugger is sweaty, he can wait. I unpack my toiletries and place nightlights around the bath. I take my time cleansing my face before sliding into the hot bath. Thirty minutes later I sneak my head around the door.

'Whoosh, whoosh'

Jesus Christ, is he going for the Iron Man record? I blow-dry my hair, pull on some jeans and a blouse, stroke some blusher on my cheeks and reapply my mascara. I open the door stealthily. I can hear the shower and take the opportunity to explore the kitchen alone. The kitchen is amazingly tidy now the cleaner has been. The dishwasher has been emptied and there is one solitary mug in the sink. I have made fresh coffee by the time he strolls in, and he helps himself to a mug.

'Have you seen the light?' he asks, taking milk from the fridge.

'I beg your pardon,' I say haughtily. 'If you mean am I leaving, then the answer is no, and before you start telling me that the vampires come out on Fridays and there are bats in the loft, forget it. You won't drive me away.'

He smiles.

'I wouldn't dream of it. Is *Binki* your real name by the way?'

Not again. I nod sullenly. He turns and takes a bottle from the cupboard.

'Right, I'll just take my medication and then I'll be in the office if you need me.'

Medication? He looks pretty healthy to me, healthier than Oliver that's for sure. The one and only time Oliver went on a rowing machine he put his back out. Mind you, everything seems to put his back out, except screwing Amanda Rowland of course. Honestly, whenever I asked to go on top he always said it was a strain on his back. Huh, I suppose that is another way of saying I'm too heavy.

'Are you sick?' I say before I can stop myself.

'Not if I take my lithium and exercise. It keeps everything well balanced.'

He grins and swallows two tablets from a container.

Lithium? Oh my God. I feel my stomach flip. He's stark-staring mad. Aunt Vera probably never left him this place at all. My heart lurches when it occurs to me that he most likely stole something from my bag that day I visited the solicitors, and he somehow managed to find out about the house. Stay cool Binki, these kinds of nutcases are unpredictable. He's probably under some delusion that I am the fraud and just someone trying to force him out of his own home. Don't give him any idea you're aware that things aren't all they seem. He probably believes he owns the house. That's about right. It all makes sense now. In all the horror movies the nutter keeps himself really fit too doesn't he? Oh my God, I'm in the starring role of my own horror movie. I'm trapped in a house with my very own Freddy Krueger, albeit better looking, but just as dangerous. Keep calm Binki. I glance behind him into the cupboard and see a row of containers. Jesus, he is on a cocktail of the things. I was lucky to survive the night. Just be nice, I tell myself while feeling my knees knock under the table. I need to search the house for chainsaws and meat cleavers as soon as he leaves, although where the hell I'm going to hide them all I have no idea. Under my bed I suppose.

'I may explore the area,' I say. Explore the local police station more like. I hope it isn't too far away. In the movies the help is always a million miles away isn't it? I hope it isn't just one local bobby who Mr Lamborghini nutcase here will most likely scalp while he's still alive. Shut up Binki. My trembling hand holding the coffee mug shakes and I wonder if I should warn the builders. He may just tip over the edge now I am here. God, it will be my fault that the builders are slaughtered. I wonder if Nathan knows. It then occurs to me that Nathan probably doesn't exist. It's probably his alter ego, you know, like in the film *Fight Club*. Don't be silly Binki, of course he does. You saw his business card didn't you? Yes, well anyone can get those on the Internet, whispers a voice in my head. Jesus, Muffy wasn't far wrong when she said he could be a sexual predator.

'You're absolutely certain you want to stay?' he asks menacingly, while shaking pills from another bottle. I wonder if he's got some Valium up there. I could do with a handful. My heart is racing so fast I feel it will burst from my chest. He picks up a breadknife and I gasp. He turns to me with one of his evil grins and I almost stop breathing.

He drops the knife onto a salami and I jump knocking my leg against the table. He slices the salami carefully, watching me the whole time.

'Perhaps you can get some shopping,' he says, casually throwing a slice of salami into his mouth and heading for the door.

'Careful with the knives, they're very sharp,' he warns closing the door behind him.

I let out a shuddering breath. I've got to get out of here, and quickly. I grab the breadknife for protection and am about to go upstairs to pack when I hear the door open. I stifle a scream and brandish the knife. Andy stands frozen in the doorway.

'Morning Mrs Ellis,' he says nervously.

'I'm not Mrs bloody Ellis,' I yell, waving the knife in my shaking hands.

He takes a step backwards.

'No, of course not. I don't know what made me say that. I'm an idiot that's what I am.'

Oh my God, what am I doing? I'm pointing a twelve-inch breadknife at a builder. I lower it slowly and smile.

'I'm sorry. I'm a bit highly strung this morning. I didn't sleep so well last night,' I apologise, lowering the knife.

'Not a problem Mrs Ellis, my wife is the same that time of the month. Well, not with the knives, but you know what I mean. No worries Mrs Ellis.'

I sigh, what's the point. I know I'm bad that time of month but I don't grab breadknives.

'Okay to make the guys a cuppa?' he asks hesitantly.

'Of course,' I say.

I decide I have to tell Andy about William.

'You do know Mr Ellis takes certain pills don't you Andy?'

He looks at me and smiles.

'Oh yeah. That's how he keeps going if you ask me. I ought to take them.'

God, don't tell me Andy is psychotic too. Perhaps the whole lot of them are crazy. For all I know this place has been turned into a madhouse. I take the lithium bottle.

'Do you know how often he takes these?' I ask quietly.

'I wouldn't know. I guess you take multi-vitamins once a day don't you? Do you have any of those chocolate biscuits Mrs Ellis? I'll replace them at the end of the week.'

Multi-vitamins? I turn the bottle around to see the 'Multi-vitamin' label. I rummage through the other bottles to see they are all vitamins and supplements. What a git. How dare he try to scare me? I search the cupboard for his chocolate biscuits and hand the pack to Andy.

'Help yourselves,' I say.

'Thanks Mrs Ellis.'

What's the point?

I grab my bag, don my cap and jacket and march to the outbuilding, slipping on the early morning frost as I do so. I feel livid. I stumble over some loose bricks and search for the entrance.

'You okay Mrs Ellis?' asks Andy, holding a tray of tea.

'How do I get in here?'

Andy points to a plastic cover and I push through it. I stop when I find myself in a neat office where the bugger sits behind a desk with two large screens. He leans back, chatting on the phone with his feet on the table and twirling a pencil in his fingers. He looks up lazily and gestures for me to wait. I wander around the makeshift office which I have to say is impressive in its tidiness considering the mayhem surrounding it.

'This is a sure investment so get it sorted ASAP. I don't want them going elsewhere, got it?'

He hangs up without saying goodbye and looks expectantly at me.

'I'm going to explore the town,' I say sweetly, aware the builders have stopped working. Great, just what I didn't want. I am sure they have their ears cocked and are listening to every word.

'Have fun,' he says, reaching for his keyboard. I open the flap to go out and stand in the doorway.

'I thought I'd look in that sex shop like you suggested. Did you say you needed more masks and whips? Do you want me to get them? I'll get more whipped cream while I'm out shall I?' I smile at the builders seductively. Two can play this game.

Ellis opens his mouth and closes it again before saying quietly,

'I don't need anything but thank you for asking.'

'Great. Don't forget your anti-psychotic medication darling. We don't want your sexual appetite suppressed do we? Not if we're buying goodies. Talking of which, I must buy more chocolate biscuits for the workmen; they do so get through them. Well, I'll see you later. Don't go near the knives until you've medicated.'

Andy looks at the others and shrugs.

'See you later guys,' I say with a wave.

What a bugger. That will teach him. I climb into Kandy and start the engine. It whines for several seconds and stops. I try again but it continues to whine. For pity's sake, what is it with my luck? This is not starting off as one of my best years is it? I try again and bang the steering wheel with my hand. I see Andy nodding his head to someone and then the bugger strolls out, walking towards me with an arrogant air about him. He opens the door and says loudly.

'I think you need me to jump you.'

I so hate him.

'Not while I'm conscious,' I retort.

He laughs and produces jump leads like a magician.

'Allow me,' he says leaning forward and brushing my knee as he reaches for the bonnet lever.

'Start her up when I give the nod.'

He walks to his Lamborghini which of course starts right away. Flash bugger. He attaches the leads and nods to me. I start the engine and it fires up. He removes the leads and grins.

'Give it a good run. I don't have time to jump you several times a day.'

'You'd never get close enough, arsehole,' I mumble. 'I'll only be an hour so don't even think about changing the locks.'

I release the handbrake and zoom off. Jump me, I don't think so arsehole. I make a mental note of things I need. Lock for bedroom door, masking tape, labels, wine, food and most importantly, chalk. It's time to draw dividing lines. I'm not leaving. Let the battle commence. I've got one hour, I can't trust him any longer than that.

Chapter Fourteen

It takes twenty minutes to get to the supermarket. I screech to a halt in the car park and curse when I see the only parking space near the entrance is a mother and child only bay. I don't know about you but just the sight of a supermarket has me grabbing an inhaler. There isn't a single parking space, unless you count the disabled spaces of which there are an abundance, and all empty of course. I look longingly at the mother and toddler space. How come they get those special spaces? It comes to something when you get rewarded for getting up the duff these days. An official looking warden as though reading my mind waves me away from the empty spaces. Bloody cheek, how does he know I don't have two little monsters at home? It's a bit discriminating if I have to bring them with me isn't it? I could be up the duff too for all he knows. I squeeze my little Kandy into a one-hour slot and sprint to the store like an Olympic runner. The bugger isn't the only one getting exercise. I've only just stepped in the door when I am accosted by a man grinning from ear to ear. Oh no, please don't hold me up. He pushes his jet-black hair from his face and I swear his hair shifts. I stare at it fascinated trying to work out if it is a wig or not.

'Good morning and how are you on this very cold morning madam?'

'Well, I'm …' I begin, my eyes fixed on his fringe.

Please step away from me.

'Just take a second I promise.' Oh really, I'm sure Sweeney Todd said that to his victims before pulling the lever.

'Today our special offer on dog food is five hundred extra Nectar points.'

Oh fabulous, I'll just pop to the pet shop and get a dog to make it even more worthwhile.

'I don't actually have a dog,' I say, moving away slowly.

'You're a cat lover aren't you?' he says pointing a finger at me.

'Well ...' I begin. I don't mind cats but I wouldn't say I love them.

'We have a special on cat food too,' he says with a broad smile, 'and cat treats.'

I'm sure my cat would be trembling with excitement, if only I had one.

'The thing is ...'

'Do you have a Nectar card?'

'Actually no ...'

He grins. That was obviously the wrong answer.

'Well let's waste no more time in signing you up.'

Quite right, let's waste no more time.

'That's very kind but I really don't have time,' I say trying to walk away.

He grabs my arm.

'Just a few seconds I promise.'

God, he smiles like Jack Nicholson in *The Shining*. I shiver.

'I'll stop by on my way out.'

'No you won't,' he snaps. 'They never do.'

God, this is a bit heavy for Sainsbury's. I'm starting to feel dead guilty that I don't own a cat, dog or a Nectar card. I give a weak smile and head for the deli counter. I fight my way past mums and their screaming children whose faces are smeared with illicit chocolate, stolen from the sweet shelves no doubt, disgraceful or what? Thieving little buggers, and to think they get priority parking. The assistant is prodding the rotisserie chickens and I consider purchasing one for dinner. She glances sideways at me and continues checking the temperature on the cooked birds with such concentration that you'd think she was performing open-heart surgery on them. I feel like telling her to give up because they look very dead to me and could she possibly pop one in a bag. I go to speak but she holds a hand up. God forbid a customer may get in the way of her doing her job. She continues with her deep concentrated efforts with the thermometer. I'm getting close to telling her where to stick that thermometer and it isn't in the chicken.

She finally looks up.

'Can I help you?' she says.

Oh how fab. I check the time and see I have been here twenty-five minutes already. I fly around the rest of the store, grabbing biscuits, bread, milk and the ultimate essentials, masking tape, marking pens, chalk, labels, M&Ms and of course, wine and Bacardi Breezers. Well, I've got to drown my sorrows. God knows I have enough of them. I skid to a halt at the checkout and sigh when I see the long queue. Bugger, I'll end up with another ticket if I'm not careful. A cheery-faced assistant approaches.

'Maybe you'd like to use our self-service checkout?' she suggests.

No not really. I'd much prefer you jump on a till actually. I look dubiously at the self-service counter and deliberate if I really want the hassle. A quick glance at the time tells me I don't have much choice. A gum-chewing schoolboy, on work experience no doubt, standing at the head of the tills gives me a false smile as I start scanning my goods. I've only scanned two packs of biscuits and the thing screams.

'Unknown item in bagging area.'

How can the biscuits be unknown? The shop stocks the things don't they? Maybe it means my handbag, not that it's unknown to me but I place it on the floor to be on the safe side. The thing goes mad, not my handbag obviously, but the machine which screams *unknown item in bagging area* for all it's worth. I feel like I've just been caught in the process of shoplifting and wait anxiously for the security men to arrive. I look at the schoolboy who stands staring into space. I beckon to him but he stares ahead, looking for all the world like a bloody zombie. I hit the back button on the screen and look around guiltily before removing the offending biscuits only to have the damn thing scream again. For God's sake, can't that vacant-faced assistant jump on a sodding till? Honestly, this is ridiculous, what happened to assistants on tills. I hate progress.

'Please place the item in the bagging area.'

I just have you stupid machine. I sigh at the lobotomised assistant.

'Remove item from bagging area.'

Trust me to get an indecisive machine. I'm close to my time limit in the car park now and all the machine keeps screaming is, *Place item in the bagging area* and *Remove item from the bagging area* alternately. I think it's trying to drive me insane. I scan the wine and it bleeps so loud I jump out of my skin.

'Assistance needed.'

Bloody men in white coats needed more like. I'll be gulping from the Bacardi Breezer any minute. If the sodding kids can do it I can. I don't mean the kids are gulping from Bacardi Breezers, obviously they're not, but you know what I mean. If they can steal sweets, I can steal a Bacardi Breezer can't I? After dealing with this premenstrual machine they should give it to me for free, a Bacardi Breezer obviously, not the machine.

'Hello, excuse me, sorry to interrupt your ...' I hesitate, not knowing quite what I'm interrupting. He looks like he's been sedated but I can't say, 'Sorry to interrupt your drug-induced trance,' can I? He stares at me like I'm an alien who has just dropped from the sky into Sainsbury's.

'Do you think you could fix this stupid machine?' I ask.

Or better still, jump on a sodding till, but that may be breaking some kind of union rule if he's in charge of self-service. In charge, that's a joke. He's as useful as a condom machine in the Vatican. Oh dear, I've become so rude since Oliver's Christmas indiscretion with Amanda Rowland. How could he?

He rolls his eyes. I'm sorry, is my request for you to do your job interfering with your laziness? I fight the urge to slap his freckled face with the mackerel I'm holding. I then become my mother.

'Now look here, I've been here over an hour now and I don't want any of your lip.'

'I didn't say nothing,' he retorts.

Cheeky little bugger. Although on reflection, he is quite right. I'm the one being rude.

'It wants to know if you're over eighteen right?' he says, eyeing my outfit.

What is that look supposed to mean?

'You can carry on,' he says politely, hitting a button that only he is allowed to hit.

I continue scanning and thankfully reach the end. I tap the pay button with a feeling of overwhelming relief.

'Do you have a Nectar card?' it asks.

Well I came close to being bullied into getting one. I swear the thing is human. It will be asking me how many times I have sex next. I hit the 'no' button only to be presented with more instructions. I fumble hurriedly in my purse for money before the thing starts a countdown and thrust a twenty pound note in the slot which it spits out immediately.

'Currency not accepted.'

Oh for pity's sake. If it doesn't accept English currency what the hell does it accept? I turn to the boy again who is now with another customer. This is terrible; I will certainly get a parking ticket. I push the twenty quid back in my purse and shove my credit card into the slot. The machine spits out a receipt and thanks me for shopping at Sainsbury. I quickly make my exit and reach the car just as the warden is looking at it. Shit, not another battle.

'Hello,' I say sweetly, opening the boot. 'Sorry I've gone over. I was giving the kiss of life to an old lady in the store.'

Now give me a ticket if you dare. No one gives a good Samaritan a ticket do they? He sneers and walks away. Thank goodness for that. I climb into the car and see slapped on the windscreen a parking ticket. For Christ's sake, is someone trying to tell me to get out of town? All I need now is to get back to Driftwood to find the bastard has changed the locks. God knows, he has had plenty of time.

Chapter Fifteen

I never really thought he would change the locks. I had after all only been gone for two hours. So when my key wouldn't turn in the lock, anger engulfed me. At that moment all my emotions came to the surface. I saw Amanda Rowland moving up and down on my boyfriend, no – correction: soon-to-be fiancé, like it was just yesterday. Her long silky hair draped across her face like a sleazy porn star. I pictured Ben Newman's features contorted in sexual frenzy as he unzipped his trousers, and then Ellis as he swallowed the pills that he pretended were lithium. How could I let all these men take advantage of me? Where's my self-worth? Aunty Vera left this house to me and he has no right to change the locks the minute I turn my back. I take a deep breath and try the key again. No matter how much I try it just won't turn. I walk angrily around to the back door and turn the knob. Of course that is still locked from this morning. He's probably changed that lock too. What a pig. I leave the shopping bags by the door and march purposefully to the barns. I stroll past Andy and his merry men who are mixing cement, and barge straight into the bugger's office. He looks up surprised and nods at me before turning back to his computer screen and his never-ending phone call.

'How dare you,' I say loudly.

He sighs and clicks his tongue.

'Can I call you straight back. Something has come up. Thanks.'

He clicks the phone off and looks up at me.

'What now, don't tell me, I moved your tampons?' he says dismissively turning his back on me to check his phone.

'I could really slap you,' I say moving closer to him and feeling an overwhelming urge to knock him off his chair.

'Well, what have I done? I've been in the office all morning.'

His eyes have hardened and he is studying me closely.

'You sleazeball, how could you stoop so low?' I yell.

'Do you mind telling me what I'm supposed to have done?' he asks gently, his eyes boring into mine.

I shake the keys in his face.

'You changed the locks while I was out didn't you? How could you? The house doesn't officially belong to either of us, we agreed that but oh no, you couldn't honour that could you and ...'

He stares at the keys and it is then that the penny drops. I close my eyes and want the floor to open up and swallow me.

'They're the wrong keys aren't they?' I mumble.

'Indeed they are,' he says quietly. 'I don't take kindly to accusations like that. I haven't been near the house.'

I'd been trying to get into the house with my flat keys. Oh my God. Oliver Weber, I hate you so much. I struggle to get my emotions under control but tears still roll down my cheeks. He lowers his eyes.

'I'm so sorry,' I whisper.

'Yep, well whatever. I've got work to do. Oh, and Andy took in a delivery for you.'

He punches a number into his phone and turns his back on me. I turn guiltily and quickly exit. I've never felt so stupid in my whole life.

'And if you could leave my shaving gel alone I'd appreciate it too,' he calls.

Oh, I could just kill myself. I open the front door with the correct keys and stand frozen in the hallway where I am met by a large bouquet of flowers. I drop the shopping bags and peek hesitantly at the card.

'I love you Binki, I'm so very sorry. All my love on your birthday. Oliver X'

The tears are flowing like a bloody tap and I can barely read the text when it comes through.

I hope you got the flowers okay Binki. I phoned a florist in town. Muffy wouldn't give me your address so I got her to give it to them. I chose the flowers though. All your favourites, I miss you so much. Please don't give up on us, I wish I could be with you on your birthday. Please come home or at least tell me where you are. I have so much to explain.

I scoop up the bouquet and search the cupboards for vases, hiccupping as I go. Everyone hates me apart from Oliver. Ben Newman hates me, he must, to do what he did and put me out of a job. William Ellis thinks I'm nothing but a spoiled brat and he wouldn't be far wrong would he? I've been acting like one since I arrived. There are two vases under the sink and a couple of empty jam jars which I fill with water. After arranging the flowers and dotting the vases around the house I unpack the shopping and set about separating the cupboard and fridge shelves. I decide William can have the top shelves and an extra cupboard seeing as he was here before me. I don't answer Oliver's text right away because I have no idea what to say. I miss him terribly and the urge to run back to him is so strong that I have to force myself to stay well away from Kandy. The thing is I still can't get the image of him and Amanda Rowland out of my head. Even a Bacardi Breezer at three in the afternoon doesn't push the vision away. I work so hard at clearing cupboards, writing rotas and sectioning shelves that by the time William walks into the house I am exhausted. He rubs his eyes tiredly and looks at the labels scattered on the table and then at me.

'I'm afraid to ask,' he mumbles, uncorking a bottle of wine from the rack. Ah, I had forgotten about the wine rack.

He opens the cupboard to get a glass and reels back.

'Where are the glasses?'

'In the joint cupboard,' I say, proudly opening it. 'This cupboard is food,' I say opening the one next to the crockery. 'The top shelf is yours, you see it is labelled *WILLIAM,* the lower two are mine, but you have another cupboard which is completely yours and you have the top two shelves of the fridge'

He studies the rota.

'Days to use washing machine, shower times and bin emptying?' he asks curiously.

I nod. He pulls a face.

'All the shelves are labelled,' I say proudly.

'We don't have scheduled times to take a pee as well, do we?'

I give him a filthy look.

'And we're sharing the crockery are we?' he asks holding up two glasses. 'Do you want wine? I imagine you need it.'

'Well the crockery is Aunty Vera's and ...'

He shakes his head and pours the wine.

'You presume so much don't you? First I try to change locks while you're out and now you mistake all my crockery for your aunt's. Everything belongs to me, including the furniture. Beds, bedcovers, cutlery, lampshades, everything. The place was empty when I arrived.'

'Oh,' I say, taking the wine and sitting at the kitchen table.

His phone shrills and I sigh. No wonder he doesn't seem to have a permanent girlfriend. At least I don't think he has. I stupidly find myself hoping he doesn't. There is something calming about him and he always smells so fresh and clean and always looks gorgeous. Oh no, this is fatal. I love Oliver don't I? I'm not getting involved with men, I must not forget that. He clicks his phone off and throws it onto the table.

'But I'm willing to share the crockery,' he says, sitting down. 'And the cupboards are great.'

'But I can't sleep in your bed,' I say without thinking.

'I didn't know you were,' he says with a smile and raised eyebrows. 'But I wouldn't kick you out if you did.'

I blush. Is he coming onto me?

'I mean ...'

'I know what you meant,' he interrupts. 'Look, I'll supply the crockery and whatnot and you just have to be nice. That's not much to ask is it?'

What the hell. Is he insinuating what I think he is insinuating? I jump up almost knocking my wine over.

'To hell with you,' I snap. 'You're just like the rest.'

He sighs and walks to the fridge.

'What have I done now?' he asks, searching the shelves.

'Have you moved the salami?'

'Don't touch my shelf,' I say.

'Don't worry, I won't go near your shelves with a barge pole,' he snaps.

'I'm not sleeping with you. How dare you,' I say, shaking with rage while wondering what he is like in bed.

'I don't remember asking you to. That's quite an ego you have there. I meant you could be nice by not shouting at me every few minutes and maybe cook dinner sometimes. That kind of nice, not give me your body nice. As lovely as you may think it is, I personally don't fancy it. As for all the rest, whoever they were, I'd prefer not to be compared to them thank you very much.'

Why does he have this knack of always getting the better of me?

'Oh,' I say.

He turns and looks at me.

'I'm sorry. I didn't mean you're unattractive, far from it. You're just not my type.'

I nod. That's what I mean about him. He can say something hurtful and then immediately apologise. He peers into the living room at the flowers.

'Is it your birthday or something?'

I take the chicken from the fridge.

'Tomorrow, it's my thirtieth.'

He takes the chicken from me and puts it back in the fridge.

'Are you serious, why didn't you say something?'

I shrug. I can't say because my whole life has fallen apart and it doesn't seem like something to celebrate. Not now, since my chance of marriage went out of the window when Oliver decided to screw Amanda Rowland can I?

'That's cause for celebration. I think you need that tonight don't you? You can have chicken tomorrow, unless you have other plans with Mr Bouquet which I'm sure you have but tonight I'm taking you out. Get dressed up and I'll meet you there. I'll book a table at Marcells, do you know it?'

Do I know it? It's only one of the most exclusive restaurants this side of London. I open my mouth to speak.

'I'm not taking no for an answer,' he says firmly. 'I'll see you there at eight. I just have some business to attend to and I'll come along after.'

Ooh Oliver was never this masterful. I wonder if the business he has to attend to is another woman. I nod obediently. I bet William Ellis would have not hesitated in knocking Ben Newman's lights out.

Chapter Sixteen

Marcells is certainly upmarket. I look at my Zara floral dress and check my tights haven't snagged, and walk purposefully towards the receptionist at the welcome desk. The soft gentle tones of a piano reach my ears, along with the excited chatter of fellow diners.

'Good evening madam. Do you have a booking?' he asks with a warm smile.

'Yes, for eight o'clock,' I respond looking past him into the restaurant to see if I can spot William. All I can see are elegant women wearing sparkling jewels. God, I hope I'm not under dressed.

'Can I take your name madam?'

'Binki Grayson,' I say without thinking.

'Binki?' he questions.

Oh good, he recognises my name.

'Yes,' I say.

'That's an odd name.'

Here we go. I must look into that deed poll thing.

'Yes, isn't it? Don't worry I did slaughter my parents.'

He smiles at me.

'Maybe look for William Ellis.'

He pulls his eyes away from me and checks his booking list.

'This way madam,' he says, leading me into the restaurant.

I follow him to where William is sitting. Note to self: all men are little shits, never forget that. This mantra I have been repeating all evening. I'm now embarrassingly saying it aloud while sitting in the ladies loo of one of the most fashionable restaurants in London. The prices on the menu scared the shit out of me. I'll have to offer him something and with the state of my bank balance it is most likely going to be my body whether he wants it or not. Not that offering my body to William Ellis is such a sacrifice. Oh Binki stop it. All men are little shits remember. God, I wish Muffy were here to reinforce this mantra. Was this how Oliver felt about brown-nippled Amanda, all lustful and out of control? Wait a minute, I'm not lustful and out of control am I? Oh God, what if I am? Oliver had taken me to some nice restaurants, but never as nice as this one. There are candles everywhere, inside and out. Our table overlooks a river, shimmering in the moonlight. It would have been so romantic if it had been Oliver. All men are little shits, I mumble to myself as I leave the loo, except William is behaving not in the least like a little shit. There is something warm and cosy about William Ellis.

William sits at the table looking out at the view, one hand lazily fiddling with the stem of his water glass. I wish I had drunk less. I sway towards him, forcing myself to stay up straight. He looks so appealing. All the women in the restaurant had given him an appraising look and me jealous stares over the course of the evening. He looks at me with a warm smile and I feel my heart melt and my legs give way. I fall quickly into my seat before I collapse in a heap on the floor. Honestly, this is ridiculous. Don't forget Binki, just because he didn't change the locks doesn't mean he didn't think about doing it. How do you know he hasn't been plotting a little scheme while you've been in the loo? It's dog eat dog and don't you forget it.

'I owe you some money,' I say gloomily.

That sex-shop job may well become a reality at this rate. My life is becoming one big sordid soap opera. I'll probably end up as a high-class call girl. I'll be the one to put Hampstead Heath on the map. Yes, that's about right. No doubt they'll make a TV kitchen-sink drama about me. *The Intimate Adventures of a Working-Class Slut*. Let's face it, there's no glamour in my life aside from William Ellis and I'm not his type, right? Well, he isn't my type either. I'm off men.

'It's a birthday treat. Thirty is a landmark. It's all downhill now,' he laughs.

God, he's irresistible when he laughs. I so need to phone Muffy before I do something stupid. Right, like I'll be in a position to do something stupid. I'm not his type am I? He was quick to tell me that wasn't he? I imagine his type is far better looking and no doubt as skinny as a rake. I'm probably the first woman he has taken out who has packed away a smoked salmon starter, roast beef with all the trimmings and an enormous chocolate pot that would have defeated your more than average woman. I blush at the memory. Of course I'm not even mentioning the amount of wine I have put away. I bet he can't wait to get me home, not in a sexual way, I don't mean. Just to be rid of the embarrassment.

'Thank you,' I say.

He waves casually to a woman who is leaving and she gives him a warm smile. He looks closely at me as the waiter pours coffee into my cup.

'So, who were the flowers from?' he asks, stirring his coffee.

'My ex-boyfriend,' I say, immediately wondering if Oliver has phoned and feeling that familiar knot of loss in my stomach.

'Ex-boyfriend,' he repeats, looking at me over the rim of his cup.

I nod.

'Everything about me is ex,' I say boldly, the drink loosening my tongue. 'I'm X-rated, that's me,' I laugh.

What am I saying? He continues to stare at me in that primeval way he has that makes you want to throw your clothes off and scream *take me take me.* Visions of him having me over the table make me shudder and not in a *Ben Newman I feel sick* kind of shudder, but rather a *Ooh rip my knickers off* kind of way. I knock back half a cup of coffee in the hope of sobering up. I'm in serious danger of ripping off my own clothes, let alone his.

'X-rated as in?' he questions softly.

'Ex-boyfriend, ex-job, ex-flat probably. It was one of those Christmases where everyone was at it, well apart from me.'

He raises his eyebrows. Oh dear, did that sound like I was hinting we get at it. All men are little shits, Binki, don't forget. Little shits. You don't want to sleep with William Ellis. Cor, like hell I don't. Little shits, Binki, little shits. The truth is I want so much to get my own back on Oliver and hurt him in the same way he hurt me. Why not with William Ellis? After all, he is a womaniser; I'll just be one other notch on the bedpost for him. Little shits, all of them.

'Little shit,' I say loudly. 'My ex was a little shit.'

'Sounds grim,' he smiles.

'Oh it was. My boss tried to give me a boner, I mean *bonus*,' I say blushing. 'While my boyfriend, or I should say ex-boyfriend, was balancing a balls on his bimbo.'

That didn't sound right did it? He widens his eyes. I sniff.

'And I got a parking ticket on Christmas Eve would you believe? Of course if Ben Newman hadn't ...'

'Ben Newman?' he asks topping up my wine glass.

Jesus is he trying to get me drunk. I put a hand over the glass.

'My boss, Ben Newman is my boss, well was my boss until he tried to have me over his desk on Christmas Eve.'

Oh Jesus, did I just wink. I felt my eye twitch in one of those uncontrolled spasm ways. I ask you, of all the times to twitch.

'Of course, if he hadn't had tried to have me over the desk I wouldn't have thrown my job in and I wouldn't have arrived home early and ...'

I'm on a roll now. No matter how much I tell myself to shut up it just doesn't happen. I throw back some wine.

'I wouldn't have found Oliver balancing balls on the bimbo,' I finish.

'Or balancing a bimbo on his balls,' corrects William.

I nod and sniff loudly.

'So, you have no home, no boyfriend and no job.'

'I know,' I hiccup. 'You don't have to rub it in.'

He finishes his coffee.

'So Aunt Vera's house came at a good time didn't it?'

I feel the hairs on the back of my neck bristle.

'What are you trying to say?'

I knew I shouldn't have confided in him. Men are little shits aren't they? What was I thinking of sharing my vulnerable side to him. He shakes his head irritably and his hair flops slightly across his face making him look even younger and even cuter, if that is possible.

'I was simply stating a fact.'

'No you weren't. You were insinuating something.'

'Here we go.'

'What does that mean?'

He gestures to the waiter for the bill, seems to smile at someone and then leans across the table and is about to speak.

'Will, fancy seeing you here,' says a cool, horsey voice.

For a minute I wonder who she is talking to and then realise it is William.

'Hello Andrea, you're looking very lovely,' he says.

I look up to see she is indeed looking very lovely, so lovely that I want to crawl under the table in shame. Her long brunette hair hangs loosely around her shoulders and sparkling diamond earrings glitter through it. She is wearing, and I use that term loosely, a black lace dress. Let's just say if I was wearing it, I'd get arrested for indecent exposure. I'd definitely need a tummy tuck before I could wear a dress like that. It clings to all her curves and flares beautifully around her thighs. A grey pashmina is draped around her shoulders. She is stunning. She gives my chocolate pot a scathing look and smiles sweetly at me but her eyes are murderous.

'Lucky you, that would have gone straight to my hips,' she smiles.

She leans delicately towards me and points to my chin.

'You have something on your face. Oh silly me, it's a pimple now I look closer. Chocolate affects me in the same way.'

I feel myself grow hot. What a bitch.

'You're looking pretty good yourself Will,' she says in a sultry voice.

He nods and then there is a dreadful silence. I feel my stomach cramp and panic engulfs me. Please God don't let me break the silence with a fart.

'Are you here on your own?' William asks and I breathe a sigh of relief. Please keep talking.

Is that hope in his voice? I look at him and realise that he is looking at her admiringly. She is exactly what I imagined his type would be and I feel my heart sink. Of course, I should have realised. Never in my wildest dreams would someone like William Ellis look at me. Of course she has nice breasts. That's the thing with big breasts isn't it? Clothes hang much better when you've got something to hang them on. When you've got two pimples like me it's plain hopeless. I'm rubbish, that's what I am. The only time I'll have big breasts is when I'm pregnant and you need a man for that don't you and I can't seem to keep one or attract one. I'm doomed to be a spinster. I'll end up like Aunty Vera, with a thousand cats, and a house smelling of cat wee and Whiskas.

What a depressing thought. I need to join the Prozac club. Maybe I should have a little breakdown and they'll shut me up in one of those lovely rehab places where I'll be given as much Prozac and Valium as I want. I shall spend my days in a haze of happiness reading self-help books. I'm bound to meet some celebs too aren't I? That doesn't sound too bad does it?

'Hello, it's nice to meet you.'

I am shaken from my reverie by a large hand being thrust into my face.

'Hi, I'm Rich,' repeats the hand.

'Are you really?' I say looking up to see a man wearing a dazzling blue tie over a white shirt. I blink stupidly and take the hand. He smiles widely revealing a row of white teeth that seem much too crowded in his mouth. 'I've always wanted to meet a rich man.'

I hear William chuckle.

'Ha, yah, I wish I was. Richard Head, nice to meet you, but call me Dick, everyone does.'

Everyone calls him Dick Head? He has a bent nose like a boxer and I find I can't take my eyes off it.

'Binki Grayson,' says William quietly, while looking at Andrea.

'Binki?' bellows the man. 'What a bloody fab name.'

Yes well, no need to make a big thing of it. Not when yours is Dick Head.

'It's an odd name,' says Andrea with a grimace. 'How did you come by that?'

I grit my teeth.

'My mother named me after her favourite novel character,' I say blushing.

'Oh, is it a famous novel,' bellows Richard. He obviously doesn't know how to control the loudness of his voice.

'Of course not,' snaps Andrea, 'or else we'd have heard of it wouldn't we?'

'Oh yes, of course,' mutters Richard. 'Well, we should get off Andy. We're off to 'Raffles' the new club that opened last night.'

'Andrea always did like the night life,' William says quietly.

I personally can't see what he sees in her. She leans down and kisses him softly on the cheek and Richard looks away. I feel a small stab of something and tell myself it is indigestion. She smiles at me.

'Let's hope you last longer than the others,' she says and then in a flash they are gone.

I look at William.

'The others?' I ask.

'Yup, let me just get this.'

He hands the waiter a debit card and gives me a shy smile.

'My ex, three months ago we had a big bust up to do with my work, but I won't bore you with the details. So it looks like we have something in common.'

What the hell does she see in Richard Head?

'I'm so sorry William,' I say softly.

'I was busy,' he shrugs. 'I got tied up with an important contract. I was hardly there. Anyway, I'm not good with commitment. The *others* couldn't cope with my work obsession either. I've let her stay in the flat we shared in Knightsbridge. So Aunt Vera did us both a favour.'

The waiter returns with his card.

'One of us a favour,' I correct.

'Quite right,' he grins. 'And may the best man win.'

Keep your friends close and your enemies closer. I wonder which one William is. I see he is thinking the same thing. I realise I can never trust him and vice versa. After all, he did disappear earlier this evening didn't he? Who knows what he's up to?

'Or woman,' I add.

If that means dirty tricks, so be it.

Chapter Seventeen

God, he even whoosh-whooshes at weekends. What the hell is wrong with the guy? I know he has to keep up his energy if he is to get through all those condoms, but blimey, can't he just get some Viagra? Surely it would be less work and at least I'd get some sleep. I turn over and groan as a pain shoots through my neck. Oh, that's all I need, a crick in my neck. These pillows are horrendous. I throw the duvet off my sweaty body and crawl to the radiator and turn it down. That's another thing, when are these heating people supposed to be coming? I guess that's something I have to sort out. I crawl back to the bed and check my Blackberry. There is a text from Muffy.

'Happy birthday sweetie. See you later. I'm leaving soon so should be with you lunchtime. Text me if you need anything.'

A decent pillow and a good night's sleep sound good. I can't wait to see her. I really should have asked her to bring my pillow. Maybe Oliver can send it. Oh no, that's a bad idea, he'll then know where I live. I could ask him to send it to the post office in the village. God, I'm thirty. I grab my handbag mirror and study my face. Thirty, how did I get to be thirty? What's more how did I get to be thirty with no sign of a marriage on my calendar, jobless and house sharing? I should be sharing a house with a husband and two snotty-nosed kids. No, that would never happen. I would never have snotty-nosed kids, yuk. This is as dire as it can get isn't it? I can't even afford decent face cream. I grab my vibrating phone. It's my mother.

'Happy birthday darling, I've transferred some money to your account. I was going to get you a calendar of naked men, but then I thought crème de lamer might be better now at your age.'

Does she have to make me sound ninety?

'Couldn't I have had both?'

I want to weep. I mean, let's face it, you're only thirty once aren't you? I'd imagined last night would have been Oliver and me together with our friends having a really good night at Romeo's. It's one of those restaurants with a small dance platform. We would have all got drunk on tequila and danced all night. After I'd opened all my cards and presents, Oliver would have given me surprise tickets for Venice or Rome or somewhere equally romantic. Instead I had spent the evening with a stranger, as lovely as that was it wasn't quite what I had hoped for.

'What are your plans for this evening?'

Just a quiet evening in with a razor blade.

'I'm meeting Muffy,' I say.

'Oh lovely, we'll give her your cream. Must dash, we're off to look at 3D televisions. Any word from Oliver?' she adds hopefully.

'He sent flowers.'

'Oh that's hopeful,' she says chirpily. 'Especially now, you know, with your body clock ticking.'

She makes me sound like a time bomb. And has she forgotten Oliver's little indiscretion already. I hang up and pull my laptop towards me to check Oliver's Facebook page and cringe at his new profile pic. It's one of him with me. I'm looking at him adoringly. It was taken in Corfu, I remember it well. We were both slightly pissed and the Greek waiter had said,

'Look loving into the eyes.'

I never was sure if he meant his eyes or Oliver's. I remember he was very sexy. The waiter that is, not Oliver, although Oliver is very sexy too, especially first thing in the morning. I always found him hard to resist in the mornings when he strolled out of the bathroom smelling clean and fresh from the shower. Oh, I do miss him. I scroll down the page and read his status.

'Missing my lovely girl Binki, bad days and bad backs.'

Trust him to get his back in there somewhere. There are several emails. No job offers from any of the agencies I had signed with which is a bit odd. I remember Ben Newman's words and feel my stomach lurch. I google *positions in sales* and see there are plenty in the city. My eyes zoom in on one company and I remember Mike Sawyer, the sales director. We'd been on some sales courses together. A polite lady answers my call and puts me through to Mike.

'Hi Binki, how are you?' he says cheerfully but I can hear a hesitancy in his voice. I feel my heart beat faster.

'I'm great actually,' I lie, forcing brightness to my voice. 'But I've left Temco. It's a bit complicated but I'm looking for another job. I see you have a vacancy …'

'The thing is Binki, I'd love to work with you …'

'I just want an interview,' I say quickly. 'I don't want any favours.'

I certainly don't. I'm not giving or receiving any favours thank you very much.

'Yeah, right, I understand, I mean totally. It's cool you know,' he mumbles.

I knew there was a reason I'd turned down his offer of a drink a few years ago. It always seems to take him forever to say a few words, that is, a few words that make any kind of sense.

'If you could get someone to ping me over the application form that would be …'

'Yeah, right, cool. It's just I think that particular post got taken, you know?'

'But it's in this week's job section. You surely haven't had applications back yet, let alone interviewed people,' I say feeling a strange sensation in my stomach. Something doesn't feel right here.

There is an uncomfortable silence and then Mike clears his throat before saying,

'Yeah yeah, you're right of course. This is a bit uncomfortable Binki …'

I can almost visualise him loosening his tie.

'This thing with Ben Newman …' he begins.

'Ben Newman,' I practically yell. 'Ben Newman, what has he got to do with this? What thing with Ben Newman are you talking about? I mean, Christ, Ben Newman.'

I feel nauseous. Does everyone who works in sales in the whole of London know about the *thing* with Ben Newman? Oh God, they don't seriously believe I would throw myself at someone like Ben Newman with the wart on his nose do they? I must seem so desperate.

'Yeah right, cool, you're right. I mean, absolutely …' mumbles Mike who must be almost strangling himself with his tie by now.

I clench my fists and fight the urge to throw my mobile across the room.

'Mike just spit it out for Christ's sake. You're doing my head in.'

There is a long sigh at the other end of the phone.

'Oh hey Binki, I'll have to call you back. The fire alarms are going off like crazy here ...'

'Oh really,' I say. I can't hear a bloody thing except him sighing.

'Yeah Christ, it's like The Towering bloody Inferno here. Better go. You know – help the others get out.'

The Towering Inferno my arse, honestly what a load of crap. Before he hangs up I hear a voice say,

'Here's your coffee Mr Sawyer.' Steaming hot obviously.

I hang up and phone six more companies. The first three I don't even get past the receptionist once I give my name. The other three claim the positions have already been filled, but I know that can't possibly be true. I hang up the phone and glance at my emails to make sure I haven't missed anything. I delete the email from the relative of the deceased African dictator who wants to put a million pounds in my bank account, and from someone called Marina, who tells me she has everything I have ever wanted, but unless she means a nice soft pillow and a job in sales then I am really not interested. I ignore the tweets from Oliver that simply say *#Missing @binkigrayson*, which makes it sound like I am either on the missing persons' register or have become mistaken for someone's lost cat. He'll be sticking posters on lamp posts next, and before I know it I'll be seeing a reconstruction of my departure from the Notting Hill flat on *Crimewatch*. I know he means he is missing me but he could have worded it better. I push the whole Ben Newman thing out of my head, telling myself it was just an idle threat. Everyone in sales isn't going to close their doors to me, surely. I sigh and roll out of my bed with another groan. I'll be walking around like the Hunchback of Notre Dame at this rate. I slip on my robe, grab the carrier bag that holds my laundry and open the door gingerly, although I don't know why as the whoosh-whoosh sounds are as loud as ever. He's like the guy in the film *Sleeping With the Enemy*. I only wish he resembled him when it came to the tidiness of his cupboards. I open the door further and a gust of cold air hits me in the face. The window on the landing is wide open. Jesus, it's like a freezer out here. I rush and close the window feeling a whisper of cold air across my feet as I pass the end bedroom. God, he's got that window open too. Honestly it's all right for him, whooshing away isn't it? I wander down to the kitchen still wondering if I should ask Oliver to send some of my things. I could sneak to the flat when he's at work and just take them I suppose, but what if she's there? That would be so humiliating. Perhaps Muffy could collect them. I'll ask her. It would be nice to have my nice soft pillow, not to mention my CDs and books. I'll ask him to pack up my candleholders too. Right, that's what I'll do. After all, it looks like I'm going to be here a lot longer than I had planned. If only I could find a job. I open the kitchen door sleepily and walk straight into Andy. Jesus, what the hell? It's Saturday for goodness' sake. The other two builders are sitting at the kitchen table sipping tea. They give me a little wave like it is the most normal thing in the world for them to be in *my* kitchen in *their* muddy boots while I'm in *my* dressing gown. Christ, I could have been in my bra and panties. What a terrible thought. They'll be coming here for dinner next. Why are they always drinking tea? Then I see it and my eyes must bulge out of my sockets. Oh my God, is that the chocolate tea pot? They've only gone and made tea in the chocolate teapot.

'Morning Mrs Ellis,' grins Andy, sipping from his mug.

'I'm not ...'

Oh, what's the point?

'What are you doing?' I squeal. 'Why have you made tea in the teapot?' I sound totally unreasonable because after all isn't that what people do? Make tea in teapots.

The kitchen door is shoved open behind me, bashing me in the bum. I turn to see William in his running shorts and top with a towel around his neck. I pull the robe together quickly and glare at the teapot.

'But that's what it's for isn't it?' says Andy, looking bemused at the other builders.

I rack my brains to remember how many M&Ms I'd left in there.

'Morning Andy,' William says pleasantly before nodding at me. 'Any tea left in that pot?'

What?

'It's not for making tea in,' I snap, grabbing it.

Andy shakes his head nonplussed.

'It's not?'

'No, it's not. It's a *chocolate* teapot.'

I place the teapot back on the kitchen counter. I see William pull a face at Andy and the other builders fight back their sniggers. I look down at the muddy floor and bite back a comment about their muddy boots.

'Perhaps you'd like breakfast too before you start work. Is a full English okay, or would you prefer continental?' I add sarcastically.

'Well, if you're offering, the lads and me wouldn't mind a …'

'I think she's cross,' smiles William, leaning across to the mug cupboard. 'Isn't that right Binki?'

I give him a filthy glare.

'I'm surprised you can manage breakfast,' I say turning back to the builders, 'considering the amount of M&Ms you've scoffed.'

A guilty look crosses their faces.

'Here, have these,' says William, handing Andy a pack of muffins. Honestly, are they here to work or just bloody eat, drink and bloody pee? Thank God, they have a portable loo outside or I'd be bathing with them next. Well at least the muffins are not from my cupboard. I'm honestly surprised he can find anything in his it is such a mess.

'Thanks Mr Ellis, we'll erm replace the M&Ms,' says Andy sheepishly.

'We thought they were old stale ones,' I hear him whisper to William.

Stale ones my arse, it didn't stop them eating them did it? I take a mug from the cupboard and ignore William's winks. I remove my jar of coffee and, being as my chocolate stash has gone, stretch to reach my half-open pack of chocolate digestives.

'Can I help?' he asks, pouring coffee into a mug.

'No, I can manage,' I say stubbornly, taking a wooden spoon from the drawer and reaching up to knock the biscuits out. I finally hit them and annoyingly they fall straight into Williams hands. It was a good catch I have to admit, but I don't want to have to feel grateful to him right now. He gives them to me and turns back to his coffee making. The familiar smell of him wafts over me and I give him a sidelong glance. He is studying a text on his phone and his forehead is creased in concentration. He looks vulnerable with his flushed cheeks and tousled hair.

'You look lopsided, like someone who has had a stroke, except your face looks normal,' he says blandly.

'I've got a crick in my neck,' I say. 'It's those awful pillows.'

He sits down to join the builders at the table.

'Ah well, I would swap with you …'

'You would?' I say happily.

'Except, I also found them too hard, which is why I chucked them in the spare room.'

And there was me thinking he was going to be nice and offer his. I open the packet of digestives and stare at them. Right, if the bugger thinks he can steal my biscuits he can think again. Honestly, he is the one with the high-powered job. I begin counting the biscuits aloud. As I thought, there are two short.

'You've had two of my biscuits,' I say accusingly, holding up the packet.

He shakes his head.

'I've not been near your biscuits or your chocolate pot,' he says dismissively, tapping into his phone.

'Teapot,' I correct. 'And yes you have, because I had eleven biscuits left and now there are only nine.'

'Oh no, call Special Branch. There are two chocolate biscuits missing. Seal the exits, nobody leave the cottage,' he says mockingly.

'Don't laugh at me,' I thunder. 'It's all right for you isn't it? With your high-powered job and bulging bank balance, while I'm living off my wedding savings …' I stop as I feel tears brimming behind my eyelids. It's not fair. Why did Oliver do this to me? He's given me this crick in my neck. I can never sleep on my old fluffy soft pillow again can I? Not if her perfumed hair has been on it. I don't care if he washed the pillow case. The scent of her will always be in that bed won't it. I hate him. I hate all men and I hate William Ellis even more. How dare he steal the little I've got?

'Well, we'll be off then Mrs Ellis', chirps Andy. As difficult as it must be to tear himself away from the drama I assume he has had enough entertainment for the time being. At last they leave, but not before one of them bends down to pick up his tool kit, exposing his builder's bum crack from his loosely fitting jeans in the process. I jump up from the table and throw my dirty laundry in the washing machine.

'I'll leave you to your biscuit investigation,' says William. 'I would help but personally I've got far more interesting things to do. I've got an important meeting with Nathan in town today. And before you nag, I haven't forgotten it's on the rota for me to empty the bins.'

Before I can reply he has left the kitchen and I hear him running upstairs. I flop onto a chair and take a breath. He's quite right of course; it is only a couple of biscuits. I never used to be this mean and hateful. I fight back my tears. I must try and be more positive. After all, things aren't that bad are they? They could be a lot worse. I could be without a home altogether and still living with Muffy. Not that much has changed of course, except I own the house I am sharing, at least I hope I own it. Oh God, what if it turns out that William is the real owner? What will I do then? No I must not think about that. Aunty Vera most certainly left it to me. I sip my coffee and look at the washing tumbling in the machine. Even if she did leave it to William surely he wouldn't just throw me out would he? One day at a time, Binki, one day at a time, it is the only way. My eyes focus on the washing as it dawns on me that everything looks blue, that can't be right can it? I definitely put my whites in. I peer closer at the suds in the machine, finally crawling towards it and watching it as it tumbles my washing around. My God, everything is bollocking blue. Panicking I turn the stupid thing off and wait the agonising thirty seconds before the automatic lock clicks and I can pull out all my white underwear, except it's not pissing white any more is it? It's all sodding blue. Absolutely everything is blue from my white frilly knickers to my lacy bra. Oh no, my new silky white camisole is blue. I stare stunned for a few seconds and then scatter them around me, my tears dropping onto my knickers. I can't take any more, I really can't. It is then I see it, a dark pair of running shorts. His running shorts. It isn't even his washing day and his running shorts are in the washing machine. I tear upstairs like a demented witch, waving my wet blue underwear in the air as I go. We collide on the stairs and he looks at me wide-eyed.

'I take it there must be a good reason you're waving your knickers at me,' he says casually walking past me. 'Don't tell me a pair of those has gone missing too. I can assure you I don't have them.'

He's wearing a pale blue shirt and tie. Even in my anger I can't help noticing how sexy he looks.

'Everything is blue,' I say, barely able to contain my anger. 'All my washing is blue.'

'Well, that's nice isn't it,' he says in a disinterested tone.

I swear it is a good thing I'm not near the cutlery drawer right now.

'This is why all my white undies are blue,' I say through gritted teeth, holding up his blue shorts.

He pulls a face before putting on his jacket.

'Ah, I see.'

I feel all the anger drain out of me and feel suddenly exhausted.

'My fault, I forgot all about you,' he says.

I raise my eyebrows and he shakes his head.

'Not forgot about you literally, but just forgot that you were using the machine too. I tend to throw things in as and when.'

His phone rings and I sigh. Bloody Nathan.

'Oh Andrea hi, no it's fine.'

He turns his back on me and I feel invisible.

'I've a meeting with Nathan but I can meet you before, no problem,' he says softly. I notice his tone changes when talking to her and I feel myself grow envious. I don't remember Oliver ever talking to me like that. He said he loved me and everything but he never spoke to me with a soft caring tone like that. He hangs up and turns to me.

'I'm really sorry. Let me know what the damage is and I'll sort it out with you later and happy birthday by the way.'

He hands me a card and walks to the front door. I turn back to the kitchen to my blue washing and the muddy kitchen floor. And there was me thinking things couldn't get any worse.

Chapter Eighteen

I push through the doorway of the sex shop dragging Muffy with me. The stuffy dark interior takes me by surprise and I wait for my eyes to adjust. Muffy looks around and nudges me in the ribs.

'What are we doing here? I thought you said you were taking me for coffee.'

'I am, after,' I whisper.

'After what?' she asks clasping my arm tightly. 'I'm not being funny Binki, but they do have these in Notting Hill you know. If I'd really wanted ...'

'Hello girls,' waves a camp man from behind the grimy till. He is wearing a tight-fitting cropped top and a long hooped earring with a skull hanging from it.

'Don't be shy,' he smiles.

'This is seedier than Soho,' Muffy grumbles. 'I thought Hampstead Heath was a nice place, if you ask me it's a bit like Skegness with sleaze. We'll be eating greasy fish and chips on a bench opposite Hampstead Heath ponds next, and consorting with the local punks.'

'Is it a strap on you ladies are looking for? In the mood for a bit of excitement are we? We have some fab ones that have just arrived.'

He holds up a black strap on dildo and I think Muffy may faint.

'Oh Jesus,' she groans. 'I wouldn't let you near me with one of those.'

I sigh.

'Muffy, we don't have that kind of relationship.'

'As long as you're very clear on that,' she says flicking through the DVDs.

I stare fascinated at the leather outfits and pink wigs.

'I'm broke,' I say.

'I don't get the connection. Do you think if you become multi-orgasmic, it will help things?'

'I need to do something. I need money. I've broken into my wedding savings.'

'You won't make much having a sex party,' she says, glancing through a porno mag.

'How about the lipstick vibrator,' offers the man, 'no one need ever know? Just pop it into your handbag, small enough for those secret moments.'

Muffy sighs.

'You don't give up do you? Thanks but no thanks. Those things get stuck.'

I gape at her.

'Stuck? You never told me that.'

'I had to use salad tongs, so now you know. Avoid secret moments is my advice.'

'Ooh salad tongs,' grins the assistant. 'Maybe we should start stocking those.'

'I'm an expert with knuckledusters too,' says Muffy, examining a mask.

I smile at the assistant and thank God the place is empty.

'I need to do something for money,' I say.

'I wouldn't say that too loudly in here doll,' says the assistant.

Muffy gasps.

'You're not thinking of ... Oh cock it Binki. I know with your name it would look good but ...'

What is she talking about? I cock my head.

'But, well look what happened to Linda Lovelace,' she finishes.

'I've got one copy of *Deep Throat* left if that's your fancy?' he says reaching under the counter.

'Oh do shut up,' Muffy snaps.

'Do I look like the next *Deep Throat* starlet to you?' I say exasperated.

'I was just seeing things like *Binki Rides Again* or *Binki Swallows It All.*

We giggle and Muffy crosses her legs.

'God I need to pee,' she chuckles.

'I'm enquiring about the sales assistant position,' I say to the shop assistant.

He disappointingly puts the video away.

'You've got to be kidding,' says Muffy. 'Christ, you'll be turning tricks next.'

'Oh right,' says the assistant brightening. 'Well it's four afternoons a week. Two until seven. You want the forms? You'll most likely get it,' he says handing me a sheet of paper.

'Do you think so?' I say, feeling flattered.

'Yeah, seeing as no one else has applied. Here, have a chocolate penis, on the house. Want a bag of them? The sell-by-date's gone so you can have the lot and a bag of chocolate nipples too. Good luck, I need a break. I'm bloody dreaming of dildos.'

'Christ,' groans Muffy as she knocks over a display of whips and floggers.

'Live locally do you? Only I don't recognise you.'

'She owns a cottage named Driftwood,' pipes up Muffy.

I thank him and pull her out of the shop.

'You can't work there,' she says, sucking on a penis.

'I may have to, there is nothing else and I soon won't have any money. Do you have to lick that in public?' I say shaking my head and dropping the chocolates into my bag. I never say no to chocolate, penis or otherwise.

'Sorry,' she smiles. 'Are you seriously broke?'

I nod ushering her into the pub. I still hadn't told anyone apart from Muffy about William. She had agreed to dig up the dirt on him. Mr Hayden had been as good as useless when it came to getting things sorted.

'We're looking into things Miss Grayson but these things take time.'

'Can't I just throw him out? He isn't family or anything. The thing is I need to sell the cottage.'

He'd chewed on his pipe and mumbled,

'I don't know how it happened. It's never happened before but it seems Mr Ellis was left the house too. I assure you, as soon as we have news Miss Grayson we will be in touch.'

The thing is I am already becoming attached to *Driftwood* and the thought of leaving it makes me miserable. I'm also getting used to William. I don't trust him mind you, but I'm getting used to him.

'Surely all you need is something unsavoury about him,' Muffy had suggested on the phone. 'You know, like in business. Then you could query his relationship with your aunt. I can't believe she left the house to him. I mean, why would she?'

I wait for her to show me the dirt on William. Don't get me wrong, I don't want to throw the guy out but what else can I do?

She sips her coffee thoughtfully and pulls several packages from a carrier bag.

'Your mum's present,' she says smiling. 'And I bought you this.'

I open the blue envelope to find two tickets to Ronnie Scott's jazz club.

'Oh Muffy,' I say, overwhelmed.

'Well, you said Oliver would never go with you and if you can't go with your mate to a jazz club on her thirtieth, when can you. It's in about six weeks' time. I couldn't get them for any earlier, but it's one of your favourite artists.'

'Oh that's great Muffy,' I say hugging her.

She lowers her eyes to the carrier bag and says.

'Oliver wanted me to give you this.'

She pulls a pink tissue wrapped gift from her bag.

'I think it's a Tiffany,' she says, scrunching her hair into a bun.

'You think?' I ask.

'I peeked. It is a Tiffany, okay?'

'God, everyone is doing well but me,' I moan.

'You got a Tiffany, be grateful. I think it is rather sweet of him seeing as you never talk to him.'

Bloody hell, what's happened to Muffy? I thought she was all up with the Hovis and off with men's heads.

'You've changed your tune. You always said he was a little shit. What happened to down with men and up with the good things in life,' I say cynically.

'Yeah well, Hovis doesn't buy you Tiffany bracelets does it? Anyway all men are little shits deep down. But I mean, look at you. You've gone downhill since you broke up with Oliver. You haven't even done your nails and when did you last shave and give yourself a face pack?'

Oh God, she's quite right of course. I've barely done anything since I've been at the cottage. I've been that depressed.

'It's all the stress. I'm constantly on edge in case he tries to change the locks or sell the house from under me. I daren't relax. You can be sure the minute I do he'll do something. So what's the dirt on him,' I ask eagerly.

'Ah yes, that's just it. There isn't any,' she says shrugging and handing me a folder.

I gape at her.

'There must be something,' I say pleadingly. 'Hasn't he done time or something? He's loaded you know, he's got a Lamborghini,' I say, making it sound like he has a nasty disease.

She rolls her eyes.

'Well yes, he's done time in France and a few other countries. Holidays I presume.'

'You know what I mean.'

She shakes her head.

'Nope, nothing like that. He's owned his own company for about fifteen years. He's very successful. All his deals are above board. He did invest money for your aunt but all legal. He was engaged for six months to someone called …

'Andrea,' I say flicking through the papers.

'Yep, how did you know?'

'I met her. It was awful so don't even go there. He still fancies her,' I say handing the info back to her.

'You sound jealous,' she probes, looking at me over her coffee cup.

'Huh, I don't think so. I'm off men remember?' I laugh.

'Well that's it. He's lived in London most of his life. He owns an apartment in Knightsbridge, the same block as your aunt so I guess that's how they met. His accountant and advisor is a Nathan Richards, a bit of a prick by all accounts but I didn't look into him too much. Oh and William Ellis owns a house in France too. No dirt I'm afraid. Geoff says you just need to sit it out. The chances are the house was left to you anyway.'

I feel quite sure it was. I just don't understand why William is so stubborn about the whole thing. It's as obvious as a wart on your nose isn't it? Oh God, why did I think that?

'And how is Ben Newman?' I say, voicing my thoughts.

'Aren't you going to open that present?' she asks, her hands twitching.

I rip at the tissue paper to reveal a small white Tiffany box. I lift the lid and we both stare at the small charm bracelet.

'Ooh it's gorgeous,' she says with a sigh.

I push it towards her and open the card. A bright pink heart sparkles at me. It flickers like a Christmas tree decoration. I open the card and Tina Turner's *You're Simply The Best* screams at me.

'*I love you Binki and I would forgive you anything,*' I read aloud. '*Please forgive me for one stupid indiscretion. Happy thirtieth birthday.*'

I scoff and slam it shut.

'I hate Tina Turner,' I say aggressively. 'And I hate being thirty.'

She fiddles with the bracelet.

'He's very forgiving Binki,' she says clipping it around my wrist.

'He's nothing to forgive. I wasn't the one doing the screwing.'

She looks uncomfortable.

'Can we go to the house? I'm dying to see it. I also want to meet this William.'

I've known Muffy for years. The only time I know her to fidget like she has ants in her knickers is when she has them on back to front or when she is holding something back from me.

'Are your pants on back to front,' I ask sharply.

'Of course not,' she says, blushing.

'Right,' I say.

'Right,' she repeats.

There is a few seconds of silence and then she says,

'Ben Newman is telling anyone that will listen that you had an affair with him. A real steamy romp, sex on the office floor and all that ...'

I stare at her. The office floor? If anyone even took two minutes to look at the state of the office floor they would know damn well that no one is going to do it there.

'All that?' I repeat.

'Over the desk, on his chair, seems you were happy to do it anywhere. You were hanging from the light fittings according to Ben Newman. I'm surprised I didn't see you dangling from an open window with your bum hanging out when I passed at lunch time.'

I bury my head in my hands. I don't believe this.

'How you got any work done I'll never know,' she finishes.

'Very funny,' I sigh.

She pulls a face.

'Thing is, he's putting it around that you're a husband stealer ...'

'What,' I yell.

She fidgets in her seat and flexes her neck.

'He asked me to tell you that your job is there for the taking but if you think anyone else will hire you then you can think again. Honestly Binki, I've heard the rumours. He makes you sound like that woman out of *Basic Instinct* but worse. Honestly, no one is going to hire bitch on heat Binki Grayson at the moment. Their wives won't let them even if they wanted to.'

I seriously don't believe this.

'It seems Ben Newman really has a thing for you and your rejection on Christmas Eve didn't go down well. I ask you though, Ben Newman, of all the men, Ben Newman.'

'Okay okay,' I say. 'I've already been turned down by two companies.'

Muffy shakes with rage.

'You should call his bluff, do him for slander.'

'Yeah, like they will believe me over a company director. Besides I don't have the money for a solicitor and frankly, as great as it would be to be on the front page of *The Sun* that wasn't quite how I imagined it.'

'I'm just thinking working in a sleazy sex shop isn't going to calm these rumours is it and you may lose Oliver for good. I'm just wondering if you should give this whole thing up, you know about the house ...'

'And give it to William? As for losing Oliver don't you think he threw all that away when he slept with his boss?'

'He may have been put in a bit of a position,' she says, sounding so unlike Muffy that I'm beginning to wonder if she has had a Stepford wife makeover.

'He was put in a position all right and I saw it,' I say angrily, feeling the tears well up again.

'You're obsessing about it and about this William ...'

Talk of the devil and he is bound to appear.

'It's him,' I squeal. 'He's out.'

'You make it sound like you chained him up,' she turns to follow my gaze. William waves from the pub doorway and I hear Muffy take a sharp breath.

'God,' she whispers, 'easy on the eye or what? No wonder you're obsessing. You never mentioned him being that bangable. Forget the chocolate tit, he can have mine. In fact, he can have both. I can cover them in chocolate no problem. Maybe you *should* chain him up.'

I shake my head in despair.

'What happened to the Hovis?' I ask.

'Fuck the Hovis,' she says drooling.

She pulls her hair from the scrunch and shakes her head seductively, her long thick hair falls around her shoulders and she pinches her cheeks. She looks fabulous and I feel like the poor relation. A fair-haired man follows behind William. He walks with a slight swagger and gives us a small lip-curling smile. He whispers something to William and I know this is Nathan. He gives me an appraising look and walks slowly towards us, seemingly ignoring Muffy. He is smart in a dark blue suit with a crisp white shirt. He unbuttons the jacket as he approaches and has sunglasses perched on his curly fair hair, which is a bit poserish isn't it, considering it's the heart of winter?

'Hello Binki. William and I just passed your car. Your tax disc is out of date.'

He smiles warmly at me but I sense insincerity in his smile.

'An unusual chat-up line,' laughs Muffy.

'It's always worked for me in the past,' he grins.

He continues smiling and points to our coffees.

'Can we get you ladies another drink?' he asks, looking directly at me.

'How lovely,' replies Muffy, not taking her eyes off William.

'He's quite right your tax disc is out of date and ...' William points to the window and I see a buggery traffic warden approach the car. I swear they are ganging up on me these bloody wardens. I shriek and dive for the door.

'Excuse me,' I shout. 'It's in the post.'

I launch myself at the warden, skidding to a halt before sending him flying. He turns and I swear I see his face drop.

'Nazi,' I mumble under my breath.

'In the post is it? It's all computerised these days lady,' he says with a sneer. 'I'll check shall I?'

I feel defeated. I'll kill Oliver. This would never have happened if he hadn't dipped his wick on Christmas Eve in someone else's ...

'Can I help Walter? Binki is a friend of mine.'

I turn to see William has followed me out.

'Hello Mr Ellis. How's that new house of yours?'

Excuse me?

'It's my house actually,' I interrupt.

William inclines his head to me.

'This is Binki,' he says.

Christ, I'm being introduced to a traffic warden now. Maybe we should all go out on a date.

'Binki?' he questions. 'You're not the girl ...'

'No, you're right, I'm not.'

'Unusual name,' he says thoughtfully.

'Yes,' I say. 'I was named after a famous literary character.'

Can you divorce your parents? Is naming your child after a Mills and Boon character grounds for matricide?

'Is it just the tax disc that is a problem Walter, or are we illegally parked too?' William says with a smile.

We, what does he mean *we*?

'Well,' grins Walter. 'The tax disc is a problem and she is just over her time limit.'

Hello, I am still here.

'How is that fund-raiser going for the youth group? I keep forgetting,' says William, pulling out his wallet.

My God, he is bribing the traffic warden.

'We always need a bit more Mr Ellis, but we're getting there.'

'Let me help with that.'

'What are you doing?' I ask.

'Why don't you just leave this to me,' William says, putting a hand on my arm.

I shake it off impatiently. Before I have time to open my mouth he has handed over fifty quid and has pulled me back to the pub.

'We'll move it in a bit Walter,' he calls over his shoulder.

'No problem Mr Ellis.'

'You can't bribe a traffic warden,' I say, pulling my arm away angrily.

'I just did,' he says arrogantly.

'How dare you patronise me. I prefer to pay the fine, whatever it is.'

'What with? Your body?'

I gasp. Oh, that was below the belt wasn't it?

'That was uncalled for.'

'So is your ungrateful attitude, you could say thank you.'

'Thank you,' I say begrudgingly.

'You're welcome, and I apologise for the body remark. I imagine it would just about pay for a ticket.'

I stare at him. He winks. I turn away. Bloody men, they all shit on you. Muffy is quite right about that. The heat of the pub hits me and I feel my face flush. Muffy looks at William and flutters her eyelashes.

'Nathan and I were saying how nice it would be if we could all go out for dinner tonight. It would give us all a chance to get to know each other better and we could celebrate your birthday at the same time.'

I know everyone well enough thank you very much and have no desire to get to know Nathan better, although I can tell by the way he is looking at me that he would like to get to know me better.

'Sounds great,' says William shaking Muffy's hand.

'Nathan Richards,' says the poser, offering his hand. I take it reluctantly. He squeezes my hand for an eternity and I make several attempts to free myself from his vice-like grip but he just squeezes more. Don't you just hate that?

'I'm Will's accountant, so I assure you that he can afford dinner and you're not thirty every day.'

I glare at Muffy. She told him I was thirty?

'Binki, what a lovely name,' he continues.

Oh well, maybe he's not so bad after all. At least I can keep an eye on William and won't have to worry about him doing the dirty on me, and it will be a free dinner.

'What do you think?' asks Muffy.

'Yes, sounds great,' I agree.

Chapter Nineteen

Muffy has eyes for no one but William. Honestly, put a good-looking man in front of her and Hovis goes out the window. I have to admit, William is exceptionally handsome but that doesn't make me forget he could be nothing but an exceptionally handsome con man. In fact, I am beginning to wonder if he and Nathan are just two con men. Just think about it, I'm left an inheritance from my great aunt and who turns up outside the solicitors? None other than Mr William Ellis, a bit of a coincidence don't you think? I imagine he and Nathan preyed on her, investing her money in their dodgy schemes. No doubt Mr charming Ellis talked her into leaving her house to him too. Yes, that's about right. Well, I'm not letting them get away with it. William has himself well covered if Muffy can't find anything on him. Maybe I'll do a little spying myself. What was he doing loitering outside the solicitors anyway? A convenient collision if you ask me.

The waiter leans towards me.

'Seared foie gras with figs poached in red wine, oriental spices and toasted sesame madam.'

'You'll have to share those,' says Nathan, seductively licking his lips.

If he thinks he is getting his mouth around my fork, he can think again. In fact, if he thinks he is getting his mouth around me he will find his balls dished up for dessert. He's a bit too forward if you ask me. I can't think why William uses him.

'Pot roast quail,' says the waiter, placing a dish in front of William, 'and the lobster for you sir.'

'And a bottle of the 2009 Chardonnay,' adds Nathan.

Nathan likes to spend William's money it seems. I relax in the warmth of a roaring log fire that is near to our table and enjoy the flickering light of the candles on the crystal glassware on the table. Nathan leans close to me and says,

'So William tells me you're in sales.' He cuts into the lobster expertly.

'I was.'

'Worked in the city did you?'

'Yes, I did.'

But now I am in the sex business it would seem, that is if I get the job.

'So you weren't an accountant?' he asks casually.

William tops up Muffy's glass and smiles at me. I smile back and try to ignore the little tingle in my loins. Con artists, don't forget Binki, con artists.

'No,' I reply. 'I was never an accountant.'

What an odd question, unless he has a fetish for female accountants.

'Why, are you running classes?' I ask.

He laughs.

'No, I just like to keep up with the competition.'

'So where in London are you based?' Muffy asks William, 'Company-wise of course.'

Good heavens, is she moving closer to him? If she gets much closer she'll be on his lap.

'Canary Wharf,' smiles William.

'Not actually in the city then?' I ask suspiciously.

Muffy gives me a sharp look.

'No, but I'm often there on business,' he says, looking into my eyes.

'Ah,' I say, leaving the word hanging in the air and sounding like Columbo.

'Which means?' asks Muffy.

Blimey, is she defending him?

'Nothing,' I shrug.

I finish my starter and spend the main course sneakily glancing at William and listening to Nathan's boring monologues about the places he has been to and his opinions on business-class travel and all of the classy hotels he has stayed in. He clearly likes the high life. By dessert I've really had enough of him.

'When I went to Saudi, this Arab sheik insisted on having me dine with him and his harem. That was a funny story. I could have been at it all night,' he laughs drunkenly. 'I tell you, I've got a great job.'

'Really,' I say, rolling my eyes at Muffy.

'Binki's got a job. Did she tell you?' Muffy blurts out drunkenly.

Oh great.

'I haven't got it yet,' I say.

'You did?' says William, raising his eyebrows.

'Why, were you hoping I wouldn't stick around?' I say emptying my fourth glass.

'Of course not,' he says softly.

'It's in a sex shop,' says Muffy loudly. She has this way of staggering news doesn't she? 'I said she'll be turning tricks next,' she adds laughing.

I throw her a filthy look as the restaurant quietens.

'Let me know when you do,' winks Nathan, wafting alcohol breath over me.

'You didn't have to do that,' says William quietly.

'I think I did,' I reply, meeting his eyes. 'I need to pay my way.'

'It's better than appearing in porn films,' giggles Muffy. 'That was her first thought, wasn't it Binki? We said the titles would be funny, like ...'

What is she saying?

'Muffy,' I snap. 'Shut up.'

'Sounds like fun,' mumbles Nathan drunkenly. 'Any perks, bet you can't match mine?'

'Chocolate penises and nipples,' giggles Muffy.

'Then again, maybe you can,' he laughs.

I'm relieved when dessert comes and the conversation has moved onto cars and how William came to have a Lamborghini.

'Can you believe a grateful client bought it for him?' says Nathan banging William on the back.

'It sounds grander than it is,' says William looking slightly embarrassed.

By the time dessert is over I realise I have drunk far too much and so has Muffy. We both stagger to the ladies and I march straight into the cubicle without even talking to her.

'Binki, I'm so sorry, I didn't mean … I've drunk too much.'

I hiccup.

'We both have,' I say flinging open the door and avoiding the mirror at all costs.

'For Christ's sake Muffy, keep your wits about you. If they are con men, don't give them any information,' I say, while wondering what sodding information I am talking about.

'Right,' says Muffy, running a brush through her hair. 'What kind of information are we talking about?'

Christ, she's becoming psychic.

'You know,' I say, opening the door to the restaurant.

'Right,' she says again.

Nathan is waiting by the table for us.

'Will is paying. I must say you two ladies look lovely.'

Lovely and pissed more like. William meets us and the waiter opens the door for us to leave.

I step outside and the fresh cold air hits me so forcefully that I have trouble standing upright and feel myself sway.

'Binki, you okay?'

I turn around and sway towards William. God I hope it didn't look like a swoon. His arm supports me, and I look into his eyes. He seems very close. If I move a fraction closer my body would be touching his. I feel my face grow hot and then his face seems to come closer. I pull back and push my hand into my bag to grab a wet wipe but pull out a chocolate nipple instead.

'Thanks but I have had plenty. Of food that is,' he laughs. 'And I prefer the real thing but thank you anyway,' he finishes with a grin.

Why is it he never gets drunk or even drinks too much come to that.

'I'm onto you, you know that,' I slur, feeling my shoes slip on the wet pavement. I grab his arm for support.

'Really?'

Oh, he is as sleazy as his partner in crime, Nathan Richards.

'I know you swindled my aunt and you deliberately bumped into me in town didn't you? I don't know what you were hoping to steal from my handbag but …'

'I was there on business Binki, and you really should be careful what you say …'

'Huh, I should be careful. You're the one who should watch your step.'

Muffy walks out of the restaurant and glances at me. She looks fabulous and I find myself feel a twinge of envy. Of course, it would be me who gets the leech Nathan wouldn't it, while Muffy gets the ever-so-gorgeous William, that's about right isn't it? What am I thinking? I couldn't care less about William Ellis could I? Not much Binki. The truth is I'm finding him the most appealing man ever, and when he said he preferred the real thing to my chocolate nipples I had to bite back offering my own.

'Everything okay?' asks Muffy.

'Fine,' I say. 'I just feel a bit headachy. I'll head back I think. I promise not to lock you out,' I whisper to William.

'I'll get you a taxi and escort you back,' offers Nathan.

Great, that's all I need.

'I should head back too,' says Muffy. 'Would you mind driving me to the station William?'

Wonderful, my best friend and my biggest enemy consorting together is what I don't need. God knows what Muffy will spill about me while under the influence. Tomorrow I am hiring a private investigator to look into William Ellis. I'll nail the little con man if it kills me.

'Thank you Nathan, but I prefer to go back alone,' I say forcefully.

I kiss Muffy goodbye, promise not to lock William out and dive into the taxi and decide, as I will be back before William, to do a little probing when I get home.

Chapter Twenty

So much for a little probing. I felt so rough in the taxi on the way home I couldn't recognise anything and kept asking the driver why he was taking such a strange route to Notting Hill. When he'd pulled up at the house I almost fell out of the cab and felt really sick.

'How much do I owe you,' I'd slurred.

'Don't worry love; the men took care of it. You just sleep it off.'

Bloody cheek, calling me love. I fumbled with the key while slumped against the door cursing William the whole time.

'The arse has changed the lock,' I mumbled, and then realised I was using my flat keys again. I stumble into the house and dash to the bathroom where I sit with my head over the bowl. Oh God, I swear I'm dying. I finally drag my reluctant body to the bedroom and search for my nightie. I bet that William Ellis has hidden it. I bet the little sod has been through my things.

'Just you wait William Ferret,' I mutter.

Somehow that didn't sound right. I wish Oliver were here. He would tell me what to do. Why did he have to go and balance a ball on his bimbo? I blame Jesus. Why did he have to be born in the first place? We'd never have this Christmas malarkey if it weren't for him. I tip my clothes out of the drawer to try and find my nightie. I grab the Ann Summers top I'd bought especially for Christmas night. With a little sob I fall onto the bed, clutching a photo of Oliver to my chest.

'I miss you so much Olly,' I whisper as the room slowly spins.

Thankfully I fall asleep and then have the worst nightmare of my life. Oliver is trapped in a big glass box with two women balanced on his balls. His wrists and ankles are bound and he is begging me to help. I struggle to get into the box but I can't, and all around me are huge brown nipples. I turn to see William with an enormous axe and I scream.

'No William.'

'It's the only way,' he says calmly. 'If we chop it off in the process it serves him right doesn't it?'

'No,' I scream, pushing him away. He shakes me and I feel like my head will fall off.

'We have to, it's the only way.'

'Get off me,' I scream.

My eyes open to find someone really is on top of me, or at least very close to me. Oh my God, a burglar. I open my mouth to call for William but nothing will come out. I'm frozen with fear and my heart is pounding so fast I feel sure the burglar must be able to hear it too. Waves of nausea wash over me and my legs feel like lead. I fumble around the bedside cabinet knocking over a glass of water. I grab my hairspray, aim it at the burglar's face and spray like a lunatic. He falls back groaning and I finally manage to scream William's name.

'Help, help,' I scream, feeling my head thump unmercifully. 'William please help me.'

'Well I would, if you hadn't have blinded me. God, what was that?'

'William?' I say.

My God, what is William doing in my bedroom? I click the light on and see William on the floor holding his hands to his eyes.

'What are you doing in my room and more importantly, what were you doing on my bed? I'm calling the police, don't move, I'm warning you,' I say, my body trembling.

'You were having a nightmare and screaming like a banshee. I came to see if you were okay. What the hell did you spray at me? I can't see a thing. Was it special rape spray? I think you've blinded me.'

'You weren't raping me?' I say suspiciously, my hand now clutching my Blackberry.

'Don't be ridiculous, if I'd wanted to rape you, I'd have done that the first night you were here wouldn't I? What is that stuff?'

'L'Oreal hairspray,' I say, jumping from the bed.

'Because I'm worth it?' he says sarcastically.

I try to ignore his boxer pants. I rush to the bathroom and soak a towel in cold water.

'Here,' I say, handing it to him. 'I'm so sorry. I thought you were a burglar.'

He takes the towel gratefully.

'You're lethal, do you know that? I only came in because I thought something was wrong.

I kneel beside him. Oh God, what if I have blinded him. He will no doubt sue me and that's all I need. He dabs the towel on his eyes and blinks.

'They don't look too bad,' I say. 'Can you see?' I ask hopefully.

Please don't let him be blind. He blinks a few times, looks at me and grins.

'Oh yes, I can see fine.'

I avoid his eyes and look down only to find myself looking at his crotch. Oh God, look up Binki, look up. He's wearing boxers and nothing else. God, he is hairy and nicely muscular. I look into his eyes and blush.

'Interesting nightie,' he says, standing up.

I gasp and put my hand to my mouth. Oh shit, shit. I look down at my Ann Summers frilly negligee and see that the bloody thing has done exactly what it said on the tin. *A quick pull on the ribbon and all will be revealed.* It has done that all right and my tits are there for all to see and in particular, for William to see.

'Oh no,' I gasp.

'He'll love it,' the assistant had said. 'Just a little tug and it opens showing everything. If that doesn't excite your man nothing will.'

Except this isn't my man and he is no doubt comparing them to Andrea's perfect specimens.

'Oh God, I'm so embarrassed,' I say.

'Don't be, they're certainly nothing to be embarrassed about,' he smiles.

'It was a Christmas present for Oliver,' I say. 'Only he didn't get to see it.'

'Oliver's loss is my gain,' he grins.

Why is he always so nice? It is so hard to detest him when he is like this. I don't even feel he is coming on to me.

'There is a chocolate nipple in the fridge,' I say to cover my embarrassment.

He grins, his red eyes sparkling.

'Won't you join me?'

'I suppose I could have a penis,' I say laughing.

'Meet you in the kitchen then.'

I watch him leave and then bury my head in my hands. I must look such a sight. I pop back to the bathroom, cringe at my reflection and splash some water onto my face. I hear him filling the kettle and after donning a dressing gown I join him in the kitchen.

'Hot chocolate?' he asks, placing a chocolate penis and a couple of nipples onto a plate.

I giggle.

'Coffee,' I say.

'Yes you're right, a much better accompaniment to a penis.'

I hand him some eye drops.

'I thought these may help.'

No matter what he wears or what gets sprayed in his face he still manages to look gorgeous.

'You saw Muffy to the station then,' I say, trying to sound casual while wondering if he kissed her, and wondering even more what it would be like if he kissed me.

'I dropped her off, yes.'

Well, that wasn't giving much away was it? He places two mugs of coffee onto the table and breaks the penis in half.

'Half a penis, or are you saving yourself for a nipple?'

'Well, I could try half a penis, I've not had one yet,' I giggle.

'You don't know what you're missing,' he winks. 'I suppose if you get this job in the sex shop we'll be overcome with the things, perks of the job and all that.'

I nod.

'Hang on a sec,' he says and disappears from the kitchen.

This is a bit disconcerting. One minute we are discussing chocolate penises and the perks of working in a sex shop, and then he has to go. Go where, and to do what exactly? Don't be ridiculous Binki, he probably needed the loo. Yes exactly, I rest my case. The door opens and I jump. He has changed into pyjama bottoms and a dressing gown, and no slippers thank God.

Slippers were always an issue with Oliver and me. He always insisted on wearing slippers, not that I have a problem with slippers you understand. My dad wears slippers but it just seems all wrong for a 29-year-old man to wear them. William is holding a box. He hands it to me and says shyly,

'This is for you, happy birthday. I would have given it to you earlier but there wasn't time.'

It's tied with a blue ribbon. I look up at him and he smiles.

'I thought blue was appropriate.'

I bite my lip and pull at the ribbon and open the box. Beneath layers of tissue paper are several pairs of white knickers, two pairs of lacy bras and the most gorgeous white camisole. I stare at them, struggling to find my voice.

'But ...' I begin.

'I took the blue ones to the shop when you were out with Muffy. They're all the right size and the camisole is silk,' he says, all hint of his shyness gone now.

I finger the camisole.

'I feel terrible,' I say. 'I didn't mean for you to buy new ones. I feel so stupid for making such a fuss over the biscuits and then the stupid washing and ...'

He waves a hand dismissively.

'It's nothing. I'm sorry for being an idiot with the shorts.'

Part of me can't help wondering when he found the time to buy them. Does this mean he didn't spend very long with Andrea, or did he ask her to go with him? I cringe at the thought. That means she now knows my bra and knickers size. As long as he didn't take Nathan with him, God, I'm not sure what would have been worse.

'Thank you,' I say looking down. After all, buying a woman underwear is a pretty intimate thing and I barely know the guy. I place the lid on the box.

'Muffy said Oliver is desperate to get you back,' he says suddenly.

He studies my reaction. I grimace.

'Well he can stay desperate.'

He bites his lip. It's the sexiest thing I have ever seen.

'Muffy said you've given up everything, your home and your job to come here. What if you find out the house wasn't left to you?'

'It was left to me,' I say sharply.

He shrugs.

'We don't have to be enemies you know,' he says softly. 'I'm not that ruthless. I've not changed the locks yet have I, and neither have you.'

I meet his eyes.

'I wish I could trust you,' I say biting into my half of the chocolate penis.

He does likewise and I feel an ache of longing in my loins. I'm missing Oliver, that's what it is. I stand up and place my mug in the sink and as I turn I find he is behind me. He leans across to put his mug with mine and our knees touch.

'Goodnight William,' I say softly. 'Thank you for the coffee.'

'Thank you for the nipples,' he says quietly, leaning towards me and kissing me softly on the cheek.

I feel like telling him he can have my nipples any time.

'Goodnight, sleep well,' he whispers into my ear.

I turn my head and his lips brush mine. He pulls away so quickly that I don't have time to savour it. He mumbles sorry and leaves the kitchen and I'm still standing by the sink when I hear his bedroom door close. Did I imagine that? It was so quick. I take several breaths to stop my heart from racing. We've both drunk too much I tell myself and then remember that William had hardly drunk anything. I slowly make my way upstairs. I stop on the landing and stare at his door. God, what am I thinking? I can't possibly go in there. I close my eyes and remember his lips brushing mine and feel a tiny shudder of pleasure run through me. I go to my bedroom and find two new pillows waiting for me on the bed.

Chapter Twenty-One

'So, I know someone who knows a private dick. I personally know a lot of public dicks but let's not go there,' says Luther taking a breath before blowing up a *Foxy Roxy* vibrating sex doll.

'Isn't there a quicker way to do that?' I say, watching her breasts slowly expand.

'It takes time to find the dirt on scumbags.'

'I meant Roxy. Isn't there a pump or something you could use?'

'A pump? Honestly sweetie, you've become filthy since you started working here, you know that?' he laughs. 'You'd never think you'd been here only five days. Anyway, it would spoil my fun. This is the nearest I'll ever get to blowing a woman and you want to spoil it for me?'

I change the DVD that has been playing for the past two hours and replace one set of tangled moaning bodies with a different set of tangled moaning bodies.

'Doesn't matter how often you change them darling, they're all the same,' sighs Luther.

I empty new stock out of a box and stare at a battery-operated vagina.

'God,' I say miserably.

'I'm sure it's no substitute for the real thing darling, not that I'd know,' puffs Luther as he disappears behind Foxy Roxy. 'So what kind of dirt are you hoping to dig up on this scumbag?'

'I don't know if I want to dig anything up,' I say thoughtfully. 'And I don't know that he is a scumbag.'

It has been nearly two weeks since the almost kiss and William has acted like nothing out of the ordinary happened. I sometimes think he is too good to be true and this makes me even more suspicious. Well, you can't blame me can you?

'I know this guy; he does a lot of undercover stuff. You want me to have a quiet word?'

I can't ask Muffy. She thinks William is the best thing since sliced bread, or should I say Hovis, and won't have a bad word said against him. I'm getting desperate to get this house thing sorted. My parents are dead keen to see the cottage and I haven't had the heart to tell them that I inherited a gorgeous hunk along with it. Although I am sure my mother would be thrilled. I've got quite a few of my things in the cottage now so it feels a bit more homely. Oliver did as I asked and sent them to the post office. The sex shop pays okay but it isn't exactly climbing the ladder is it? But what else can I do? Wart on the nose Ben Newman has well and truly finished my sales career at least for the time being. The thing is, I don't know what I'll do if William Ellis really does own Driftwood. I'll never be able to rent anything on what I'm paid here.

'Well ...' I begin. I stop when the door opens.

'Yours,' says Luther. 'I've two more to blow yet, not to mention masking the dummies. You can deal with the wanking pervert. I'll pop the kettle on.'

I turn to the customer and grasp the counter when I see the wanking pervert is none other than Oliver. I want to grab a whip from one of the mannequins and give him a good flogging. What an arse, he comes all the way to Hampstead Heath and the first place he goes to is a sex shop. I'm finally seeing my once prospective fiancé for the wanking pervert that he is.

'Well you're certainly showing your true colours,' I snap while thinking how handsome he looks in his striped shirt and jeans.

'Dirty mags, or is it DVDs you're after. Or maybe you're just looking for a huge-nippled woman. There are plenty of adverts over there and most of them are quite cheap. Or is it dominant female bosses that take your fancy?'

'Muffy wouldn't tell me where you lived so I came here to say ...'

'Or perhaps you're into something far kinkier now. Our BDSM shelves are over there and ...'

'Muffy told me where you worked,' he says bluntly. 'I think you're losing your mind.'

I see. He screws his boss on Christmas Eve and then wonders why his girlfriend is losing her mind. He stares at my name badge and shakes his head.

'Binki, here to serve your sexual needs,' he quotes despairingly. 'Have you gone totally mad, and you're calling me the pervert?'

'I wasn't the one caught humping,' I shout.

Luther rushes from the back and skids to a halt.

'Difficult punter darling?' he says glaring at Oliver. 'We have security,' he adds nervously. 'Big burly black men.'

In fact the only security we have is a rusty panic button and for some reason Luther seems to think mentioning big burly black men is a good deterrent. Personally I think big black burly men are his fantasy.

'Christ,' groans Oliver. 'Big burly black men, surely that's racist isn't it?'

'No worse than being a sexist punk,' says Luther with a bravado I know he is far from feeling.

'Luther, this is my boyfriend,' I say.

'Ah, you're the wanker who shagged the boss,' says Luther, giving Oliver the once-over.

'I rather think that isn't any of your business,' snaps Oliver, pulling me to one side and knocking over a display of DVDs in the process. 'Have you gone mad telling everyone our personal business?'

He looks down at the battery-operated vagina.

'They're on offer,' I say stupidly.

'Jesus,' he mumbles, picking up the DVDs and placing them neatly on the shelves while trying to ignore the pictures on the covers.

Luther heads towards him.

'Do you want that one mate?' he says pointing to the one Oliver is holding. 'I can throw another in. Two for a tenner this week, double your pleasure. You get a free chocolate nipple too. All treats here. We've got one called *The Spanking Pirate-esses of the Caribbean.* Right up your creek so to speak,' laughs Luther.

I cringe. Oliver rolls his eyes before saying,

'Disgusting. I seriously don't believe you shared our intimate secrets with a stranger.'

He's a bloody fine one to talk isn't he?

'No more disgusting than screwing your boss in our bed,' I say, tears welling up. 'And Luther is my friend.'

'Your parents are appalled, you know that?'

'You told my parents I worked here?' I say, stunned.

God, that's likely to give my dad a stroke. That's about right isn't it, both my parents collapsing after hearing their daughter is working in a sex shop. To them it's like selling my body. I'll get the blame of course, not Oliver. If he hadn't have been at it in the first place I wouldn't be here. Well, I suppose Ben Newman is to blame really. If he hadn't have tried to get me over the desk I wouldn't have left early, and Oliver wouldn't have been caught, and I wouldn't be working in a sex shop and consequently my parents wouldn't be wheeled off to A&E with my dad suffering a stroke all because their daughter is working in a porno store. This whole thing gets worse by the day doesn't it? How could Oliver even consider telling my parents? He's the one who's gone mad.

'They're on special offer actually,' quips Luther. 'All our pirate ones that is, they don't sell that well.'

I glare at him. This is a disaster, a complete disaster.

'We're all worried about you,' says Oliver. 'Muffy said you're becoming obsessed about Aunty Vera's cottage.'

Thanks a lot Muffy.

'And that you're sharing it with some guy called William,' says Oliver. 'I'm not happy about that.'

Huh, like it is anything to do with him. I wasn't too thrilled about you sharing our bed with Miss Brown Nipples either. I bite my lip to stop myself saying anything.

'There's nothing you can do until the solicitors get it sorted so why don't you come home. I'm sorry about everything Binki.'

'So you should be,' pipes up Luther. 'I mean come on dude, doing it in your own bed, that's a bit crass.'

'And what business is it of yours,' snaps Oliver. 'Christ, it comes to something when I get given advice from a pissing sex-shop assistant.'

What a rude bugger.

'I'm a sex-shop assistant, if you don't mind,' I say. 'What are you doing here Oliver?'

Oliver takes my hand whipping up a multitude of emotions within me. Somewhere in the back of my mind is a little voice whispering *give in, give in*. It would be so much easier to pack up and go home and continue my comfortable life with Oliver. It wouldn't take long to find a job. In fact maybe Oliver would now go and punch Ben Newman's lights out. It would be such a relief to forget about William and whether he is up to something fishy, and not have to watch porno films all day. Not that I watch porn all day, obviously I do a lot more than that, but it would be nice not to have to listen to other people at it, especially as I am never at it myself. Oh the temptation to give in.

'Binki, I want you to know I am very sorry,' he says raising his voice above the loud moaning of an orgasmic woman.

'Hold on a sec,' says Luther. 'I'll just turn her down a bit.'

I've got a bad feeling about this. Oliver sighs and we wait until the orgasmic woman finishes her moment of ecstasy.

'And, well the thing is ...' Oliver says.

'Go on,' eggs Luther while I am silently pleading for him not to do so.

'The thing is,' continues Oliver, 'I love you and I miss you and, and ...'

Oh God.

'Binki, will you marry me?' he finishes, producing a single solitaire set in a white gold band.

Oh my God, he's done it. He's only gone and proposed to me in the middle of a sex shop. This seriously could only happen to me.

'Oh babe, I've been well and truly screwed,' says the horny woman in the movie.

You and me both, I couldn't agree with her more.

Chapter Twenty-Two

'Five years I've worked for the company Binki, what was I supposed to do? There was the promotion staring me in the face. I couldn't throw the job away.'

I try to take in what Oliver is saying while staring at the diamond solitaire which sits between the condiments on the café table. The waitress looks at it enviously as she places our order in front of us. Perhaps she would like to marry Oliver. God knows I'm not sure if I want to. I'd made him wait until I finished my shift and agreed to have something to eat with him at the local café. Yes I know, very romantic. But Oliver kind of took all the romance out of it when he proposed during *Debbie Does Dallas* don't you think?

'So you slept with her to keep your job?' I say stiffly, pushing a bacon sandwich away as visions of Brown Nipples assault my brain.

'It was Christmas,' he says, reaching for the ketchup and dripping it onto the white gold solitaire. 'I'd drunk too much. She said she wanted to discuss the promotion. The next thing I knew ...'

'Oh of course, I keep forgetting it's okay to get your leg over at Christmas. I must be the odd one because I actually didn't get my leg over at Christmas at all,' I snap, grabbing the salt pot and knocking the ring towards Oliver's plate in the process. I swear one of us will end up eating the thing before this sodding lunch is over.

Oliver dips a chip into his egg yolk.

'That's not what I heard,' he mumbles.

The waitress seems to spend forever wiping down the table next to ours. She is probably waiting for the wonderful moment when I ecstatically scream *Oh yes, I will*, and obviously doesn't think it at all odd that Oliver is proposing over egg and chips in a cheap café just around the corner from a sex shop.

'What does that mean?' I snap.

He squeezes tomato ketchup onto his plate, the bottle making a farting noise as it does so.

'Ben Newman,' he says accusingly with another squirt of ketchup. I snatch the bottle from him, accidentally spilling a drop on his shirt. He looks down and then back up at me wide-eyed. Blimey, I've squirted him with ketchup, not stabbed him in the chest with my cutlery. The waitress wanders over with a teapot.

'More tea?' she asks.

'Oh my God,' she adds when she sees the ketchup stain.

Now, she thinks I have stabbed him too. I'm not surprised the way he is clutching his chest.

'It's ketchup,' I say with a sigh.

'For Christ's sake,' Oliver moans, dabbing at the stain with a serviette. 'This is a Viktor and Rolf.'

The waitress rushes over with a wet cloth, smiles, glances at the ring and asks if we need anything else.

'Is everything okay with your food?' she asks, looking at my uneaten bacon butty.

'Fine,' I nod.

'I expect you're too excited to eat,' she smiles.

Well something like that. I smile back.

'Ben Newman,' I hiss as soon as she is out of earshot. 'Are you serious? Have you seen him?'

'Well maybe men with warts on their noses turn you on. How do I know? You have been behaving oddly the past few months.'

'But bloody Ben Newman,' I say.

How could Oliver even think I could shag Ben Newman? In fact, how could Oliver think I would shag anyone while I was with him? But Ben Newman, I mean, bloody Ben Newman. I've got to be desperate haven't I?

'I wouldn't shag Ben Newman if you paid me a million pounds, and besides Oliver, I've always been faithful, which is more than can be said for you.'

He lifts a steaming mug of tea to his lips and lowers his eyes before saying.

'That's not what Ben Newman says. Apparently you were at it all the time, that's what Muffy was told. Rumours are you wouldn't back off and that he finally had to ask you to leave.'

What a lying wanker.

'So it seems,' he continues, 'that we were both shagging the boss, but at least I did it for a promotion. It will make you happy to know that it totally buggered my back.'

I don't believe I am hearing this. Am I supposed to sympathise with his bad back now.

'So it's okay to be unfaithful as long as it is with your boss and if you get a promotion out of it?' I say, biting into my bacon sandwich before the waitress asks again if the food is okay.

'Of course not, I never actually said that ...'

'And I never shagged Ben Newman. I don't care what he's telling everyone.'

'Well ...'

There is silence while Oliver eats his chips and I fiddle with the bacon sandwich to look for bits of bacon that haven't congealed into fat. He finally gives a weak smile and says,

'Did you have a nice birthday? Did you like the bracelet? I thought ...'

He hesitates as a lad wearing a baseball cap stops at our table.

'Hi,' he interrupts. 'You work in the sex shop don't you?' He grins, before spitting out his chewing gum and sticking it on our table.

'Actually ...' begins Oliver.

'I ordered two movies, *Titty Titty Bang Bang* and *Forest Hump,* are they in yet?'

'Jesus Christ,' groans Oliver.

I could go to the loo I suppose. It's as good an idea as any. Maybe they have a window I could climb out of.

'I'm not sure,' I say vaguely.

In fact, I'm not sure about anything. A month ago I was a normal person. I'm still a normal person but you know what I mean. I had a normal job and a normal boyfriend. Well, he seemed normal, and a normal flat, and yes maybe I had a weird boss but I didn't know that until Christmas Eve. In fact, come to think of it maybe I don't have a normal boyfriend either. What kind of normal boyfriend sleeps with his boss to get a promotion?

I guess the only thing I had that was normal was my flat. Mind you, all that was much more normal than what I have now wasn't it? Now I share a house with a man I don't know and I work in a sleazy sex shop, and live where strange men come up to me in cafés and ask if their porn movies have arrived right in the middle of my boyfriend's marriage proposal. I have a big bag of chocolate penises in my fridge. Okay on my shelf in a shared fridge, but the point is I have them. How normal is that?

'I'll pop in and check, shall I?' asks the man.

I nod and look at Oliver. We sit in silence for a time and I nibble at my cold bacon sandwich. The waitress watches us from behind the counter.

'Well, what do you say? I love you. I'm sorry. It won't happen again. I was foolish. I forgive you for Ben Newman and ...'

'Forgive me?' I say stunned. 'I wouldn't shag Ben Newman if he was the last man on earth.'

'That's not what ...'

'I don't care what Muffy heard. I didn't shag Ben Newman, but you did shag Amanda Rowland. I saw you remember?'

'And I was a fool and I know that, but be fair Binki, I'm putting up with a lot too. How do you think it looks you sharing a house with some guy you hardly know, and working in some sleazy sex shop?'

'I don't care how it looks,' I say defiantly.

'And you have let yourself go,' he says looking at the waitress who nods at him supportively.

'Let myself go?' I echo.

I don't believe what I'm hearing. He coughs uncomfortably.

'Well, your hair looks ... well it doesn't look as nice as it used to.'

God, Wesley said he had taken twenty years off me. I've a good mind to ask for my money back.

'And you've got a pimple on your chin. You never had pimples before.'

I feel the pimple self-consciously. Yes well, I've never been this stressed before have I?

'And I couldn't help notice ...' he hesitates.

How much more? I'm beginning to feel like Frankenstein's sister.

'In the sex ...' he glances at the waitress and lowers his voice. I'm starting to wonder if something is going on between these two. 'Shop,' he continues, 'that you haven't shaved your legs.'

I don't believe this. He pushes the ring towards me.

'But for all that, you're the only woman I want,' he finishes.

Well that's wonderful isn't it? Oliver loves me despite my scarecrow hair, pimples and hairy legs

'Please Binki, let's start again. There's no one else for me. We can put all this behind us, please say yes,' he says, taking my hand.

'Oh congratulations,' squeals the waitress. 'It's so romantic. We've got fresh custard tarts. I'll bring two, on the house.'

Well I guess it makes a change from champagne. The truth is I want to say yes, I really do, but it's not only the memory of Amanda Rowland that haunts me but I can't get William Ellis out of my head. It's not like I fancy him or anything, it's just I can't get the memory of that almost kiss out of my head. I know I should, he probably kisses women all the time. You only have to check the contents of the bathroom cabinet to know what he gets up to, but anyway, I'm not his type, isn't that what he said? But he has also said he wouldn't kick me out of his bed. Then there is also the question of *Driftwood*. Kiss or no kiss, I can't trust William Ellis. He could be nothing but a con artist for all I know, but more importantly, can I really marry a man who cheated on me? I could try and forget Amanda Rowland, although that is easier said than done especially if Oliver carries on working under her, do you see what I mean? I can't shake off that vision of her sprawled on top of him. I must try and put it all behind me and get back to my lovely life in Notting Hill, and have my lovely dream wedding and my lovely 2.4 children, whatever 2.4 children means. I always wanted children. At least I'd have big breasts for nine months. Come to think of it I could have big breasts all the time, although of course that would mean having 10.4 children or something like that. On reflection, maybe breast surgery would be easier. And not to mention after having all those kids I'd end up with such a huge vagina that Oliver would disappear inside there and end up finding someone else like Amanda Rowland, not inside my vagina obviously, that would be a bit gross and it would never be big enough for Miss Brown Nipples but you know what I mean, and there we would be, full circle. So how can I possibly agree to marry him? Apart from anything else, how could I possibly marry a man who proposes first in a sex shop and then again in a café over egg and chips? It's no good. I push the ring back.

'I really don't know,' I say.

His face drops and he looks so miserable that I have to fight back the urge to say *Oh alright then*. Sometimes I am so stupid. Fortunately the waitress returns with our celebratory custard tarts before I can say anything.

'Congratulations,' she says cheerfully, unaware of the gloomy atmosphere. 'I've brought two orange juices on the house.'

Yes well, custard tarts and orange juice just about sums up Oliver and me doesn't it?

'But why?' asks Oliver.

'Because you just proposed,' says the waitress with a big smile on her face.

'Why don't you know?' he says ignoring her.

I grimace.

'I said no,' I whisper to the waitress.

She looks at the custard tarts as though debating whether to take them back.

'Don't worry we'll pay for everything,' I say, wondering why the hell I am discussing custard tarts and orange juice at a time like this.

'Because it is so sudden and ...' I continue, talking to Oliver.

'Sudden? You were bloody expecting it Muffy said.'

Muffy? Whose bloody side is she on now? Honestly, you can't trust anyone.

'Yes well, that was before you balanced Amanda Rowland on your balls,' I say.

He stands up and snatches the ring from the table.

'I'll let you think things over. I can't apologise for ever Binki. I said I'm sorry. I've got a good job now and we can have a nice life together, have kids and everything.'

So, bonking Amanda Rowland got him the promotion did it? That's just great, isn't it? I must remember to tell our kids that we owe their good fortune to Daddy's great ball-balancing act. I can hear our children now,

'Is Daddy balancing again, Mummy?'

I'll spend half my life pretending to the children that Daddy is in some kind of circus act and the other half rubbing Deep Heat into Oliver's back.

'Wonderful,' I say, 'I'll let you know, must dash, leg waxing and all that.'

I storm out of the café, brushing past the open-mouthed waitress and leaving Oliver with the complimentary custard tarts. I hope he leaves a tip.

Chapter Twenty-Three

I arrive home to find the house in darkness. The office lights are off too so I assume that William must be out. I fumble nervously with the keys and as always, feel relief as the key turns. I really should trust William when he says he won't change the locks. I head for the bathroom and stop in the doorway. What the hell? William has moved my candles from around the bath and left them in a pile on the floor. They were bloody expensive *Wax Lyrical* scented candles. Has he got no taste? A wet towel lies in a heap beside them and the bathroom cabinet is wide open. He was no doubt in such a rush to grab his condoms he had no time to shut the door. Honestly, why can't he be just a bit tidier? I scoop his razor from the sink and put the top back on his shaving gel, and shove them back into the cabinet. I slam the lid of the loo back down and then glance at myself in the mirror. Ugh, Oliver wasn't far wrong. I am a physical disaster. I pull open the cabinet again and fight the urge to look on William's shelf to see if the condoms have gone. I shake my head and reach for my razor. I close the door, replace the candles and run a bath. I guess Oliver is right, I have gone to pot a bit. My skin is most certainly saggy. God, when did that happen? Can you get facelifts on the NHS? Surely if you're depressed to the point of suicide they'll help. Mind you, with the state of the NHS waiting lists I'll be bloody ninety by the time they get round to it. I peer at the pimple on my chin and curse when I see another looming at the side of my nose. Great, I'm starting to look like Ben bloody Newman. That expensive face cream Mum bought me hasn't done much has it? Twenty minutes later I am relaxing in a lavender-scented bath with nicely shaved legs and a green clay face mask on my skin. That should see to the pimples. The more I think about Oliver as I soak in the warm water in the flickering light of the candles the more certain I am that I still love him, but

I'm also certain that I cannot marry him. At least not while he works with Amanda Rowland. But if he gives up his job at Mansill Enterprises then what? Supposing Amanda Rowland refuses to give him a reference? What if he is doomed to work at Mansill for the rest of his life? God, what if he has to bonk Amanda Rowland for the rest of his life just so we and the children can eat. *You'll never work again Oliver. Why throw away a good career, when all you need is to be nice to me every now and again,* I can hear her drawl in that low sexy voice of hers. I so hate the bitch. Although I suppose she couldn't have had sex with Oliver unless he had allowed it could she? Was he sexually harassed? She probably said he wouldn't get the promotion unless he slept with her like in the *Disclosure* movie.

I reluctantly step out of the bath and put on my towelling robe. I'll need to give Oliver an answer soon. It's ironic that after waiting all this time Oliver finally proposes and I didn't even get a good look at the ring. I wander into the kitchen and sigh. The sink is full of the builders' mugs and used teabags. I open the fridge and take out a chocolate penis. I'm in serious need of a chocolate fix. I notice a bottle of whisky on the counter and wonder why it is there when I turn and bump into William. I almost jump out of my skin.

'God, no wonder you get hairsprayed,' I say, feeling my heart race.

'You're a bag of nerves,' he says. 'Sorry I didn't mean to scare you. Do you want a drink?'

He is wearing a striped shirt. The top button is undone and his tie hangs askew and I've never seen him look sexier. His hair is tousled where he has obviously been running his hand through it, and his eyes are heavy. He looks tired. He must have made good use of the condoms this evening is all I can think. God, if Oliver was at it like William he'd spend half his life in traction. I feel a little pang of jealousy at the thought of William with another woman and then tell myself it is just hunger pangs, after all, I didn't eat my bacon sandwich did I? The memory of lunch reminds me of the engagement ring and I sigh. I spot William's phone on the counter and see to my amazement that it is turned off. He looks at me and smiles. His breath smells of whisky and it occurs to me he has had more than one glass already. How long has he been home? It can't have been that long.

'I wish you wouldn't move my candles from the bath,' I say, taking the glass he offers.

'Okay, next time I won't. I'll just fill them full of water when I shower.'

Sometimes he can be so irritating.

'Also, do you have to leave wet towels on the floor? There is a towel rail in the bathroom you know.'

'You're not my wife,' he snaps.

'Thank God,' I retort, feeling stung by his words. 'Maybe you can tell Andy and the cleaner that too. It insults me to be called *Mrs Ellis*.' I down the whisky and shudder.

He leans across me to the freezer and removes some ice.

'Whatever,' he says walking back into the living room.

'And perhaps you can ask them to wash up their mugs too,' I say. 'And ...'

He thumps his whisky glass down onto the coffee table.

'Look, I've had a really crappy day. I'm not blaming you but I don't want to come home to a nagging woman. So can you back off please?'

What a nerve.

'How dare you,' I say angrily. 'You move my things and leave a mess for me to clear up and now you call me a nag ...'

'It was only a towel,' he protests.

'Shaving gel with tops off, and razors and ...'

'No wonder your boyfriend had another woman,' he snaps nastily.

I stare at him stunned and feel tears prick my eyelids. How could he? What a hurtful thing to say. What a bastard.

'I'm sorry,' he says quickly, 'I didn't mean that. I'm a bad-mouthed pig when stuff goes wrong with the business.'

I stiffen and back away from him.

'I'll have you know that Oliver came here to propose to me today,' I say proudly while not feeling in the least bit proud.

'Oh,' he says.

'Yes. He proposed in the shop.'

He smiles.

'Original, you have to admit,' he grins. 'Did you accept?'

I grimace.

'I'm still thinking about it?'

'Ah.' He picks up the whisky glass, downing the contents in one. 'Seeing him later are you?'

'I might be,' I say. 'Not that it's any of your business.'

'No, of course not, I just thought you might want to take that green stuff off your face before you do.'

Oh my God, oh shit and bugger. I've had the bloody face mask on the whole time. I feel my whole body grow hot. What must I look like getting all huffy with him with green muck all over my face?

'You look like Shrek.'

'Shit,' I exclaim. 'Why didn't you say something?'

'I just did,' he laughs.

I dash to the bathroom, gaze in the mirror and groan. Buggery bollocks. I scrub the mask off and stare at my flushed face. Oh, well at least the pimple has gone. There is a light tap on the door.

'I'm sorry Binki, I didn't mean to mock. If you're not going out do you want some nachos? I'm sticking some in the oven? I'll share mine.'

'Okay,' I say softly.

I pop some dangling earrings in and smooth down my baggy smock top. Maybe William will be able to give me some advice about Oliver. After all, it's always good to get a man's perspective. Perhaps he will be able to explain how Oliver got into that position with Amanda Rowland, I don't mean underneath her of course, although I am sure William does that all the time but not with Amanda Rowland, of course.

As I enter the kitchen he is grating cheese onto the nachos. I notice the whisky bottle is almost empty.

'So, did he go down on one knee over the vibrators?' he asks.

He takes a bottle from the wine rack and I'm tempted to say that he has already drunk enough but bite back the words. William Ellis is not someone to be lectured.

'Not exactly, and anyway it was hard to hear him over *Debbie Does Dallas,*' I smile.

I glance at his phone and see it is still off. He rubs his eyes and sips from a glass of wine.

'I would make a side salad but I've only got a cucumber, but it's yours if you want it.'

Ooh what an offer. I stifle back a giggle and realise the whisky has gone to my head.

'Well, if you're offering,' I say before I can stop myself.

Our eyes meet and he winks.

'Okay you can have my cucumber if I can have your cherry tomatoes.'

God, this is more sexual than the videos in the shop. I stretch across him to my shelf in the fridge. He doesn't move and I have to lean against him to reach into it.

'I have an avocado,' I say shyly, conscious of his body. 'No salad dressing though.'

'I'm happy to have an undressed salad,' he says huskily. I feel my hands tremble as I take the avocado. He moves away and my heart is racing. It never raced like this when I was with Oliver. I watch him chop the cucumber. I open my cupboard and take out a French stick. He looks at it and pulls a face.

'Ah, I just have a stale roll, but if I had a French stick it would be all yours.'

God, he is seriously flirting with me.

'You can share mine,' I say.

'You're a very sharing person,' he says clinking our glasses. 'To your future engagement, you're saying yes I take it?'

'I'm not sure; there is still the matter of ...

'The bonking bimbo,' he finishes for me.

I nod. He turns to the oven and says softly.

'He was a fool.'

I have no idea how to respond so say,

'It seems really odd not having your phone bleeping every few minutes.'

He lifts the nachos from the oven. I put two plates out and we sit at the kitchen table.

'I'm not in the mood to take calls tonight. I lost a big contract this afternoon. Not only a contract but a hell of a lot of my own money too. It's a complete disaster.'

'Oh William,' I say, taking his hand. 'What happened?'

The warmth of his hand sends a surge of sexual desire through me and I know I should move it but I can't. He takes a gulp of wine.

'I don't know,' he shrugs. 'It was a sure deal. I had an investor who was keen to put five million into a company I recommended ...'

'Five million,' I gasp, almost choking on my wine.

'The company is called Optimun and they are doing really well. It's not that unusual to invest that much money in a company that's flourishing. They've just landed a big international order but they needed capital to expand. I brokered a good deal for them and the investor. It was a sure win-win for everyone. I even put money in myself. Then today out of the blue my investor pulled out. It's a disaster. The company will lose the order and will probably go under. At best there will be a lot of lay-offs; a lot of people will be made redundant.' He stops and sighs heavily.

'I don't know what made him back out but Nathan says he is adamant. He's agreed to meet me for dinner to discuss it on Friday but I don't expect him to change his mind.'

'Why don't I come too,' I say and bite my lip. I must have drunk too much. I'm feeling bold and reckless.

He looks thoughtful. God, he is sexy, I cannot believe that ex-girlfriend of his let him slip through her fingers but then of course I barely know William Ellis. He slides his hand from beneath mine and removes his tie throwing it onto the table. Ooh, I'm definitely up for a game of strip poker if that's what he's doing.

'The thing is ...' he stops.

Stupid me, how could I have been so silly. He is obviously taking Andrea isn't he? Let's face it if you want a woman on your arm, she's most certainly the one.

'It's fine,' I say quickly. 'It was a stupid suggestion. Obviously you're ...'

'No, it might be a good idea. The thing is I've always gone to these things alone. But Roche, the investor, is a family man so it might look good to have woman with me. Nathan ...'

'Does he have to be there?' I interrupt. 'Do you even need to tell Nathan?' I add cautiously, knowing how much William trusts him. Personally I wouldn't touch him with a bargepole.

'Roche has made it quite clear that no one else from the company is to be there, so it might be best not to mention it to Nathan.'

God, it's bloody hot in here again. I slip off my cardigan.

'We need to get this heating sorted,' he smiles, rolling up his shirt sleeves.

The strap of my smock top slips slightly and he stares blatantly at my bare shoulder.

'We'll be eating dinner naked at this rate,' he laughs, his eyes twinkling.

I blush. I know I should pull the strap back but somehow I can't bring myself to.

'I was in sales,' I say, 'and I understand a little about business. If I can look at the background I may be able to help.'

He grins.

'I'll give you access to everything I have,' he says, relaxing back into his chair.

Oh yes please.

'In fact, why don't I show you all I have tonight?'

Oh my God, he is seriously flirting with me.

'Obviously the sooner I see all you have the better,' I say, openly flirting back.

I look at him over the rim of my glass. His eyes meet mine and hold them for a second before he drops them and says,

'I'm sorry about the comment earlier. I think Oliver was mad to do what he did.'

'You do?' I say softly.

He nods and stretches his hand to touch mine.

'I've drunk far too much and am in serious danger of making a pass at you, and that's the last thing I want to do.'

That's bloody great isn't it? Maybe I am like an anorexic in reverse. When I look in the mirror I see a reasonably-attractive woman that someone would like to make a pass at when in reality I am one big turn off. I do get through a lot of M&Ms and they've got to end up somewhere. I bet they've all gone to my arse. It most likely looks like one big M&M but as I can't see it I wouldn't know would I? That's the problem with your bum isn't it, it's impossible to see, but the truth is there must be something wrong with me sexually. Let's face it, Oliver couldn't do it with me unless I wore a stupid sailor outfit and cooed *arr, tie me to the rigging Cap'n.* Then when we finally did get going I'd need my vibrator and for some reason Oliver always got defensive, like I was insinuating he wasn't good enough. Like making me wear a sailor hat and crotchless shorts isn't saying the same thing? So, we then have this mammoth vibrator search while Oliver does all kinds of things to keep the erection going, like my exciting body isn't enough to keep it up. By the time I do find it, the bedroom floor is littered with my undies and God knows what, and then the bloody thing doesn't work because one of the batteries is missing. I finally give up and fake an orgasm so Oliver doesn't say,

'It comes to something when I get replaced by a bloody vibrator.'

Why can't he just accept me for little old me is what I want to know? Okay, maybe my backside does looks like a giant M&M and I really should weigh myself, especially after I've scoffed my way through a bag of out of date chocolate penises. Still mustn't complain, at least I'm getting some penis. I take a gulp of wine. That's another thirty calories. I can't win.

'I know you've only been here a couple of weeks but I really like having you here, I don't want to blow a good friendship by doing something stupid,' William says, pulling me out of my reverie. 'Besides you've just been proposed to.'

A good friendship, is he serious? All we've done so far is insult each other.

'Right,' I say, picking up the dishes. 'I'm not sure whether to be insulted or flattered.'

I pull the strap back onto my shoulder and stack the dishwasher. I suppose it would be pointless to suggest a game of strip poker now wouldn't it?

'Binki,' he whispers, 'you should be flattered.'

I feel his warm breath on my neck and shiver, my desire for him so strong that my hands tremble. He kisses me gently on the cheek and a multitude of emotions consume me. The fresh smell of him combined with the whisky intoxicates me. I'm his for the taking.

'Friends,' he murmurs into my ear.

I nod and turn to the dishwasher.

'Are you going to forgive Oliver?' he asks, handing me my glass.

Perhaps I should forgive him. Maybe it wasn't his fault. Maybe it was my fault for not being exciting enough or for being *Binki, not the best shag in town*. Why does everything sound like a porn movie with me? Even *Binki of the Caribbean* with the stripy tights and the anchor motif has a porno sound about it. But there is nothing porno about me, I can't even find a vibrator without wrecking the bedroom in the process. Even the search for the batteries would totally deflate his erection. There's a limit to how long you can keep it up isn't there? I wasn't that great in the kitchen either. My idea of an impressive meal was a bowl of pasta with a Jamie Oliver sauce thrown over it. I never greeted him sexily in the mornings either. I should have worn my silk robe more and clipped my hair up sexily but instead I'd wander in wearing my terry towelling dressing gown with my hair sticking up and last night's mascara smeared across my face. Seriously, can anyone blame him humping Amanda Rowland, especially if there was a promotion in it for him? I need to make more of an effort. I'm sure we've got the *Kama Sutra* somewhere. That should liven things up. I'd better do something about my inner core muscles though, or I'll never take the strain. Then again I'm not sure Oliver's back can take the strain either. Oh this is just awful, only a few days before Christmas I was dreaming about my fairy-tale wedding and planning the invitations in my head. I'd imagined Olly and me huddled on the couch with old Christmas films playing on the television as we'd looked through the designs together. I was expecting an engagement ring on Christmas Eve and not the sight of Amanda Rowland doing gymnastics on my boyfriend's cock.

'Do you think I should?' I ask William.

'That has to be your decision. I'll get the Optimun papers for you. Good bedtime reading,' he grins.

William walks unsteadily from the room. I finish my wine, put the glass carefully into the dishwasher and turn to find William standing right behind me. He gently slides the strap of the top off my shoulder. I shudder.

'It looks better that way,' he says softly.

He places a pile of papers on the table and picks up the wine bottle.

'I'm off to bed before I do something very stupid. And no matter what Oliver says or did, you're one very sexy woman Binki Grayson. I always speak the truth when I'm drunk. I shall now take my drunken self to bed.'

He turns at the door.

'We're still on for Friday dinner?'

I nod. He grins and closes the door behind him. *I'm one very sexy woman* I repeat to myself. Well, that's something to celebrate with an M&M isn't it? I lift the lid from the chocolate teapot and see the builders have replaced my stash. I smile, throw a handful into my mouth and make a decision to phone Oliver in the morning. Maybe it is time to talk things over like adults and I don't mean in the manner of an adult movie, although maybe that would not be such a bad idea.

Chapter Twenty-Four

A loud drilling in my head wakes me with such a start that I almost tumble out of bed. Christ, what is that noise … Is my head exploding or something? The room is like an icebox. I shiver and pull the duvet over me and see the scattered papers on my bed. I check the time on my Blackberry and curse. It's nearly ten. I've two missed calls and two texts. I struggle to get my brain into gear and then the memory of William's words, his whisky drinking and the almost kiss comes back to me and the discovery I'd made when going through his papers last night on the investment deal with Roche. I scramble to get the papers together. The drilling is even louder now and it isn't in my head. I can't believe how cold it is. We've gone from the Sahara Desert to Scott Base in the Antarctic. It's all extremes in this house. I must have been reading William's papers until three this morning and I still couldn't make anything add up. I'm no accountant but I've done a few figures during my time in sales and something about the figures in these papers seems wrong. At first I thought William was on the fiddle, but surely he wouldn't have shown me the figures if he was, unless he thought I would never understand them. I didn't understand everything and the deal seemed pretty straightforward, it was the other papers that William had obviously given me in error that didn't make sense. Mixed in with the papers was William's accounts ledger. I wouldn't have taken too much notice but I was stunned to see just how well William's business was doing. I found myself glancing at the entries. It was then I noticed something strange. Quite a few expense claims were repeated. For example, there was an entry for expenses for Nathan for hotel accommodation in Japan and another entry for the flights, but the same entry was repeated a few days later. Surely it would have been sensible for Nathan to have stayed in Japan rather than spend all that money returning a few days later, but the strange thing was another claim for a taxi fare from Tokyo to Kawasaki on the day before the second flight, and even I know that Tokyo is in Japan and unless Nathan is superman he couldn't be in London one minute and riding in a taxi in Tokyo the next. I really should return the accounts to William. I'm sure I wasn't meant to see them. He was after all somewhat pissed last night, gorgeously pissed I must admit. I pull my mind from the memory of his hand on my shoulder. How do I approach William? I can't accuse Nathan of swindling can I? Although I don't trust the guy and surely William checks the accounts himself. He obviously didn't mean for me to see them, but the thing is I have. My head spins with my thoughts and when my phone buzzes I grab it gratefully.

'Binki, it's me,' says Oliver, sounding pained.

I can hear the clicking of computer keys and laughter in the background.

'Have you given my ... well, have you thought things over?' he says in a low tone.

Oh dear, I've barely given it a thought if I'm honest.

'It's a lot to think about Oliver.'

'Of course it is,' he hisses, 'that's why I imagined you may have been up most of the night thinking about it. It's one of the most important decisions of your life.'

It certainly is. So I'm not going to make it while half-pissed am I?

'It's just the children I've been thinking about,' I say, draping a woollen shawl over the jumper. What's wrong with this heating? I'm normally walking around in a bikini.

There is silence apart from the clacking of keys and the ringing of phones in the background.

'Whose children, and what have they got to do with us?' Oliver asks finally.

'Our children, how do I explain your ball-balancing tricks with your boss and the late nights at the office?'

He exhales so loudly down the phone that I think he may burst out through the mouthpiece like some horror film character.

'We should talk. I'm taking my parents out tonight and I've got to close a deal with a client tomorrow. I'll book a table at Romeo's for Friday, say about eight?'

Oh dear, he would have to say Friday wouldn't he.

'How about Saturday?' I suggest, pulling on another pair of socks. I'm starting to think a whole family of poltergeists have moved in. I watch my breath condense in front of my eyes.

'They're always packed on a Saturday, you know that. How can we have a quiet talk?'

My teeth are now starting to chatter.

'I can't make Friday,' I say.

He groans.

'I suppose you're doing a shift in that disgusting s ... shop aren't you?'

'You can say the word Oliver,' I sigh. 'But no I'm not doing an extra stint in the *s* shop.'

'Not in the bloody office I can't.'

'Oh no, you can't say it but you can sure hint at it between you and your boss can't you?'

'Don't start that again. So why can't you make Friday?'

Well, firstly if I don't do something about this bloody heating I'll be dead by Friday.

'I'm having dinner with William ...'

'What?' he bellows. 'I knew it. Your parents said I shouldn't allow you to stay there alone with him.'

'I'm thirty years old Oliver and amazingly neither you nor my parents can tell me who I can be alone with. I'm having dinner with him and one of his clients, I'm just helping out,' I say shivering for all I'm worth.

'Why can't we do Saturday evening?' I offer.

God, all these meals out I'm having. I'll end up the size of a small bungalow.

'Well I suppose it will have to do then,' he grumbles.

'I have to go before I develop hypothermia.'

'What ...'

I hang up, pull my coat from the wardrobe and looking like Mr Blobby race downstairs to find the source of the noise, and almost go flying over a toolbox on the kitchen floor.

'Sorry Mrs Ellis, I'll get that out of your way in a jiffy,' says a middle-aged man in dungarees. 'Been a bit of a bugger this has. I'm gonna have to get you a new one. I did tell Mr Ellis it may take the best part of the day. Couldn't have picked the worst time of year could you?'

The back door swings open and Andy strolls in. He takes one look at me, fights back a smile and says,

'Okay to make tea, only John here hasn't had one yet. He's replacing the boiler. That will make things better, less of a sauna in here. I said to John here, you and Mr Ellis don't need much to get yourselves heated up in this house.'

He roars with laughter while I stare deadpanned at him. I bloody hate builders. I didn't before but then I had never met any until now.

'Please help yourselves,' I say sweetly. 'After all, you normally do.'

'Right, thanks Mrs Ellis, oh by the way Mr Ellis said as there is no heating he will work at the Wharf.'

Well that was kind of him to tell me wasn't it?

'Okay to take a biscuit?' asks Andy.

I fight back a sigh.

'Feel free, watch some telly if you like, make yourselves at home and put on a DVD.'

Another builder enters and gives Andy a knowing look. If they think they can help themselves to my M&Ms they can think again.

'Yeah, talking of DVDs Mrs Ellis…'

'I'm not …' I begin but think better of it.

Andy scratches his cheek, and says,

'Steve 'ere, said his son saw you in that shop, you know, the adult one …' he hesitates. God, I think I preferred it when they were after my M&Ms.

'Well, we were wondering about the DVDs like, whether they can be borrowed by friends and family.'

Friends, family and builders you mean. I don't believe I'm hearing this.

'Sadly Andy, drinking our tea and eating our biscuits, and of course my M&Ms, doesn't quite make you family,'

Fortunately my phone rings and I grab the chocolate teapot and make a quick exit.

'Hi doll, I was wondering can I swap shifts with you. My mate has got tickets for the Zodiac club tomorrow night. Can I do your shift this avo and you do mine tomorrow.'

'I was hoping to get warmed up later,' I say.

'Blimey babe, I didn't know those films did that much for you,' laughs Luther.

It occurs to me that this would be the perfect opportunity to pop to William's London office. There may be a good chance that Nathan won't be there and maybe I could snoop around a bit on the pretext of wanting to find out all I can about Roche before our dinner on Friday.

'That's great Luther. I've got some things I need to do today anyway.'

* * *

I decide not to put Kandy through the manic journey to Canary Wharf and get the underground instead. It was not one of my best decisions. I spend the entire tube journey standing squashed against a pole with a man pressed up against my arse. Maybe that is some women's dream journey but I'm not quite that desperate. I can't believe how my life has changed since Christmas Eve. There I was one minute the soon-to-be fiancée of Oliver Weber, successful surveyor with a promotion just around the corner. Of course we all now know that Oliver had a lot more than a promotion around the corner don't we? I was a proud tenant of one of the most sought-after flats in Notting Hill and I had a good and respectable job as senior sales assistant for one of the biggest advertising companies in London. Everything was going swimmingly. And then poof, bloody Christmas arrives with vicious spiky Christmas trees, a randy boss, the devil incarnate, disguised as a traffic warden, and an out of control boyfriend; a nightmare Christmas if ever there was one. I push through rotating doors into the plush interior of the Canary Wharf office block and am met by a very friendly doorman.

'Good morning madam. May I be of service?'

I look around the building with envious eyes. Soft furnishings line the foyer and smartly dressed employees wander back and forth carrying folders and looking very important. I used to look like that once. Now I wear a low-cut top with a name badge saying *Binki - Here to serve your sexual needs,* and looking very unimportant. I don't mean I'm wearing it now, obviously. Christ, I wouldn't have got past the doorman if I was. No good applying for a job here is there? No doubt Ben Newman has put the word around here that man-eating Binki Grayson is on the loose looking for a job and someone's husband to go with it. Oh God, what if William heard that too? This is so embarrassing. I daren't give the doorman my real name; I'll be thrown out on my ear.

'I'm here to see William Ellis,' I say, giving him my most appealing smile.

'That's the third floor. The lifts are just over there. I'll need to search your bag if you don't mind madam.'

Oh crikey, I hadn't thought of that. I struggle to think of what may be in there that would certainly give away my identity. I hesitate for a second and his smile begins to turn into a frown.

'Just trying to remember if I've got my spare knickers in here,' I say, feigning embarrassment.

There's only my driving licence and credit cards with my name on. He isn't going to rummage through my purse. That's far too small to hold a bomb isn't it?

'Yes, well we can't be too careful can we?' he says with a smile.

'No quite, my mum always said I should carry a spare pair.'

God, what am I saying? Someone just kill me.

'Yes, I meant we can't be too careful when it comes to security these days.'

Absolutely, I have to agree. Even I thought I looked like your typical maniac when I glanced in the mirror the other day. So if anyone has something to declare it's bound to be me right?

I hand my handbag over. He rummages through it, pulling out Oliver's Brands Hatch voucher that I had forgotten about. The doorman hands back my bag.

'Can't be too careful,' he repeats.

'No, I agree.'

After all, you should see the size of my handbag. I could get a Kalashnikov in there and a few grenades and it still wouldn't bulge. I wander over to the lifts feeling perspiration from my armpits. Honestly, this is ridiculous. I'm not a terrorist. I'm just Binki Grayson infamous man-eater. I see the doorman looking at me curiously as I hesitate at the lift entrance.

'Third floor,' he says again, nodding.

I give him a friendly wave and step into the lift. The doors close and open again after a few seconds. I am not sure the lift moved as everything looks the same, except the doorman has changed into a pretty blonde at a shiny oak reception desk. She gives me a broad smile and I do try to smile back but all I can think is *bitch, how come no one wants to have you over a desk.* It then occurs to me that maybe William does have her over the desk. I shudder as I approach her.

'Hello, can I help?' she asks pleasantly.

'I'm here to see William Ellis.'

She opens an appointment book. Oh bloody great.

'What time is your appointment?'

This is worse than the doorman.

'I don't actually have an appointment. I was ...'

She shakes her head, her sparkly diamond earrings swinging wildly with her.

'Mr Ellis is very busy I'm afraid. He doesn't see anyone unless they have an appointment. Can I get him to call you? What was the name?'

'Binki,' says a man from behind me.

Good God, I didn't even open my mouth. I turn to see Nathan walking out of the lift.

'Hey, what are you doing here?'

It's said with a smile but there is suspicion in his eyes. He looks very handsome in a pink striped shirt and well-cut jacket, if you're into that kind of bloke.

'You're certainly a sight to brighten my day,' he says. 'Let me give you a tour. William's at lunch with a client. Lucky bugger, he always gets the lookers for lunch where I always get the old duffers,' he laughs.

I find myself wondering who *the looker* is.

'So what brings you here?' he asks again.

I rack my brains, come up with nothing and say,

'Curiosity.'

He nods.

'Well you know what they say about curiosity and the cat,' he says leading me through a door.

'So this is *Ellis Financial Investments* and here is my office.' He opens the door to a tidy large office with a massive desk in the centre of the room. I bet that's seen some action. Oh what's wrong with me, just because Ben Newman tried to get me over the table it doesn't mean everyone is doing it. Further down the corridor he opens another door where two women are busy typing away on their computer keyboards.

'Where the work really gets done,' he laughs.

I feel his hand slide around my waist and move away from him. He drops it quickly and stops outside another door.

'And this is William's office. Best to knock, you must know all about that.'

I feel my face grow hot

'What does that mean?' I say sharply.

He opens the door, peeks inside and says with a grin,

'No action here. He really is at lunch.'

'How dare you,' I say angrily.

'We've all heard the rumours darling, and rumours I'm sure they are. Look, I don't approve of men harassing women at work but you can't expect William to give you a job just because he knows you.'

I turn around to face him.

'I'm not here for a job,' I snap and walk to the lift.

The lift pings as the doors open and William strolls out. His warm brown eyes widen at the sight of me.

'Hey,' he smiles.

'I've been showing Binki around,' Nathan says.

William's eyes light up. He seems genuinely pleased to see me and I feel my body relax.

'Great. That heating guy hasn't blown the house up has he?' he laughs.

I follow him along the hallway, feeling Nathan's eyes boring into my back as I do so. William stops and turns to him.

'The lunch went well, can you get the contracts over to Wildings before she changes her mind, and I'll need you to get on to Tokyo to find out what's holding up things their end. Any word on that new company you mentioned yesterday?'

'I'll chase up Tokyo now. Any news on Roche by the way? Did he agree to meet with you?' asks Nathan casually.

I pretend to fiddle in my handbag and William avoids my eyes.

'No, nothing from Roche, we'll have to cut our losses on that one but I'm not sure how we'll cope with it. Anyway, let me know the news from Tokyo and copy me in on any emails.'

I sense Nathan is being dismissed and within seconds William has ushered me into his office. For some stupid reason I feel an overwhelming urge to cry but instead I say,

'I'm not here for a job and I don't know what you've been told or what you think of me but I'm not a man-eating bitch who spends her life sprawled over her boss's desk. So, if that's what you're expecting, you couldn't be more wrong.'

I finish and fall into an armchair. He looks at me and shakes his head.

'As amazed as you may be, that was the last thing on my mind, actually it wasn't on my mind at all …'

For some reason I feel disappointed.

'I'm not appealing enough to be sprawled over your desk, is that what you're trying to say?'

He sighs.

'Whatever I say is going to be wrong isn't it?'

He clicks a button on his desk phone.

'Jen, could we have two coffees in my office. Thanks.'

He sits opposite me.

'Actually, the thought of having you sprawled across my desk is very appealing, but I don't sprawl women over my desk.'

He doesn't? That's good to know isn't it?

'Not even at Christmas?' I say.

'Most certainly not at Christmas,' he smiles.

Oh dear, I've gone and made a total fool of myself haven't I? A middle-aged lady with dark-rimmed glasses and red permed hair comes in with a tray of coffee, places the cups on the table and leaves without saying a word.

'That's Jen, my PA and I can assure you I have *never* had her sprawled on my desk at Christmas or at any other time of the year.

I laugh and look into his warm smiling eyes.

'So what brings you here, apart from telling me you don't sprawl over desks?'

'I wondered if I could look at anything else you have on Optimun and anything on Roche, I would like to be as informed as possible on Friday, if that's okay?'

He clicks his fingers.

'Ah, that reminds me, Roche wants to take us to this exclusive place he likes in Chinatown. It's bound to be upmarket so you'll need a cocktail dress, which I'm happy to pay for.'

I go to protest.

'You're helping me out and I want to buy the dress, okay.'

He opens a drawer and removes a bottle of aspirin.

'I don't know about you but I've got a hell of a hangover from yesterday. The last thing I need is to be here but Driftwood was like an icebox.'

A brilliant idea occurs to me and I rummage in my bag and with a flourish, produce the gift voucher for Brands Hatch. Well he does have a Lamborghini so he is sure to enjoy this and I'm certainly not giving it to Oliver now.

'Do you want to go Brands Hatch?' I ask.

He looks at the ticket and his eyes light up.

'Are you kidding? Is that one of those experience gifts where you actually get to race cars around the track?'

I feel so happy. I'd been so looking forward to this response from Oliver on Christmas Day and it did occur to me, it seriously did, to give it to him when we met yesterday. I'm so glad I didn't.

I nod.

'It was Oliver's Christmas present and I've swapped shifts with Luther, so today is officially my day off. So ...'

He grabs the ticket like a child.

'Let's do it. It'll only take an hour to get there. I've got a few phone calls to make and a couple of things to settle before I leave, so why don't I get Jen to show you to the filing room and she can pull out the stuff on Roche for you,' he says buzzing her.

'What if Nathan sees me there?' I say anxiously.

'He's got a meeting this afternoon, so that's unlikely,' he smiles.

I feel bubbles of excitement in my stomach. A day out with William, how much more exciting could my day off be. He doesn't fancy you Binki, remember? He thinks you're nice enough but just not quite his type. I find myself wondering just what I'm lacking that doesn't make me William Ellis's type. No worry of him ever pinning me against a desk anyway, although hold on, now I think back didn't he say *the thought of having you sprawled across my desk is very appealing but I don't sprawl women over my desk.'*

Oh my God. I was so focused on the fact that he doesn't sprawl women across his desk that I totally overlooked what he had said. Oh – My – God.

Chapter Twenty-Five

The file room turned out to be a little treasure trove and the fact that William was more than happy for me to wander around in there reassured me that he had nothing to hide. Even though William had assured me that Nathan would be in a meeting I did find myself on tenterhooks much of the time and was forever glancing behind to check I was alone. When the door opened at one point I almost jumped out of my skin. It was just another member of staff who nodded kindly and left when they found what they needed. They were obviously unaware that I was Binki Grayson the famous boss-eater. I continued searching through the accounts in my furtive style feeling like that woman out of *Erin Brockovich*. I photocopied all of last year's accounts and added stuff I'd found on the merger with Roche, and was about to leave when the door opened and William walked in. He'd changed from his shirt and tie into jeans and a cuddly chunky grey jumper and it is all I can do not to enfold myself within it.

'Right, let's buckle up and do Brands Hatch,' he says smiling.

Ooh, and I get to go in the Lamborghini too. Am I glad I left Kandy at home, as loyal as she is, I really don't want her cramping my style today do I? My phone vibrates and I pull it from my bag. Oh no, it's Oliver.

'Oliver, it's not a good time.'

'When is a good bloody time then? This morning was a bad time and now is a bad time, when is it not a bad time?'

'I'll meet you downstairs,' says William quietly, diplomatically closing the door.

'Oliver, please don't be horrid, I didn't mean ...'

'Do you want to meet for a late lunch?' he interrupts. 'I can get away for a bit. Maybe a walk across Hampstead Heath, give us a chance to talk?' he says earnestly.

Why now, why does he have to phone now? This is just awful. Guilt consumes me. Oliver my potential husband phones as I am about to take another man out with his Christmas present. Great, now I feel like a prize bitch. Not only am I giving another man my boyfriend's gift but I'm turning down lunch with my boyfriend to go out with the other man. This is not good. Perhaps I am turning into the woman everyone believes me to be.

'I can't get away right now Oliver, I'm …'

'Don't you want to spend time with me,' he says petulantly, making me feel even guiltier. I hug my Optimun papers to my chest and take a deep breath.

'Yes of course I do. I just can't spend time with you now,' I say.

'Why not?' he snaps.

Oh dear, I hate lying.

'I'm going out with William, we're …'

'What?' he bellows. 'I don't believe this. I've bloody proposed to you and every time I ask to see you it's not possible because you're busy seeing someone else. I don't know why the fuck I bother with you.'

'Oliver, it's not like that. I'm helping him with some business. This is good for me. I don't want to work in a sex shop forever do I?'

Well it's only a little white lie isn't it? The worst that can happen is that I'll get a pimple on my tongue according to my mother. I am helping him with his business and it is true that I don't want to work in a sex shop all my life. I don't really want to be working in a sex shop at any time in my life actually, but that's something else. The only thing I missed out was that I'm not helping him with his business *today*, so in theory, I haven't really lied at all have I?

'Binki, I really want to announce our engagement. What do I have to do to make you say yes?'

Leave Mansill Enterprises so you never see the bitch Amanda Rowland again would be a good start.

'Oliver, could we talk about this on Saturday over a nice romantic dinner?'

Christ, more food. This bungalow is turning into a house.

'Do you still love me Binki?' he asks quietly.

I feel my heart lurch.

'Yes Oliver, I believe I do.'

And that's the truth. I do love Oliver Weber. The big question is, am I *in love* with him?

* * *

I will never travel any other way but in a Lamborghini. It's just fabulous. Can those babies move, but even nicer is the cosy space you have next to the driver, and not to mention that everything is at the touch of a button. Of course, once you're on the motorway the damn thing drives itself. Honestly, you could have full-blown sex between Watford and Luton while driving, and still make it to your destination on time. Maybe I should offer that as an advertising campaign and get myself a job with Lamborghini. On reflection maybe that is not the best angle to go for, it doesn't look that great with my past reputation does it? False reputation, that is. Even I'm beginning to believe I'm guilty. I enjoy the drive immensely even though William makes frequent calls on his hands-free phone. It's got tinted windows too, perfect if you were on the run, which of course we're not but you know what I mean. He finally finishes his call, and says,

'Do you want to choose some music?'

I'm almost terrified to push any buttons in case I catapult myself out of the bloody car. I imagine Lamborghinis are fitted with ejector seats. That is probably how he gets rid of his girlfriends when he has had enough of them. Oh well I'm safe. I'm not his girlfriend, so he won't eject me. I'm right though aren't I? Who knows what this Lamborghini baby can do. There are probably James Bond sniper rifles in the glove compartment and spike-producing tyres. In fact the whole thing may well bloody self-destruct if primed. God, I think I'll stick to Kandy. At least she plays it safe. That's not strictly true actually. She doesn't play at all, not since I lost the code for the CD player but at least she'll never eject me.

'There,' he says smiling, pointing to a compartment and accidentally brushing my leg with his arm. Well I presume it was accidental. There are so many compartments and buttons in this car that it resembles a woman's handbag. I push the button to open the compartment and take out a leather case of CDs, and am stunned to see one by Tony Bennett.

'You like Tony Bennett?' I say amazed.

He looks sheepish.

'I suppose I could pretend they're my dad's but I'll own up. They're mine. I don't think you have to be over sixty to like him.'

'I love Tony Bennett. Oliver would never let me play him. He said I was ageing before my time.'

'Put it on then. We'll have a Tony Bennett fest.'

I push the CD into the player and he fiddles with the buttons.

'This is my all-time favourite,' he says, turning up the volume. I fight back the urge to straighten his tousled hair and then gasp as Tony Bennett begins to croon *It had to be you*.

'It's my favourite too,' I say. 'I used to decorate the Christmas tree playing this. I always turned it off when Oliver came in of course.'

He begins to sing along and before I know it I am joining him. For the next fifteen minutes we sing along happily. *Lady and The Tramp* comes on and he laughs.

'Happy to be the tramp?' he says.

'Absolutely,' I say, giggling.

I'm having so much fun and we haven't even reached Brands Hatch. I've never had this much fun with Oliver, singing Tony Bennett songs would be an anathema to him but then I never feel Oliver is my friend, just my lover and boyfriend, and of course soon-to-be fiancé. The sign for Brands Hatch looms ahead and William lowers the volume.

'Here we are. This is where the fun begins.'

We park the car and an attendant approaches us just as William's phone rings.

'How are you?' he says winking at me. 'Yes, I am, she's a very good friend of mine. Binki Grayson. We've just arrived at Brands Hatch actually.'

A pause.

'Her gift actually,' he laughs. 'You can be sure I will. Yes of course, one second.'

He hands his phone to me.

'Piers Roche,' he says with his hand over the mouthpiece. 'He wants a word with you. I'll find out where we go.'

He climbs from the car and leaves me staring at the phone. Oh shit, I don't want to blow anything. Supposing Piers Roche has heard of me. Oh for God's sake I'm Binki not sodding Beyoncé.

'Hello,' I say.

'I hear you're joining us for dinner tomorrow. I hope you like Chinese?' he sounds younger than I thought he would. He has a kind, gentle voice and I immediately feel comfortable with him.

'Yes, I love Chinese. We're looking forward to it very much,'

'Just make sure that brilliant investment consultant doesn't kill himself. Lucky bugger, I'd like to be in his shoes. You must tell me all about it tomorrow. Good, Chinese suits you. It's my favourite place in Chinatown. I think you'll love it. I'll see you tomorrow Binki, interesting name by the way. You're not the girl ...'

'No,' I say quickly. 'I'm not, same name different spelling.'

He laughs.

'Right, well you two have fun. See you tomorrow.'

William pokes his head around the door.

'Okay. I'm all booked in. Let's go. How did that go with Roche?'

'He sounds nice,' I say.

He nods.

'Yep, he's an okay guy. I was looking forward to doing business with him. Anyway, we'll see.'

He takes my hand and helps me from the car.

'I thought we'd go to a hotel I know that's not far from here when we've finished. I'll buy you dinner, my way of saying thank you.'

'You don't need to do that,' I say, thinking that if I eat any more that small bungalow is going to turn into a bloody mansion.

'It's what friends do, right?'

Friends? Yes, I suppose that's what we are, house-sharing friends. After all, I'm as far from William Ellis's type as any woman could be. It's probably safer having someone like William as a friend than a boyfriend anyway. I sigh and allow him to take my hand again, the connection sends a strange thrill through my body and when he removes it and drapes his arm around my shoulders the effect is like an electric shock. I realise I may not be as content as William to be just friends and I wonder if the time has come to say yes to Oliver and move out of Driftwood. After all, what choice do I have? Unrequited love is the worst thing right?

Chapter Twenty-Six

Watching someone race an *M3 Master* supercar around Brands Hatch track is perhaps more terrifying than actually doing it. I spent most of the time praying, realising that if William Ellis got killed during an adventure experience it would be entirely my fault. I'm sure his family would not thank me for the funeral experience that would follow. William, on the other hand, loved it. I had to take photos of the M3 Master, him posing by the M3 Master and him getting into the M3 Master. He insisted on having his instructor take a photo of the two of us next to the car and then another of him in the car. I'm surprised he didn't want to hump the car and have a photo of that. It may have been a cold day but I was sweating from cheering and waving as he came around each lap.

'That was amazing, seriously amazing. Thanks so much Binki. I really enjoyed that,' he says, lifting me high in the air.

He's still wearing his protective clothing but has removed his helmet, and he looks flushed and happy and also the most gorgeous I have ever seen him. He is buzzing and hands his phone to the instructor.

'Can we have one together, do you mind?' he grins pulling me close to him.

Ahead of us I see a woman and can't help smiling as I watch her flick her hair behind her ears before approaching William. I feel my heart sink when I realise she is exactly his type, slim, thick blonde shoulder-length hair and with pheromones so strong that even I could fancy her. Her bright blue eyes are highlighted with Kohl and she gives William such a dazzling smile that I'm almost blinded.

'Oh hi,' says William, 'would you mind taking a photo of the three of us?'

He hands her his phone and I'm amazed that he barely gives her a second glance.

'I'll hope you'll send a copy for our Facebook page,' the instructor says cheerfully.

'I was wondering if you had time to share your experience with us today,' the blonde woman asks, flicking her hair back and fluttering her eyelashes like a mating peacock.

William looks to me, raises his eyebrows.

'It's up to you,' he says. 'Do we have time or do you want to go straight for dinner?'

'It will only take a few minutes,' she says brusquely, turning to me.

William smiles warmly at her and I see her melt before him.

'I'm sure it will take longer than a few minutes. Can we email our feedback to you? I assure you I will do it first thing tomorrow. I had a brilliant time though, I can tell you that much.'

My God, is he turning her down. Can't he see she is coming onto him? I watch her struggle to hide her disappointment as she hands him a card.

'This is my personal account, if you could send it there,' she says with a shake of her hair.

I try to copy her seductive hair shake and feel an earring drop out, shit. You see, I just don't have it do I? William glances at the card and slides it into his wallet.

'Sure, no problem,' he says turning his back on her.

He takes my arm like it is the most natural thing in the world and we walk to the Lamborghini. I shiver as a few flurries of snow fall around us.

'Snow,' says William. 'Don't you just love it?

He looks thoughtful and then says,

'You want to go ice skating at Hampton Court Palace. It's an open-air rink and great fun.'

I cock my head. I haven't been ice skating since I was a kid. He sees my hesitation, clicks the door to the Lamborghini and says,

'No, you're right it's a stupid idea.'

'No,' I say quickly, 'I'd love to. I really would. I've not been for years.'

'Right let's Tony Bennett it to the ice rink and then I'll take you for dinner.'

Oh dear, the mansion is now turning into Buckingham Palace.

Chapter Twenty-Seven

I'd actually forgotten how much fun ice skating was and what a great atmosphere there is at a skating rink. Hampton Court Palace looks magical and the light dusting of snow makes the winter wonderland beautifully romantic. Children wrapped in hats, gloves and scarves are giggling happily even when they fall over. The snow which has become a steady flurry is making it more exhilarating and, although I hate to admit it, I am struggling to stay on my feet. William's hysterical laughter at my attempts makes it all worthwhile. I've never heard him laugh so much and his laugh is infectious. He's on a high and my previous opinion of him is changing with every passing minute. He is far from the legendary womaniser despite attracting more attention from women than any other man I know and I am indulging in the pleasurable thought that these women think he is my boyfriend. He's an accomplished skater, which doesn't really surprise me. I'm sure I've spent more time on my arse than on my feet, and when I manage to stay on my feet I'm so busy enjoying my status as potential girlfriend of sex-god Ellis that I fail to notice I am careering towards the barrier and the bad news is I haven't quite mastered the art of turning or stopping, and I end up crashing straight into it.

'Having a good time?' he asks helping me up.

'I am, but I'm not so sure about my body though,' I reply, dusting myself down and wondering how I must look to him in my bobble hat and knitted mittens. He grins and pulls me into the centre of the ice rink.

'Some time tomorrow I think your body will remind you of the great time you had this evening,' he says.

A screaming teenager comes hurtling out of control towards us and William steadies me as I attempt to move, saving my bruised backside from another tumble.

'My backside certainly will,' I laugh.

'It will need a good massage with Arnica,' he grins.

'Are you offering?' I say before I can stop myself.

He looks into my eyes and bites his lip.

'It's the least a friend can do,' he says softly.

I'm about to reply when another unsteady skater, who looks like he is making rapid semaphore as his limbs are moving so erratically, knocks me into William's arms. I feel his warm breath against my cheek and his gloved hand on the small of my back. We seem to do a little turn on the ice while in each other's arms before he releases me.

'I guess that was our Torvill and Dean bit,' he says shyly.

'Not quite Bolero, but we were good,' I say forcing a laugh.

'If you're hungry we could eat now,' he asks warmly.

I have to admit the thought of the nice warm Lamborghini is very appealing and although my mind tells me I could skate for hours, my legs and bum are screaming for me to stop. God, I am so unfit. Oliver always said I was. After this dinner, well after the dinner with Piers Roche on Friday, or after Saturday's dinner with Oliver, I will go on a diet. I'll have salads. In fact, I will start tonight. After all, I don't have to eat chips with everything do I?

'I'm happy to carry on if you want to,' I lie.

He grins and wrinkles his nose.

'I think both you and I know you've had enough. Besides it is getting late and the snow is getting heavier.'

'And I don't want my bobble hat to shrink,' I smile.

'Absolutely not,' he laughs.

He leads me off the ice taking my hand and giving it a little squeeze making me feel all warm inside. I take the opportunity to study my reflection in the changing room. My cheeks are pink from the cold and my hair has gone wild from being under the bobble hat, but my eyes shine and I look good. I run a brush through my hair, splash some water on my face and walk outside to meet William. He opens the door of the Lamborghini for me and I climb into the warm interior. He already has Tony Bennett playing. He clicks his phone on and apologises when it rings.

'I'd better phone Nathan. He's left five messages. It won't take two seconds.'

He starts the car and puts the phone onto hands-free. Nathan answers immediately.

'William where the fuck are you? I've been trying you all afternoon.'

I see William wince and I remember him saying that I swore a lot, what a blooming cheek.

'I've been out with Binki. We've been ice skating and racing around Brands Hatch,' he says, smiling at me.

Blimey, it sounds like we've been on some kind of keep-fit marathon. I must mention this when I see Oliver. Then again, I'd better not mention the Brands Hatch thing, not that he'll ever know that was his present of course but knowing me and my big mouth I'm bound to let it slip.

'You've been what?' asks Nathan, irritation in his voice. 'For Christ's sake William, we've had a bloody crisis here while you've been racing cars like bloody Clarkson.'

What a bloody nerve. William turns the music down with a mumbled apology.

'Well, that's why I pay you an extortionate salary Nat, to deal with those crises,' he says his voice hardening.

There is silence and I wait for William to speak but he doesn't.

'Yeah right, but you were supposed to be here to sign the papers for the Brignall deal. I did tell you about that yesterday.'

'Well I wasn't there was I? Was that your crisis?'

'It was a deadline. We agreed to sign today or we'd lose the deal. The thing is William, if you're going to dilly-dally off with that Binki all the time, who I have to say, is not your type ...'

William clicks the phone off hands-free and pulls the car over. I feel myself go hot and try to pretend I haven't heard. Just what is it about me that makes me *not William's type* is what I want to know. Okay, so I'm not a petite brunette with long legs and huge breasts. But I've got curves, maybe a few too many I admit, but I've got them all the same. They're just a bit out of proportion at the moment but nothing that less food and a few minutes on a running machine can't fix. Ben Newman said I've got cute dimpled cheeks and a nice tight arse. Ben Newman? Why am I thinking about Ben Newman? What does he know, my arse looks more like a giant M&M if you ask me. All men like tight arses don't they, it's a fact isn't it? Or is it my age? Christ, I'm over the hill at thirty. Mum is right, the clock is ticking and I do want babies, obviously not just anyone's babies and I suppose Oliver would produce reasonably nice ones, although not as nice as William would. Oh God, I'm so depressed. I thought with Aunt Vera's inheritance something nice was finally coming my way. I guess it did in the guise of William Ellis but just about everything else couldn't have gone more wrong could it? I feel like I'm rubbish at everything. I can't skate, I can't keep a boyfriend, I can't get a decent man to shag me over a table, I can't get a decent job. The only thing I can attract is a man with a wart on his nose and the only job I'm capable of is selling porn. I'm not fit, in fact I'm not fit to be alive, period. I sigh heavily as William is saying,

'I'll phone him myself. Okay you arrange it. No I can't do Friday, I'm busy.'

I pretend to fumble in my bag. I could do with a tissue. I see my phone has a text and quickly read it. It is from Oliver.

'Love you babe, can't wait till Saturday when I know we will sort everything out.'

I turn the phone off and blow my nose quietly. William hangs up the phone abruptly and makes another call before starting the engine. He turns and says softly,

'On Nathan's behalf I apologise.'

'It's fine,' I say.

It bloody isn't though is it?

* * *

'So you really think I should forgive Oliver?' I say.

All my resolve went at the sight of the menu and William didn't help when he said their Steak and Ale Pie was the best, which of course I had with chips.

'I didn't say it would be easy,' he smiles, 'but if you still love Oliver?' he adds questioningly, looking into my eyes.

The waitress approaches us for the umpteenth time to ask William if the food is okay. Why she doesn't just ask him to shag her and be done with it is beyond me.

'Yes, it's perfect thanks,' he says before turning back to me. My face feels flushed from the wine but I'm getting desperate to talk to someone about Oliver. I do love him, at least I think I do. I've never been more confused in my life.

'I think I do,' I say. 'In fact before the Christmas thing I'd have said that Oliver was my whole life.'

He nods thoughtfully, dropping his eyes.

'I doubt if those feelings have died,' he says softly.

Is it possible to fall out of love just like that? If only Oliver hadn't been so stupid.

'If you want my opinion you need to take a step back. You need to take stock of your situation and what you feel for Oliver, use the fact that you live at Driftwood as an asset to get Oliver to pursue you ...'

'You make it sound like a business deal,' I interrupt.

'It is. Between now and your wedding day Oliver needs to see how much he values you, and win you back in the process. In the meantime you stay at Driftwood and date Oliver at the same time,' he says stealing one of my chips.

'If you're eating my chips then I'm having some of your smoked salmon,' I say.

'You make that sound like a business deal,' he smiles. 'But it's an idea isn't it?' he says, looking into my eyes, 'and I was thinking if it goes well with Roche then I may be able to offer you a job with me, and I won't be needing a reference from Ben Newman.'

He offers a fork of smoked salmon to my lips.

'Really, are you serious?'

Maybe things are looking up.

'Yes, I'm going to whisk you away from fluffy handcuffs and blindfolds, and get you back to a job that is more suited to your skills.'

Ooh, you can tie me up with the fluffy handcuffs whenever you want Mr William Ellis, is all I can think. I must stop drinking or I'll be making a pass at him at this rate. I'm so bloody randy it's unbelievable. I've not had sex since before Christmas, and my period is due and I always get randy this time of the month. Just wait till Saturday Binki, then you can shag the balls off Oliver. But can I, that is the question? Can I let him touch me after, well you know, the Amanda Rowland business?

'Mmm,' I say. 'It all sounds perfect, except Oliver is really not happy about me living with you.'

The waiter refills my glass before I can stop him. Damn and double damn. I suppose I don't have to drink it.

'But then he has nothing to fear does he, because I'm not your type am I?' I say boldly.

'Nathan was out of order saying that Binki, I'm sorry.'

'You've said it too,' I interrupt.

He looks embarrassed. I've not seen him look this way before and I put my hand on the radiator as a cold chill runs through me. Please don't say anything to hurt me, I silently plead, I don't think I could take it.

'Binki, whatever I said in the past I didn't mean. We bantered a lot when we first met, and I knew you had a boyfriend so I didn't …'

He hesitates. Didn't what?

'Anyway,' he continues, 'you're one of the nicest women friends I've ever had, and I know you love Oliver and you deserve someone like him …'

'I do? I deserve someone who shags his boss on Christmas Eve,' I say bitterly as the waitress approaches for the fourth time.

'Erm,' she flaps, 'is the …'

'Yep, still great, just like five minutes ago,' says William.

'No, obviously you deserve better than that, and he was a fool but if you love him …' he continues, looking at me intently.

'Yes,' I say solemnly. 'I suppose I do still love him.'

'Then, isn't this the perfect time to see if you can make it work? It won't happen if you move back, but if you take it slowly and we make sure Oliver knows that you and I are just good friends.'

'House mates,' I say dully.

'Yeah,' he smiles. 'Driftwood wouldn't be the same without your labels and rotas.'

I guess that means a shag tonight is out of the question.

'I'm getting the bill before this woman throws herself onto my lap,' William says as he signals to the waitress. 'As *she* really isn't my type,' he laughs.

I look at the waitress as she approaches. She isn't his type? But she has the big tits and the legs that come up to her armpits, she is your stereotypical long-legged blonde, and she is ten times prettier than me. If I'm not his type, and she's not his type then what the hell is his type? Oh my God, he's not a closeted gay is he? No, Andrea is his type, sophisticated, elegant, fashionable, and confident with an air of grace that I could never carry off. Maybe Andrea is the one for him.

So, my perfect boyfriend turns out to be my best friend and house mate, and Oliver has to win me back while I live at Driftwood. All I can say is thank goodness for the chocolate teapot. Every woman should have one for the times in life when things get complicated. *When the going gets tough the tough get chocolate* is my motto.

Chapter Twenty-Eight

'He's playing our song,' William whispers in my ear.

William leads me through the throng of people. A pianist's recital of *It had to be you* is almost drowned by the hubbub of talking and laughter in the bar. Piers Roche waves as we approach giving William and me a warm smile. He is older than I imagined. His grey hair is expertly styled and he has glasses perched on his head. He takes my hand and kisses it softly. I chose to wear a knee-length black cocktail dress that I had bought last year for a friend's wedding. I'd refused William's offer to buy me a dress, feeling it would not go down well with Oliver. Well that's an understatement; he would have a hundred canary fits if he found out that William was buying me dresses. I had accessorised it with a pearl bracelet and pearl studs and a white pashmina. I wanted to look good for William as I knew this meeting with Roche was important, and had spent forever on my hair, using my curling tongs for so long I'm surprised they didn't blow up. I'm wearing a pair of high-heel black court shoes and if it wasn't for William's arm I feel sure that even the walk to the bar would have had me falling flat on my face.

'William, good to see you,' he says shaking William's hand warmly.

'Good to see you too,' smiles William, draping an arm around me.

'And this is Binki I take it?'

I nod.

'You look stunning my dear. Let me get you both a drink. What's your tipple Binki?'

Would it sound awful to say *anything will do*?

'White wine, champagne ...' he offers.

'White wine sounds perfect, thank you.'

'And the *Highland Park* for you if I remember correctly William. I know it has been a while but I recall that was your tipple.'

'And you have an excellent memory,' nods William.

Roche gestures to the barman and leads us to some couches in the corner of the bar.

I follow William's lead carefully balancing on my heels.

'Have you been here before Binki?' Roche asks. 'It's nice for a pre-dinner drink. But my favourite Chinese restaurant serves up the best food, and you never feel alone there. My wife died two years ago,' he says, his face darkening. 'There's nothing worse than dining alone in a stuffy restaurant.'

'I'm so sorry,' I say.

He shrugs and turns to William.

'How was Brands Hatch?'

'Brilliant, absolutely brilliant,' smiles William.

'Lucky bugger, I'd love to have a go at that.'

He sips his drink and then says,

'So, I don't get it William. I heard from a trustworthy source that Optimun is on the verge of collapse. Now, it's not like you to get things wrong but you know me, I don't take chances.'

William nods and sips from his whisky.

'I'd be interested to know who your source was.'

Roche laughs.

'I'm sure you would.'

I bite my lip and say,

'Because whoever they were you can't trust them. Or should I say you can't trust where they got their information from. Optimun is far from on the verge of collapse. In fact it was going to flourish with your investment. They have received a government-backed order and have already scaled up their production plant ready to deliver. I've been through the details myself and everything is in order, it's a rock solid investment for you and even William has put a lot of his money into the company, and I believe you know William is not one to take chances either.'

Ooh I sound dead knowledgeable don't I? But having looked through a lot of Ellis investment consultant's accounts, I am starting to think that Nathan is not all he seems.

He looks at me over the rim of his glass and raises his bushy eyebrows.

'You sound very sure about it. What makes you think my source is unreliable?'

I open my mouth to reply when a small commotion at the bar and the sound of my name stops me.

'Well, well, if it isn't Binki shagging Grayson.'

The hairs on the back of my scalp bristle and I feel my hands tremble as Ben Newman sways towards us. Oh my God. Of all the restaurants in London he has to be in this one. He appears to be with four or five businessmen, all looking just as pissed as him. I'm surprised they let him in. Don't they have rules about warts on noses? I try to breathe slowly but I find I am almost gasping for breath. William looks at me curiously.

'Ben Newman,' I whisper.

He nods and puts his drink onto the table as Ben Newman gets closer.

'Well,' he drawls lazily scratching his chin, and appraising me. 'Of all the gin joints in all the towns in all the world, she walks into mine.'

'Bad accent mate,' laughs William. 'And actually maybe it is the other way around and you have stumbled unwelcomingly into hers.'

Oh this is terrible. I so wanted to make a good impression for William. This really isn't going to help him clinch the deal is it?

'I'm so sorry about this,' I whisper to Roche.

'Don't worry, I'm rather enjoying the drama,' he smiles.

'And who might you be?' snarls Newman, his alcohol-fumed breath washing over us.

'William Ellis and this is Piers Roche of ...'

Ben Newman laughs loudly.

'You don't want to employ her mate. No one in bloody London will employ her. She's just a shagging bitch who hankers after other men's ...'

William jumps up and grabs Ben's arm.

'Now you listen to me. This is a respectable establishment, so what the hell you're doing in it is beyond me. Now, I know how you sexually harass women at work and if you don't shut that filthy mouth of yours I'll shut it for you. Now you back off or believe me I can make sure *you* never work again and don't underestimate who you're dealing with. Do we understand each other?'

Ben shakes off William's hand.

'She fucking harassed me,' he says scornfully.

Roche laughs.

'When did you last look in the mirror,' he comments dryly. 'Even I only have to look at her and then you to know who did the harassing. Now I'd take William's advice if I were you or I'll have you thrown out of here with a click of a finger.'

I bite my lip to stop myself from laughing. Ben lurches himself at me and hisses,

'You bitch. Landed on your feet, didn't you. Slept with them both, threesome was it?'

Now that is funny. I can't get one man to sleep with me, at least not one worthwhile, and Ben Newman is suggesting I've been having threesomes with William Ellis. You've got to laugh haven't you?

'Yes, that's right Mr Newman. It's just been one long orgy for me since I left Temco.'

'Right,' says William taking Ben's arm.

'It's okay dickhead, I'm going. The clientele in this place is enough to make me puke.'

He pulls his arm away and stumbles to the exit. His business colleagues look embarrassed and they follow a little distance behind.

'I can't apologise enough,' I say again, feeling myself blush.

Roche finishes his drink.

'Let's have dinner shall we, my chauffeur is waiting outside. Let me take you to the best place in Chinatown.'

I look at William and he shrugs. We assumed Roche had changed his mind about the Chinese when he had asked us to meet him here. Fortunately there is no sign of Ben Newman as we step into Roche's silver Mercedes. We drive to Chinatown and turn into Wardour Street, finally pulling up outside a tatty looking restaurant with Peking duck hanging in the window. I look around for a smarter place but see that Roche is already heading for the door. He surely isn't serious.

'Here it is,' he says laughing. 'You don't get food better than this.'

We join a queue with other people dressed in jeans and sweaters and I look down at my cocktail dress in despair.

'I hope you don't mind roughing it,' Roche smiles. 'Normally it's only a five minute wait.'

I grin at him.

'If you can, I can,' I say pulling my pashmina closer around me. He turns to William.

'I'm with her,' laughs William, removing his tie.

How embarrassing. It's like he's testing us. After a few minutes we enter the hot restaurant to be met by a harassed waiter. The strong odour of Chinese food hits us and Roche sniffs appreciatively.

'Upstairs, upstairs,' the harassed waiter shouts.

In these heels, God, I don't think so.

'Could we not have that table there?' I ask, pointing to an empty table.

'You not argue with waiter. Upstairs I say.'

'But,' I protest.

'You not like, you leave.'

Roche laughs.

'I think it best not to argue. The thing I love most about this place is the service.'

And what service would that be exactly?

'Or lack of,' I mumble

We clamber up two flights of stairs and are directed to a long table where several diners are already seated.

'I hadn't realised you'd invited others,' William says dubiously. I hover anxiously, wondering if William is going to suggest we leave.

'What?' asks Roche, removing his jacket. 'Oh I don't know any of these people. You always sit at a large table here. Good fun don't you think?'

We arrange ourselves so William is sitting opposite Roche and I am next to him. On the other side of me sits a man in jeans and a hooded jumper.

'Hello, I'm Alex,' he says warmly. 'I'd recommend the Won Ton soup.'

'I agree, it is the best,' agrees Roche.

The waiter approaches to take our order and trips over my handbag.

'Oh I'm so sorry,' I say, leaning down to push it under the table.

'Tsk, trying to kill the waiter,' he mumbles throwing paper mats in front of us.

'What you want?' he snaps.

I look at William who bursts out laughing.

'I guess champagne is out of the question?'

'Bring your own yes?' asks the waiter.

Roche pulls two bottles from the carrier bag he was carrying. I wondered what was in that.

'For the table,' he says.

'Cool,' says Alex.

'Cheers mate,' says another sitting opposite William.

'I'll have a Tiger beer,' says William.

'Me too,' I say slipping off my shoes.

'Make that three,' says Roche. 'Bring glasses for the champagne too please.'

'You want caviar too maybe?' snaps the waiter.

William laughs and winks at me.

'Forget the caviar, we'll opt for the Won Ton soup, three of those,' orders Roche. 'It is indeed superb.'

The place is buzzing with waiters shouting everywhere and customers laughing along with the clatter of cutlery. I remove the pashmina and relax my shoulders. The truth is I am far more comfortable in a place like this. We clink our beer bottles and I feel myself relax.

'So, tell me about Optimun and why I should invest in a company that's about to collapse,' says Roche.

'I don't ever advise unless I know it's a sure thing. Whether you're investing five pounds or five million. I know my companies. If there is even a whisper of a problem I'd never recommend it. You know me Piers,' says William.

'I also hear you got money problems.'

I nearly choke on my beer. I meet William's eyes to try and gauge his reaction but there is nothing. He puts his beer down and leans forward towards Roche.

'There is only one thing I've got a problem with and that's lying. My dad taught me everything I know about business ...'

'And he was a good businessman and we all miss him. It's sad when a boy loses a father so young like you did but that's ...'

'And the biggest lesson he taught me was to always be honest in business. Without your investment Optimun will go under, I'll be frank. It was on the strength of your investment they got the contract. They will lose that now. I've lost money. But when I brokered you this deal it was with honesty and integrity. The company was doing well.'

'I was advised that I would do better to go with Lansdowne. Apparently that company is really taking off according to my sources ...'

'I don't know who your sources are but they're badly informed,' William says with a smile. 'Lansdowne is a flash in the pan. It will do okay but most of the guys on the board are wide boys without a clue what they're doing. I'd never advise you to invest in a company like that. Your sure investment is with Optimun ...'

'You order main course now?' interrupts a waiter, plonking our soups onto the table.

'Erm in a minute ...' I begin.

'We got queues downstairs, you hurry yes.'

'They're discussing business,' says the guy next to me.

'We restaurant not bloody office,' yells the waiter before tripping over my handbag again.

'Move dangerous thing,' he demands, making it sound like a grenade.

'Excuse me,' calls a lady at the opposite table. 'How much longer will our food be?'

'You leave if you not like,' he says walking off.

I laugh with Roche and study the menu.

'I think we should order our main course. I fear for our heads otherwise,' says William.

'There must be reason why your source misled you,' I say quietly, tasting my soup which is superb just as Roche had promised.

The dumplings are sumptuous. To think I was worried how I would eat when I lost my job. I've eaten more in the last few weeks than I have in years.

He nods.

'So, have you met William's accountant, Nathan?' he asks, making direct eye contact with me.

I bide my time and sip some champagne.

'Yes, I don't know him very well though.'

William is discussing our main order with the waiter and Roche leans closer.

'I see him a lot at the casino. I get the feeling he's not too lucky sometimes. Just a feeling, you know what I mean?'

I nod.

'So you can say to me hand on heart that I can trust William?'

'Yes,' I say in a heartbeat and realise that I mean it.

'I suppose you would say I should trust her,' he says to William.

'She's one of the best friends I've got,' William says smiling at me. 'I trust her.'

Roche nods.

'What did you order us lad?'

'King fried prawns in sizzling sauce, roast duck Cantonese style and lobster with ginger and spring onions. I remember the last time we ate out together that was your favourite.'

Roche's slaps his thigh.

'And it still is.'

The rest of the evening flew by with great food and great company. Our table was the most raucous in the restaurant and the food just kept on coming. Forget the small bungalow and just think Downton Abbey. I'll have to invest in a whole new wardrobe at this rate. Roche was sharing jokes with Alex, and William was explaining investments to another couple on the table.

'I'm getting the bill before Piers beats me to it,' William says, laying his arm on my shoulder sending a tingle through me. It isn't desire, it isn't lust, but it's something I can't quite define. It's like a familiarity. It's as if I have known him all my life. How can it be possible to be more comfortable with William than I am with Oliver? I watch him talking to the waiter and at that moment a woman approaches him. William turns and begins chatting to her, his face animated. I see her hand him something, a card or a piece of paper, her phone number I imagine. More condoms to be purchased, no doubt he has shares in Durex. He sees me looking and gives a little wave. I wave back and find myself wondering what Oliver is doing right now. Is he out at dinner, maybe even chatting up a woman like William? Is he feeling fed up that I'm taking so long to accept his marriage proposal? The ring was lovely, I had to admit. Just the kind of ring I had always dreamt Oliver would give me. I'll need to talk to him about a few things before I say yes though. This whole sailor malarkey has got to stop for a start, unless Oliver can transform himself somehow into Johnny Depp for thirty minutes. I'm no prude. I'm more than happy to look at the odd blue movie if that helps, although I have to admit that two weeks working in the sex shop has rather made me a little immune to them. I may as well be watching *Red Dwarf* for all the effect they have on me. Of course we can't live in the Notting Hill flat. God knows how we will get out of the tenancy agreement. Perhaps Oliver can find new tenants for the landlord. Then there is the matter of Amanda Rowland. God, by the time we get this lot sorted I'll be thirty-five and my body clock will no doubt have stopped by then. Why is romance so complicated? No, the real question is, why are men little shits?

'Hey kinky Binki, how are you doing?'

I turn at the sound of my name to see Richard Head swaying towards us, Andrea at his heels looking so casual that I want to crawl under the table and hide myself and my black cocktail dress from the whole world. What the hell is happening? Have I accidently clicked something on my Facebook page that tells the whole bloody world where I am? I barely ever bump into anyone when I'm out and tonight I'm seeing just about everyone. Christ, my sodding parents will walk in next. And what the hell does he mean by *kinky* Binki? They have both clearly had too much to drink. They are with a group of others that have followed them from the top floor. It looks like they have just come from a five-year-old's birthday party minus the party bags. One of the group holds a bunch of balloons and is draped with a *Just Engaged* sash. Richard is barely able to walk in a straight line and Andrea's cheeks are flushed bright red. She is wearing a floppy wool fedora on her head and a thick multi-coloured poncho over her jeans. They were obviously leaving, what a shame they didn't quite make it to the door.

'*Kinky Binki*,' repeats Piers, laughing.

Andrea leans brazenly across him almost falling into his lap. Her eyes are bloodshot and her mascara has run slightly making her look almost evil.

'Piers, how are you darling, it's been months since I've seen you. I didn't know you were here. We've been on the top floor celebrating Kat and Jools' engagement. You know what it's like upstairs, up the bloody stairs.'

She goes to kiss him on the cheek but loses her balance and ends up giving him a slobbering kiss on his neck.

'Ah, didn't you know,' she slurs. 'Binki works in a sex shop, *kinky Binky*, get it?' she giggles.

Piers looks at me.

'I thought you were in sales,' he says, frowning.

I'll kill the bitch.

'Flavoured condoms and porn DVD sales maybe,' laughs Richard. 'Hey Binki, do we get discount as we know you?'

Right that's it.

'Hello Richard,' I say sweetly. 'How did you get here? Did someone leave your cage open?'

He stares at me like an imbecile.

'I don't get what you mean.'

'Well don't think about it too much it might sprain your brain,' I snap.

'You don't have to get on your high horse darling,' snorts Andrea. 'It's not our fault you work in a sex shop is it?' she sways towards me and grabs the back of Piers's chair.

'Oh I feel sick. Where's William. Where's my Will.'

'I don't know what you mean about a cage,' says Richard dreamily, bumping into a waiter. 'I'll sit here next to you mate,' he says to Alex.

'This is Richard Head,' I say sarcastically, 'but everyone calls him Dick Head.'

'Well, if the name fits,' laughs Alex.

'You sit down, over there, at table,' shouts the waiter.

'Don't you bloody shout at me, you obnoxious chink, I've just spent over seventy-five quid in here,' Richard snarls leaning dangerously towards me.

'Okay, you've overstepped the mark now,' says Roche, standing up.

'You sure have Dick Head,' says Alex, also standing up. 'I know they're bloody rude to us but that's what most of us come here for. If you don't like it you should go somewhere else. No need to be racist.'

'William,' shrieks Andrea as she sees him walking towards us. 'Oh, Will honey I feel so rough.'

He catches her as she falls into his arms. Very conveniently I have to say. Richard drops his head onto the table.

'Oh God,' he groans.

'Will, honey can you take me home. I'm so sorry Will ... I'm ...' whines Andrea.

'Yes, okay I'll take you home,' says William without a moment's hesitation.

'I'll call a cab for you,' Roche says, 'and I'll take Binki back, and as for you, William, you've just paid the bill haven't you.'

William smiles glancing at me but I turn away.

'I'll sign the contract; send it over in the morning and William, let's keep this between us until it's all legally settled. We don't want it to upset the markets do we, not yet?'

William shakes hands with Roche.

'It's a deal, you have my word.'

William turns to me a grin on his face.

'I'll see you later.'

'Oh, don't rush,' I say spitefully.

'Will, can we go,' moans Andrea.

Within a few moments William and Andrea have gone, as well as the engagement party revellers and the restaurant quietens.

'A sex shop huh?' Roche asks.

'Yep, you should visit. A free chocolate penis with every purchase,' I say, not even trying to hide my sarcasm.

'I'll be there tomorrow,' laughs Alex, pouring the last of the champagne into a glass.

'So you're not in sales? What was all that about this evening then?' asks Roche.

'Up until Christmas I was a senior sales assistant at Temco and I was good at my job. I had everything Piers, and then some prick of a boss decides he wants me over his desk on Christmas Eve and I say no. He has since made it impossible for me to work anywhere, and if that wasn't enough I went home to find my boyfriend screwing his boss in our bed. But all that aside, you should sign that contract. I may work in a sex shop but I don't lie.'

He studies me. I feel a lump in my throat and knock back half a glass of wine to calm me down.

'The guy in the bar,' he says.

I nod.

'What's his name?' he asks, wrapping my pashmina around my shoulders.

'Ben Newman,' I say miserably.

'Leave him to me.' He nods and leads me from the restaurant.

'William is a good guy but he isn't one to commit. He's too work focused. You may not need this advice but there it is for what it's worth.'

I climb into the Mercedes and say,

'No I don't need it. I'm accepting my boyfriend's marriage proposal tomorrow.'

And it was done. The decision was made and it was that simple. I suddenly knew it was the right thing to do.

Chapter Twenty-Nine

'There must be something you like,' says Muffy, squeezing herself into a *Spandex all in one*.

'There was, that black dress that you said was too sixties,' I say, opening a bag of M&Ms.

'It's perfect if you're planning a sixties themed wedding but personally I can't see Oliver in a paisley shirt and kipper tie,' she pants and scrutinises herself in the mirror. 'Besides, the going away dress is as important as your wedding gown.'

She looks down at the Spandex.

'Christ, do women wear these all day long. I'd need to carry smelling salts.'

'I wish you'd stop eating those,' says Mum pointing to the M&Ms. 'You'll never get into your wedding dress.'

'What wedding dress?' quips Muffy, 'She hasn't bloody chosen a wedding dress yet. This will be the only wedding where everyone will be dressed up except the bride,' she huffs.

She adjusts her silk bra before slipping a dusty blue ball gown over her head.

'There's plenty of time,' I say.

'Two and a half months is not long in wedding terms. Will you tell her Bella?' pleads Muffy.

'She's quite right darling. It will be here before you know it,' agrees Mum.

'And you'll be walking down the aisle like Lady Godiva will you?' quips Muffy.

'At least it will be different,' I smile.

Muffy twirls in front of us almost knocking the M&Ms out of my hand with her chiffon scarf.

'Well, what do you think?'

'You look like Camilla Parker Bowles on tour in India,' I say, studying her.

She sighs.

'Let me try it. I don't mind looking like Camilla Parker Bowles at your wedding,' says Mum excitedly.

'Do you want to look like sodding Dawn French when you waddle down the aisle?' snaps Muffy, snatching the M&Ms from me.

'She's quite slim now,' I say, sipping iced water from a glass the assistant had given me.

We're in *Victoria's Bridal*, for that *perfect outfit for that perfect occasion,* is what the brochure says. Mum disappears into the changing room to turn herself into Camilla.

'I don't know what I want,' I say honestly.

'Apart from bloody M&Ms,' Muffy says scornfully.

The truth is the excitement I had always imagined I would feel preparing for my wedding kind of evaporated the minute Oliver and I started looking at invitation cards. It isn't Oliver's fault either. The past three weeks since I accepted his proposal he has been so romantic, too romantic if I am honest. You know that kind of puke into a sick bag romantic. He sends me little text hearts every hour on the hour, to the point where my Blackberry got clogged up. In fact I am surrounded by hearts and flowers. There are flowers all over the house and little heart notes which say things like, *You've made me the happiest man in the world* and *Thinking of you.* He even sent me a huge heart card that the post lady couldn't get through the letter box. He's actively looking for another job and struggling to find a tenant for our flat so we can move into the dream house we have found just around the corner from Muffy. I should be ecstatic, I know. I'm walking around with a huge rock on my finger and I'm acting like I lost a thousand pounds and found a tenner. William's deal with Roche has gone without a hitch and once the final details are sorted by the solicitors it will be made public. I have a great job working for William. I fall out of bed and straight into my office chair in the offices next to the house. William is seeing Andrea again, I think. Well, he is seeing someone. Don't worry, I'm not counting his condoms or anything but I imagine they are going down at an alarming rate. He whooshes more than ever so something is giving him that extra energy. I'm not whooshing at all. And the way I have been going through the chocolate teapot I really should be whooshing at something. Oliver and I are using a bit of energy having sex of sorts. It's all a bit embarrassing really and I'm sure I shouldn't feel like this with my future husband but somehow I can't quite get Amanda Rowland out of my head. I'm sure I will, and of course it doesn't help that we do it in hotel rooms because I won't go near the flat. We must be the only engaged couple with a shared flat who are spending a fortune having sex in hotel rooms. I can't imagine what the receptionists at these hotels think. We only ever stay a few hours. I'm wearing an engagement ring. Honestly I must look a right slag having it off with someone while engaged to someone else. We do try and alternate the hotels. Oliver seems to like the sordidness of it as each time the hotel gets cheaper and cheaper. Well, we are preparing for a wedding remember. We'll be shagging in a Travelodge soon. Still that's fine as even they have a kettle and coffee sachets which is about all I fancy afterwards, well that and a few M&Ms. Muffy is right though I really should stop eating them. The worst part is that I just want the sex to be over as quickly as possible. Nothing he does sexually seems to work and I'm starting to wonder if I should see a sex therapist. The other problem is that Oliver thinks everything is great. I'm so keen to get it over with that I fake orgasm so often even Meg Ryan could learn something from me. I am seriously good. I even do that build up stuff really well, you know the moaning and the 'oh don't stop, don't stop,' stuff, when in fact he isn't doing anything to stop, but it all sounds good and then my finale is truly worthy of some kind of award. Apart from screaming 'Yes, yes, yes,' like a banshee and thumping the mattress, which may be a bit over the top, I seriously think I could easily win one of those awards they give to porno stars. Actually, if my job with William doesn't work out I should consider a career in the porn game. Of course the M&M addiction would have to be curtailed. A nice bum is crucial in the porn business. I should know, I saw enough of them at the sex shop. Still, I suppose once I get into that business I'll be doing lines of cocaine, never mind the M&Ms.

'I know I complained about you working in that sex shop but God Binki, it's turned you into a really dirty bitch. You're coming all over the place these days,' said a satisfied Oliver.

So, now he thinks I'm multi-orgasmic. What's worse he thinks he barely has to do anything to make it happen. That doesn't bode well for our marriage does it?

'Well,' asks my mum emerging from the changing room looking like the queen mother, when she was alive, of course.

'Great, you look perfect,' I say.

Muffy holds up a wedding dress and the assistant gasps.

'Oh, this is a one-off, the designer is new but in a few months you won't be able to get any of her designs. The demand will be massive. I predict …'

'Try it on at least,' urges Muffy.

My phone rings and I pull it from bag and feel my heart flutter when I see it is William.

'Hi,' I say.

'I'm just back from Holland. How are you doing?'

'I'm in *Victoria's Bridal* with Mum and Muffy. We're looking at dresses.'

Do I sound as bored as I feel?

'Give Oliver my love,' says Mum.

'Sounds riveting,' he laughs.

'Did it go well in Holland?'

'Yeah, really well and I bought you two family bags of M&Ms at duty free. They're in the teapot.'

I smile.

'I didn't know Oliver was in Holland,' whispers Mum to Muffy.

'It's William,' mumbles Muffy trying on a flowered hair accessory making her look like a Druid.

'You're not wearing that,' I hiss. 'You like a Satan worshipper.'

I will miss Driftwood when I am married to Oliver. I should really chase up the solicitors to find out if the house is mine or William's but I somehow can't bring myself to. I don't want to know who owns our house any more because in my mind, that's what it is, *our* house. The night following the dinner with Piers Roche, William had officially offered me a job at Ellis Enterprises.

'I can't find my purple striped shirt. I've got a meeting later and I really wanted to wear that one. Have you seen it?'

I smile.

'It's in the bathroom, hanging behind the door.'

I hear his footsteps on the stairs and he laughs.

'Ah, how did it get there?'

I sigh.

'Right, will I see you later? Are you doing anything with Oliver tonight?'

I bite my lip. Oliver was planning on taking me to dinner.

'No,' I lie.

'Great. Roche's investment with Optimun is all finalised and the news hits the *Financial Times* tomorrow. We should go out and do something to celebrate.'

'Yes,' I hear myself say. What the hell am I doing? This is a bad start to my marriage, but William is just my friend right? It isn't like I'm having dinner with another man is it?

'I'll book that place opposite the ice rink. See you later.'

I hang up feeling my heart racing. Roche's words run through my brain *he isn't one to commit, he's too work focused.* He's quite right, it's all about work. What do I tell Oliver? Surely he will understand if I say I want to celebrate this deal with William. After all, I did kind of help him to get it.

'This veil works perfectly with the dress too,' says the assistant excitedly.

'It is beautiful,' says Mum, tears forming in the corner of her eyes.

'Are you crying?' I say.

'Of course not, it's the glaucoma,' she sniffs.

'You don't have glaucoma.'

I walk into the dressing room, strip off and step into the dress. It's soft material cool against my skin. The assistant zips up the back while cooing at me.

'Oh madam, you look stunning.'

I stare at myself in the mirror and I have to agree. I step out of the dressing room and Muffy and my mum gasp.

'Oh my God, you look so Grace Kelly,' says Muffy.

'Before she died I hope,' I say.

'Oh my,' whispers Mum with a hand on her heart.

Okay, it looks nice but I'm not royalty and the bloody lace at the throat is a bit itchy and I'm about to say that when Muffy says,

'And the lace bit at the throat, God, it's the final touch.'

It's the final irritation more like, but they are right, it's perfect. My fairy-tale wedding dress, the one I had dreamt of wearing since I was a child. It gathers in beautifully at the waist and then billows out fabulously. I don't look at all like your typical marshmallow bride. The sleeves are lined with little pearl buttons and fall just below my wrist.

'I bet it costs the earth,' I say depressingly.

'Two thousand,' whispers the assistant.

'Two thousand,' I gasp.

'We're paying for the dress, don't forget,' says Mum quickly. 'It's our wedding gift.'

'But two thousand pounds, you couldn't possibly.'

'You only get married once,' says Muffy.

Hopefully, but I hate to mention that statistics disagree with her.

'Well,' I say hesitantly.

'We could give a small reduction,' says the assistant.

'How small?' asks Mum.

'Fifteen per cent, that reduces it a fair bit."

I study myself in the mirror and visualise walking down the aisle. It is perfect, but two thousand pounds, Christ, when I think what two thousand pounds could buy. I suppose it is special isn't it, your wedding day? I could always put it on eBay afterwards.

'She'll take it,' says Mum, sensing my hesitation. 'And I'll take this dress and scarf.'

Honestly, I really don't understand why everyone is in such a rush. It isn't like I'm up the duff or anything. The only reason we're having the wedding on the 3rd May is because Oliver's friend, who manages the events at the Dorchester, said he could give us a special deal for that day as there is some building work going on that afternoon and no one else will book it. Everyone seemed to go crazy when we got that offer. *Oh my God, to have your reception at the Dorchester, what a dream Binki,* Muffy had said, and for Muffy to say that it must be something. She hates weddings and all that goes with them. So I'm getting married in nine weeks' time because the Dorchester has building work. I'm sure it makes as much sense to you as it does me.

'I should get a hat?' says Mum thoughtfully.

'Amanda,' calls the assistant. 'We need this adjusted.'

Oh great, the woman adjusting me is called Amanda. Well, that's about right isn't it? Amandas seem to have a habit of adjusting my life.

'Can I get you other ladies another coffee?'

Mum nods and Muffy grabs a dress from a rail.

'I'll try this on,' she says merrily.

I follow Amanda into the changing room and glance down at my engagement ring and with a knot in my stomach I phone Oliver.

'Hi honey, how is the dress thing going?'

I cringe. I so wish he wouldn't call me honey. There is something so American about the *honey* thing isn't there. I imagine us greeting each other in the evening.

'Hi Honey, how was your day Hun? '

No, I can't really picture it. I'm just not a *Hun* type of person.

'It's going okay. Mum has found a nice dress and Muffy is kind of ...'

'How about you, did you choose the wedding dress?'

'I think so, just a few minor adjustments and ...'

'Hang on babe,' he interrupts and his voice becomes muffled. Oh why do I think Amanda Rowland has entered his office?

'Oliver?' I say, trying to keep the irritation from my voice.

'Sorry,' he says. 'Something came up.'

As long as it wasn't your cock that came up. Binki stop it, you can't spend the next nine weeks leading up to your marriage like this or the next sixty years of marriage either. Christ, sixty years.

'Helen was asking about your wedding shower,' he continues.

Who the hell is Helen and what the pissing hell is a wedding shower? I know Oliver works for an American company and all that, but I'm British and proud of it, well, most of the time anyway. But you know what I mean. We don't have showers here do we, unless you're talking about downpours of rain.

'Well I hadn't thought of having one ...'

'It's the done thing these days; all women have them before their wedding day. I suppose we should compare diaries and get these things sorted. I need to book my stag night too. Anyway we can talk about it over dinner. I'd better get on Binki.'

Amanda doing a slow striptease is she? Oh God, I have got to stop this. What kind of marriage will I have if I don't trust my husband?

'Do you mind if we leave dinner tonight …'

Amanda spins me around.

'It needs to be tighter in the waist,' she says.

'Why?' he asks.

'It's a bit loose,' I reply.

'I meant why do you want to cancel dinner?'

'How does that feel?' asks Amanda.

I glance in the mirror. It makes me look very slim actually. A shame I can't wear it every day.

'Great,' I whisper.

'It's just, do you remember that deal William did with …' I say into the phone.

'Christ, not bloody William again. What is it with him?'

Oh dear.

'I think we should try it with a good bra,' suggests Amanda.

'Oliver, William is just a mate and well, the deal is being announced tomorrow in the Financial Times and …'

'But that deal was weeks ago …'

Amanda disappears to fetch a bra and I fan my hot face.

'It takes a long time to finalise these things and anyway he's celebrating it tonight and I'd like to go and …'

'Oh, so others will be there?'

I hesitate. There will be other people in the restaurant so it isn't strictly lying if I say yes is it? And William and I are just friends and I can have dinner with Oliver any night. I live in the same house with William so I don't know why Oliver is getting so uptight over dinner anyway.

'These should cushion your breasts perfectly,' says Amanda returning.

'Who are you talking to?' asks Oliver.

'The assistant adjusting my dress, and yeah I imagine there will be other people there.'

'So I can come with you?'

Shit.

'I think it's just people involved in the deal and stuff and …'

'In other words I'm not invited. Look honey, you've got to ask him to chase up his solicitor. That house is most certainly yours. We can sell that and really reduce the mortgage we take out on our house. I don't understand why it's taking so long.'

'I did phone Mr Hayden but he was away skiing. They promised he would phone me as soon as he returned. One of Muffy's friends said it could take up to a year …'

'Can you hang on a minute Hun?'

What did I say about the *Hun* thing? It's started already.

'Look I have to go Binki, there's a problem here. In fact I may have to work late so maybe it's for the best. Phone me later won't you? '

Work late, the two little words that send a little chill through me. I've got to stop this. I've got to stop translating *working late* into *fucking Amanda* and *something's come up* to *Oliver has a hard on* or I'll drive myself insane.

'Oh sorry, did I prick you?' Amanda says as she pins the hem.

You see, I just can't get away from it can I? I'll ask William for his advice. A man's perspective will help me see sense.

Chapter Thirty

I watch the ice skaters glide gracefully around the rink and am transported back to the day that William and I went skating. I don't imagine anyone watching us from this restaurant window would have seen anything quite as graceful that day. It seems such a long time ago that we were at Brands Hatch, and now just a few weeks later I am engaged to Oliver and sporting a huge sparkling bling on my finger. The problem is I am carrying around as many doubts as I am carats.

'Binki.'

William's voice seems to come from a distance. I turn my head from the window and see the waiter by our table.

'Sorry, I was miles away. I haven't even looked at the menu.'

William cocks his head.

'We'll share a Fettuccine Carbonara and a green salad, and olives and bread to start. Thank you.'

'Wow,' I say laughing. 'You know what I want better than I do.'

He checks his phone and then leans back in his chair. He's still wearing the purple shirt but has removed the tie. As usual he is causing his usual stir and the women in the restaurant are finding it hard not to glance at him.

'Did you choose the dress?' he smiles.

I pull a face.

'Yeah apparently I look very Princess Grace of Monaco.'

'Hopefully before she died,' he laughs.

I stare at him.

'That's what I said.'

He smiles and pushes some papers across the table.

'Signed sealed and delivered.'

I clink his wine glass with mine.

'We should have ordered champagne,' I say.

'We still can,' he says, lifting his arm. I reach out to stop him and our hands touch and I'm shocked at the feelings that shoot through me, it's like I've been struck by lightning. His face gives nothing away so I presume he felt nothing.

'It's fine,' I say.

He sips from his glass and I feel his foot touch my leg and quickly pull it away.

'Roche's having a big bash tomorrow night but I said I imagine you and Oliver have something on.'

Oh God, I can just see Oliver agreeing to that.

'I think we have,' I say, leaning back as a waiter places the olives and bread on the table.

His phone rings and I see Andrea's name flash up. I turn away and pop an olive into my mouth. I go to pop another one when I remember the wedding dress. Sod it I suppose I'd better not eat the bread either. He clicks the phone off without answering it and pushes the bread towards me.

'It's not like you not to tuck in. Do you feel okay?'

I sigh.

'Apparently there are only so many dress fittings you can squeeze into the space of eight weeks and Muffy says I must not gain weight.'

'One dinner won't make much difference.'

He's quite right of course. I dip the bread in the saucer of oil and laugh as a couple slip over on the ice.

'That's cruel,' laughs William.

'I know, but I bet people laughed at us.'

'So how is Andrea?' I ask, not giving a fig if she is covered in psoriasis.

'She's fine. I'm sure that's as much as you want to know isn't it?'

'And how's Dick Head?'

'I don't know actually. She's not seeing him any more.'

Ah, which can only mean she is seeing William instead. Oh, well, I guess they are a good match.

'So, what's Oliver doing tonight?' he asks as the waiter places the Carbonara onto the table.

'Working late,' I say and wait for the waiter to grate parmesan onto our plates before blurting out,

'Christ William, do you think he is screwing Amanda Rowland?'

He cringes.

'Are you trying to put me off my pasta or something? Oh, talking of nipples, Luther said they have tons and he knows what a chocolate addict you are. They're going to go stale. Can you imagine stale nipples and penises? Anyway the upshot of it is he asked me to ask you if you want them for the chocolate teapot. They're back at the house because I presumed the answer would be yes. So wedding dress or no wedding dress you've got a hell of a lot of chocolate at home and that doesn't even include my M&Ms'

He smiles and I feel myself go all warm at the words *at home*. Oh why couldn't William be the committing type? I stupidly feel myself come over all weepy. Oh for Christ's sake. It's that bloody background music they're playing and all those lovey-dovey ice skaters that's doing it.

'And no, I'm sure he isn't screwing Amanda Rowland,' he says, putting his hand on mine. 'He's marring you. You've only got to look at that ring on your finger to know he loves you.'

His phone rings again and this time *Vicki* pops up. Who the hell is Vicki? I'm surprised he had time to fit me in.

I pull my hand away sharply.

'You're sure you've got time to have dinner with me. I feel like a gooseberry here. Are you running your own private dating service or something?'

He laughs.

'When do two women constitute a dating service? I am allowed to see women you know. Don't forget I've got all those condoms to get through. You never stop talking about them.'

I feel my body relax.

'I know. We never seem to talk now do we?' I say petulantly.

'We talk every day,' he says, biting into a piece of pasta.

'Yes, but that's about work. So how is your love life?' I ask sipping from my glass.

He runs his hand through his hair and smiles.

'Well, Vicki is very keen but I'm not sure. She talks about vampires and stuff ...'

I burst out laughing.

'Her most valued possession is her complete box set of *True Blood*. I don't know what she's on about half the time. Andrea is cagy, after last time and so am I ...'

He hesitates and smiles at me.

'You're the woman I see the most of these days and it's nicely uncomplicated. Nathan comes back from Dubai tomorrow and things went really well with that merger by the way. I've got to tell him about Roche. I'm not looking forward to it. He'll be hurt that we shut him out.'

'It was what Roche wanted,' I say, feeling my heart drop at the thought of Nathan returning. Hopefully he'll work at the office in Canary Wharf.

We eat in silence for a time and I watch the ice skaters with envy. I look up to see William studying me. He turns away and tops up our wine glasses. I remember Oliver's words about the house and reluctantly broach the subject.

'William, Oliver asked about the house. It would reduce the mortgage if it turns out the house is mine and ... Oh God William, I don't really care who it belongs to but I guess we need to find out and ...'

He places more salad onto his plate and then onto mine.

'Yes, you're right, I should chase mine up. I'll call them first thing tomorrow okay? I've got to go to Manchester tomorrow but I will do it, I promise. Now let's celebrate the Roche deal. How do you want to do it?'

'I thought we were celebrating,' I say surprised.

'With dinner, absolutely not, you must be joking. Apparently a new jazz club opened in Soho last week and tonight is a Tony Bennett special. They've got a band, a singer and I think it will be a brilliant night and it *had to be you* to come with me tonight. So what do you say? We'll get drunk on tequila and both have mammoth hangovers tomorrow, but you saved the deal and we should celebrate. Let's face it, I won't be able to take you out when you're a married woman.'

I gawp at him and burst out laughing.

'Do you realise in the whole time I've known you that is the most you have said to me?'

He looks embarrassed and runs his hand through his hair.

'I guess I want you to come,' he says softly.

And I so want to go. I want to spend as much time in William's company as I can. I try not to sigh when his phone trills. He gives me an apologetic look and begins talking business. I finish the Carbonara and remember Andrea's words, *let's hope you last longer than the others.*

'Sorry about that,' he says, hanging up. 'I've just got to call them back on the way to the club. The papers are in the car. Is that okay? You are coming to the club?'

I nod.

He grins and beckons to the waiter.

'We'd better crack onto dessert then.'

Of course, once Oliver and I are married I won't be able to see William, at least not socially. I'll see him at work. Then of course if the house does turn out to be mine then I won't work at the offices any more because Oliver will want to sell Driftwood. I wonder if I can actually bring myself to sell Driftwood. Maybe we could rent it out to William and that would make everything perfect. I could still work for William, and William would have the offices and the house and the rent money would pay our mortgage. Surely Oliver would be happy with that?

* * *

'Jesus,' I mumble. 'Is that me?'

I stare at my reflection and am speechless. Christ, I wish I had meet Rhona a few weeks ago. I could have given Amanda Rowland a run for her money. I've been totally transformed. I seriously could be on the front page of *Elle*, okay maybe that's a bit adventurous, maybe *Woman's Own* but crikey, you should see me. Mind you, after the amount of tequilas I've drunk there is a good chance I'm not looking even half as good as I think am, but right now I couldn't give a shit. Rhona is the American singer at the club but it turns out that during the day she is a professional make-up artist and she has just given me the makeover of my life. She adjusts my hair and stands back to appraise her work.

'You look stunning darling. Every man in the room will want to shag you.'

It's been a brilliant evening. The jazz club was buzzing when we arrived and things just got madder as the evening wore on.

The band was terrific and Rhona was fabulous. After one too many tequilas William was demanding they play *The Lady is a Tramp* and she responded with *I'll be your tramp any day baby*.

Rhona had said to me, *Darling, I can turn you into Miss Glamour* and the next thing I knew I was in the ladies and being transformed.

My lips are a beautiful red, and she has somehow given me high cheekbones. My flimsy eyelashes are long and full. She pulls me out of the loo and towards William who is standing by the piano. He glances at me, turns back to the piano and quickly back to me.

'Wow, what happened to you?'

'You need to hang onto her William. There won't be a man in this place who won't want a piece of her ass.'

I smile shyly and flutter my eyelashes at him.

'Want a piece of ass?' I say seductively.

I've had far too much tequila but it is a celebration after all.

'Don't tempt me lady.'

He glances at his watch.

'It's 2 a.m. I think you and I should head home don't you?'

I nod. I am beginning to feel tired. Oh God, I never phoned Oliver and I never thought to check my phone. I quickly check my Blackberry to see two missed calls and a text.

Tried to phone you to see how your evening was going but you must be out of signal or something. It's ten here and just finishing. I'll phone you in the morning. I love you. Xxx

Ten, what the bloody hell was he doing until ten. Working my arse, well if he has been balancing bloody Brown Nipples on his balls that will be the end of that and …

'Binki, did you hear Rhona?'

'I'm sorry,' I say throwing the phone into my bag.

'I said one last song before you go. William said it's got to be *It had to be you.*

Everyone cheers when the song is announced and William twirls me into his arms.

'One dance, Miss Glam? You know we haven't danced all evening?'

I look around.

'There isn't a dance floor.' I smile.

The music starts and he pulls me close.

The next thing I know we are moving together and William is singing the lyrics into my ear. He twirls me twice and then pulls me back into his arms. I've never felt more at home anywhere than I am feeling now in his arms, and I've never felt happier in my whole life. I feel a stab of guilt for enjoying my evening with William so much. He whispers in my ear,

'Thank you for making the evening so special. I couldn't celebrate that deal with anyone other than you and enjoy it like this. You know exactly what that deal meant to me. Thanks so much for being such a support.'

And that's it isn't it? He's the best looking guy in town who could have anyone and I'm the one woman who understands him, knows where his shirts are and helps with his business without making any demands on him. I'm the perfect friend and you know what I'm starting to think? I'm starting to think sod this for a game of soldiers. I pull myself away from him gently.

'I think it's time to leave, you're right. I'm really tired.'

He nods and goes to fetch our coats. I consider texting Oliver but when I try I realise I can't even see the screen.

'I'll call a cab, says William pulling his phone from his jacket.

He takes my hand in his and we head for the door.

'Hey you guys, when is the wedding?' calls Sam the pianist.

'What?' we say in unison.

'Your wedding, when is it?'

We look at each and William raises his eyebrows.

'You've got to be kidding. She's marrying someone else mate. She'd never ever put up with me.'

Oh, William, you couldn't be more wrong.

'Anyway, I'm not the marrying type,' he adds before pulling me to the cab.

William spends the journey checking his phone and I text Oliver apologising for it being so late but that we had gone on to a jazz club and I hadn't heard the phone ring. The cab pulls up at Driftwood and William pays the driver. As we enter the house I sense he is shy with me. I wander into the kitchen and peek into the chocolate teapot where I see the two family-size bags of

M&Ms. His washing is on the floor next to his suitcase. I glance at it, feeling my head throb from the tequila.

'It's not my washing day until tomorrow,' he says looking at me.

'Quite right, I'm off to bed,' I say smiling, as an overwhelming urge to throw myself into his arms engulfs me.

'Okay, night Binki, sweet dreams,' he says softly.

I turn and walk unsteadily up the stairs and enter my bedroom, closing the door behind me before leaning against it. God, this is awful. My body seems to be on fire. I glance at the bedside cabinet and groan when I realise I have no water. I open the door and walk straight into William who has just reached the top of the stairs. We stare at each other and I sense he moves closer to me but I can't be sure.

'I was just going to get some water,' I say shakily. I feel sure my legs will give way if he continues staring at me like this. I force myself to look away and down at my engagement ring. His eyes follow my gaze and he says.

'I'll get it for you, I need some too.'

He turns and I sigh. I cling onto the door knob and wait for him to come back. He returns a few moments later with two glasses of water. I take one and smile.

'Thanks.'

I am about to go back into my room when his voice stops me.

'Binki,' he says softly.

I bite my lip and turn slowly.

'Yes.'

Please don't try and kiss me I pray, please don't. I know I will lose myself totally if you do. I daren't do this, there is no future. I'll lose everything if I do. I feel my hand tighten on the door knob.

'Thanks for tonight. It was a brilliant evening and ...' he fumbles and looks down at his water.

'I just wanted to tell you that you looked fabulous tonight, you know, really stunning and I felt really proud to be with you.'

I swallow and lick my dry lips.

'Thank you,' I say finally.

He leans towards me and my heart begins to beat so fast that my breath catches in my throat. His lips brush my cheek and travel slowly to my neck where he stops and pulls himself back.

'Sleep well,' he whispers before disappearing down the hall and closing his bedroom door. I close my door and for the first time since moving into Driftwood, I lock it. I fall onto my bed and feel tears run down my cheeks.

'Oh William, it really *had to be you*.' I whisper.

I take the photo of Oliver and hug it to my chest. I can't throw this away. I can't. William said himself he isn't the marrying kind. He's married to his job. We had too much tequila that's all it was, but this time I don't believe it. I know if I knock on his door right now he would let me in. Maybe he is wondering if he should knock on mine. I climb into bed without removing the make-up Rhona had so carefully applied and check my phone, but there is nothing. I check the time: it is now three in the morning. I'm marrying Oliver, I tell myself forcefully, pulling off my dress and dragging the duvet over me. I want babies. William is just a playboy. He's not the marrying kind, he certainly isn't father material. He has barely got time for the women in his life, let alone a wife. Maybe life with Oliver won't be as exciting as it is with William but you can't have excitement all the time right? Shit, it's no good. I've got to phone Muffy. I don't care if it is sodding three in the morning. If I don't I'm likely to be balancing myself on William Ellis's balls in the next ten minutes. Her phone rings and rings. God, she will kill me. Finally, she answers with a sleepy voice,

'Who the fuck is this? Do you have any idea what the time is? If you're trying to sell something you can bugger off.'

'It's me,' I whisper. 'I need help before I do something totally stupid.'

'Shit, Binki, it's bloody three in the morning, why aren't you sleeping like normal people?'

'Because I can't and if you don't do something I am in danger of throwing my body at William Ellis.'

'Fuck,' she shrieks.

Yes, well that is one way of putting it.

She curses.

'Hang on, just give me a sec. I've got to get my head around this. You do realise you interrupted me and Bradley Cooper shagging don't you?'

'I'm sorry.'

'Do you know how hard those kinds of dreams are to come by?' she grumbles.

'Yes, I know.'

'So why tonight of all nights do you want to jump on William's bones?' she asks, yawning.

'Because I've had too much tequila and I think I have finally realised that my best friend is actually the right one and I ...'

'I'm your best friend,' she says hesitantly.

I shake with frustration.

'No, I mean my best male friend is Mr Right, except he's Mr Wrong isn't he? Convince me. He even said he isn't the marrying kind. He'd be a crap dad wouldn't he? And then I'd lose Oliver, all because of a stupid one-night stand, which won't mean anything to William right? But he remembers to buy me M&Ms and things and tells me I look stunning and, oh God ...' I stop and take a deep breath.

'Don't you think you've answered your own question, but I do need to point out one thing you have overlooked,' she says calmly.

I flop onto the pillow.

'What?'

'Supposing you do knock on his door, just supposing, and just suppose you and William do it, did it not occur to you that it would then be the end of a great friendship? You can't go back to being friends once you've shagged can you? It just doesn't work does it? So you'd have lost Oliver and if William isn't the marrying kind you haven't gained anything but you have lost him as a friend haven't you, which sort of means you lose everything, but then I'm half asleep, you're pissed and we could both be talking a load of crap.'

Oh God, she is so right, so absolutely right. Why didn't I think of that?

'You're right, you're a hundred per cent right,' I say drunkenly. 'i'm going to sleep now.'

'Oh you're welcome. Don't worry about me and Bradley will you?'

I click off the phone and turn off the bedside lamp. Thank God for friends.

Chapter Thirty-One

'Oh God,' I groan. 'I'm never drinking tequila again.'

I drop my head onto the desk and wonder if I can take more aspirin. How William managed to get up so early and drive to Manchester is beyond me. I imagine it wasn't easy as he left me a little note saying, *I sure hope you feel better than me this morning. I'll overlook all errors you make at work today.*

'You okay there Mrs Ellis?' asks Andy, walking into the office.

I lift my head from the table. I could barely face the shower this morning let alone applying any make-up. For me to face someone without mascara is almost unheard of. But after scrubbing off last night's wonderful makeover I couldn't face applying more. I don't have the energy to correct him and I have to admit, sometimes being called Mrs Ellis sounds rather nice.

'No, I think I'm actually dead and someone warmed me up without my permission.'

I pull the laptop towards me and try to focus on the sales figures I had been working on and throw two aspirin in my mouth, along with some M&Ms.

'Tony bought some doughnuts; we thought you might like one.'

I pull a face. God, I must look horrific if the builders feel so sorry for me that they want to share their doughnuts

'That's so kind of you. Do I look that bad then?'

'Tony thought you did.'

Great, the builders pity me. I take the doughnut gratefully.

'We were going to work on that last outbuilding today, now we've finished that wall. But if you'd prefer we ...'

'No carry on, honestly it's okay. I'll just overdose on M&Ms and aspirin,' I smile.

I click on the office kettle when there is the sound of tyres on gravel as a car pulls into the driveway. A car door thuds and

Nathan walks into the office. Oh no, just when I needed some peace and quiet.

'Hi, how was Dubai?' I ask, holding up a mug. 'Would you like a coffee?'

'Dubai was great, why did you miss me?' he smiles but the smile doesn't reach his eyes.

'You look rough,' he says dryly.

'I feel rough. William and I went to a jazz club last night and we had too much tequila.'

'Is that right? Celebrating something were you?'

He slumps into the chair and looks at me across the desk. I push the coffee towards him and hesitate. My head begins to thump more and the builders start banging and I feel I might puke.

'Yeah, kind of,' I begin.

'It's okay,' he smiles. 'William called me this morning on his way to Manchester. Great merger, it must be the biggest William has ever pulled. He always was a lucky tosser.'

I feel a little flutter of anxiety in my stomach.

'Nathan,' I begin.

'Was it you that told William to shut me out of the deal? Do you know how long I've worked with William?' he says fiddling with the staples on my desk. 'Well do you?'

'Nathan ...'

'William never kept anything from me until you came along.' He looks livid.

God, I wish William was here.

'And to think I brought you a little something back from Dubai,' he says sardonically.

'That was very kind of you, thank you,' I say in my friendliest voice while all I want to do is to tell him to sod off.

He sips from the mug of coffee and takes my doughnut.

'I really liked you. That Oliver is nothing but a wanking wimp ...'

I stand up and grab the table.

'I think that's enough Nathan, I don't want to hear you insult Oliver. I don't want to hear you insult anyone come to that.'

I fall back into my chair.

'How about you and I have dinner tonight, I know nice places too and …'

'Thank you Nathan but I'm seeing Oliver tonight. We have wedding planning things to do. You know that kind of boring stuff.'

I try to smile but it doesn't work and it comes out as a half-smile, half-grimace and I imagine I look minging, I mean, me without make-up is minging on its own. I can't seriously believe any man would want to take me out to dinner right now.

'Oh yes, the wedding. How is the house hunting?' he shouts above the building work.

I sip my coffee and look at him over the rim of the mug.

'Fine. It's going fine.'

He chews his lip.

'So where did you William and Roche do the dirty deed?'

I'm either still slightly drunk or there is something very odd about Nathan this morning. He seems ridiculously cross over something that he should be really pleased about. He works for the company after all. Okay, maybe it was irritating to be shut out but that wasn't my fault, so why is he being so aggressive?

'Nathan, it wasn't a *dirty deed*, and I think you should talk this over with William …'

'Huh, that's a laugh. William doesn't talk things over with me any more. Oh no, you're flavour of the month aren't you?'

He stands up abruptly, knocking his coffee mug over and spilling the contents onto my papers. I rush to mop it up when he grabs my hand roughly.

'I think we should go out for dinner tonight darling and you can tell me what other little secrets you and William are sharing.'

I pull my hand away and feel myself shake. I see Andy standing at the door and nod to him.

'Okay to make tea is it?' he asks, but I can tell from his look that he is really asking me if I'm okay.

'Yes, it's fine Andy,' I say shakily.

Andy turns away and I look up into Nathan's face.

'I'd like you to leave my office Nathan and discuss this with William later,' I say, trying to hide the tremble from my voice.

'You want me to leave your office?' he smirks.

I nod. He laughs and turns towards the door.

'You want me off your premises do you?'

I don't reply. He fumbles in his pocket and produces a small wrapped gift. He throws it onto the desk.

'For you, the bloody fool that I am, but it's yours. I'm dead do you know that? William could have coped without that deal. But you had to poke your nose in didn't you? I had it all set up. I had a nice little deal for Roche and it would have cleared all my debts ...'

'*You* told Roche not to invest in Optimun?' I say shocked. 'Why did you do that to William?'

'Because he's loaded darling, and he can afford it. I'm up to my eyes. I've got every loan shark in the country after me. If you'd left things alone Roche would have gone with Lansdowne Enterprises and I'd be out of debt by now.'

My fuddled brain tries to register what he's saying. Lansdowne the competitor to us for Roche's investment?

'You owe money to Lansdowne?' I say wide-eyed.

'Don't sound so innocent sweetheart. You think William has never ever done a dodgy deal?'

Actually no I don't.

'I owe Charles Lansdowne half a million in gambling debts but don't let that worry you darling. All I needed was Roche to pull out from Optimun and I would have cleared everything. That was the deal I had with Lansdowne, but you two put your heads together and pushed me out.'

'William would have been ruined,' I say.

'And I'm not? I'm not fucking ruined?' he says nastily, sweeping papers from my desk. 'Enjoy the present.'

'Thank you. Now please leave my office,' I say.

He shakes his head.

'The bastard didn't tell you did he?'

Why do I not want to hear this?

'Didn't tell me what?'

'This isn't your office darling, and this isn't your house either. William found out weeks ago the house was left to him. It's all official, above board, the whole lot, but he took pity on you. Why do you think he gave you a job? You've been done up like a kipper too, haven't you?

He slams the door so hard that the room shakes. I fall into my chair.

William owns the house? He's known for weeks? I try to take in what Nathan had said, but my hung-over brain struggles to comprehend it. Has William been lying to me? I have a vague notion that my Blackberry rings but I don't really hear it. Even yesterday William lied to me when I asked him to contact his solicitor, and he had promised to chase them up today. I grab the office phone and call Hayden and Carruthers, solicitors of repute. Samantha answers in her bright cheery voice.

'Hello, this is Binki Grayson …'

'Mr Hayden is still skiing,' she says in a tired voice.

I have visions of the old man bombing down the slopes like a steam train, puffing his pipe and leaving bellows of smoke in his wake. I somehow doubt he is skiing but hey.

'Yes, I'm aware of that. I'd like to talk to Mr Carruthers,' I say firmly.

'But Mr Hayden handles your …'

'Look, I don't care who is handling my case. If you don't put me through to Mr Carruthers I shall sue your solicitors of repute for negligence because I know that you have information that has not been passed to me and should have been,' I say with a conviction I do not feel.

I don't really know if they have any information. They'll end up suing me for defamation of character. God, I wish my head didn't ache so much.

'I don't understand …' she stammers.

'No, you don't. That's why you should put me through to Mr Carruthers.'

'One moment Miss Grayson,' she says haughtily, putting me on hold. Oh I see. I don't even get asked now if I am okay to hold.

'Miss Grayson,' says a man's voice. 'Roger Carruthers speaking, how can I help you?'

I take a deep breath.

'You or rather Mr Hayden were handling my late aunt's affairs and …'

'Yes, I have that paperwork in front of me. I'm not sure what the problem is Miss Grayson? I hear your intention is to sue us.'

Shit.

'I have your case as closed. Is there something we have overlooked?'

How can it be closed when they haven't told me who owns the house?

'But no one got back to me about the last will and testament, and who owns Driftwood,' I say stupidly.

'That letter was sent to you, let me see, yes just over two weeks ago. I'm sorry if you didn't receive it. Shall we send you a copy?'

For Christ's sake, I don't want a bloody copy. I want to know if I own the sodding house.

'Who owns Driftwood?' I ask.

'Mr William Ellis. I'm so sorry we thought you had that notification.'

I hang up.

I drop my head onto the desk and burst into tears.

Chapter Thirty-Two

I sit in the kitchen with my suitcase beside me. The chocolate teapot is in front of me with just one penis and two nipples left inside. I have had more penises in the past few hours than I have ever had in my life. In fact, I'll probably never have that many penises again. I have had a chocolate penis orgy. Frankly, I don't think I ever want a penis again, chocolate or otherwise. I had removed the family-size M&Ms and left them on the kitchen counter. I had ripped off all the labels in my frenzy and almost yanked a cupboard door off in my anger. Fortunately Andy had been around to fix it. Poor Andy, he just couldn't get his head around how Mrs Ellis couldn't own Driftwood, and it just got too complicated to explain. I'd opened a bottle of William's whisky and left twenty-five pounds by the bottle, figuring it couldn't have cost much more than that. I want nothing from him, nothing at all except the truth.

I'm back where I started. I have no home and no job. I came close to phoning Luther to see if he had filled my position but couldn't bring myself to do it in the end. I fiddle with the little diamond bracelet that Nathan had brought back from Dubai and idly wonder how much I will get for it on eBay. I hear the sound of tyres on the gravel and take a large swig of the whisky. A car door slams and I hear his key in the lock.

'Anyone home,' he calls.

The front door slams and he is opening the kitchen door. He stops at the sight of me.

'Hey, how you doing,' he asks walking to the fridge.

He opens the door and I see his shoulders tense.

'What's happened to the ...'

He turns and sees my suitcase. He bites his lip and flops into the chair opposite me.

'Who told you?' he asks simply.

'Nathan. He said you told him about Roche and ...'

'I haven't spoken to Nathan today,' he interrupts.

'And I am supposed to believe what you tell me. You've done nothing but lie to me,' I say, my voice breaking.

He sighs heavily.

'It's the truth. I haven't spoken to him. He must have seen it in the *Financial Times*. I don't know why he is so upset or why he'd want to take it out on you,' he says removing his tie.

I sniff and pull a tissue from my bag.

'Because he wanted that deal for Lansdowne, you see he owes Charles Lansdowne a lot of money, gambling debts apparently. He's been stealing from you too. I was going to talk to you about it tonight but ...

He takes my whisky glass and finishes the contents.

'What an idiot,' he mumbles.

'How could you tell *him* about the house and not tell me?'

'I never told him about the letter. It came to the office and as it wasn't marked personal it was opened and given to him. He wouldn't have known otherwise.'

'Why didn't you tell me William?'

He sighs and pours whisky into the glass.

'What was the point? You didn't want to go back to the flat did you, and the wedding is only eight weeks away and ...'

'But I had a right to know that this wasn't my house William.'

He sighs.

'And what happened to the letter my solicitor sent me?' I say quietly reaching for the glass the same time as he does and our hands touch. I want to scream. How can he have this effect on me by just touching my hand? I am so angry with him but as soon as any part of his body touches me I totally lose it. I pull my hand back sharply. He throws back the remaining whisky in the glass and says, 'I hid it from you.'

'What! Why did you do that?'

He leans across the table to reach for my hand but I pull back.

'It was wrong. I'm sorry. It's just everything was going so well, you were working here and ... Oliver would have demanded you left and ...' he breaks off, lowers his head and mumbles, 'I'm sorry.'

'I've lost everything William, everything,' I say, starting to cry.

'Binki, please don't,' he says softly, getting up from his chair.

'Don't touch me,' I snap, holding my hands up. 'I couldn't bear it.'

He flops down in his chair looking dejected.

'You don't have to leave the job ...'

'Of course I do. I'll have to look for another job, go back to the flat where ... I lost trust in everyone William, but I thought I could trust you,' I say barely able to see him through my tears.

'I thought you were my friend.'

I grab the suitcase and head for the door.

'Binki, I am your friend,' he says quietly.

'I'll never understand why you did it,' I say.

I sense him behind me.

'Because I didn't want you to leave,' he says bluntly.

I turn to face him and his eyes meet mine.

'I've never had so much since you've been here. It feels so natural being with you and I can always be myself. There was never any pressure and I honestly thought I was helping by having you stay until the wedding. Why can't you stay? What would you have done if the house was yours? Were you planning on kicking me out of the offices?

'Of course not, I was thinking you could rent them,' I say, sniffing and fumbling in my handbag for a tissue.

He fetches some kitchen towel and hands it to me.

'Don't leave,' he whispers.

'I can't stay here. I can't lie to Oliver, and once he knows he'll want me to leave. I'm an engaged woman. Give this back to Nathan when you see him. I don't want his presents.'

I hand him the bracelet. He opens his mouth to speak but his phone rings. He pulls it from his pocket and I see Andrea's name light up the screen. He clicks it off. I turn to the door but my legs feel like jelly and I wait for him to say something, anything but he doesn't.

I lift my suitcase into the boot and climb into Kandy and without glancing back I pull out of Driftwood's driveway.

Chapter Thirty-Three

'Hey guys how are you getting on?' I swear this bed salesman's smile is stuck onto his face. He even talks with his mouth in a smile a bit like a ventriloquist. I bet he has jaw ache at the end of the day. I suppose things could be worse, I could be doing his job.

Actually *us guys* have not been getting on too well for the past few days but I'm not going to tell a bed salesman ventriloquist that am I?

'Yeah okay, this one seems nice,' says Oliver, glancing for the umpteenth time at his watch.

'It's a great bed this one isn't it?' says the smiling salesman.

'This mattress does wonders if you have back problems,' says the salesman.

'Perfect for you then,' I quip to Oliver.

'My back's fine now,' says Oliver wearily.

Yes, well it would be wouldn't it? Seeing as he isn't the one sleeping on a blow-up bed that slowly deflates overnight, usually coinciding with me needing to pee. I find myself rolling around like a beached whale trying to get off the bloody thing just to go to the loo. It's like doing bed Pilates. I then have to switch the pump on to blow the thing back up and of course, that wakes Oliver. So we've both been walking around like zombies for the last week. Trying to have sex on the damn thing is a feat all of its own. We're fine until Oliver gets a bit frantic and then the thing deflates in one big massive whoosh, as does Oliver's erection, leaving us both flaying around like beached whales trying to get off the goddamn thing. I swear getting out of quicksand would be easier.

'Well mine isn't,' I snap.

The salesman coughs softly.

'These orthopaedic mattresses are the best things invented if you ask me. My mother-in-law, right, she had this crippling back problem, spent a fortune on podiatrists ...'

'I thought they did feet,' says Oliver, absently glancing at his watch again.

'No, they massage your back,' says the salesman, looking puzzled. 'Her feet are okay.'

Like we need to know this, I mean for Christ's sake. I want to tell him I don't give a shit about his mother-in-law's feet or her bloody back. I just want a decent night's sleep in a bed that Amanda sodding Rowland hasn't slept in. In theory she shouldn't have slept in any of these beds, but knowing that little trollop who can say? God, I've become such a bitter woman since Christmas, and this is without a pending period. I dread to think what I'll be like then. I only hope Oliver survives.

'She's not looked back since she bought this mattress,' he says nodding enthusiastically.

'Right,' says Oliver.

The salesman continues to smile at me as a child pulls his trouser leg.

'Hey mister, my mum said you're giving out lollies.'

'Yes, in a minute son,' he replies the smile still pasted on his face.

'I want it now. If you don't give it to me now I'll tell my mum I hate these beds and want to go somewhere else.'

Little sod. I'm determined that our kids will never turn out like that.

'I'll leave you guys to try it out, be back in a sec,' he says, walking away with the little sod clinging to his trouser leg.

'Why you can't sleep in the bed we have is beyond me,' Oliver grumbles.

'You know why?' I snap.

He just doesn't get it. He really doesn't. Even if he had the bed fumigated I still couldn't get in it.

'Anyway, we'll need a bed when we move into the new house,' I say.

'If we get the mortgage offer, that is. We hadn't planned on taking out such a large mortgage, remember? We were banking on your inheritance weren't we?'

'Well I'm sorry that you're not marrying a millionairess.'

He shakes his head.

'Don't be ridiculous, I only meant we may not get the house. We may have to rent somewhere first, which means we'll be stuck with two beds if it comes furnished. Of course if you hadn't have been so pedantic about the flat we could have stayed there, now of course it has new tenants.'

How is it everything is my fault? I wasn't the one caught screwing someone else, I'm the one out of a job and sleeping on a blow-up bed. I swear my core muscles are the strongest they've ever been though. Maybe I could start a whole new exercise craze called *Bed Pilates.* I could do a good line in faulty blow-up beds.

'Are you trying this one?' asks a lady behind us.

'Oh no, we're just talking about it. Please go ahead.'

Christ, how many people have lain on these beds. I shudder at the thought as my eyes wander to an overweight sweaty woman. Christ, I bet these beds are full of bed lice and all kinds of bugs. I watch the sweaty woman fall onto the bed I had been coveting and cross that one off the list.

'Look Binki, I've got to get back. As great as it is lying on beds with you I really can't afford to put my job on the line can I? Not now.'

I roll my eyes.

'Is that another dig at me?'

'Of course not, look you choose the bed and I'll see you tonight. Good luck with the interview, let me know how it goes.'

He quickly kisses me on the lips and flies from the shop. I sigh and look around at the beds.

'Any luck?' asks the smiling salesman worriedly, his eyes following Oliver's fleeing body.

'He has to get back to work,' I say.

I glance over at the four-poster bed in the far corner of the room and point to it. It's totally impractical and way too big, but I've always wanted to see what a four-poster was like to sleep on.

'I'll try that one and then I'll let you know which one I've chosen,' I say walking towards it and not really hearing his response. I fall onto the bed, stretch my body and close my eyes. My mind drifts to the interview. God, I hope I get this job. The agency seemed very keen to get me an interview with this company. Let's hope Ben Newman hasn't been on the blower to them. I remember Piers Roche saying *leave him to me*, and I think back to the night of our Chinese dinner and sigh, and then remember my emotional departure from Driftwood. William and I were due to have dinner with Piers tomorrow to celebrate his birthday.

'I hate celebrating alone,' he'd said.

I sigh and turn over on the bed. Oliver had been thrilled when I'd turned up at the flat although his face had dropped when I'd told him that the house didn't belong to me. In fact he had banged on about me taking legal action as surely I was entitled to the house. But of course I was no more entitled to that house than anyone else. Aunty Vera left it to William and I am in do doubt that he did more for her when she was alive than I did. It's been over two weeks since I left and I haven't heard from him. Well, there is no reason why I should is there? Some days I miss him so much though. I'm still doing my washing on my designated washing days as it seems somehow comforting, and I miss his whoosh-whooshing sounds in the morning and the smell of his whisky. I even miss the bloody builders. Now that is a bad sign right? My phone rings and I pull it from my bag.

'Hey it's me,' says Muffy brightly. 'I thought I'd phone and wish you good luck for the interview. I'll see you at one at Georgia's brasserie. Are you still up for lunch?'

'Yes, looking forward to it.'

'Don't be fucking stupid, what the hell would we do with a four-poster bed?' says a voice beside me.

I turn to see the fat sweaty woman studying the bed with her husband who is less sweaty, but just as fat.

'I thought it might be romantic, you know,' he replies in a dull voice.

'Romantic, what the fuck is wrong with you?'

Yes, things could always be worse. I could have been born her. God, what an awful thought.

'Where the hell are you?' asks Muffy.

'In a bed shop,' I say in my most depressed tone.

'Nice class of people you mix with in bed shops,' she giggles.

'Yes, fortunately one doesn't have to get into bed with them.'

'Save that for the job interview darling,' she laughs.

'Muffy,' I exclaim.

'Only kidding, see you at one, and I've got an extra hour to go for the fitting with you. See you laters.'

I get up with a sigh and approach the salesman.

'The special back one over there,' I say pointing. 'How long does it take to deliver?'

'Delivery on that one is two weeks,' he says whipping out the paperwork.

Two weeks. God, I'll need a hell of a lot more than an orthopaedic bed by then. I'll probably be looking at a new hip. Why does everything take so long in this country?

'Is that the earliest?'

He looks pained.

'That's a very good delivery time, most shops don't ...'

'We'll take it,' I say, pulling out my credit card making a mental note to get a puncture repair kit on the way home.

I leave the bed shop and realise I only have an hour before my interview. I dash into Debenhams and check my make-up. I'd chosen to wear a smart navy suit with a pale blue blouse on Muffy's advice.

'The last thing you want to do is walk in looking like the most fuckable woman ever.'

'What does that mean?' I'd questioned.

'It's just with your reputation and everything ...'

'What reputation? I didn't bloody do anything ...'

'No, but the way the rumours have spread you may as well have done and don't wear flats. Make sure you have heels okay? That way you'll look sophisticated and chic.'

Isn't it bloody sod's law? Ben Newman makes the pass at me and somehow I'm now the biggest slapper in town. 'Honestly, it comes to something when I have to dress down so people don't think I'm the slapper I never was.'

'All I'm saying is, you don't want to walk into an interview dressed like you're clearly up for it.'

Yeah right. My reflection looks back at me and I grimace at myself. I look about as unfuckable as a woman can look. I can't imagine any man wanting to sprawl me over a desk. Not that bosses spend their time sprawling their sales assistants over their desks of course. I think it was just my bad luck to work for Ben Newman. I run a brush through my hair, reapply my make-up, tell myself I can get this job and leave Debenhams. It's a twenty minute walk to the offices of Alpha PR, and I'm fifteen minutes early which is perfect. I stroll in and stop when I see a line of women sitting in plush leather chairs in the reception area, and they all look very fuckable. In fact they are so rosy cheeked they look post-coital, post-orgasmic and fuckable. Christ, I must look like some prim snooty spinster who's never had sex in her life and would faint at just hearing the word. Shit and no time to change or have a quickie with Oliver so I at least look a little post-coital. Oh bugger it, another job down the drain. I approach the reception desk feeling all the other women's eyes like little daggers, in my back. Just wait until I see Muffy. She'll get it in the neck for sure.

'Hello,' I say quietly to the receptionist. 'I'm here to see Martin Lucas. My name is Binki Grayson.'

She looks up and smiles at me.

'Ah yes, Binki, do take a seat.'

Do I have to? Can't I just hide in the loo until this lot have been in? After all, my chances are zero aren't they? No one will hire me when they have all these glamour pusses to choose from. Oh, what am I thinking, not all men are like Ben Newman.

'Are you here for the receptionist job?' the girl next to me whispers.

I sigh with relief.

'No, I'm here for the senior sales assistant position,' I whisper back.

What a relief. I try to work out which of these women is my competition, but it is impossible.

'Binki Grayson,'

I turn to see a tall, long-legged woman holding a folder. I stand up, ignore the curious eyes that follow me and approach her.

'Yes, I'm Binki Grayson,' I say.

'Follow me. Mr Lucas is ready to see you.'

I follow her into an office which houses a large oak desk and three comfortable leather armchairs. The man seated at one stands and extends his hand to me.

'Martin Lucas, nice to meet you Binki, that's an unusual name?'

At least he didn't say *Ah Binki, the anytime anywhere girl*.

He gestures for me to sit.

'Yes, my mother is a great Mills and Boon reader and I'm the product of one of her favourite characters unfortunately.'

He laughs, and I take the opportunity to study him. I don't think he looks like a Ben Newman. He has brown hair which is greying at the temples. He wears a wedding ring and there are photos of his wife and children on the desk. Best of all, there isn't a wart in sight.

'It's unique,' he says opening a folder. I'm presuming he means my name and not the contents of the folder. This is the folder that no doubt is full of my sexual exploits with Ben Newman, sex over the desk, and oral sex under it. Not to mention the crazy shagging on the office floor and the hanging from the light fittings. Christ, I wish I had that kind of energy. Oliver would be thrilled I'm sure. Right now I can barely do it on a bed, although it has to be agreed that at the moment it does rather feel like I'm having sex on the high seas in a life raft. I'm surprised Oliver hasn't wanted me to wear the sailor outfit. I feel myself blush as Martin Lucas lifts his head from my folder. It must be like reading *The Confessions of an Office Slut*.'

'Mr Lucas, my last job ...'

He flicks through the folder.

'At Temco,' he nods.

I feel myself blush even more. Oh God. I rummage in my bag nervously.

'I do have a glowing report from my previous job before Temco,' I say pulling papers from my bag along with a chocolate penis which before I can stop it, has rolled across the floor and landed at his feet.

Bollocks and piss it. Well, that's that then. I've just confirmed that everything he has heard about me is true. I like cock so much I even carry one around with me, I could die of shame and scoff the whole penis, I feel that depressed. He leans down and picks up the penis, handing it to me with a smile.

'Cheap chocolate,' he says.

'They are quite reasonably priced. Actually they were freebies from my last job,' I admit truthfully.

Well, it's all out in the open now isn't it? I've lost the pissing job anyway so why bother even trying.

'The thing is, my boss at Temco ...

He lifts a hand and stops me mid-sentence.

'Piers Roche advised me I'd be crazy not to employ you.'

Piers Roche? How did he know I was applying for this job?

'Piers Roche,' I echo.

'You didn't give references in your application. You just mentioned that Ellis Financial Investments was the last place you had worked. I phoned Mr Ellis who was in a meeting with Mr Piers Roche at the time, and they both gave you glowing references.'

'They did?'

'I have two more people to see but having looked through your portfolio, you seem ideal. You're exactly what I'm looking for Binki Grayson, and I'm talking office skills. I'm sorry to hear of your experience with Temco but rest assured nothing like that goes on here.'

I can't believe my luck, although I rather wish William and Piers Roche had not had a say in it. Still, this is not the time to be proud is it? Otherwise Oliver and I will end up living in a *big fat gypsy caravan*, and although Victoria Beckham might be happy to live with David in a dustbin I'm afraid I couldn't even stretch to a campervan as fond as I am of Oliver.

'When would you be able to start?'

'Immediately,' I say and bite my lip. Was that too quick a response?

'I don't have a job to give notice to.'

I'd told Luther I couldn't come back. Oliver had put his foot down quite forcefully on that one. *No fiancée of mine works in a sex shop*, he had said and I'd felt quite touched until he had added, *what would our friends think?*

'I was going to ask about your strengths and weaknesses but a reference like that from Piers Roche is more than enough for me.'

He stands up and I quickly follow suit not wanting to outstay my welcome. Now if I can just walk to the door in these heels and not fall arse over tit there is a good chance the job is in the bag, and we may be able to get that mortgage and move out of that damn flat which I swear is covered in a film of Amanda Rowland's perfume.

'We'll be in touch,' he says, shaking my hand. 'I only ask that when you start, you bring in more conventional chocolate for your break.'

I smile and thank him. I make it safely to the door and want to scream *I've got a job*. Still, mustn't get too excited, after all he did say he has another two women to see but it looks hopeful. I clip-clop in my heels to Georgia's brasserie. Muffy is sipping a latte.

'Well,' she says, looking hopeful.

'I think I've got it,' I say, kicking off the shoes and stealing the freebie biscuit from her saucer.

'That's great Binki,' she says, gesturing to the waitress.

'Piers Roche and William gave references apparently.'

Her eyes widen.

'I thought you wanted nothing from William Ellis, except his body of course,' she says slyly.

'I do not and I never have wanted William Ellis's body unless it is on a slab,' I say bitterly.

'You liar, and why did you give him as a reference?'

'I didn't. I just said he was my last employer. I couldn't put Ben-wart-on-the-nose-Newman could I? His reference would be how good I was at having sex over a leather couch and up against the accounts drawer. It goes without saying I couldn't mention the sex shop but a chocolate penis fell out of my bag. He took it rather well actually, and it wasn't the final nail in the coffin as I thought it would be. Apparently, he phoned William after seeing he was my last employer and he was in a meeting with Roche and it seems they both said glowing things about me,' I say, taking the menu from the waitress.

'So, you're totally over William?' she says, looking at me closely.

'There was nothing to get over. I don't know what you're on about.'

'So, you won't be in the least bit bothered by this then,' she says, pulling a folded piece of newspaper from her bag and pushing it across the table.

'William is engaged. It was announced this morning in *The Times*. Andrea's doing most likely. I can't imagine ...'

'What!' I exclaim, grabbing the cutting. 'He can't be. He's not the marrying kind.'

'He obviously is now,' says Muffy, ordering two salads. I don't want salad, I need chocolate.

I stare at the cutting and feel a rollercoaster of emotions run through me.

**Laurier and Mervyn Garcia are proud to announce the
engagement of their daughter
Andrea Garcia to William Ellis**

'But ...' I begin.

She couldn't handle his work hours, I thought. He isn't the marrying kind I thought. Seems I think a lot of fucking rubbish doesn't it. Andrea, I mean Andrea, long-legged, everything positioned just nicely thank you very much, Andrea. Bitchy horrible Andrea, how could he? Is he trying to throw his life away? Has he gone totally crazy? He could at least have given Vicki a chance. Chances are she would have grown out of *True Blood*, or William could have got into it. Bloody Andrea will always be after his blood, that's for sure. I don't believe this, I really don't.

'Two Waldorf salads,' says the waitress, placing them in front of us.

'Can I have a double chocolate ice cream with whipped cream?' I ask

The waitress gawps at me.

'Cock it,' groans Muffy, 'I knew I shouldn't have told you.'

'*Now*, you want the ice cream *now*?' asks the waitress.

'Yes, ASAP in fact,' I say.

'You'll never get into the dress if you go on like this. You'll be walking down the aisle like Gemma Collins. You'll be the star of your own TV show called *My Big Fat Notting Hill Wedding*.

'I'm not that overweight,' I scoff.

'Yet,' she quips.

'But Andrea, I mean why the hell would he get engaged to her, aside from the long legs, big tits and well-proportioned body and shaved pubis ...'

'How would you know about her pubis?' asks Muffy, tucking into her salad.

'It's obvious. She's Miss Perfect isn't she?'

'She doesn't shave her pubis actually,' says Muffy quietly.

I widen my eyes.

'And how would you know about her pubis?' I say stunned.

She shrugs.

'Okay, I follow her on Twitter,' she says stabbing a lettuce leaf with her fork.

'You what?' I say disbelievingly.

She sighs.

'It's not what you think, she tweets beauty advice. It's good stuff, that's what she does and ...'

'I'm really not interested,' I say petulantly.

'You asked how I knew ...'

'God, she puts stuff about her pubis on there?'

'Not exactly, anyway you hate Twitter.'

'Yes, because you can't say anything in 140 characters. It's bloody frustrating.'

I feel a stab of envy and hate myself for it. I suppose she will go to dinner with William and Piers now, instead of me. My ice cream arrives and I push the salad to one side.

'I still can't believe he got engaged to her. I mean her of all people.'

'I imagine he got engaged to her for the same reason you got engaged to Oliver. He's in love.'

She raises her eyebrows.

'So did you get a bed?'

I nod miserably.

'A thing with an orthopaedic mattress, dead exciting,' I say. 'The bed man had a permanent smile stuck to his face.'

I stuff my mouth full of ice cream much to Muffy's disgust.

'Do you think I should invite him to the wedding?' I say thoughtfully. 'After all, it seems a bit off not to.'

'The bed salesman,' she says with a grimace. 'Well, I suppose you could. A bit unusual but ...'

'Not the bed salesman stupid. William. Do you think I should invite *William* to the wedding? God, I wonder if he'll invite us to his.'

I push the ice cream away.

'Don't you want that salad?' asks Muffy, eyeing it hungrily. How anyone can covet a salad is a mystery to me. I shove it towards her. My phone is ringing and I pull it from my handbag. It's Oliver. Shit, I forgot to tell him how the interview went. Honestly, he seems to be the last person on my mind these days. That can't be right can it?

'How did the interview go?' he asks.

'I think I got the job,' I say proudly.

'Well done, I knew you could do it. Well done honey, I'm proud of you.'

I smile and feel a warm glow run through me. I do love Oliver. I only wish I felt sure I was in love with him. He will make a good husband and a brilliant dad.

'I've got an interview at Munroes next week. They want a senior surveyor, the agency thinks I've got a good chance,' he says, sounding dead chuffed.

'That's great Oliver, it really is. I bought a bed too, the sleigh one.'

He's really trying.

'Oh yeah did you hear, Ellis has got engaged.'

He had to go and ruin everything didn't he? I pull the ice cream back towards me but what was left has melted. I debate the penis but even I have principles and would never suck one that has been around a bit and let's face it that one certainly has.

'Yeah, Muffy mentioned it,' I say dismissively. 'I'd better go Oliver, Muffy only has an hour and we have the fittings today.'

I click off and beckon the waitress. Muffy pushes my hand down.

'Unless it is the bill you're getting, forget it.'

Honestly, I thought friends were supposed to be supportive.

'Let's pay for this lot and get to the fitting, and you'd better pray that sodding dress still zips up. I don't know how many fittings I can cope with.'

Don't you just hate weddings, and even more so, other people's weddings? I wonder if William will invite us. Oh God, I hope not.

Chapter Thirty-Four

One week later and I'm dieting for England. The dress doesn't fit. I've dipped into the chocolate teapot one too many times and even with a spanx it still won't bloody zip up.

'Don't worry,' Andrea had said, the dress fitter Andrea that is, not the other one. I wouldn't let her near my body with a bargepole.

'We'll have you looking like Kate Moss when you walk down the aisle.'

Muffy had scoffed.

'Huh, work wonders and shit miracles do you? Perhaps you can make me look like Angelina Jolie while you're at it.'

To make matters worse we are dining with Oliver's parents this evening at a posh restaurant, and I just know I'll be tempted by the menu.

'Is that what you're wearing?' Oliver asks as I walk out of the bathroom. I look down at my long black skirt and white cashmere cardigan.

'Yes why?'

'It's just a bit …'

'A bit what?' I say defensively.

'I don't know, it's okay, I just think that cardigan makes you look a bit dumpy.'

A bit dumpy, oh my God, I look dumpy. I rush into the bedroom and look at myself in the mirror. I suppose I do look a bit dumpy.

'I'll have to change.'

He sighs.

'There isn't time now. You'll have to go like that.'

Like that, meaning *dumpy* I suppose. I grab my coat and handbag and waddle my dumpy body out of the doorway. Honestly weddings, they are such a stress. There is such pressure to look perfect. The closer to the day we get the more nervous I am that the dress won't fit, or if I do squeeze into it then it will burst open at the back as I am halfway down the bloody aisle. I keep wondering if William has his wedding date and find myself scrutinising the newspapers for an announcement, but there is nothing. Twice I've come close to phoning him on the pretext of thanking him for the reference but I always stop at the last digit. Then I type a text, thanking him and asking how things are, only to delete it after staring at it for about half an hour. Twice I've been tempted to drive past Driftwood but chickened out at the last minute. I did read in the FT that he had replaced his accountant. There was a short piece on Nathan, saying he had been offered a terrific opportunity in Dubai, which he could not turn down and as much as they hated to part company they both felt it was for the best.

Oliver rests his hand on my knee and I place my hand over his. Things have been a lot better between us since the new bed arrived. What a difference a bed makes. Tonight is a celebratory dinner to toast my new job and Oliver's job offer at Munroes, and that we have finally got our mortgage offer. Muffy had quipped *you're very much becoming Mr and Mrs Average*.

Oliver's phone rings and he removes his hand from my knee to answer it.

'Hi, really, blimey that's a bonus. I'll just tell the driver. See you there in fifteen minutes.'

He hangs up and leans forward to the driver.

'Could you take us to Marcells instead? Thanks mate.'

Oh no, why are we going to Marcells?

'I thought we were going to *The Manor*,' I say, trying to stop the tremble in my voice.

'Apparently they've had a fire. Luckily they managed to get their customers into other restaurants. Marcells is pretty upmarket. We were lucky to get rebooked there.'

Oh please don't let William be there. Why am I being so stupid? Why should he be there? There are a hundred places he could be. Anyway, he probably isn't even eating out tonight. Most likely he is getting a Chinese, he likes that and we often did that on a Friday. My heart sinks at the memory. The taxi pulls up outside Marcells and Oliver's parents, Sylvia and Robert, are waiting outside. Sylvia enfolds me in a crushing hug.

'How are you darling?'

'Fine, how are you?' I say untangling myself.

'Have you gained weight?' she says, holding me away from her and studying me intently. Of course she would have to do this in public wouldn't she? Anyone else would have had a quiet word in the loo, but not my future mother-in-law.

'Yes she has,' replies Oliver.

Why is it I feel not only fat but invisible all at one and the same time?

'Oh dear, is the dress going …'

'It's fine,' I say hurriedly. 'The dress fits perfectly.'

Well, it will eventually so I'm not lying as such.

'Oh dear,' she mumbles.

'Shall we go in?' says Robert, my future father-in-law.

I'd prefer not to but seeing as I have no choice. God, it would be tonight that I look dumpy wouldn't it? Of all the nights that I could bump into William it is the night I look dumpy and overweight. I must be if Sylvia noticed. I'm beginning to think this Kate Moss thing is something of a dream on the part of Andrea. My phone rings and I pull it from my bag as we enter the dining area.

'I'm at my beauty therapist having my nails done,' says Muffy.

'I need to know this do I?'

'Okay, no need to be sarky. She's got the answer to your bridal dress problem.'

I walk past the red velvet curtains that cover the windows and peep behind one to see the river and remember how William and I gazed out of the window when we were here. I follow Oliver and his parents to a table at the back of the room.

'She knows how to perform miracles does she?' I say, allowing the waiter to pull back a chair for me.

'Colonic irrigation.'

'What, I'm not having anything poked up my arse thank you very much,' I say, totally forgetting I am with Oliver and his parents. There is a brief silence and I blush furiously.

'Erm, can I call you back later Muffy. I'm out for dinner with Oliver.'

'Yeah sure, I'll book you in, you can always cancel. You should give it serious thought.'

I hang up and smile at Sylvia.

'Muffy,' I say, like that explains everything.

Robert nods and asks the waiter for champagne.

'Well, what a night huh, not only do we have a double celebration but we get to do it here. Who gets this kind of luck?'

Oh I do, I really so do, I think as I see William stroll into the restaurant with Andrea at his side. Another couple follow behind them and William turns to smile at his male companion as he passes our table. I try to duck under it but I've been pushed so far into the corner that it's all I can do to get my legs under the table let alone my whole body. Bugger it. He turns back and our eyes meet. I shrug stupidly and give a little wave. He seems to freeze for a couple of seconds and Andrea nudges him while laughing with the other woman and flashing her diamond engagement ring for all she's worth. William gives me a little nod, at least I think it is me he is nodding at, and then he is gone. I see Andrea's chiffon dress disappear around the corner. My heart is thumping and my hands are trembling. God, what is wrong with me.

'Someone is looking down on us,' laughs Robert.

And who would that be, because whoever it is they certainly have it in for me. The waiter pours the champagne and hands us menus.

'Perhaps not too much for you dear,' Sylvia says softly. 'Alcohol is the worst thing when it comes to calories. I'm on the five-two diet aren't I Robert? This is one of my five days when I can eat whatever I like. I've lost pounds, haven't I Robert, it's marvellous. I'll send you all the details.'

God, three comments in the space of fifteen minutes regarding my bloody weight, surely this is a record. I don't mind Muffy going on, well I do really but it's a bit much when you can't come out for dinner without having it rubbed in. I find myself looking at the assortment of salads on the menu while trying to remember where the loos are, and if they are anywhere near where William is sitting.

'Here's to Oliver and his fantastic new job, well done son, and to our lovely future daughter-in-law on landing her new job,' says Robert, raising his glass and clinking against ours. I knock mine back in one go. God, I hope I don't have to hold it in all night. I really couldn't bear a weight comment from Andrea.

'Fabulous menu,' murmurs Robert.

Sylvia looks up from hers and says,

'Talking of menus dear, Oliver said you're going for the salmon as the main course for the reception. I thought we all agreed duck, it's much nicer, and salmon is so common. Everyone has salmon don't they? I know your parents prefer it but ...'

'Oh yes, I was going to tell you,' adds Oliver, gesturing to the waiter. 'Could we have a bottle of the house red?'

I remember William ordering our wine by name and in fluent French too. Oh I wish I could go and speak to him. If only he had come alone.

'Binki.'

I look up to see Sylvia waving her hand in front of my face.

'Are you with us dear?'

I wish I wasn't.

'I think Mum is right, duck would be far more original don't you think?'

'But we've already chosen the menu,' I say feebly. 'And most people will eat salmon won't they. The thing is ...'

'Well, of course they'll eat it darling, but do you really want to be like everyone else?' says Sylvia firmly. 'I'd like my son's wedding to be a little bit original. I'll phone your mother.'

Great. And why can't I have sodding salmon at my wedding? After all, it is my wedding isn't it?

'Good, that's that sorted, now what are you having Robert?' she says dismissing me.

I fight back a sigh and grab my wine glass. I order a hot chicken salad and feel decidedly more depressed than I did when Ben-wart-on-the-nose offered me his Christmas bonus. That feels so long ago now, and so much seems to have happened since then.

'The sea bass is supposed to be amazing here,' says Oliver.

God, I'm dying for a pee but I can't possibly risk walking past stick-thin Andrea, or should I say waddling past her. Honestly, I feel that fat the way everyone keeps talking about my weight.

'Do you want a starter?' Oliver asks.

I'd love one.

'Oliver don't tempt the poor girl. She's got an important dress to get into, isn't that right Sylv,' laughs Robert loudly.

Are these people really going to be my in-laws?

'I'll just have some bread,' I say.

'Oh, that's the worst dear,' says Sylvia with a tut-tut.

God, why don't they just throw celery sticks at me?

'So,' says Robert. 'Munroes is a nice little number. Gets you away from ...' he stops embarrassed and glances at me.

'Well, we don't want to dwell on little mistakes do we,' says Sylvia, breaking open a roll.

There are a few seconds of silence. A little mistake, is that what she sodding calls it? Personally I call it a huge mistake. A bloody *how much bigger could it get* mistake.

'Excuse me, I need the ladies,' I say, squeezing past Oliver.

'You okay?' he whispers.

I straighten my clothes and attempt to walk with my head held high to the loo. *Keep looking ahead* I tell myself. I pass tables without looking to see who is sitting at them. I feel certain I hear Andrea's laugh but it seems a little distance away. I dive into the ladies and stare at my reflection in the mirror. My cheeks are flushed from the champagne and my eyes are sparkling. I turn and twist my head to see just how big my backside is in the skirt. It doesn't look *that* bad, or maybe I am just kidding myself and the cardigan looks okay in my opinion. Maybe a little tight around the bust but blimey it makes a change for me to look big breasted. I look like Nigella Lawson in one of her cashmere cardigans. I hear footsteps approaching and dive into a cubicle and sit on the loo. I listen as two women chat about their fabulous evening at such a posh restaurant and look down at my shoes. I'm not that dumpy. Okay, I'm not a stick insect and never have been and don't know if I even want to be. And if I want sodding salmon at my wedding surely I should have salmon shouldn't I? It is my wedding after all and also a special day for my parents. Maybe I'll have beetles for the starter. They're a delicacy aren't they? Maybe not in this country but they are somewhere. That will be fun, watching Sylvia crunch her way through a plateful of beetles. But why should my parents eat duck? What's happened to me anyway? I've become so insignificant, I'm amazed I haven't disappeared into the wallpaper. Mind you, didn't Muffy say I was bloody stupid when it came to men? I supposedly *loved too much*. God, that's a joke. I'm now beginning to worry that I don't love Oliver enough. How do you know if you love someone? I suppose it's all subjective. I would hate not having him in my life but I could cope with not living with him. Do all married couples feel this way? I'm sure this is all wedding nerves. I bet if you asked any woman how she felt six weeks before her wedding she would say exactly the same. I'm marrying a man that I love dearly but is that good enough? I've a good job. I could rent my own flat and buy an Amanda Rowland-free bed all for myself. I don't have to be a desperate 30-year-old do I? Maybe the clock is ticking but it isn't going to blow up if I don't walk down the aisle by the time the clock strikes thirty-one is it? Do I want to be married to a man who thinks I look dumpy? More importantly, is it normal to be giving oneself a pep talk while sitting in a posh restaurant's loo? The door bangs as the women leave and I scroll through the contacts on my Blackberry and pick out three of my closest friends, apart from Muffy.

'Mel, hi it's Binki.'

'Hey Binki, how are you …? Oh God, hold on. Ben, no, you can't pe-pe there. Shit. Bloody three-year-old has just pissed on the new rug. I don't know why the fuck we have a potty. It might as well be the dog's drinking bowl. How you doing? Wedding plans coming on well?'

'Yeah great, I just want a bit of advice really,' I say with a false laugh.

'Christ, not sure I'm up to that but fire away.'

'How did you feel six weeks before your wedding? I mean, did you have doubts?'

She laughs.

'Doubts, bloody hell, I was planning the great escape for weeks before. Mind you, if I'd known what I know now I'd have taken that escape tunnel.'

'Oh really.'

'Ben, put that back. It's not a toy. He's got the sodding vibrator now,' she says wearily. 'Mind you, it's the most it's been used all year. Look honey, don't listen to me. It's a bad day. It'll be great.'

'Right,' I say.

'Better go, before he throws the thing down the loo or something. We're looking forward to the big day by the way. We bought the Buddha painting on your list, nice, different.'

Ah, that was one of Oliver's. I was rather hoping no one would bother.

'Great, thanks.'

I scroll down quickly to Francesca. She answers immediately.

'What? I'm really not interested in what you have to say.'

'Fran, it's Binki,' I say hesitantly.

'Oh Binki, I'm sorry I thought it was Ted. I didn't bother to look at the screen. We've just had this huge row. Can you believe he called me fat?'

Yes, I can actually.

'I'm premenstrual so of course I'm bloody fat aren't I?'

'Yes, I mean ...'

'Oh look, can I call you back? That's him trying to get through. I'm not having the bugger call me fat ...'

'Erm, yeah, of course.'

The phone goes dead and I drop it back into my bag. I'd get better advice from the loo. I leave the cubicle and again check my reflection. I open the door and peek outside to check all is safe. I sound like a wanted woman. The coast is clear and I walk with head held high back to the table and squeeze back into my corner seat.

'Your skirt is tucked in your knickers,' sighs Oliver. 'The whole world just saw your black panties.'

Shit. Well not the whole world exactly, that's a slight exaggeration. You couldn't get a bus load of people in here let alone the whole world.

'Let's not draw attention to it,' whispers Sylvia.

'I don't think many people noticed,' adds Robert.

They don't have to make it sound like I moon shined the whole restaurant. It's a small *skirt in knickers* catastrophe, not the *News at Ten* headlines.

My salad arrives and I look enviously at Oliver's sirloin and Robert's sea bass. Sylvia has opted for a chicken and mushroom dish and I covet her roast potatoes like I've never coveted anything in my life. I'm about to put a forkful of salad to my mouth when I see William approaching and drop the lot down the front of my cardigan.

'What's wrong with you tonight?' asks Oliver.

I quickly brush the bits of lettuce off my cashmere cardigan, and lift my red face to William. 'I thought it rude not to come over and say hello,' says William in that soft gorgeous voice of his. I hadn't realised how much I'd missed it until now.

'Hi,' I say shakily. 'This is Oliver, and this is William.'

Oliver gives William a long stare before extending his hand.

'Oh right, nice to meet you. Congratulations on your engagement by the way.'

I feel a tomato slide down my cleavage as William looks at me.

'Thank you and congratulations to you too,' he says, looking into my eyes.

'Hello, I'm Sylvia, and my husband Robert.'

Sylvia leans across, almost knocking my wine glass over. That will be the next thing, what with salad down my cleavage and my knickers on the outside of my skirt I must look a right mess. William shakes hands with Robert, and Oliver says,

'This is William, Binki's previous boss,' with a look that dares me to mention he is the same guy I shared a house with.

'Nice to meet you and good to see you Binki. Did you get transferred from *The Manor* too?' he smiles.

'Oh no, we were already booked,' says Oliver.

I snap my head round to look at him. How can he lie like that?

'I'd better get back,' William says.

I want to say so much but all that comes out of my mouth is,

'It is nice to see you.'

'You too,' he responds.

And then he has gone. I wonder what the going rate is to hire a hit man to knock off Andrea. I need to talk to Muffy, or maybe I should pop back to the ladies, the restaurant loo is a good listener. I pull the tomato from my cleavage and knock back some wine as I remind myself of the facts: William is marrying Andrea and I'm marrying Oliver, and the truth is, if we're looking at the evidence your honour, I wouldn't be marrying Oliver if I thought I had a chance with William, but I don't have a chance because: (a) He is engaged to Andrea. (b) According to Piers Roche, he is not the marrying type and (c) According to Nathan, I'm not William's type. So there you have it. The whole thing is out of the question and I can't hanker after someone I'll never be able to have.

'Here, have some of my sirloin,' says Oliver, wrapping an arm around me. 'I know what you fancy.'

Actually, I think he doesn't know at all.

Chapter Thirty-Five

'Good luck.' Oliver kisses me on the cheek, grabs his briefcase and flies out the door of our flat, tripping over my shoes as he does so.

'Oh Oliver, can you phone Douglas today and check he's got the flowers organised?' I ask, placing the breakfast dishes into the sink.

'What flowers?'

God, men, they should be drowned at birth.

'For the buttonholes, he's supposed to be organising that. Get him to phone my dad if he's unsure.'

I don't want to be thinking about carnations and buttonholes. Today is my final dress fitting and if the dress doesn't fit I'm in real shit street. Muffy's dress is organised and Fran's little boy's outfit is sorted. My mum is finally happy with her hat and the car is booked, and the honeymoon arranged. Two weeks in Tuscany. It's all we could afford with the new house and everything, but I'm happy. Everyone seems to think we should be flying to the Caribbean or something. I mean why? Isn't that where all the other newly-weds will be? A touch overcrowded with hand-in-hand doe-eyed lovers don't you think? The Dorchester has everything perfectly organised and all I've got to do is pray the dress fits. I've not been near the chocolate teapot. In fact Muffy has taken it away and hidden it somewhere. She promises to return it after the wedding. I'm attending the fitting alone and I am quite relieved to be honest. The thought of hearing everyone's groans if the zip doesn't do up is too much to bear. Muffy couldn't make it as she has an important meeting and I purposely didn't tell Mum it was today. So Amanda the fitter, who fortunately prefers to be called Mandy, and I will have to groan together and come up with a Plan B, which we probably should have come up with months ago but hey ho. I feel sure I've lost tons of weight. I feel lighter. Of course it could just be wishful thinking. God, I feel sick. I've got no idea what I will do if it doesn't fit. I walk into the bathroom and see Oliver's towel folded neatly over the rail. His shaving gel sits on the shelf with the lid on, and his toothbrush stands erect alongside his special sensitive gum toothpaste. I brush my teeth, forcing myself not to think of the untidy bathroom back at Driftwood, but of course you do don't you? It's impossible not to think of something when you tell yourself not to think of it. I wrap my scarf around my neck and throw on my woollen poncho. The weather is milder today so I leave my hat and pull my hair into a messy bun. I head out of the flat to face the dreaded fitting and walk along the streets of Notting Hill enjoying the busyness. Turning into Portobello Road I spot a market stand with a load of beautiful teapots. The temptation to buy one is overwhelming. I could have one for M&Ms and another for chocolate buttons.

'Three quid darling and they're real china. No rubbish 'ere. I'm practically giving them away,' says the stallholder.

The thought of chocolate sends a craving through me and I hurry past. I'm determined to overdose when on my honeymoon, on chocolate, I mean, in case you thought I was talking suicide. Marrying Oliver isn't that terrible. I take the bus to Knightsbridge. The closer I get to the shop the more my stomach churns. I stop at Starbucks and order a latte and then quickly change it to a skinny latte. Honestly, as if what I drink now is going to make any difference. My phone bleeps with a text as I leave Starbucks and I fumble in my bag for it. I pull my phone out as I turn the corner and bang, my latte and phone are knocked out of my hand, and my handbag slips from my shoulder as I collide with a hard firm body. I feel myself lurch backwards as I try to recover the handbag. The latte splashes over my hand, down my poncho and onto my boots. Déjà vu or what?

'Can I call you back Andy,' says a familiar voice.

God, I don't believe this. I look up into William's eyes.

'Perhaps if you hadn't have been chatting to *Andy* in the first place this wouldn't have happened,' I say, rubbing my poncho with a tissue. 'Don't you have an office to go to?' I smile.

'I think you walked into me. You're making a terrible mess of your poncho,' he responds.

I can't stop my heart from thumping and I feel sure he must be able to see it pounding away through my clothes. I dust off the bits of tissue and lift my head to look at him. His grey eyes are twinkling and he is grinning. His appealing cupid's bow affects me the way it did the first time we met. He is wearing a dark blue suit, again, and carrying a rucksack and I feel like I've travelled back in time. He scoops up my phone and the bottle of aspirin.

'I think you've lost a few of these.'

'Well that's the suicide cancelled then isn't it,' I laugh. 'I was looking forward to that too.'

'I'm sure things aren't that bad,' he says, his hand touching mine softly as he hands the bottle to me.

'To be frank it is. I'm on my way to my final dress fitting at *Victoria's Bridal* and last time it wouldn't zip up. I've done everything apart from having my flesh surgically removed. If the thing doesn't fit this time I don't know what I'll do.'

He pulls a face.

'Oh dear, sounds nerve-wracking,' he says, rolling his eyes.

'It's all right for you men. You just buy a better suit don't you?'

I drop my mobile into my bag and hesitate. I'm running late but I don't want to say goodbye.

'Are you off to a meeting?' I ask.

He shakes his head.

'Just left one, was going for a coffee actually. Maybe I can get you another?'

He looks at me hopefully.

'I'm late for the fitting but … Well you could come to the fitting with me. They do great coffee there actually, and chocolate biscuits,' I say boldly, feeling my shoulders tense in anticipation of him saying no.

He looks thoughtful.

'Unless you have somewhere else you should be,' I add quickly, making it easier for him to say no.

He bites his lip and feelings I really shouldn't have run through me.

'No, I haven't. Isn't Muffy meeting you there?'

I shake my head.

'She had a meeting.'

'Okay, let's do it,' he smiles.

He tucks my arm through his.

'Lead the way.'

Sophie doesn't bat an eyelid when I walk into *Victoria's Bridal* with William. She settles us on her cosy white couches and gets us coffee.

'So, we'll let you get your breath and then we will try the dress, and I feel certain it will fit. I can see you have lost weight,' says Sophie.

I feel a bit more confident. William removes his jacket and takes off his tie, reminding me of when he had done that in the kitchen at Driftwood.

'How is Driftwood?' I ask

'Quieter now you're not there,' he smiles.

'I wasn't that noisy.'

Sophie hands a plate of biscuits to him.

'For you only,' she says to William. 'Now, let's get this fitting done before us girls both collapse from anxiety.'

Oh God, any confidence I may have felt left me with that one sentence. I follow her to the fitting room.

'You won't leave will you?' I call over my shoulder.

'I'm going to enjoy my biscuits and while I'm at it I'll eat your share.'

'Bastard.'

He laughs and my heart beats even faster. My whole body is a tremble. I can't believe he is marrying that beauty-tweeting bitch bloody Andrea.

'God Binki, you're shaking all over. It will be fine. If it doesn't fit we'll do something. There are always ways around these things,' consoles Mandy.

I'm barely thinking about the dress now if I'm honest. I look at it hanging on the stand and check my reflection in the dressing room mirror. I look radiant and it's not often I think that about myself I can tell you. Tendrils of hair have escaped the messy bun and hang loosely around my neck. My cheeks are flushed and I do look a bit slimmer, not loads but hopefully, please God, enough to get into the dress. I slide out of my clothes and exhale as Mandy takes the dress from the stand.

'Ready?' she asks.

I feel like I'm being led out to a firing squad instead of going to try my wedding dress for the most important day of my life. I nod nervously and step into the dress. She gently pulls it up and I slide my arms into the cool fabric and slip it over my shoulders. It fits snugly on my hips and I take a deep breath.

'Right,' says Mandy, and I feel her yank the zipper. I will myself not to hold my breath. It has to fit without that. The dress gets tighter as she pulls up the zip and then ...

'It fits,' she cries.

I fight the desire to literally cry myself.

'Oh Binki, it's beautiful and it fits a treat. Look,' says Sophie.

She twirls me around and I come face to face with myself in my wedding dress. It hangs perfectly and I really do look like a fairy-tale princess. Before I realise what she is doing she has whisked open the curtains and is saying to William,

'So what do you think?'

William slowly puts his coffee cup down without taking his eyes off me. He opens his mouth to speak and closes it again.

'You don't like it?' I say. 'It's supposed to give me a *Grace Kelly* look, you know, before she died remember,' I say.

He swallows.

'You look sensational, and a hundred times more stunning than Grace Kelly,' he says finally.

I smile.

'Really, you're not just saying that?'

'I never lie, remember?'

'Once you did,' I say softly.

'It wasn't strictly a lie I just held back the truth,' he smiles.

Our eyes lock and I think we would have stayed that way had Sophie not pulled me back to the dressing room.

'Right, let's get this off and do a final veil check and then you can have a chocolate biscuit if your brother has left any.'

I don't correct her and neither does William.

'I've put two to one side,' he calls.

I see my phone flashing in my bag and remember the text from earlier. It is from Muffy.

'Sweetie, can you phone when you get out of the fitting. I feel like shit and had to go home, gone down with some bug. Do you

think Oliver will go with you to Ronnie Scott's tonight? God, I'm so sorry.'

Shit. I was so looking forward to that too. Oliver sitting through an evening of jazz music is almost unthinkable. God it's like asking him to sit through *Strictly Come Dancing*. I tap in her number.

'Hello,' she says croakily.

'Just checking you're really sick,' I say.

'God, I'm not sick, I'm dying. I think you should make arrangements for a stand-in maid of honour,' she groans.

'You'll survive,' I laugh.

'I've never puked so much in my life. Do you think Oliver will go?' she asks anxiously.

'Yes, of course he will. If not my mum would love to, so don't worry and at least I have the tickets,' I lie, knowing that Oliver hates jazz and that my mum probably would come but under sufferance.

'Dare I ask, did the dress …'

'Yes,' I say excitedly, and am about to tell her about William when she breaks in with,

'God, I'm going to puke again. Phone me later.'

The phone goes dead. I toss it back into my bag and throw on the rest of my clothes before joining William.

'I'll get the veil and we'll have a fiddle,' says Mandy.

'Sounds delightful,' I say.

'You have everything else, the something borrowed, and the something blue?' Sophie asks.

'I see what you mean about it being easier for us men,' laughs William.

I reach across him for a chocolate biscuit, expecting him to move back slightly but he doesn't, and my face comes close to his. He smiles at me shyly. I grab the biscuit and lean back feeling my legs tremble.

'Mum is giving me the something borrowed but I have still to get the something blue.'

'Ah,' says William, 'that's on me then. What's the usual blue thing women have for their wedding?'

Sophie laughs.

'That is such a *man thing* to say, but usually a garter unless you have one already Binki?'

I shake my head. God, I can't let William buy me a blue garter for my wedding day, Oliver would have a thousand canary fits, no two thousand more like if he knew. She brings a tray of garters for him to look at, and he rolls his eyes.

'Not what I imagined I would be doing when I woke up this morning,' he says, fingering the lacy garters and affecting my loins in a way they haven't been affected in years.

'It seems fitting that I of all people should buy you something blue,' he laughs holding up a particularly pretty garter. 'Just remember not to wash it with your white jumper. How about this one? Do you want to try it?' he asks.

I shake my head, thinking it is perfect and exactly what I would have chosen myself.

'Your brother has good taste. I'll put it with the rest of your things,' says Sophie.

I sip my coffee. I'm finding it hard to know what to say to him. I want to ask him about beauty-tweeting bitch Andrea but I can't.

'I've been demoted from husband to brother it seems,' he laughs. 'I can't imagine what Andy would make of that one.'

His phone rings and he excuses himself to take the call. It's obviously Andrea. I wonder if he will tell her he is with me.

'Right, let's try this veil,' says Sophie.

I follow her over to the dressing room again as two women enter the shop. I slip into the dress again and she settles the veil on my head and fiddles with it for a bit while I wonder if I should ask Oliver to come with me to Ronnie Scott's but I know he will hate it.

'I'll come if you can't find anyone else. Have you asked your mum?' he says.

'I'll do that now. How is your day?' I ask, slipping on the garter to see how it looks.

'Bloody manic actually. I probably wouldn't be able to get away in time anyway. How is the fitting, was it okay?'

'Yes, everything fits.'

'Phew,' he laughs. 'Just a few more days and we'll be relaxing in Tuscany.'

The garter looks lovely and I stare at it for several seconds before saying,

'I'd better go, we're adjusting the veil.'

'Okay Hun, see you later, text me what you're doing.'

I spot William wander back into the shop and the two women turn to look at him. One nudges the other and giggles. He smiles at them and looks around for me.

'Trying on the garter,' I say.

'Come and see,' says Sophie.

No! I really should tell her he isn't my brother. This is getting out of hand. Nicely out of hand I admit, but out of hand all the same. He pops his head around the curtain and I lift the dress timidly, and give him a glimpse of the garter. He nods approvingly.

'I hope Oliver appreciates it,' he says, pulling the curtain.

Ten minutes later and I'm finished. I tidy my hair, apply some lipstick and hug Sophie warmly. The whole time my thoughts have been on William. He has been with me for nearly two hours, surely he will have to leave soon. He is sitting relaxed on the couch when I come out, chatting about work on his phone. He gives me the thumbs up and finishes the call.

'Is that it? Your wedding officially sorted?'

I nod.

'Yep.'

I'm struggling to think of ways to keep him here but bloody nothing is coming to mind. Aside from having a sudden fainting spell I'm totally buggered, and in a few minutes I'll be saying goodbye and who knows when I'll see him again. We leave the shop and step outside and I shiver. It was so warm in the shop that I had forgotten how chilly it was outside. I wrap my scarf around me and push my hands into my poncho pocket.

'Well,' says William, looking down the street.

'It was nice seeing you and thanks so much for being a support,' I say.

'It was fun,' he says hailing down a cab.

Oh no, think of something Binki, but nothing remotely sensible comes to mind. The cab pulls up beside us.

'Can I drop you somewhere?' William asks.

Yes, off Tower Bridge sounds a good idea. He moves towards me and I put my arms around him with the intention of giving him a goodbye hug. His arms pull me closer and his lips nuzzle my neck.

'Have a great wedding,' he says into my ear and then steps into the cab. My hand reaches out to the door before he can pull it closed and I lean in and hear myself say,

'I don't suppose you're free a bit later. I've got tickets for Ronnie Scott's. It's Muffy's birthday present to me, but she's gone down with a stomach bug and Oliver hates jazz and ...'

'Get in,' he says.

'What?' I say.

'Get in the cab.'

'Right,' I mumble, throwing in my bag.

Chapter Thirty-Six

So here I am again in yet another restaurant talking to the loo. I'm beginning to think that restaurant loos are not given anywhere near the credit they deserve. They are not mentioned at all in any self-help book. I should write my own self-help book called *Loo Therapy,* or words to that effect. I find it is a great place to be really mindful, and no one interrupts you. You can sit on your little toilet seat safe in the knowledge that no one will disturb you and you can have your own little meltdown in your own little public loo, which is precisely what I'm doing now. Have I gone totally insane? What am I doing? I'm having dinner with another man, who I'm not only deeply attracted to but am beginning to think in love with too. I'm getting married in five days and what is worse, I've not told Oliver the truth. When he'd texted and asked if I was okay for Ronnie Scott's, I simply said *yes,* and when he presumed I was going with my mum I didn't correct him. I'm being unfaithful to my husband and I haven't married him yet. Not that William and I have done anything apart from have dinner but I swear if he swept everything off the table and sprawled me on it, I'd be his for the taking. He can have me with the soup of the day any time. This is awful. What's worse is that I'm sure he was seeing Andrea this evening. Of course I can't be sure. He had assured me that he had nothing important on this evening.

'Nothing I can't get out of,' he had said, but on returning from my second loo therapy session I overheard him finish a conversation with her,

'Apologise for me will you Andrea? And we'll do dinner with them together next week. I couldn't say no to this proposition, Phil will understand. I'll see you later.'

He had hung up quickly on seeing me. I've now left him to pay the bill and order a taxi where we will drive to my flat so I can change for Ronnie Scott's. I'm praying Oliver hasn't come home or I might have trouble explaining who is in the waiting taxi outside the flat. I keep trying to tell myself that everything about the evening is completely innocent, but I know that just about everything is far from innocent. Admittedly we've kept our dinner conversation to basics like work, the offices at Driftwood and how they are finally finished, but we're both acutely aware that we have been dishonest with our prospective spouses and there is only one reason you would do that, right? Which means this whole evening isn't completely innocent is it? I reluctantly leave the loo and my little private therapy session and walk back to our table where he is waiting for me.

'Ready?' he asks.

'I should pay my half of the bill,' I say, putting on my poncho.

'No way, I'm getting a free ticket to Ronnie Scott's. The cab is outside.'

He takes my hand like it is the most natural thing in the world. He tips the waiter and says,

'Thanks Louis, see you next time.'

'I hope so Mr Ellis. Good evening madam.'

I smile and feel William's arm slide around my waist as he directs me to the cab. The drive to the flat is short, and thankfully Oliver isn't home. I pull my best evening dress from the wardrobe. You know the one, the little black dress that always comes out for weddings, christenings, bar mitzvahs and of course, jazz evenings. I tie a silk white scarf around my neck to complement the dress, and pop some pearl studs into my ears before redoing my make-up and hair. I slip my feet into a pair of black heels and finally throw my coat over the whole lot while a little voice in my head whispers *It's not right you know*. Why is it these little voices try to put a damper on everything? It's a night at a jazz club not a night in a Travelodge, although I am wondering which would be preferable, and that's a first because I have never craved a night at a Travelodge before, even more so after my exploits in them with Oliver. As usual William is on the phone when I step into the cab, and continues to stay on it the whole journey to Ronnie Scott's. He finishes as we pull up and pays the driver before I have a chance to reach into my bag. When I complain he smiles.

'If I remember you always were a bit slow getting that purse out,' he says.

'That's not true,' I protest as he takes my arm.

'You look nice by the way.'

I'm glad it's dark and he cannot see my blushes. We enter the club and I'm immediately swept along by the atmosphere. A prettily dressed woman is offering around a tray of *Baileys*.

'Ben Bailey is our artist tonight. A little treat,' she says. William goes to take two glasses but I shake my head. Just a taste of anything that looks like chocolate will tip me over the edge.

'I've got to get into that dress in five days' time,' I say, fighting the temptation.

For us addicts anything that reminds us of the smooth melt-in-the-mouth creaminess of chocolate is an absolute nightmare. Seriously, I could snort a whole tin of cocoa powder right now, I feel that desperate.

'I was trying hard not to remember that?' he says quietly.

I turn expecting to see his usual smile but there isn't one. He guides me to the bar and orders a Bacardi Breezer and a whisky. We don't speak for a time and just sip at the drinks.

'Sorry,' he says finally, 'I should have asked if you wanted a wine or something?'

'This is perfect,' I say.

He turns on his stool to face me.

'When is your wedding?' I say quickly.

Why the sodding hell I said that I do not know. He looks a bit taken aback and shakes his head.

'I don't know. We're not organised like you. I guess we'll just do it one weekend when we've got nothing else on,' he replies gesturing to the barman for another whisky.

'I would have invited you. It's Oliver and ...'

He rests his hand on mine.

'It's fine. I'm happy to know you'll be wearing my garter,' he smiles.

Right Binki, chapter one of *Loo Therapy* should be titled *Don't fall in love with your best friend,* and should follow with *Never go to a jazz club with your best friend*, especially if he is a man, and more importantly, do not let said best friend buy your wedding garter. But most of all make sure you drink only one Bacardi

Breezer even if he drinks two glasses of whisky. But of course, I haven't written the book yet so I can't follow its advice can I? I have a second Bacardi Breezer. Second chapter should be titled *Jazz music is a No No*. Unless you hate it of course, because the artist may ask for requests and your best friend requests your favourite song *It had to be You* and you feel so sodding sad and fumble around in your handbag pulling out everything from a lipstick with the top off to a pair of frilly knickers which you end up blowing your nose on because you can't find a tissue until finally your best friend will hand you a tissue which you take and your hands that touch will somehow stay together for the rest of the evening. His hand is warm and I feel I should move it but somehow I can't. As the club empties he turns towards me, unclasping his hand from mine as he does so.

'Do you come to Ronnie Scott's a lot?' he asks simply.

'Oliver doesn't like jazz, so no not really.'

'But you do?'

'Yes I do,' I smile.

'Me too,' he says. 'We both like jazz don't we?'

He pulls his phone from his pocket and turns it on. It bleeps immediately.

'Yes,' I say.

'I think we missed something of an opportunity somewhere along the line,' he says adding softly, 'C'est la vie.'

Before I can respond his phone rings and lights up with Andrea's name, and he shrugs apologetically. I turn my Blackberry on which also rings with a voicemail message. Before I can check it, my phone rings again and Oliver's name flashes onto the screen and I also find myself thinking *c'est la vie*.

I ask the cab driver to stop the cab at the end of my street. I know it's stupid, I'm sure Oliver isn't looking out of the window but if he is, and sees me saying goodnight to William, well let's be honest, it doesn't bear thinking about. I fumble in my bag to William's chuckling.

'Don't start. I'm paying,' he says, putting his hand on mine.

I sigh.

'I wish you wouldn't keep doing that,' I say before I can stop myself.

'Paying for cabs? I've been doing it for years. I can't be bothered to drive around town ...'

'Putting your hand on mine,' I say softly.

I won't see him again I'm sure. I really can't imagine Oliver and me having dinner with Mr and Mrs Ellis, aka William and Andrea, or out for an evening bowling with Andrea and William can you?

'Right,' he says quietly, removing his hand.

The cab driver clears his throat.

'I should go,' I say lifting the door handle. 'Thanks for a wonderful evening.'

I'm about to open the taxi door when I feel his arms around me and his lips crushing mine. My body melts and I just drown in the kiss which feels so perfect that it can't possibly be right. I can't think and my body arches towards him. He releases me and I open my eyes to find myself looking straight into his.

'C'est la vie,' he whispers. 'I always leave things too late.'

He opens the door for me and I sit feeling like Kate Winslet on the life raft, calling to Jack in the film *Titanic* and wanting to scream *come back, come back*.

'Maybe one day we'll have a coffee for old time's sake,' he says.

I nod. For the first time in my life I can't speak. If I attempt to I am sure it will not be anything coherent. I climb from the cab and before I can say goodbye the door has closed and the cab is pulling away. I watch it until it disappears around the corner and make my way slowly to the entrance of our flat.

Chapter Thirty-Seven

'Cock it,' yells Muffy, skidding towards me as her foot lands on a stray heated roller.

'Oh, there it is,' says Wes, who had agreed to be my hairdresser for the day, at an exorbitant fee I might add.

'Have you seen my pink lipstick?' Muffy asks, limping around the room. 'Christ, I think I've got three degree burns from that bloody thing Wes.'

Wes winds the stray roller into my hair and surveys me.

'Right, I'll have a tea darling while they do their magic,' he says, disappearing to the kitchen. I feel so sick I'm sure I will throw up all over the wedding dress. It hangs outside my mum's wardrobe and the veil and wedding train lie on the bed in my parents' spare room.

'Are you doing my make-up Muffy?' I ask anxiously. 'How much time do we have?'

Muffy flops onto the bed and sighs.

'About three hours, plenty of time. I'm bloody exhausted and your parents have got the heating up so high. I feel like I'm going to pass out, and my foot is throbbing like buggery.'

'Mum can you turn the heating down?' I yell, feeling perspiration running from my armpits. I sniff under my arms and groan.

'I'll have to shower again,' I moan.

'Just do the arms and spray with loads of deodorant,' says Muffy, falling back onto the bed.

Her hair is freshly washed and hangs beautifully in gorgeous waves. Wes is going to put it in a chignon at her neck and dress it with the pearls we had bought at *Victoria's Bridal*. I feel sure she will look a hundred times more stunning than me, and I really don't mind. I finger the pearl earrings and necklace that sit in the white satin of a box that Oliver had given to me last night.

'I want you to know that you have made me the happiest man in the whole world,' he had said.

I had opened the box to find the pearls.

'I want to see you in only these on our wedding night,' he had said huskily.

I fiddle with them and jump at a knock on the door.

'What was that?' calls Dad from the other side.

'I asked if the heating could go down,' shouts Muffy.

What the sodding hell is my dad doing here? Why isn't he at the church making sure everything is going okay? He knows I don't trust that bloody Douglas, who is no doubt already pissed on rum. He's another one into the pirate malarkey. If he and Oliver had their way I swear we'd have been dressed as bloody pirates for the wedding. God, I hope he hasn't got Oliver playing that stupid pirate game. When those two get together they get so immature.

'Christ Dad, why are you here?'

I open the door where he is hovering outside.

'I didn't know if you'd be dressed,' he says. 'Didn't like to come in.'

He's wearing his dressing gown and slippers. I nearly faint at the sight. This is a disaster, a complete and total disaster.

'Why aren't you dressed?' I yell. 'You should be dressed and checking everything is okay at the church, Mum, where are you?' I shriek.

'I was practising my speech, and anyway I'm taking you to the church in the car,' says Dad frowning, 'but not for a few hours yet.'

'Oh no,' I cry.

'Christ Binki, take a Valium or something. You're overstressing,' says Muffy forcing herself from the bed.

Mum bounds up the stairs, panic written all over her face.

'You know what Douglas is like, he's worse than Oliver with his pirate stuff. They'll get playing that stupid bloody strip the pirate game to see who can destroy the boat first and capture the woman and then Oliver will never get ready and ...'

'Good God, what on earth are you on about,' says Mum. 'What boat and what woman?'

Oh for God's sake.

'It's an online game,' sighs Muffy. 'All very boring, the woman strips every time you hit the boat, you know, men's stupid games.'

'I've never seen that one,' says Dad.

'And you never will,' says Mum firmly. 'Now, what's the panic?' she asks breathlessly. 'Does the dress not fit?'

'What is Dad doing here in his dressing gown,' I say, sounding hysterical. No, that's not true. I *am* hysterical.

'Well, he lives here dear,' says Mum.

For God's sake have they gone totally insane? They're too young for dementia so it has to be insanity doesn't it?

'I know he bloody lives here but today he is supposed to be at the church, checking everything is okay, preferably in a wedding suit as opposed to his sodding dressing gown. I don't trust Oliver's best man, I told you that,' I snap, bursting into tears. 'It's my wedding day, the happiest day of my life,' I sob.

'Yes, one can see that,' says Muffy dryly.

'It's all going wrong,' I say. 'I knew it would. Oh God, give me the bloody chocolate teapot Muffy.'

She holds her hands up in front of me like a traffic policeman.

'Now calm down Binki. You said no matter what happens or how much you beg I was not to give you the chocolate teapot. Not until after the ceremony. You'll overdose when you're this stressed.'

'I don't care what I said,' I say walking menacingly towards her. 'Give it to me now.'

'Christ,' says Muffy backing away. 'She's bloody possessed.'

'Bernard, get dressed now and down to the church,' instructs Mum. 'And make sure you're back here by twelve.'

'But ...' interrupts Dad.

'Now Bernard,' she says firmly.

'Right,' says Dad disappearing down the hall.

'Can you turn the heating down?' yells Muffy. 'I swear the Sahara is cooler than in here.'

Mum grabs my arm and sits me down.

'Now listen to me dear. You have three hours. Your dad will be back in plenty of time. Douglas phoned to say everything is fine his end. The buttonhole flowers are all ready, there have been no problems. You just have to make yourself beautiful.

Now, do you want Sylvia to come round and help, she just phoned and …'

'No,' I yell.

'That's just as well because I told her we had a houseful as it was.'

'Hello Mrs Grayson, do you have any Earl Grey sweetie? I can't possibly drink PG Tips,' calls Wes.

'Just coming dear,' calls Mum. 'Are you okay if I go down to the kitchen, you won't do anything stupid will you?'

Do something stupid? I'm already doing something stupid. I'm bloody marrying Oliver aren't I?

Chapter Thirty-Eight

Meanwhile back at the flat

'Arrr, the hair of the scurvy dog me matey?' suggests Douglas, pulling a bottle of champagne from the fridge along with a slab of cheese.

'This and some cheese on toast will do the trick.'

'Put that back you wanker, that's for when we move into the new house.'

'The cheese or the champagne?' laughs Douglas, making Oliver's head thump even more. 'Or maybe both, I have to give it to you; you two know how to live.'

'Don't get anything down that shirt either. That's all we need right now,' groans Oliver.

'You need to chill out mate. Christ, if this is what marriage does, you can keep it.'

Douglas puts the bottle back and rummages through the cupboard for a bottle of rum while Oliver drops two more Alka Seltzer into a glass.

'I blame you for this hangover. What the fuck did you lot put in my drinks last night?' he asks while throwing a carefully aimed parrot at Douglas.

Douglas laughs.

'Don't ask me mate, buggered if I can remember. After that fourth vodka and fifth lap dancer I'd had it. Christ, that brunette was a goer. Wore me out she did. I won't be doing anything for a while.'

Oliver buries his head in his hands. He'd never had a hangover like this in his life. What the hell had he been thinking of? He'd promised Binki he wouldn't drink too much and he'd probably drunk more than he ever had in his whole life. Will he ever learn?

The last time he had drunk too much look what had happened? He thinks back to that lunchtime on Christmas Eve and feels that small tingle of excitement that always follows memories of that day. It was a mistake but he hasn't forgotten the mind blowing sex. He loves Binki, but she certainly lacks something in that department. He seriously hopes after the wedding and once they are settled in the new house things will pick up in that area. If not he may have to convince her to seek some kind of help. He can't spend his married life spicing it up by thinking about a one-night stand, or in this case a one-afternoon stand. It's not his fault he knows that, because Christ, when she does explode she's like a firework display, so he's doing everything right. She's just not very adventurous and he can't for the life of him understand why the pirate fantasy doesn't work for her. Amanda had been dead keen to try on the outfit. God, what is he doing? The last person he should be thinking about right now is Amanda. He does miss her tight little arse walking past him at the office though. He shakes his head to push the memory from it and feels his head thump.

'Bloody good night though wasn't it?' laughs Douglas, giving up the search for the rum and filling the kettle instead.

'Black coffee for you sonny boy. Need you looking like something on earth to meet the old ball and chain.'

'It's not a bloody prison sentence,' Oliver snaps throwing back the Alka Seltzer.

'Trust me there won't be nights again like last night and while I remember you need to get that lap dancer's phone number off your iPhone, and her text message.'

'Shit,' mumbles Oliver, scrambling for his phone. The flat intercom buzzes and Douglas goes to answer it.

'Maybe it's her, one last quickie,' laughs Douglas.

'Christ, I didn't did I?' Oliver groans.

Douglas opens the door to the florist holding boxes of carnations.

'Great, shove them in the kitchen will you.'

The fragrance from the flowers makes Oliver feel nauseous, and the text from the lap dancer doesn't help either. Christ, he hopes nothing happened with her. It's no good asking Douglas, his memory of last night is worse than his own. Still, this is what happens at stag nights isn't it? It's bloody expected that the groom will end up wasted. That's one good thing. If he was that pissed then the chances of him having done anything were pretty slim.

'Jesus, I'm going to throw up,' he declares, rushing to the bathroom.

'Best thing mate, get it out now. You've got a few hours yet before your life is over.'

Oliver retches over the toilet bowl still holding his phone. It bleeps and he glances at the screen and sees it is a text from Amanda. Great, just what he didn't need today.

Chapter Thirty-Nine

'God, I want to cry,' says Muffy. 'You look like a real princess. You really do.'

Even I don't recognise myself. Muffy has performed miracles with make-up. I have acquired high cheekbones and thick long black lashes, and if I don't resemble Grace Kelly I certainly look like a film star. I only wish I could look like this every day, not wearing a wedding dress obviously, that would be a bit weird, I mean looking glamorous like Andrea always does.

'I look amazing,' I say, my voice sounding miles away and not belonging to me at all.

'It's all down to Touché Éclat darling,' says Muffy.

The dress fits to perfection. The lacy sleeves stand out against my pink painted fingernails. Wes has done wonders with a few heated rollers and a styling brush. I look stunning and I find myself thinking how I wish William could see me. Mum spreads the train around me so Dad can take photos. Muffy stands beside me and we hug for a picture and she then kisses me on the cheek.

'I'd better go. Come on Bella or else the bride will be there before us.'

Mum gets all tearful.

'I'm so proud. Now don't rush her down the aisle Bernard. Take your time,' she sniffs.

'The car is here. We'll go when you're ready, okay?' says Dad. 'I'm just going to check I've got everything. You just close your eyes and relax. It's going to be wonderful.'

I take Dad's advice and close my eyes, except for the occasional peep at myself in the mirror. I tell myself I'm getting married. It only seems like a few moments before Dad says,

'Ready, love, we should go.'

I look up at him in his smart new suit and smile.

'I think so,' I say.

God, I've never been so unsure of anything in my whole life.

'This is the first day of the rest of your life,' smiles Dad.

Shit and double shit. This feels like the *last* day of the rest of my life, the last day of being Binki Grayson and the beginning of the rest of my life with Oliver and lots of mini Olivers or Olivias. But it is the right decision isn't it? He's a good man. I'm thirty, and how many good men are there out there? Apart from the odd few with bloody warts on their noses, or God forbid, warts somewhere else, and the divorced and desperate men. What's left at my age? No, Oliver is the right one. He's stable and in a good job, unlike William, who never knows what will happen from one day to the next. One day he could have work and the next ... What am I doing? I shouldn't be thinking about another man on my wedding day. I've chosen the right man. He loves me and I love him. I can sort out the being in love thing afterwards. There are loads of books I can read and maybe Oliver can see someone about his pirate fetish. That's not normal but everyone has their oddities, right?

All the neighbours are standing at their gates as I walk towards the white Rolls-Royce.

'Congratulations darling, good luck', they cheer.

Dad helps me into the car and folds the train around me before climbing in.

'Alright love?' he asks.

I nod while wondering if it is normal to feel so unsure on the most important day of your life. I glance down at my engagement ring and finger the pearls in my ears.

'I feel a bit sick,' I whisper into my dad's ear.

'I've got some water, will that help?'

I nod and he hands me a bottle of sparkling water. Great, the last thing I want to do is go belching down the aisle isn't it? I shake my head and hand it back.

'How about some nice calming music?' says the chauffeur. 'I have it especially; you'd be surprised how many nervous brides I've had in this car.'

I lay my head back and take a deep breath as he pushes a CD into the music player. I'd just inhaled and was about to exhale slowly when Tony Bennett's *It Had to Be You* begins to play. I snap open my eyes, exhale and stare at the chauffeur, is this some kind of joke? I mean of all the bloody songs he must have in his little collection he chooses to play this one.

'Perfect huh?' he says, smiling at me through the rear-view mirror.

He begins to sing along.

'Played this at my own wedding, what's your song?' he asks.

I feel Dad pull his jacket sleeve up to check the time on his watch and all I can think is, this is *our* song. Not Oliver's and mine but William's and mine. I struggle to think of a song that Oliver and I share and realise we don't actually have one. We'd chosen to start the dancing with W*hen a Man Loves a Woman* but I was surprised Oliver didn't want to start it with *Yo Ho, Yo Ho, a Pirate's Life For Me*. God, have I gone completely mad? I'm marrying the wrong sodding man and it takes me to be in the bloody wedding car to finally realise it. I can't marry a man who plays pirate computer games, not to mention playing them for real during our lovemaking. Most of all, I can't marry *someone* just because I'm thirty and I ought to be marrying *someone,* most of all I can't marry Oliver because I love someone else. I may not be able to marry William and maybe William doesn't want to marry me, well, I'm quite certain William doesn't want to marry me. Who would want to marry me when they can marry someone like Andrea, with her big breasts and stick-thin legs, not to mention her natural elegance and sophistication which I could never ever hope to achieve? But just because I'm not Miss Perfect it doesn't mean I have to marry Mr Not-So-Perfect does it? I don't have to settle for second best just because the clock is ticking do I? Of course you do, whispers a voice. He's waiting for you. The reception is booked, the food is prepared, all the guests are arriving, and presents have been bought. In other words, your face is on the tea towel now. Christ, can you imagine if there really were tea towels with Oliver's and my face on them? I cringe at the thought. Plus, continues the voice, your dad is in the car with you, Muffy is waiting at the church, the vicar is primed and ready to go. You can't back out now, and besides do you remember what your wedding dress cost?

Oh fuck it.

'Dad, can I use your mobile?' I say breathlessly.

He shakes his head.

'I didn't bring it dear.'

Shit, shit.

'Do you want to borrow mine love? Everything all right?' asks the chauffer.

No everything is as wrong as wrong can be.

'Yes, I mean no, everything is not fine but yes, can I borrow it for a sec.'

The minute he hands it to me I realise I don't know Muffy's number. Oh for God's sake. How can I not know her number? I hate technology; it makes me not know my best friend's phone number. She's just down as *Muffy* in my contacts. That's not natural is it? Why didn't I bring my bag? Because brides don't carry bags, you idiot, whispers the voice. God, I hope Muffy has her phone with her.

'Here we go,' says the chauffeur and I see the church approaching. Oh buggery fuck. Muffy stands at the entrance all smiles, holding her bouquet delicately in her hands, and the photographer is positioned ready to capture the moment that I step out of the Rolls. I scrutinise Muffy to see if she has a bag, but there is nothing. Oh, buggety bugger it all. Douglas waves and rushes into the church, no doubt to tell Oliver that the bride has arrived. God, this is getting worse by the second.

'You've got to get out Dad,' I say.

'Yes, I know dear, give me a moment and then Muffy and I can help you out with the dress.'

Dear God, please don't let my dad have a heart attack.

'Dad, you need to get out and Muffy needs to get in. I'm the one not getting out of the car.'

'What?' says Dad and the chauffeur in unison.

'Oh no, I hate it when this happens,' moans the driver.

'I don't understand,' says Dad halfway between getting out of the car and staying in it.

Muffy stands by the door looking confused. She peeks in almost headbutting my dad.

'What's going on?' she asks.

'She's not getting out of the car,' says the driver.

'Oh God,' she groans.

'Do you have your Blackberry,' I hiss.

'What,' she says fiddling with the bouquet, like she doesn't now know what she is supposed to do with it.

'Do you have your Blackberry?' I repeat pushing Dad out of the car.

'Oh dear,' he mumbles. 'Is it that you can't get out of the car or ...?'

'I can't go through with it,' I say with a little sob. 'Tell Oliver I'm terribly sorry.'

'Oh cock it,' groans Muffy.

'Is that a yes?' I snap.

'What?' she asks helping my dad from the car.

'Do you have your ...' I shout.

'Yes,' she yells.

'Get in.'

'Hang on a minute,' says the driver.

'Don't worry you'll get paid,' I say.

'Christ Binki, have you lost your mind?' asks Muffy, hesitating by the door.

'Oh dear, oh dear, what do I tell your mother?' says Dad.

I can't stand this. I pull Muffy into the car and she almost falls into my lap. The photographer captures the moment with a shot of Muffy falling into the car.

'Just drive,' I shout to the chauffeur.

'But ...'

'Please,' I beg.

He shoots off and Muffy looks at my dad appealingly through the back window.

'Just wait until I tell the wife about this one,' grins the driver.

'Please turn that music off too,' I plead.

'Where are we going?' asks Muffy. 'You're not Julia Roberts doing a scene from *Runaway Bride* you know. Christ Binki, you can't just jilt him at the altar.'

'She jumped on a horse,' I say.

Muffy pulls off her headdress.

'Well I'm glad we clarified that. You still can't jilt him at the altar, I mean cock it all Binki, you've had weeks to call it off.'

'Cock it, that's a new one. I must tell the wife,' says the driver.

'It's all your fault,' I say pointing a finger at him.

He looks at me through his mirror.

'What did I do?' he asks defensively.

'Yes, what did he do?' asks Muffy struggling to get the pearl garland back into her hair.

'He played *It Had to Be You,* that's *our* song.'

'We don't have a song,' Muffy says, looking confused.

'Not *our* song, of course we don't have one. It's the song William and I shared, and I realised ...'

'Oh God,' groans Muffy. 'Not bloody William.'

'Who's William?' asks the driver.

'Do yourself a favour and keep your eyes on the road. You really don't want to hear any more of this because it just gets worse,' groans Muffy pushing her hand down her cleavage and producing her mobile like a magician.

'I've seen everything now,' he grins.

'Eyes on the road,' she reprimands. 'We need to turn back and you have to marry Oliver, phone Douglas now. Tell him you had last minute nerves but you've realised it was silly and you're on your way back,' she says firmly, handing me the phone.

I stare at her.

'Turn around now, sorry what's your name?' she asks the driver.

'Max,' he says.

'Turn around now Max.'

Max swerves to take the next turning.

'No,' I scream. 'Muffy what the hell are you doing? I need to tell William it is him I love. Even if there is no future in it, I don't care. I have to tell him and I can't marry someone I no longer love. Max, keep going to Hampstead Heath please.'

'Bloody hell,' he mumbles doing a three-sixty degree turn in the middle of the road.

'Christ,' mumbles Muffy. 'Binki, William is marrying Andrea today. You can't tell him anything and you can't throw away your one chance of marriage. You may never get another one, and Oliver is a good man isn't he?'

What does she mean William is marrying Andrea today, he can't be. He would have told me, surely. Oh God no, he can't be?

'He can't be?' I whisper.

'It's all over her Twitter page,' she says softly, taking the phone off me and scrolling into it.

'This morning, first thing: *so excited, can't believe the big day is here. See you all later.*'

'That doesn't mean she's getting married,' I say, feeling a small sense of relief.

'A bit later: *can't wait to see William in his top and tails, so sexy.*'

'Still doesn't …' I begin.

'Ten minutes ago: *Car arriving soon & we'll be on our way to the church. Love my dress so much, thank u Carla #wedding*'

'That clinches it,' says Max.

'Shut up Max,' I snap.

'He's marrying Andrea, and that's it Binki, and you should marry Oliver,' says Muffy, putting her hand on mine.

'Good advice,' says Max.

I glare at him through the mirror.

'Sorry,' he mumbles.

I close my eyes and remember the last time I had seen William, and our kiss in the taxi and his words,

'C'est la vie, I always leave things too late.'

I must not do the same thing. I can't leave things too late. It's the first day of the rest of his life, what if it is a mistake? He loves me too, I feel sure he does.

'I still have to tell him. I'm sorry Muffy. If you don't want to come with me I understand but I have to do this.'

I hold my breath. She pulls off the headdress and says,

'Phone William.'

I frown.

'I don't know his number. It's in my phone.'

She sighs.

'Okay, let's try to find out where the church is. Maybe she has updated. Hang on.'

I wait patiently.

'Okay, latest update: *On our way to St Andrews Church. Feel like a princess #wedding*

'Where is St Andrew's church?' I lean forward to ask Max.

'There are loads,' he stammers.

'In Hampstead Heath?' asks Muffy.

'I don't know, about six I think. Is it Catholic? If you knew that we could eliminate a few, but you can't be sure it is in Hampstead Heath. It could be anywhere,' says Max.

'Oh God,' I groan.

Muffy sighs and scrolls through the stream again

'Do you think William would marry in a Catholic church?' she asks.

I shake my head.

'I don't think so, but maybe he would for Andrea.'

Her phone rings making us jump.

'Fuck, it's Oliver,' Muffy shrieks, throwing it into my lap. I click the off button quickly.

'This is terrible,' Muffy groans.

I scroll through the stream again and see a new update.

'One of the oldest churches in England, how cool is that? Pics to follow. #thebigday'

Max bangs the steering wheel.

'It could be the one in Launcester Street,' he says, 'that's old.'

Please God, please let it be the one.

'Let's go,' says Muffy.

Chapter Forty

Meanwhile at the church

Bernard stands stunned and watches the Rolls-Royce disappear around the corner. He would still have been standing there if Bella hadn't come out of the church to see what was going on. Douglas, seeing her leave taps Oliver on the shoulder.

'All systems go me matey. I'm just checking everything is shipshape before ye walk the plank.'

Oliver doesn't reply and Douglas grimaces. His friend had barely spoken since leaving the flat. Mind you, he can imagine the poor bugger is feeling pretty rough. Let's face it getting married is the same as castration in his opinion. If you can only give it to one woman what's the bloody point of having it? A woman in every port was Douglas's motto. If you can make a hundred women happy then that's your duty, surely.

'Just be a sec,' he whispers to Oliver.

Oliver nods and then sighs. He feels sick and can't stop thinking about the texts Amanda had sent him. He ought to phone her but his brain is in such a whirl. Christ, of all the bloody days.

Douglas follows Bella outside to see Bernard and the photographer standing on the kerb. He looks around for Binki and Muffy. Maybe the car has broken down, that can happen but what the hell has happened to Muffy? She was here five minutes ago. Bella shrieks and buries her head in her hands. Oh God, this isn't bloody good, then again if this means old matey getting off the hook that's not such a bad thing.

'Everything okay?' he asks, knowing full well if there is no bloody bride then everything is far from okay.

'My daughter must be having a breakdown,' sobs Bella. 'I can't think of any other reason for her behaving in this fashion.'

'What fashion would that be?' asks Douglas.

'She threw me out of the car and asked me to tell Oliver she's really sorry but she can't go through with it.'

'Is there a problem?' whispers the vicar as he approaches Douglas.

'She's not turning up mate,' Douglas replies.

'Who is going to tell Oliver,' sobs Bella.

'Tell me what?'

At the sight of Oliver, Bella throws herself into his arms.

'For goodness' sake Bella, pull yourself together, it's a wedding not a funeral,' says Bernard.

'It may as well be,' cries Bella. 'She's thrown her whole life away.'

'She's not coming, me old matey,' says Douglas to Oliver, before whispering, 'A lucky escape if you ask me you jammy bastard.'

'Where is she?' Oliver asks Bernard.

'No idea son, she pulled Muffy into the roller and they shot off. They've probably gone back to our house,' says Bernard.

'Oh God,' sobs Bella. 'The neighbours will think she's been jilted and not the other way around.'

'Perhaps best not to rub it in,' whispers Douglas, looking at Oliver's ashen face.

'Give her a bit of time, you never know ...' begins Bernard.

'I've another wedding in an hour,' butts in the vicar.

'Oh, yes of course, stupid, I just thought ...'

'Bernard do shut up,' snaps Bella.

'Do you want me to give her a bell?' asks Douglas. 'You know, just to make sure she isn't coming back?'

'She doesn't have her phone,' says Bernard.

'I'll call Muffy,' says Oliver calmly.

They all look hopefully on as Oliver taps in Muffy's number. A few seconds pass before Oliver says,

'She's not answering.'

'Douglas, can you phone the Dorchester and tell them the reception is cancelled. Bernard, do you mind telling the congregation. I can't face going back inside.'

'Of course not,' says Bella putting a comforting arm around him.

He nods at her and gently releases himself.

'I need a walk,' he says.

'I'll kill her Bernard, I swear I will. What can she be thinking of,' Bella sighs.

'I imagine she has decided that she doesn't want this to be the first day of the rest of her life,' he says philosophically, walking towards the church.

Douglas and Bella watch Oliver stroll away from them with his head bowed.

'Poor bugger,' says Douglas searching on Google for The Dorchester's phone number while thinking lucky old sod.

'I hope he doesn't do anything silly,' says Bella worriedly.

Fortunately he can't now, Douglas thinks with a grin.

Oliver turns the corner out of sight of the church and takes a long deep breath. Bloody hell, he can't believe it. She has bloody jilted him. God, he couldn't have planned it better if he'd tried. Not only will everyone feel sorry for him but they'll understand perfectly when he turns to Amanda for comfort. Christ, he can't believe his luck. He really thought he was going to be the bad guy. He feels like sending Binki a bouquet of flowers. He only hopes she doesn't go and change her mind. Christ, what a day. Jilted at the altar and discovering he is to become a father all on the same day calls for a large rum.

Chapter Forty-One

'This is the oldest is it?' asks Muffy with a tremble in her voice. 'It doesn't look that old.'

'Well I'm not an expert on churches. I've just driven to a lot. This is the oldest St Andrew's in this area that I know of,' says Max. 'Are you sure you want to do this?'

No I'm not sure at all. In fact I'm starting to think it is the worst idea I've ever had. Guests are arriving and I feel my nerve go. Perhaps I should just go back and marry Oliver. I hope he's okay. I did try and phone him but it just went into his voicemail. I'd apologised profusely, saying it was the best thing for both of us. Of course I don't imagine he feels it is the best thing at the moment. I'm trying so hard not to think of all the presents and the food, not to mention the honeymoon which has been booked and paid for, and all the guests that have travelled to get there. I turn to Muffy.

'Update,' I say.

'There isn't one,' she says, looking at her phone.

'Go in and check,' I say, giving her a little shove.

She gapes at me.

'What, are you serious? Have you looked at me lately? I'm dressed like a bridesmaid. It's not like I'm incognito is it? And the last I recall, Andrea Garcia didn't ask me to be one at her wedding.'

What's she talking about? It's the best incognito ever surely. No one will look twice at a bridesmaid will they?

'But they'll be expecting bridesmaids won't they?' I say. 'So no one will think it odd.'

She shakes her head.

'Yes, but they're not expecting other people's bridesmaids. I rather think Andrea Garcia will recognise her own bridesmaid, or are you hoping she may have forgotten who they are? Christ Binki, I can't believe we are even seriously considering this.'

I suppose she has a point.

'There's no sign of the bridal car so you could quickly nip in, pretend to be a bridesmaid and check it's the right wedding ...'

'Check it's the right wedding? What am I, the dumbest bridesmaid on earth? I'm not going in there on my own. What if William is there and ...'

'Max? I ask.

'No,' he says waving his hand. 'Driving the getaway car is as far as I go.'

Shit. I've got to do it haven't I? Honestly if you want something done right do it yourself. I'll never forgive myself if I don't tell William how I feel.

'Right,' I say, opening the door determinedly.

'Bugger,' says Muffy. 'She's only bloody going through with it.'

I clamber from the Rolls with Muffy behind me. I realise I'm still clasping my bouquet and throw it back into the car. I grab Muffy's hand for support and find it hot and sweaty.

'Hold the train,' I say.

'What?' says Muffy straightening her headdress.

'My wedding train, you'll have to hold it.'

I walk as fast as I can towards the church with Muffy following behind. I reach the heavy oak doors, take a deep breath and push them open. The coolness of the church makes me shiver. The congregation turn and there are a few hushed gasps. I look ahead to the vicar who is holding a baby over the font. Oh shit, it's only a sodding christening. He looks at us and confusion creeps slowly across his face. I cringe as his hands shake and the baby's head touches the water. Bloody hell, he's going to drown the poor little thing.

'Hello,' I say.

Well, what else am I supposed to say?

'Did I muddle up? Oh no, I didn't, surely,' he says. 'Not again.'

'Again?' I whisper to Muffy.

'Christ,' says Muffy and quickly puts a hand to her mouth and mumbles, 'shit.'

'Sorry,' she continues, 'I didn't mean to say that. What I meant to say was ...'

The baby's head seems to dip further into the font.

'Oh God,' Muffy cries and bites her lip and then finishes with, 'Oh Jesus … I'm so sorry.'

I roll my eyes.

'What I mean is, wrong church, sorry for the Christ Jesus, stuff.'

'Muffy, you're just making things worse,' I whisper.

'I didn't then?' asks the vicar, sounding relieved.

'No, certainly not,' smiles Muffy pulling me backwards by my train. 'It isn't you, absolutely our cock-up, totally.'

'Muffy,' I say despairingly.

'Must dash,' she says.

The church is silent and all eyes on us, and all I can think is God, we're too late. By the time we get to the right church it will all be over. I will never be able to tell him how I feel and will live my whole life carrying that burden.

'Come on, we don't have much time.'

'Right,' says Muffy. 'Oh, and congratulations on the baby by the way.'

I pull her by the arm and we race as fast as anyone can race in a wedding dress, back to the car.

Chapter Forty-Two

'Go,' I shout to Max, pulling my dress into the car and hearing a rip.

'Oh my God, that was awful,' groans Muffy.

'It's just a small tear,' I say.

'I don't mean the dress, that whole pantomime back there. How could I have blasphemed three times in as many seconds?' she says, slapping her forehead.

'Where to now?' asks Max.

I feel tears prick my eyelids.

'I've no idea,' I say and burst into tears.

Muffy takes my hand and with the other checks her phone.

'Ooh, there is an update: *Quick Éclat touch up. Can see church now, don't you just love those arch gates. Can't wait for William to see me.*

'St Matthew's, not St Andrew's,' says Max. 'It's the only church with the arched gates.'

With a screech of tyres he turns the car around to bursts of car horns.

'But she must know where she is getting married,' I sniff.

'Let's face it, she is so full of herself that she probably got it wrong,' snorts Muffy.

I shake my head. I don't believe a bride forgets the name of the church where she is getting married. She'll be forgetting the name of her husband next. With a pain in my heart I realise I've lost everything. The man I love as well as my best friend. I've no home to go back to and I've deeply hurt the one man who really loved me. I'm the biggest bitch on earth. I don't deserve happiness.

'Shit,' says Max, banging his hand on the steering wheel. 'Roadworks. Of all the bloody times, okay girls, hold onto your bridal gowns.'

He swings the car around and Muffy and I slide across the back seat. Muffy's chignon is askew and escaped strands of hair stick to her neck.

'How do I look?' I ask.

'Amazingly, still rather stunning, I think it must be the adrenalin,' she says breathlessly.

Before I realise it Max is careening around a corner and heading towards a church with arched gates. My throat tightens and my heart begins to beat so fast I can hear it in my ears, and feel sure Max and Muffy can hear it too. There are lots of cars parked outside the entrance and with a pang I see William's Lamborghini.

'This is the church then,' says Muffy following my gaze.

My hands and legs are trembling so much that I can't move.

'I can't do it,' I say, feeling an overwhelming urge to throw up.

'Right fine, let's go Max,' says Muffy firmly.

'No,' I cry.

I've got to do it. What's the worst that can happen? I could open the door and find William and Andrea are already married of course. Or I could be in time and maybe they haven't started yet. I could ask to have a quiet word with William. He's his own man isn't he? William would never go ahead with something if he was unsure. If he knew I loved him, if he knew we had a chance together. Oh for Christ's sake Binki, stop bloody analysing everything.

'You're right,' I say. 'I can't do it. I can't just walk in there and ruin his day. They're probably married now anyway.'

I fumble for a tissue and Max hands me one.

'I'm going in,' says Max, sounding like an SAS agent. 'I'll give the thumbs up if the wedding hasn't started or a down if it has.

'Oh God,' I groan. 'What if I can't do it?'

'Then I guess you've lost them both, Oliver and William. Which means you're stuck with me, surely that's an incentive to do something. Let's face it, you're buggered if you do and buggered if you don't now. The fact is you've lost Oliver and that was no great loss I suppose and …'

'But this could lose me William as a friend …'

'Grow up Binki, once he's married her you can't be friends, and he knew that once you married Oliver you couldn't be friends too. So you've got everything to gain and nothing to lose, right?'

We both look to Max as he exits the gates with a *thumbs up* sign and a wave to hurry.

'It's now or never Binki,' says Muffy, squeezing my hand.

Everything that follows seems to happen in slow motion. The walk to the church seems endless and it feels like I am in a nightmare where the nearer you get to something the further away it becomes. I feel certain the church is moving back all the time. Oh God, I'll never reach it, I'll never get to the doors in time. I've got no idea what I'm going to do when I reach the doors anyway. I can't just open them and shout *Stop the wedding. I'm in love with the groom.* If I do, supposing William says *but I don't love you.* I imagine I'll faint at that point and won't know much about what happens after that. I'm finally at the doors and all we can hear is the mumbled tones of a man's voice. It's the vicar performing the ceremony. I look at Muffy and Max and with a nod we all push the doors open.

Chapter Forty-Three

The door creaks loudly and the congregation turn to look at us. The vicar is seemingly unaware of us and all I can focus on is the back of Andrea's head, and her outstanding wedding dress which makes mine look like it is off the peg from Primark. My eyes move to the back of William's head. I feel Muffy's hand on my arm and she begins to shake it and I realise I can't just stand here looking like Grace Kelly, as lovely as that may be.

'If any of you can show just cause why they may not lawfully be married, speak now or else forever hold your peace.'

'I do,' I shout. 'The groom loves me and I love him.'

The congregation murmur in response. Everyone turns to survey the woman in her wedding dress standing at the door. Oh God, what must I look like? It's like I've come all dressed, ready to take over from the bride. Jesus, I want the floor to open up and devour me. Andrea spins around to see who has shouted, except it isn't Andrea. It takes me several seconds to take it in. For a moment I find myself wondering why William is marrying this woman instead. Muffy reels at the side of me and Max leans out an arm to support her, and it all kind of confirms the fact that I'm at the wrong bloody church, again. Once is a mistake, but twice is just bloody stupid isn't it? The groom turns slowly and looks at me. I gasp. I've never seen this man in my life, or maybe I have somewhere. He looks kind of familiar, but he isn't the man I love. I cringe, and feel my body go hot. Oh God, I just said he loves me and I love him. Piss it. It most certainly is the wrong sodding wedding.

'Jools, who the hell is this woman?' screams the bride.

'I've never seen her in my life,' he stammers.

'Well, she seems to think she knows you,' she says, beginning to cry.

Sod it. I rush down the aisle towards her but my train gets stuck on a pew and I am yanked back.

'It's a mistake, I'm so sorry. I thought someone else was getting married. Please forgive me. I don't even know Jools. I've just jilted my own groom because I realised I loved someone else and he's getting married today and ...'

At that point I see William standing at the side of Jools and I gasp. I'd been so intent on the sodding groom that I had not noticed the best man. Piss it. How could I have got everything so wrong? I'll kill Muffy.

'I'm so sorry,' I say, my eyes falling on a woman in the front row. She raises her fist. Andrea? Is that the sophisticated, elegant, fashionable and confident with an air of grace Andrea? She looks the ugliest I have ever seen. Her eyes are glinting dangerously at me. She looks amazing in a fabulous white satin dress which clutches her slim waist perfectly. A beautiful garland of flowers is grasped in her other hand and I now realise she was never the bride but just a sodding bridesmaid. Muffy takes my arm and Max lifts the train and I begin to walk from the church just like a real bride, minus a groom of course. The church doors open and I see my mum, Oliver and Dad standing outside.

'Fuck,' says Muffy, 'this is a bit intense.'

'You phoned my parents?' I say.

'I thought you might need some support,' she says lowering her eyes. 'I didn't think they would bring bloody Oliver with them.'

'I'll get the car started,' says Max, making a quick exit.

Honestly, you'd think we'd robbed a bank the way he's carrying on. I try not to meet Oliver's eyes. I'm beginning to think if there was a horse nearby this may be a good time to jump on it.

'Binki.'

I stop at William's voice and turn. Oh, he looks so gorgeous wearing his starched white shirt and black bow tie and the way his hair flops casually over his forehead. It's all I can do not to throw myself into his arms. The congregation turn their heads to me and then back to William. I feel like I'm on centre court at Wimbledon, although thankfully there is no balls-balancing going on here.

'Hello,' I say. Well, what the hell else is there to say?

'Sorry about all this,' says Muffy. 'It's been a hell of a day. I think I should get her home.'

He doesn't take his eyes off me.

'You didn't marry Oliver?' he says simply.

I shake my head. I so wish he would smile. He looks so serious.

'I almost did and then Max, the driver, you don't know him,' I say stupidly and see a small smile cross his face. 'He played *It Had to Be you* and I suddenly knew that it did. That for me it had to be you. I totally understand that you're marrying Andrea but I just had to tell you.'

My voice is shaking but the sense of relief at finally telling him is so great that my whole body seems to give way and I clutch at a pew to support myself.

'You'd have stopped my wedding?' he asks.

I see Andrea push past the bride, sending her falling into the arms of the groom.

'Yes, I'm so sorry,' I say, realising how selfish I've been.

I turn to look at Oliver who gives me a weak smile. I'm about to apologise again to him when Andrea is upon me like a wild cat, pulling at my veil with one hand and slapping with the other. I am sent reeling, but fortunately reeling into William's arms, which is the silver lining I suppose. Muffy screams and my mum rushes forward. They both try to pull her off me but I hear the rips as she tears my dress.

'You bitch, you man-stealing bitch. Everything they say about you is true. You only want other women's men. Can't get a good one for yourself is that it?' she cries.

'Andrea,' says William, gently grasping her hands in his. She struggles against him as the congregation gasp. Mum takes my hand and pulls me towards the door.

'We need to get you out of here. I don't know what you're thinking of,' she says sharply.

'Yes, let's get the hell out of here,' agrees Muffy.

Andrea pulls one hand from William's grasp and slaps him hard around the face also. The congregation wince in unison.

'How could you?' she asks. 'I could have anyone, you know that don't you? There are plenty of rich men in the world you know? You're not the only one.'

'I was under the impression you were marrying me because you loved me, not because I was rich,' William says angrily.

She grits her teeth and finally pulls herself away from him.

'You were a good catch William, what the hell has love got to do with it?' She pulls the solitaire diamond ring from her finger and throws it in his face. 'I wouldn't marry you if you were the last man on earth,' she hisses.

She gives me a filthy look and marches to the door, giving Muffy a shove as she does so. I look at William with a grimace. I can't imagine what I look like now. Any resemblance to Princess Grace I imagine, has well and truly disappeared and I look more like the bride of Chucky.

'I'm so sorry,' I say to William. 'Muffy follows Andrea on Twitter and it sounded like it was her wedding.'

'Don't be, I came close to stopping yours.'

I take a sharp breath.

'You did?' I say in a high-pitched voice.

'Attending this wedding today was unbearable. Knowing as I heard Kat say 'I do' that you would be doing the same thing just a few miles away. It was torture.'

I open my mouth to speak but nothing comes out.

'I need to say something,' says Oliver walking towards us.

'This is all highly irregular,' says the vicar loudly.

'It's fine,' says the bride. 'I'd rather it got sorted and then we can all carry on.'

I turn to Oliver.

'I'm so sorry Oliver, I ...'

'Amanda's pregnant, it's mine. I didn't find out until this morning. I was going to jilt you. Frankly, I couldn't have been more relieved.'

I gape at him. Muffy shakes her head and mumbles,

'Little shit. I always said you were a little shit.'

'You were going to jilt my daughter?' Mum says quietly.

'Lucky escape if you ask me,' mumbles Muffy.

'Don't get upset Bella,' says Dad.

I pull the ring from my finger and hand it to him.

'I think you should have this,' I say. Knowing Oliver he will recycle it if he can.

William takes my hand and pulls me into the vestry.

'Can you give us a few minutes,' he says.

The coolness of the church and the shock of Oliver's words have set me trembling so much that I find I can't stop shaking. William pulls me into his arms and his lips brush my neck and I feel that familiar tingle that only he can produce.

'I've missed you,' he whispers. 'I've missed everything about you. I keep buying M&Ms for the teapot and then remember you're not there any more. I can't play Tony Bennett any more without thinking of you. I can't go to a jazz club because they remind me of you. I don't even ice skate any more. You're everywhere. I didn't want to spoil things for you if it was Oliver you loved. It would have been selfish of me. Binki, the truth is nobody else gave me a thrill like you. With all your faults, I love you still. You see it had to be you, wonderful you, only you.'

I feel the tears forming and take a deep breath.

'I thought,' I say fighting back my tears, 'that I wasn't your type, that I was not big breasted enough or ...'

'I've seen them remember. They're perfect,' he smiles.

'That work was more important and ...'

'You worked with me. I've missed you so much in the office. Everywhere feels empty without you.'

'Oh William,' I cry, wrapping my arms around his neck.

'In fact I've decided you're the only one I would ever consider sprawling over my desk, that's if you don't mind of course?'

'Is there a bonus in it?' I smile.

'Well I'm sure one could be arranged.'

I lift my face and close my eyes as his lips come close to mine. In my head I can hear the song *It Had to Be You* playing as his lips touch mine.

'I love you,' he says gently, clasping my hand in his.

'I love you too,' I whisper.

'Not your best dress though, I have to say I've seen you in better.'

'You don't like it?' I say acting surprised.

'I did before, but ...'

He lifts my chin and looks into my eyes.

'Binki Grayson, will you do me the honour of marrying me but preferably in a different dress.'

I try to smile but I can barely see him through my tears of happiness.

'Yes,' I say.

There is applause from behind us and I turn to see Mum, Dad, Muffy and Max in the doorway.

'I couldn't have wished for anything better,' I hear Mum whisper to Muffy. Honestly, my mum.

'God moves in mysterious ways,' nods the vicar.

'Well, even if he turns out to be a little shit at least he'll be a rich little shit,' Muffy says.

'Muffy,' I snap.

'Just saying,' she smiles.

William laughs and takes my hand.

'Shall we make our exit? Call it a practice run.'

We leave the vestry to the applause of the congregation. I already feel married and smile when I know I still have that pleasure to come.

Aunty Vera left me the best inheritance ever. I can somehow imagine her looking down from heaven. It wouldn't surprise me if she planned the whole thing; she always was a bit of a minx. Thank you Aunty Vera, I couldn't have wished for a better legacy.

The Dog's Bollocks (A Romantic Comedy)

On arriving home after a friend's posh wedding, launderette worker Harriet, finds her life changed when she discovers her flat ransacked

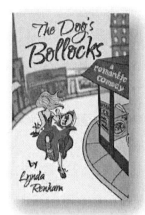

and her boyfriend missing. In a matter of hours she is harassed by East End gangsters and upper crust aristocrats. Accepting an offer she can't refuse, Harriet, against her better judgment becomes the fiancée of the wealthy Hamilton Lancaster, with dire consequences. What she had not bargained on was meeting Doctor Brice Edmunds.

The Dog's Bollocks is Lynda Renham's funniest novel so far. A cocktail of misunderstandings, three unlikely gangsters, a monkey and a demented cat make this novel a hysterical read. Follow Harriet's adventure where every attempt to get out of trouble puts her deeper in it.

Pink Wellies and Flat Caps

(A Romantic Comedy)

Alice Lane has everything; a wonderful fiancé, a responsible job and a lovely flat in Chelsea, but after she has a bra fitting her life goes tits up. Homeless, and with just a sparkling engagement ring as a memory of her previous life Alice accepts a live-in farm manager s job and discovers that things actually can get worse. Come with Alice as she makes her hilarious career change and struggles to cope with her moody employer, Edward. But can Alice turn her back on romance and resist the dashing Dominic or will the past come back to surprise her?

Coconuts and Wonderbras

(A Romantic Comedy Adventure)

Literary agent Libby Holmes is desperate for her boyfriend, Toby, to propose to her and will do anything for him and if that means dieting for England then she'll have a go. However, when Libby's boss introduces her to her new client, Alex Bryant, her life is turned upside down. Alex Bryant, ex-SAS officer and British hero, insists Libby accompany him to Cambodia for a book fair. What she hadn't bargained for was a country in revolt. Libby finds herself in the middle of an uprising with only Alex Bryant to protect her, that is, until Toby flies out to win back her affections. Come with Libby on her romantic comedy adventure to see if love blossoms in the warm Cambodian sunshine or if, in the heat of the day, emotions get just too hot to handle.

Croissants and Jam

(A Romantic Comedy)

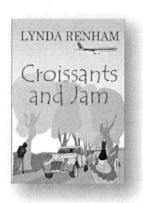

Annabel Lewis (Bels) has two days to get to her wedding in Rome, but her journey is beset with one disaster after another as fate takes its turn. Will the stranger she meets on the way get her to her wedding on time or will he change her life forever? Come with Bels on her humorous romantic journey to see if she marries Mr Right or if destiny takes her in a different direction.